busman's holiday

For Amy

Alison

Billy

busman's holiday

by

Billie Watson

First published in Great Britain in 2004
by W. Watson Publications
PO BOX 639, Aylesbury
Bucks, HP22 6YQ

www.wwatson.net

ISBN 0-9547599-0-7

Printed and bound in Great Britain by Antony Rowe Ltd,
Chippenham, Wiltshire, UK.

About the Author

Billie Watson worked in the home-entertainment business before taking up writing.

For Miller, who never stops believing

An Eternal Question

Which pair do you like?' asked the mother of her eight-year-old daughter.

'I can't decide,' replied the little girl, fidgeting on her mother's hand as she stared through the shoe shop window.

'You're no help,' said the mother, taking her offspring into the store.

A little while later, they were back on the street, the new sandals slapping the surface of the pavement with a steady beat.

'I don't like these ones,' said a little voice as they reached the grocers.

'Are they hurting you? Is it your toes?'

'No. I just don't like them now. I want the other ones!'

'Look here, young lady. These are the ones you chose. You wanted these sandals and you're going to wear them, whether you like them or not.'

The terse tone brought on a flood of tears, which did not subside until the groceries were packed into the car. The silence of the homeward journey was only broken a little later by a question from the little girl.

'When will I know what I really want? Is it when I grow up?'

A smile creased her mother's face as she glanced at her little one. She considered her reply carefully, knowing a good answer was required.

'When you grow up, you will know what to choose most of the time. But now and again, it will be difficult.'

'What do I do then?'

'Listen to your heart. It will tell you what to do.'

The little girl placed her hand on her chest, asking, 'What if it's my heart that's asking me what to do? What do I do then?'

Chapter One

Bob Sinclair drove the tour coach through the rolling Cumbrian countryside with an easy firmness. He looked in the internal mirror: empty velour seats rowed behind him, headrests bedecked with clean white squares, 'Scotia Tours' in blue lettering stitched into each one.

Wrap-around sunglasses shielded his eyes from the glare of the early-morning July sunshine. The radio station forecast a clear sky for the day ahead.

A carpet of lush green countryside undulated through the windscreen as Bob wound his way eastwards. Dry-stone dykes hemmed sheep and cattle in the arable lower ground, giving way to the heath-covered escarpments touching the horizon.

Twelve years of coach driving flowed from his mind and body into the Volvo 7550 through the driving controls; steering-wheel, gear stick, brakes, clutch and accelerator. Second-by-second, instructions transmitted to the eight-ratio gearbox, down into the 12.1 litre turbo-diesel engine.

Driving skill and mechanical energy were all perfectly combined by the time they reached the 22-inch tread tyres, which smacked along the tarmac. The 7550, by many people's standards in the tourist coach industry, was a solid performer; an all-round bus which Bob had personally deemed his favourite over the years.

Included with the standard features were adjustable seats, refrigerator, radio-cassette CD PA system, two 15-inch video monitors, air-conditioning, and a reading lamp for each seat.

But Bob's vehicle had added modifications; an extra toilet to create a ladies' and gents' facility, four tables, an extra luggage rack at the front and extra legroom with a footrest. The result was seat capacity reduced from the standard 53 to 28 – normal for any tour company selling itself as a luxury operator.

For Bob, there was something else this coach possessed; a fine paint and livery job to reflect the tour operator's distinguished image.

Deep, dark, rich metallic blue with the words 'Scotia Tours' in white Celtic lettering embellished the vehicle. Below the windscreen was the tour company's slogan: '*Take the low and high road to Scotland with Scotia Tours*'. Discreet thistles and flags finished off the striking look.

Next to other coaches, Scotia Tours 001 stood head and shoulders above them all, giving Bob a surge of pride as other drivers commented on the classy look of his charge.

The A69 to Newcastle, Tyne-and-Wear, was a bustling journey, typical for the first day of the working week. Trucks, vans, cars, buses and the odd farm tractor pushed along the transport artery, hauling the occupants to their respective jobs.

The road passed through small hamlets, skirting the larger villages, bypassing small towns; all built with the same flint stone plundered from Hadrian's Wall.

Bob recalled this detail from a previous excursion, the guide's comments returning to him. He was impressed at his own memory for such detail; he could easily adapt to being a tour guide.

'Shit. Bollocks!'

'Language, Mother,' commented Jane Smythe as she freewheeled her little car off the A69. The dissipating energy from the stalled engine was sufficient to bring her into a lay-by. Steam rose from the bonnet.

'I'm going to be late,' exclaimed Alison Smythe, her agitation visible by the light film of perspiration on her forehead.

'Calm down. You don't want to be wound up for the interview'

'What bloody interview? I won't be there in time.' Alison's large almond eyes rolled upwards, a sure sign of anxiety. But then again, thought Jane, was she never not anxious. Ever since she had been little, Jane could easily recall many incidents of her highly strung mother 'losing it', much to her daughter's embarrassment.

'I'll call Dad. He can get here in twenty minutes,' said Jane, dialling her mobile phone.

'He's out. Gone over to Barry Higgs to see some piece of machinery.'

'But he'll have his mobile.'

'You'll be lucky, he's always forgetting it.' Alison smoothed down her serge blue skirt, eager to keep it looking fresh.

The dial tone kept ringing.

'Told you so.'

Jane let go a long sigh.

'What's that for?' asked Alison defensively.

'We just need to keep calm and come up with a way to get you to your meeting.'

'It's not a meeting, it's an interview. You might go to meetings in your job, but that's not my world.' Alison rolled down the window, eager for fresh air.

Jane felt a twinge of sympathy for her mother, a woman who had dedicated her adult life to being a full-time mother and wife. Here she was now, attempting to join the workforce, applying for jobs with diminished confidence and trepidation.

'Look, I'm sure they can reschedule it?'

Alison swivelled to look at her youngest daughter, taking in the sweet demeanour she had inherited from her father and felt the compulsion to kiss her.

'It's not the impression I want to give, Jane,' replied Alison haughtily. 'I'm going to be there on time, whatever it takes.' Getting out of the car, she straightened her smart outfit before walking to the roadside.

Jane had never seen her mother attempt to thumb a lift before; somehow this behaviour seemed below her. But there she stood, rigid, determined and if Jane was honest – scary. Not scary as in 'old bat' scary, but more 'headmistress' scary; the piercing personality which radiates authority and little warmth.

Fearing this must have been the case as no one was stopping to pick her up, Jane joined her mum, whose firm-faced expression did not seem to be encouraging any roadside chivalry.

'Mum, come on, this isn't you.'

No reply.

'Mum, I'll call the AA, and they can drop you off for the interview.'

'No need, sweetheart,' replied Alison with a smile, her thumb dropping.

As if from nowhere a large metallic-blue coach swept into the lay-by with a throaty deceleration and a hiss of air brakes.

'You wait here for the AA man. I've an interview to get to.'

Bob Sinclair loved the road before him – the miles disappearing under his coach, devouring tens of thousands of miles every year. He relished the certainty of repeating the same route every month, especially his run; *Scotland*.

Even after eight years of driving coach parties along the length and breadth of this country, he never grew tired of the breathtaking scenery – the castles, the lochs, the rivers and the ever-changing firmament of the weather.

He also liked being on the move, always had; he needed the change around him, the bend in the road so to speak. This bend in the road was not restricted to his driving, but also extended to the tour parties he drove for. Every two weeks, between April and September, a group of 18 individuals would climb aboard his luxury bus for a ten-day tour: 200 people over the duration of the season. Travellers he would get to know well, especially in the evening as Bob lodged in the same hotel as the tour party.

He liked the feeling of dependency it gave him to transport these people on their holiday, being part of their overall enjoyment. After many years, he was able to anticipate their reactions – knowing a purple-heather clad vista would appear shortly, slowing to a crawl to let their eyes feast on a beautiful mountain range as they turned a corner. The passengers' murmurs of appreciation would roll down the coach and wash over Bob like a warm wave, triggering a sense of real satisfaction.

As far as he was concerned, he had the ideal job: a job where new discoveries were around the next corner, just around the bend in the road.

The smartly dressed woman trying to hitch a lift from the lay-by caught his eye.

Pulling in, he swung the door open and waited for her to appear.

'Where are you headed?' he asked.

'Botley – it's about twenty minutes from here,' replied Alison, stepping up into the coach.

'I know it, it's on my way. I can drop you off.'

'Mum, are you going to be okay?' asked Jane from the doorway.

'This kind man is going to help me, I'll be fine.'

With a nod, Jane returned to her car.

'The name's Bob, Bob Sinclair,' informed the driver in his usual confident tone, getting out from his seat. Alison could see he was easily six foot one, maybe six foot two and fit with it. Not a typical coach driver's build with a stomach overhang, but a flat abdomen. He was a handsome man for his mid fifties.

'Alison Smythe,' she responded unsure of where to sit.

'Please,' Bob motioned to the guide's seat. 'And put this on, it's a communicator so we can speak without having to shout.

I'll need you to direct me to where you want to be dropped off.' Bob handed Alison an earpiece with a little microphone attached. She struggled to put it on the right way until Bob helped. He seemed to exude confidence, radiating waves of capability.

Slipping into the traffic again, Bob's voice poured into Alison's right ear.

'An important meeting to make?'

'An interview actually, with a doctor's practice. Receptionist.'

'You like dealing with people then?'

Alison detected the driver's accent was southern, maybe London.

'I do, but it's been a long time since I've been for a job.'

'Nervous?' Bob glanced over at her, his clear blue eyes in sync with his sympathetic smile.

'I am. In fact I don't think I'll get it,' she replied dolefully, but conscious she was staring at him. No doubt about it, he was an attractive man.

'Where are you headed?' Alison was keen to change the subject.

'Scotland. Picking up a tour party at Newcastle, and then straight to Edinburgh.'

'I love Scotland, it's beautiful. We've been on holiday there a few times.'

For the next fifteen minutes, they exchanged conversation on their travels, mostly Bob relating a few comical stories about some of the local people he had met. His infectious geniality captivated Alison, and although he kept his eye on the road, the driver managed to lock eyes with his only passenger on a few occasions.

No complaints, she was enjoying his warm gaze. The type of look a woman does not mind from a man; a soup of flattery and desire.

Alison's peals of laughter rode into Botley and she had to stifle her giggles to give Bob directions to the doctor's practice.

'Here you go,' said Bob finally pulling up outside.

'Thank you so much Bob. You're a life saver.'

Bob felt a big wet kiss on his forehead and the body heat from his departing passenger. 'Hold up, I've got something for you,' he called, pulling a little wrap of heather from his windscreen sun-visor.

'I can't take that, Bob. It must be your lucky keepsake?'

'I want you to have it, honest.'

The purple-headed shrub was clasped into her palm by his large hand, his eyes emanating more than friendliness.

At that moment, a part of Alison wanted to just stay on the coach, to keep going. It was like feeling the tug of a kite line, the wind pulling, daring you to free the airborne toy to see where it may go. But good sense prevailed, and Alison felt herself reel in the compulsion to remain on the tour coach.

Pushing her thoughts of escaping out of her mind she stepped off the coach.

'Alison, about that heather,' shouted Bob as he fired his bus into life. 'I don't think you'll need it for this interview, you'll get this job anyway, believe me. I just wanted you to have it.'

The doors swished closed and he was gone, taking temptation with him.

Alison Smythe walked into the doctor's practice without one ounce of anxiety in her body. She positively glowed when Doctor Reid called her in. Every answer she gave in the forty-five minute interview bristled with confidence, and the relaxed smile she flashed impressed her prospective employer.

When she got a call that evening to say she had the job, she whooped with joy and confused her husband with the words she used when toasting drinks.

'Here's to Bob Sinclair, a knight in driving armour, a knight of the road.'

Joining the traffic outside Botley, the Scotia Tours coach was now fighting through the rush hour.

Averaging 40- to 50-miles per hour, Bob's speed caused

traffic at his rear to jockey for the chance to pass him. Like prancing deer, bristling with tension, cars waited till a clearing formed, allowing them to bolt past.

For Bob, glancing in the mirror, the constant trail of traffic looked like a tail on the body of his bus. This posed no problem until certain links in the tail decided to break free and overtake him without enough clear road ahead. He could spot them, the reckless impatient ones, trying to detach their vehicles from the stream of cars; a jerkiness to their driving. By anticipating such foolhardiness, Bob would be able to protect his coach.

He sighted one at 9.17 a.m. A white saloon car, no doubt a company vehicle, the front chrome grill edging into Bob's mirror as the driver nudged out slightly to check for safe passage, only to swerve back in as oncoming traffic swished past.

Bob slowed down.

Moments later, the driver decided to make his move on a short tree-lined straight. As he was halfway along the coach, its engine racing, an articulated truck swung round the corner into view from the opposite direction – tons of rolling steel bearing down towards the reckless vehicle.

Bob assumed this would be the signal for the white saloon to decrease speed, give up the overtaking attempt and take refuge behind the coach. But it kept coming and so did the lorry – the two vehicles set to collide.

Jamming on the brakes rapidly, the steering-wheel shuddering in Bob's hands, his body lurching forward with the force of the coach coming to a near stop.

Within only seconds to spare, the car managed to swerve in front of Bob and avoid an accident.

The lorry thundered past, the driver's face crimson in fury, mouthing expletives. Bob's anticipation of the situation had allowed a controlled breaking manoeuvre, causing an identical reaction in the traffic behind.

He remained calm, a thin film of sweat trickling down his brow. Such poor driving was a common occurrence and he reacted in the usual fashion, making a note of the rear number plate of the offending vehicle as it sped off.

Half-an-hour later, Bob felt in need of a rest and a cup of tea. Sure enough a crude sign by the road indicated a mobile café half a mile ahead. He knew from experience it was a good one. He pulled into the generous lay-by where 'Johnny's Tea Stop' was situated – a boxy white van with a smoking chimney and a middle-aged couple serving the usual selection of fast food for the weary traveller.

A few lorries were parked up, a transit van and a white saloon car.

As Bob turned off his engine, he checked the number plate with the one he had noted earlier. It matched. The driver, a man in his mid-to-late twenties, was leaning against the car, talking into a mobile phone, his sunglasses pushed up onto his head. He had 'sales representative' written all over him; the checked shirt, the silk tie, the nimble body movements of a man who had been trained to sell on reflex.

Bob made his way to the rep, who was now joining the queue at the van and stood behind him. The smell of grilled bacon and burgers wafted over everybody. The squelch of sauce bottles could be heard coming from the front as orders were placed with a red-faced woman, who was quickly buttering bread and rolls from a large margarine tub.

As Bob tapped the checked-shirt shoulder, the young man turned round to face his six-foot-one inch frame.

'Remember me?' asked Bob in a soft but firm tone.

'Sorry mate. No,' said the young man uneasily. He sensed confrontation. Others in the queue turned their heads, smelling hostility over the bacon fat. Bob slipped off his sunglasses.

'Remember my bus?' He indicated over his shoulder. The young man felt like he was in a western movie – the scene where the lone cowboy walked into an inhospitable saloon. He took in the appearance of the questioning cowpoke, noting that the bus driver had a natural authority that came with his age. He filled his burgundy blazer with a straight physical firmness the young man recognised as ex-army. His own father had the same uniformity of stance – now a retired officer from the forces. He braced himself for a bollocking.

All was quiet as Bob slowly reached into his jacket and pulled out his wallet, from which he pulled out a photograph. He handed it to the young man.

The photograph was of a blue saloon car – the front and roof crushed and mangled.

'That was my *son's* car, involved in a road accident two years back,' said Bob in a matter-of-fact tone. He pulled out another photograph and gave it to the white saloon driver, whose stomach was audibly churning.

The second photograph was a seaside-holiday snap of a pretty woman in her late twenties, holding the hand of a young boy; both were smiling.

Only the sound of passing traffic cut the silence.

'That's my son's wife and my grandson. The car accident made her a widow and left him without a daddy.' Bob's voice was sorrowful.

The young man felt the blood drain from his face as he looked up at Bob. A dry mouth prevented any response, if indeed one was expected.

Bob took the photographs back and stared straight ahead while the young man walked to his car, head bowed, and drove off slowly.

The other travellers nodded at Bob and in thoughtful silence waited quietly to be served.

Chapter Two

Jenny Jenkins sat by the window in the small travel agents, waiting to be seen by one of the two young female travel advisers – one blonde, one brunette. The blonde was busy with a middle-aged couple, and the brunette was helping two Asian lads find a holiday they both could agree on.

Being a Saturday lunchtime in July, the store was busy with people chasing last-minute deals.

Hawkins Travel was an independent agency, and the shop had a comfortable feel, unlike the high-street multiple chains, which Jenny loathed. They never took time with their customers – too eager to slot you in, make a booking and wave you out.

Jenny and her late husband had booked many holidays here over the years, sitting with the owner Stacey Hawkins, pouring over the catalogues before choosing a sun-drenched destination. Many happy holidays.

Jenny had known Stacey since primary school. They'd been in the same class till Jenny had left to go to the local girls' grammar at the age of twelve. Although Stacey went on to Allerton Secondary, they had stayed in touch. But then again – Allerton was a small Yorkshire town – everybody stayed in touch.

On this sunny day though, Jenny had stared through the window before entering to see if Stacey was there. On seeing the two young girls only, she was relieved and decided to go in.

Anxiety still swirled around inside her, a nagging sense of dread. An overwrought 48 hours had brought little sleep.

Times like this she felt so alone; like other widows she presumed.

The blonde girl looked over at Jenny briefly as she entered. She was finishing with a couple, who were taking brochures home to make a final decision. The woman waiting to be seen looked familiar to her, but she could not place her face.

Jenny sensed the look and felt agitated. This was the look she'd had from countless strangers since Friday, and the reason for her visit to Hawkins Travel.

She took a seat before the blonde, who was called Vicky, according to her name badge. She could now get a good look at the woman sitting before her who seemed a little edgy, tired, preoccupied. She was attractive, slim and looked good in blue jeans. Her shoulder-length hair was chestnut and Vicky could tell the cut was expensive.

Very little make-up, she did not need much, her clear complexion and fine bone structure were enough. Difficult to place an exact age – could be anywhere from early to mid forties, probably older. People were aging well now, mused the travel adviser.

'How can we help?' asked Vicky, her smile making Jenny a little more relaxed.

'I need a break. I'm afraid it's last minute. Leaving tomorrow, if possible. Jenny's voice was apologetic.

'Okay, well let's see what we can do,' replied Vicky turning to her computer screen and tapping on the keyboard, her chunky gold bracelet glittering.

'Your options are limited because of the time of the year – cancellations are all we have left.'

Jenny nodded and put her handbag down on the floor: she had been clutching it on her lap.

'Any idea of budget?' asked Vicky, her eyes switching from Jenny to the monitor screen and back again.

'Around four hundred pounds,' replied Jenny, a little embarrassed. 'And something here in this country. I can't be bothered with the hassle of airports.' She thought of the three-thousand-pound holidays she and her husband used to take; Mexico, Egypt, the Caribbean.

'For that price, I think our best chance is to look at some coach tours,' responded Vicky.

The other travel adviser had finished with the Asian lads, wishing them a good trip as they left the shop. Jenny noticed her name badge said 'Claire'. She stood up briefly glancing at Jenny.

'Are you okay if I take my break now?' her Yorkshire accent was heavy, just like her make-up.

'Sure,' said Vicky, her gaze fixed on the screen. Claire turned to go into the rear of the shop. Remembering something, she turned to Vicky.

'Did you bring in last week's *Herald*?' she asked.

Jenny felt her frame tighten at the mention of the local weekly paper.

Vicky fished around under her desk, and from her handbag handed Claire a folded newspaper. Claire disappeared into the back of the shop.

The two travel advisers failed to notice the trace of fear in Jenny's eyes as the paper was exchanged. While Vicky was busy taking down information from her computer screen, Jenny was thinking about the absent travel adviser; imagining her making a coffee, lighting a cigarette, and settling down with the *Herald*, laying it out on the table.

How long before she got to page two? thought Jenny. Four or five minutes if she was lucky.

'Okay. First of all, I have a space on a tour in Scotland departing...'

'I'll take it, just the thing,' interrupted Jenny, speaking quickly.

Vicky sensed desperation.

'But don't you want to hear about other options or the agenda for this one?'

Jenny shook her head, producing her credit card.

'Scotland – I've always wanted to go there It's ideal,' she responded, forcing a smile.

'Okay, let's get some personal details,' said Vicky, intrigued at the speed of this transaction. 'First off, you need to get to Edinburgh quickly – the tour started today, but you can catch it there.'

'No problem, I'll get the train tomorrow, or even tonight.' Jenny glanced to the rear of the shop, no sign of the brunette. Maybe she'd gone straight to the classifieds, not interested in the local news.

Five minutes later, Jenny stepped outside the shop, holding a brown manila envelope with details of the Scottish coach tour inside.

Her car was parked across the road opposite the parade of shops; a mini-supermarket, newsagent, off-licence and chemist. Jenny tended to use all of them, but not today – she would use a petrol station on the ring road to get what she needed.

As she unlocked her little blue hatchback and slipped in behind the steering-wheel, she did not see Vicky and Claire standing at the window, staring at her through a gap in the adverts.

'That's her?' asked Vicky as she looked at the photograph of a woman on page two of the paper Claire had handed to her when she had come back from her break, seconds after Jenny had left.

'I only got a quick look at her,' Claire replied, straining to see Jenny's face as she drove by quickly.

'Yeah,' confirmed Vicky, as she looked again at the photograph, 'same woman – that explains why she was in a hurry to get away from here.'

'What trip has she gone for?'

'Scotland.'

'Doesn't look the type,' added Claire.

'What, to go to Scotland?' quizzed Vicky.

'No, to be getting up to the things the paper says.'

'You can't always trust what the papers say.' Somehow Vicky felt sorry for the woman. Although she'd seemed uptight, Vicky had sensed warmth in Jenny Jenkins – warmth and kindness.

'Watch where you're going, I don't want to end up down that banking,' growled Gregory Spittlewood to his first wife.

A part of Miriam Ash would have loved to let go of the wheelchair she was pushing, sending her ex-husband careering down the grassy slope of the beautiful gardens they were in. He was being a right bugger on this trip, and it was only the second day.

The traffic from Edinburgh's Princess Street above was just a murmur, passing above the city gardens which nestled below the city's castle. The mid-morning sun felt good on Miriam's face as she strolled along with her wheelchair-bound charge.

'It was your driving, I never trusted your driving. Did you ever get a license?' His tone was derisory, almost bordering on cruel.

'That was years ago, Greg. You were never in the car with me, so how could you judge my driving?'

'Did you get a license, answer the question?' He turned to look at her, his eyes narrow slits as he squinted against the sun, the brightness of the day giving his skin an even more sallow look.

'No, I didn't,' replied Miriam.

'I'm surprised. You always seemed to get what you wanted – one way or another,' stated Gregory snidely.

He felt his wheelchair come to an abrupt stop and Miriam's taught face swing into his. Her words came fast and furious.

'What is it with you, always taking pieces out of me. Dig, dig, fucking dig...'

'But I thought that was the deal, removing the extra, taking it all away, slicing off the bits you didn't want,' spat Gregory, gripping his wheels.

'The deal! That was then! Not anymore you ungrateful... I'm not here today because of some arrangement...'

'I didn't ask you to come back...' but his words trailed in the light breeze as he watched Miriam's slim back walk away towards some steps. Turning his wheelchair in the opposite direction, Gregory quickly sped along the path.

She watched from the bottom of the steps as he abruptly stopped and turned to look up at the castle towering above. His sharp nose piercing the air, his pale lips drawn tight.

Miriam took a seat on a nearby bench. Forcibly quelling her flames of anger, she sought sympathy for a man so wrought in bitterness and hurt.

She couldn't really blame him, who could? There he was, trapped in a wheelchair, dependent on others, robbed of his mobility at the age of fifty-five; Gregory Spittlewood, a talented, brilliant man, one of Britain's first pioneering plastic surgeons.

A group of American tourists trundled past, all trainers and loud voices. One of the men gave her a look and smiled. She still looked great for fifty-three, even if Gregory's skills as a surgeon had had something to do with it.

That was the deal he had referred to. As their marriage was coming apart in the mid-seventies, he was getting his first practice off the ground in Harley Street and needed all the money he could beg, borrow and steal. It had been her idea to propose 'maintenance' in the literal sense. Over the coming years, whenever she required plastic surgery, her first husband would perform the operations free of charge.

Every eight or nine years, she had booked herself into his clinic, easier when he came out to New York and Los Angeles where she had remarried.

A friendship formed through the scalpel, a good natured understanding of each other at whatever point they were at in their lives. As he made his incisions, Miriam made her own into his emotional state at the time: where was he at with his love life – still going for blondes, or still losing money at the casinos and on the horses.

A candid exchange throughout her treatments, even when the bandages were coming off; the ex-husband and wife picking through each other's lives.

Gregory's work left no scars, only an invisible line of care over the years, a tracing of mutual welfare they both felt for each other.

'Some change for a cup of tea, mister?' asked the drunken tramp. His alcohol stained-breath engulfing the wheelchair-bound man, the former surgeon felt himself begin to retch. He tried to back away, but the matted-haired man held one of Gregory's wheels tight.

Miriam was at his side in seconds, a pearly toothed smile disarming the beggar as well as the pound coin she flicked towards him.

'Are you okay?' asked Miriam quickly.

'Yes, I was coping.' But Gregory did not sound convincing.

The Scotia Tours coach pulled in front of the Northern Regency Hotel, a cream-coloured Edwardian building situated on the north side of Newcastle's city centre.

It was 9.45 a.m. and Bob had made good time since the encounter with the reckless driver. He let the engine die, dropped down from the vehicle and lifted up the luggage door. Opening a cardboard box half-full of purple heather, Bob pulled a sprig out and wrapped the stems in silver paper. He smiled to himself, no doubt about it, the heather worked a treat on the ladies. Returning to the driver's seat, he inserted the shrub into his sun-visor.

Entering the hotel, a modern interior of smoked glass, chrome railings and marble flecked tiles, Bob looked for the tour party. By the concierge's desk was a stack of luggage, and by the quantity Bob guessed it belonged to the party he was here to pick up. They would be finishing their breakfast.

He was on his way to the reception desk, when he heard a voice behind him.

'Scotia Tours?' The enquiry was clipped.

Bob wheeled round to see a young man in his mid-twenties approaching. Average height, slim build with plain features, sporting a stubbly goatee beard, he was dressed in the same burgundy blazer, grey-flannel trouser uniform Bob wore.

Who was this? thought Bob. Where was Elspeth?

'Hi, you must be Bob,' the young man said.

'Yes.'

'Marc Ryder.' Bob sensed the trace of a Liverpool accent.

Bob extended his right hand to shake Marc's; an action which quickly prompted Marc to do the same.

'Is Elspeth here?' Bob asked, enquiring after the guide who he had taken this tour with for the last four years.

'Can't make it. Shingles.'

'How is she?' Bob was concerned – he liked Elspeth, and they made a good team.

'Don't know. All I know is she'll be off sick for a few weeks.' His reply was tinged with frustration, and Bob sensed this young man was not a willing stand-in.

'Have you done this tour before, Marc?'

'Yeah, but only as part of my induction training.' Marc continued. 'I was due in Ibiza this morning with my usual crew.' He was referring to the other reps on the 'Med Squad', the division of the company running the Mediterranean holidays for the 18 to 35 age group. 'Got a call from my supervisor, and because my training file said Scotland...'

'Put Ibiza out of your mind, no use in wishing you were there,' interrupted Bob, his attention caught by two couples in their mid-to-late fifties, approaching from the direction of the breakfast room.

Marc looked sternly at Bob. This was not what he wanted to hear. Instantly, he took a dislike to the coach driver. The feeling was mutual. Bob did not care for the whining goatee.

As the two couples drew closer, Bob could tell they were Scandinavian. The smart casual clothes were good quality and not drab. All four moved in unison. The two males, the two females, a tight little unit, just like their visits to the gym; moving around the equipment in a synchronised fashion.

Bob respected the Scandinavian attitude – the effort to stay current as middle age arrived.

'Marc, when are we departing?' asked the taller of the two men in good English.

Marc scanned his watch, but Bob beat him to the answer. '10.30 a.m., sir. Let me introduce myself. Robert Sinclair. I will be your coach driver for the trip.'

The little party beamed back at Bob, as his piston-like hand shook theirs, extending reassurance via a firm grip.

'Good to meet you, Robert. I'm Mats Andersson, my wife Gisela,' said the tall man, indicating the slim, short-haired brunette.

'Adam Frick,' said the shorter, stockier man, pushing his rimless glasses further up his nose.

'Lotta Frick,' added his tanned blonde wife, her eyes fixing on Bob's with a perceptive stare.

'Robert, the luggage,' quipped Marc, sarcasm heavy on the *Robert.*

Bob excused himself from the group and made his way to the portly concierge, hovering over the pile of suitcases with two of his underlings.

Soon the coach was loaded with luggage and 15 passengers. Like the couples Bob had met, the group's average age was between mid-fifties to mid-sixties. One exception was a 28-year-old woman who was accompanying her 67-year-old aunt who was working in a replacement hip.

The party majority was Swedish, with two Danish couples and an English couple. What typified the group was not so much nationality but the gender ratio; 12 out of the 17 were female.

Bob had his own theories on why coach-tour holidays appealed to women – the enjoyment the fairer sex derived from talking to each other, for one.

Coach seating was the key, two women sitting beside each other. This allowed conversation to be more free flowing, thinking out loud talking, lubricated conversation without the face-to-face reading that tends to punctuate and possibly inhibit.

Bob sat in the driving seat as the party boarded and used this opportunity to greet everybody with a smile and a 'good morning'.

It was also a good opportunity to get a measure of the group he would be spending the next ten days with.

Like the couples in the hotel lobby, this was a polite young middle-aged group. Bob noted how well the women looked. Two of the women in particular caught Bob's eye with their attractive disposition. Last on the bus, a woman of medium height, sunglasses pushed back on her honey-haired head, giggled with her friend who was slightly taller with a dark bob.

'Good morning, ladies,' welcomed Bob, unconsciously straightening his tie.

'Good morning, Mr Driver,' replied 'honey hair' in a Cheshire accent, her cheeky smile flashing at him. 'Eva Nelson. But don't let the accent fool you, I'm Swedish!'

'Very Swedish,' piped up 'dark bob' in a knowing voice, as she rummaged in her handbag to retrieve her mobile phone.

Eva continued, 'I was two years in Knutsford in the seventies. Kinda stuck in my English.'

Dark bob introduced herself in a low husky Swedish accent, 'I'm Christina and you are...?'

'Robert Sinclair, but call me Bob.' Bob felt his face open with a grin.

'Where do you want us to sit, Bob?' asked Eva, unbuttoning her turquoise cardigan that formed half of a matching twin-set.

'I kept these two seats especially for you.' He turned and indicated the two empty seats directly behind him.

'Good,' added Christina, 'we can see what you see, Bob.'

'The best view in the bus, ladies,' he replied as they sat down. In turn, Bob had a fine view in his internal mirror – both Eva and Christina had nice tanned legs, which they displayed, especially when cross-legged.

Ideal. I-fucking-deal!

They both laughed at some message on Christina's mobile phone, while returning his glances via his rear-view mirror.

Bob felt a current of energy drive through his body, a little surge of expectancy increasing his physical presence – of which he had plenty. His sheer maleness exuded through every pore, his sexual centre span like some mirror ball – reflecting back female lust ten fold – strengthening his pull on their desires. Bob conveyed strength and capability, a sureness of himself, which easily transferred to those around him – both men and women, but especially women.

Attractiveness of this sort in such concentration was a potent force on the opposite sex – power Bob wielded on a daily basis – mostly for his own gratification.

There was something even more attractive about this aspect – taking what he wanted – as much as a tour coach driver can get.

Marc moved down the aisle, counting heads to make sure all were aboard and with a nod to Bob took his seat at the front of the coach.

The diesel engine came to life. Bob moved the vehicle out onto the road, feeling the added weight of the passengers and the luggage.

The forces at work on his fully laden coach needed careful handling – the entire driving process had to be planned, controlled and accurate.

Braking and accelerating required a smooth approach. Bob took his craft seriously and took pride in delivering a comfortable journey for his precious human cargo. The first leg of the journey, he took a little slower to bed his passengers in, gain their confidence in his driving, for their well-being was in his hands.

The A1 to Edinburgh from Newcastle was often a frustrating traffic-clogged run, and the excursion to Bamburgh Castle on the Northumbrian coast was a welcome break in the middle of the day. The castle, one of England's finest, sat perched on a basalt outcrop, jutting out into the sea with views of the Farne Islands and Holy Island.

Marc felt the pressure of providing the first tour narrative, and was dependent on reading from a company manual.

'Dating from the sixth century, the castle was typical of many in England and Scotland, having many ups and downs. Most castles never recovered after the invention of the cannon, and it was only the rich who restored a few in the late

19th and early 20th century. Bamburgh was one of these privileged few.'

The party listened carefully, then split up to take a brief tour of the castle before local tea rooms tempted visitors with the aroma of hot lunchtime dishes.

By 2.30 p.m., the coach was back on the road, pushing north into Scotland through the border country. The green undulating valleys with their granite farmsteads and sheep-filled fields pressed into view.

The passengers commented on the Norse-sounding place names as the signs swished past.

Marc Ryder could not offer any commentary to the passing scenery as he had his head buried in the tour manual, trying to cram in the information he would need for the Edinburgh section of the trip.

The party would probably not have paid too much attention in any case; they were busy getting acquainted with each other. A sociable hum of Scandinavian conversation drifted down the coach. Bob liked the sound of other languages, and although he understood nothing of what was being said, he found the steady stream of noise a soothing background for his driving.

He glanced in his mirror. Eva was sleeping, her head against the window, propped by a Scotia Tours cushion. Christina looked up from her magazine. She caught Bob's eye in the mirror and smiled back before returning to her article. Her tanned legs looked even better than the last time Bob looked.

Just after 4.30 p.m., Marc's droney voice began emanating from the PA system. Standing at the front, microphone in hand, the manual lay open on his seat providing a script of description. 'Welcome to the capital city of Scotland; *Edinburgh!*'

They were descending down Lothian Road, a broad dual-lane thoroughfare into the centre of Edinburgh; a bustling main artery that pumped with the city's lifeblood of people and traffic. Rising up from either side of the bus, the fine

Victorian and Georgian architecture exuded stately pride in sandstone brick and granite facades.

'Built on seven hills, like Rome, the city has 16,000 buildings listed as architecturally or historically important.' Marc paused to catch his breath. His memory was holding out on what he had read so far. 'As you can see, approaching on the right is the dominant centrepiece to this fine city, Edinburgh Castle.'

Everyone looked over to see the skyline fill with the high-walled fortification, tiered ramparts rising high on the black craggy stump that was once a volcano.

Marc paused to let the party soak up the view and sat down relieved that no questions had arisen. The hotel was only five minutes away.

The coach turned onto Princess Street. Traffic lights, which ran along the street allowed Bob to crawl along steadily and give his party the opportunity to take in this magnificent city, which they did, just like others before them.

Arthur's Seat rose into view – a 251-metre miniature mountain set on the far side of the Old Town. Bob knew such sights gave an ideal start to the tour, and he always felt at this point that the show was well and truly underway.

His own made-up phrase skipped through his head for the second time that day.

I-fucking-deal!

Chapter Three

Jenny sank into her train seat on the 6.35 p.m. from York to Edinburgh with a mixture of exhaustion and relief; five minutes to departure, people boarding, luggage being hoisted onto overhead racks, silent goodbyes mouthed through the windowpanes.

Her window seat had a fixed table, and a couple of youths sat opposite; a boy and girl. They looked alternative, thought Jenny; a threadbare look for the young man with piercings, the girl had dreadlocks. They were immersed in each other, tangled like vines.

The train started into life with a heavy jolt, they were pulling out on time.

Jenny felt she could relax a little now, let the anxious knot inside her unravel a little, unspool as the miles clicked past. Her native part of Yorkshire was slipping away as the train sped northwards. The distance would make a difference, she thought.

She felt bad about leaving a message on the answer phone at the dental practice where she worked. Or should that be where she used to work.

They would not be surprised at the message on Monday: *Jenny here, sorry to do this, but I won't be in for a few days. A family crisis. I'll call you.*

She could visualise Sally Arkright smugly taking the news to Mr Ainley, her boss, who would raise one bushy eyebrow and then ask Sally to organise cover, her meat-slab face grinning with these instructions.

Family crisis! They would all know the real meaning, and the dentist partners would be relieved that Jenny would not be showing for work.

She would have to resign; she could not sit at the front desk, patients coming and going with their knowing smiles or disapproving looks.

The practice would ask her to leave anyway – they could not have a receptionist like her. How was it the paper put it? *Respectable neighbour by day, providing a sleazy service by night.*

It all felt so unfair, that bloody rag. Sleazy service: how dare they judge her about what she did in her private life – with the utmost discretion. No one ever got hurt, it was all a bit of harmless fun for grown ups.

It was a shame about her little receptionist job though. Mr Ainley was good to work for; a sweet-natured man who always seemed to appreciate Jenny's efficiency, the way she handled the difficult patients, soothed the nervous ones with her sympathetic smile and always had the correct records at hand.

She took pride in her role, pride in everything she did; running away like this felt alien. Jenny had never run away from anything before. It must be instinct, she thought, or was it shame? Her mind, her emotions, were overwrought. She needed to relax, to try and switch off.

Jenny rummaged in the oversized handbag she used for travelling. The CD Walkman given to her by her son Peter was in a side pocket.

Sweet Peter. She wondered how he was doing in Dubai; he had been working there for nearly a year now. One good thing about the location, he would not be reading the *Allerton Herald*.

Thinking about Peter sparked a positive feeling. His thoughtful articulate speech came to mind at the party she had organised for him before he left for the new job abroad. In front of family and friends, he had stood between his parents, an arm around each, and proclaimed, 'From this fine clay, I was fashioned, a vessel, who is thankful for such substance.'

He had looked at both of them. He was proud. They were proud.

Slipping on the headphones, Jenny checked to see if her *Best Of Supertramp* was in the player. She skipped to track three, *The Logical Song*.

The song's lyrics had been her favourite since she had got into the band. As she had grown older, this particular song had become her own private anthem whenever she was in need of a boost.

The Yorkshire Dales sped past outside. With the music in her ears, an underscore to the rural scenery, Jenny felt an undertow of sleep tug at her consciousness. The couple had slipped into this state too, their heads resting against each other. They looked peaceful and together.

Jenny propped her summer fleece against the window and closed her eyes. She so wanted to sleep, as a proper night's rest had evaded her since Friday.

The music faded and she drifted off.

Her dreams were short, disjointed with no real substance until she settled into one channel of vivid dreaming. She was back in her kitchen, a winter-evening blackness outside. The room was filled with smells and cooking heat. The front door opened and she heard the familiar metal clunk of John dropping his car keys onto the hall table. Jenny had had this dream before; the ones about John were reassuring.

His broad frame came through into the kitchen, taking off his suit jacket and tie, his tallness forcing him to bend down to peck her on the forehead as she greeted him. As in the other dreams, he looked the picture of health, never the gaunt figure he had become as the cancer had eaten through his lungs.

Now they were eating. Jenny took in his broad face, the strength of his features, the sandy hair which made him look younger than he was. But it was his piercing blue eyes that were his best feature. They had always melted her, even when she was angry at his frustrating stubbornness.

He looked up and asked, 'Have you checked the site?'

She heard her reply, 'No.' and felt the atmosphere in the dream shift from warm to cold.

'Better check then.' He got up and headed for the little study across the hall. The cold feeling was turning into fear, an emotion that propelled her after him. But he had locked the study door. She could see him through the square glass panes of the door frame, his back to her, the computer monitor flickering.

Jenny's heart was pumping, rapid beats of despair as an image of her naked self flashed onto the screen, full frontal, moving in a jerky dance. Then her name and address in big, bold luminous letters passed over her digital body.

JENNY JENKINS, 25 ELGIN GARDENS, ALLERTON.

John's head and body turned in the chair, his face was incredulous at first, and then rage stabbed its way across his features.

'What have you done...what have you done to our website?' Through the glass, Jenny could hear the question bellowed.

She felt herself turning, but it was as if her feet were glued in treacle – moving was impossible, slow and laboured. RUN AWAY, her mind screamed.

She pulled herself forward into the lounge, aware of John coming after her. As he caught her at the back of the sofa, she felt his weight bear down on her body and she flipped onto the cushioned seats. But now it could not be John forcing her head into the armrest, the upholstery filling her face, breathing in the fibres; John would never have pushed her around like this.

She felt a barking angry voice in her ear as an arm held her down.

'You stupid woman. What have you done to the bloody site?'

The arm across her shoulder blades pushed harder. The fury continued.

'I told you to be careful, I told you again and again, discretion is the key, if we keep it discreet...'

Jenny felt herself lift, not from the sofa, but from the horror of the dream.

She awoke with a start, jolting in her seat. Her breath came in little gasps; a light film of sweat bathed her forehead and palms. The anxious knot inside remained, wound tighter with the beating of her heart.

The carriage was now lit up, outside only the blackness of night covered the window. No lights were visible. The train must be in the countryside.

Jenny checked her watch; it was nearly nine o'clock. Her sleep had been deeper, longer than she thought. She felt some calmness return, the relief of reality over fantasy.

A yearning for John inhabited her, a hollow turning of emotions, like gears and cogs turning with no purpose.

The couple were no longer across the table. Their belongings gone, they must have departed at an earlier stop. Something else had disappeared – her Walkman. The headphones were still over her ears, but the unplugged cable lay at her side.

She did feel angry a few seconds later. To add insult to injury, her Supertramp CD had been left. The shiny disc lay abandoned on top of her magazine.

The breakfast in the St Andrews hotel was very good, especially the scrambled eggs. Bob had accompanied the eggs with brown toast, fresh orange juice and a bowl of bran flakes.

He usually ate on his own before the tour party guests sauntered into the restaurant. It was a preference he had allowed himself after coming out of the army in 1972. Barrack breakfast was eating with a 'pack' of men, the only bug-bear about army life. Bob liked his own company first thing in the morning; the breakfast table was his moment of solitude.

He made his way through the hotel lobby and onto the street. It was another clear blue sky day. The morning sun glinted off the cream Georgian frontage of the hotel. A veil of moisture was lifting across the city, evaporating in the sun's rays.

Bob took a stroll onto George Street to soak up the city: a city which had been part of his life since 1965. Then he'd been a raw recruit of twenty when he'd enlisted with the Argyll and Sutherland Highlanders.

A Scottish regiment with a glorious history stretching back to 1794; Waterloo, the thin red line of the Crimea campaign, the Zulu Wars, the Somme. The regimental motto's were *Ne Obliviscaris* – Do Not Forget, and *Sans Peur* – Without Fear.

Bob was to find these very apt for his first year with a platoon of 'Jocks', who kept reminding him he was *English*, a *sassanach*; a man who should have joined a regiment south of the border.

But Bob had grown up listening to his Scottish father's tales from the Second World War, and of the *glorious Argylles*. Sinclair senior's love of the regiment had made an impression on the young Bob; so much so, he specifically requested to join them when entering the army. His father had been very proud.

But Bob was not prepared for the abuse he received from his fellow soldiers, the insults and pranks. But growing up in the streets of south London stood him in good stead to give as good as he got.

He won the 'Scottish bastards' over with his determination, his ability as a soldier, a quick sense of humour, and most of all, with his boxing gloves.

Bob settled many a score in the ring with the satisfaction of seeing one of his tormentor's bloody faces hitting the canvas as he punched him out. 'Without Fear' became his personal motto.

By the time he had been in Edinburgh for six months, he had six good friends around him in the platoon, friends he still had today. Winning respect from a Scot was hard work, but once they gave it, they never took it away.

He looked up at the castle that frowned back from its rocky stump and decided he would visit it today, tag along with the tour party. Normally, he would amuse himself on his day off, take in a few bars, relax.

Jenny Jenkins joining the tour party came as a surprise to Marc.

Only on reading the fax he had forgotten to pick up from reception the night before, did he realise there was not only one additional person joining the group, but three.

Now he had to meet this Jenkins woman, leaving less time to read up on the day's excursion. Then again, he wished he wasn't here at all, and his aggrieved state was manifesting itself as it usually did in these situations; small white heat lumps appearing on the back of his hands. With severe stress, they spread to his back, causing a terrible itching sensation.

Jenny waited in reception and watched the comings and goings of the hotel guests. A woman pushing a man in a wheelchair took a table not far from her. He looked sullen, but was smartly dressed in a crisp white shirt and light tan jacket. She wore designer jeans and a white polo shirt with plenty of jewellery.

'Gregory, would you like a coffee?' twanged her transatlantic accent.

He nodded without looking in her direction.

Jenny now realised how little she knew about the tour, the itinerary, places she would be visiting.

The hotel was a good omen for the trip – very pleasant and comfortable.

A young man in a burgundy blazer with a goatee beard appeared in reception and approached her, a thick lever arch file under his arm, looking a little agitated.

'Jenny?' he enquired.

'Yes. You must be Marc,' Jenny replied standing up, smoothing down her denim dress, slipping back on her right

open-toed mule which had unconsciously slipped off.
He did not shake her hand as she expected. 'I have the
itinerary here. It's got all the excursions we run.' He produced
a clutch of typed sheets. The guide then noticed the man in the
wheelchair.

'Scotia Tours?' questioned Miriam as she passed Marc,
coffees in hand. 'Hi, I'm Miriam, and that's Gregory. Did you
get our message?'

At closer range, Jenny could see this woman had had major
cosmetic surgery, the fastened down look of skin tissue
stretched and fixed to some concealed point. Jenny noticed
the falseness extended to her breasts which seemed too large
for her slight frame.

Marc acknowledged their presence and immediately
launched into his talk.

His brusque manner did not invite any questions, but Jenny
had one. 'Today's excursion? What is it?'

'Edinburgh Castle. It's a short walk from here.'

'The coach? Does it have a hydraulic ramp? That's why we
booked with you?' asked Gregory, speaking for the first time.

'Yes, Mr Spittlewood, and our driver is very capable too.
He'll be around to help.'

'I take it all the hotels are geared for wheelchair access?'
chipped in Miriam looking at both Marc and Jenny.

'Yes, they are,' replied the guide.

'And, if I need some specific help with Gregory?' continued
Miriam, looking directly at Jenny, waiting for her to offer her
name.

'I think there is a misunderstanding. I'm one of the party,
I'm not with Scotia Tours.'

A high-pitched peel of laughter came from Miriam's
sculpted face, 'I'm sorry, forgive me, silly me.'

Jenny prayed the rest of the party were not like this woman.

Marc distributed some more information to the new
members of the coach party and turning to go asked, 'You
might also want to attend the dinner show tonight. Will I put
you down?' He forced a smile.

'Love to. What's the theme?' enquired Miriam.

'It's a Scottish...' He paused trying to find a description for something he did not have a clue about.

Jenny helped him out. 'Scottish night...claymores and bagpipes I bet.'

'You've got it, that's the thing.' Then he was gone.

Gregory extended his hand towards Jenny with a slight smile. 'Pleased to meet you young lady.'

'Jenny. Call me, Jenny,' she replied, unsure if Miriam's smile was genuine.

The views from the ramparts of Edinburgh Castle were spectacular. The city's carpet of historic buildings stretched out underneath the gaze of the party, all the way to the sparkling strip of blue sea – the Firth Of Forth.

The panorama took in Princess Street and the gardens running parallel – the green space cutting a swathe of colour through the heart of the city.

The Scott Monument's jagged blackness jutting into view competed with the twelve columns of the National Monument on Calton Hill for the skyline. All around, spires and domes conveyed history, the orderly design of the new town, rubbing shoulders with the Old Town's closes, wynds, vaults, steps and cobbles.

Marc asked for the attention of the party; they huddled around the large medieval cannon that stood next to St Margaret's Chapel. The clutch of Scandinavians, milling together, strained to understand Marc's accent. They had a newly pressed air to their appearance; this being the first day of proper excursions – the day when a holidaymaker believes the vacation has started in full – the men, adorned with cameras, the women with makeup.

Marc was struggling with the tour facts on the castle, the information he'd memorised the evening prior was slipping out of his mind like change through a torn pocket.

He had also not expected the driver to come along. Marc had caught Bob's smug little smiles when he had stumbled over some historical account. The guide's hands were itching constantly. With raised voice, he launched into the origins of the cannon. 'Don's Meg is a cannon which was forged in...'

'Mons Meg,' corrected Bob, loud enough for everyone to hear from his position at the rear of the group, 'Mons Meg.'

'Mons Meg,' continued Marc, his neck growing red under his collar, 'was built in France...'

'Belgium,' interjected Bob again, who now had come to stand at the front of the party. Mats and Lotta stood next to him; they saw the, 'if looks could kill look' dart between Marc to Bob.

Marc paused, forced a smile, and turned to look at the cannon. 'I think you will find Belgium was part of France when this piece of artillery was created.'

A good bluff, thought Bob, and on that basis did not continue with his comments. He let Marc ramble on.

Jenny stood at the back of the group, but she was not listening to the verbal spat that was taking place. Her head swivelled around to take in the atmosphere of the grand overbearing fortification. It was good to be in the company of people, to enjoy the anonymity of being with strangers.

They would become less like strangers each day, but for the moment, she felt safe in this little pocket of people, their polite smiles reassuring her to stay.

The party began moving, the huddle falling into a column as it moved to another part of the castle. One of the Scandinavian men was pushing Gregory, a relieved Miriam in tow. Jenny decided to explore on her own, and broke away in the opposite direction.

Bob lingered at Mons Meg with Eva and Christina.

'You are very knowing about this big gun,' stated Eva, running her hand over the black metal casing.

'I had to clean it on many occasions when I was stationed here with the army.'

Bob pulled his camera from its case. He had Eva in his

sights. With mock shyness she leant with her back against the cannon. Eva beckoned Christina to join her.

'The army? When was this, Bob?' enquired Christina, adjusting her cream blouse to look its best.

'The seventies.' He fiddled with the lens to get them into focus. Their outfits complimented each other. Both had print skirts on; Eva's pastel blue, Christina's pastel yellow. Eva wore a white top with a V-neck showing off her cleavage.

'Smile, ladies.' The camera clicked. 'Hold it. That's good.' Bob moved closer to them. 'Christina, can you put your arm around Eva?'

Christina did. 'You look like two school girls on a field trip.' They both laughed and Bob caught the moment on film. One for the album, he thought.

Marc herded the group into St Margaret's Chapel. He noted the group had reduced and was relieved to see the driver was missing.

'As you can see, this is a very old building, nine hundred years old. The architecture is Norman and St Margaret's Chapel survived all the battles the castle underwent. The castle was demolished several times, but not the chapel.' Marc was pleased with his commentary. He allowed himself a smile, another couple of words and they would move on.

'Mr Ryder?'

Marc's hackles bristled. The fucking driver had shown up, now standing to his right. 'Yes, Bob.'

'Why did the chapel survive when everything else was destroyed?'

Marc did not have the answer. He had read it, but not retained it. All eyes were on him, silence filling the little room. His silent prayer for an answer went unheard.

'Religious significance spared St Margaret's,' pronounced Bob. 'No invading horde could desecrate this holy place.' He sounded a little holy now.

Marc could take no more, but before he could say anything, Bob interjected again with an open question to the group.

'My question was a little unfair. This is Marc's first tour of Edinburgh. I can add a little more light to this place if you want?'

Christina and Eva chimed, 'Yes.'

Not waiting to hear the ditty, Marc stormed out of the chapel, his heat spots on fire.

Jenny stood in the half-moon battery, soaking up the sun; its rays flowing into her body, the heat slackening the tautness in her frame.

Her eyes closed, she leaned against one of the huge cannons that poked through the battlement wall. Moving at a quick pace, Marc brushed past her, rubbing his hands.

Two minutes later the party, led by Bob, caught up with Jenny and she decided to rejoin the group, falling into step with a couple that appeared to be her age. 'Was it interesting?' she addressed them both.

The man answered. 'Yes. Mr Sinclair knows his history.' He was a handsome fifty-something, but with his sandy hair, he looked younger. 'I'm Henrik, this is my wife, Pernille.'

'Pleased to meet you, I'm Jenny.' She shook both their hands. Pernille was the attractive equivalent of Henrik. Both had light grey eyes, fair hair and smooth complexions. She too was probably older than she looked.

'Is this your first time in Scotland?' Jenny enquired.

'Yes. Friends recommended we make the trip,' replied Henrik in perfect English.

'It's wonderful,' added Pernille. 'Denmark is so flat, we have come to see the mountains.'

'You're Danish?'

'We are,' proclaimed Henrik proudly.

'There is another Danish couple on the tour,' informed Pernille.

'The rest,' Henrik lowered his voice. 'Are Swedes.' He raised his eyebrows.

Pernille smiled.

The party had reached the car park where Marc stood at

the battlement wall, facing out across to Princess Street. His composure regained a little, he waited to see Bob's next move with the party. Bob broke away from the group and walked over to Marc.

'Finished?' Marc seethed. 'Or do you want to do the whole fucking tour today?'

'Marc, these people have paid good money for this trip. They deserve proper facts, accurate information...'

'Not fucking fair. Not fair. I have been dropped into this one.' Some spittle from Marc's mouth flew onto Bob's shirt.

Bob felt a twinge of sympathy for Marc. 'Calm down, I was making the point...'

'Make your point by disappearing. I can manage!' Marc's voice was raised.

'Keep your voice down.' Bob did not want a scene in front of the party. 'Fine by me, you're on your own.'

Marc did not say another word. He quickly walked over to the group where he addressed them all. 'We can proceed to the Royal Mile now,' his voice edgy and rattled. 'You are free to explore on your own if you wish. Those continuing with me, please raise their hands?'

The majority of the group took this option. Eva, Christina, Henrik, Pernille and Jenny declined the offer.

'Follow me,' instructed Marc, turning on his heel and setting off at a quick pace in the direction of the Royal Mile.

Eva and Christina joined Bob at the car park wall overlooking Arthur's Seat.

'Bob,' asked Eva, 'I don't suppose you could give us a mini-tour?'

'Sure. No problem. But first ladies, we need a little drink and I know just the place.' They took one of his arms each, and in step headed off to the Grassmarket district, a big fat grin on Bob's face.

Jenny, Pernille and Henrik agreed to seek out a tearoom for some refreshments. Just off the Royal Mile, opposite Parliament Square, they discovered Mackay's Teas. The smell of tea, coffee and fresh baking filled their noses as they entered.

Two grey-haired women were busy serving customers. One of them waved them over to a table at the window.

'What cakes do you have?' Jenny asked passing a waitress.

'Come to the counter. You can choose what you fancy.'

Pernille touched Jenny lightly on the arm. 'Let's take a look.'

The two women peered into the glass fronted display counter where the freshly baked produce was neatly arranged. Jenny decided on a slice of ginger cake, Pernille on a scone with cream and jam. Two large creamy coffees completed their order. Henrik had already opted for macaroni cheese.

'Jenny,' asked Pernille. 'Are you on your own for this trip?'

Jenny was used to this question since John's death. 'I'm widowed.'

She always answered this question in a matter of fact way, it seemed the only way to answer. Her coffee and cake arrived. She took a small spoon to the cake, popping a thin slice into her mouth.

'Sorry to hear this, Jenny,' sympathised Pernille. Henrik echoed his wife's comment.

'Life goes on, Pernille,' explained Jenny. 'I have become quite independent. My friends have been wonderfully supportive.' The latter part of the sentence about friends did not seem to ring true since last week; a feeling of isolation fleetingly inhabiting her. Jenny felt Pernille squeeze her hand gently.

'Good for you.' Pernille smiled warmly.

The woman was a genuine person, a giving person and Jenny liked this very much.

Henrik wiped his mouth. 'I lost my brother last year. He was only forty-two. It made us all appreciate what life was about.'

'John was fifty-two. Lung cancer. It only took three months from diagnosis to when he passed away.' Jenny paused before continuing. 'The thing was, I was the one still smoking. He'd given up three years earlier.' She smiled philosophically. 'I gave up the day the doctor told him it was lung cancer.'

'Henrik gave up just last year,' informed Pernille. 'Now he can't stop eating.'

Henrik shovelled his macaroni cheese into his mouth and thought about dessert.

'We all need a vice,' added Jenny. 'It's only human.'

'If you don't mind me asking, what's yours, Jenny?' Pernille was intrigued.

'Oh, too early to say, Pernille. I need to get to know you better.' Jenny half whispered her answer with a mischievous look.

Pernille laughed and vowed to uncover the English woman's secrets.

They chatted easily for another forty-five minutes, exchanging life and family histories. Henrik was a civil engineer, working for the Swedish government. Pernille had gone back to work after their son and daughter went to senior school. She worked in the administrative department of a large hospital in Stockholm.

Jenny talked about her son, Peter, and her beloved John. She fondly recalled their childhood sweetheart romance, growing up in neighbouring streets, losing touch while he was at college then striking up their relationship again in their early twenties when they met at a party.

Conversation between Jenny, Pernille and Henrik came easily. They made each other feel relaxed and Jenny looked forward to the Danish couple's company over the coming trip.

Both women sensed they liked each other; female frequencies meeting, wavelengths matching, like-minded signals converging. Pernille and Jenny related to each other in the tacit responses only women understand.

Leaving the tearoom, they continued their exploration of the Royal Mile together, Jenny feeling like her old self again,

Pernille pleased she had found some good female company for the holiday.

Jenny did not have anything to read for her trip, so they stopped off at a large bookstore, packed with tourists.

Henrik disappeared into the transport section of the store to seek out a classic motorcycle book, while Pernille and Jenny browsed the fiction shelves.

'What kind of books do you like?' enquired Pernille.

'A good love story...with plenty of realistic sex.'

'Me too!'

They both giggled like schoolgirls, and set about looking for a likely title.

'What about this,' offered Pernille. 'Mitch Alexi was a successful corporate lawyer in a Boston law firm, used to getting his way until he met Cassia Armstrong, his new boss. From the boardroom to the bedroom, this stormy romance spills off the page with corporate excess, glitzy parties, sizzling sex...'

'A tale of everyday folk then,' commented Jenny as she spied a book on the shelf she had read. A little charge of daring skipped through her. Should she mention the book to Pernille, or would it say too much about herself?

Jenny decided not to fetch it down from the shelf. Maybe a Scottish travel book would be a better investment.

Seconds later, Pernille nudged Jenny. She turned to see her holding the book: *A Tail Of Two Women*.

'My friend recommended this to me,' stated Pernille.

Not being able to resist, Jenny took the book and immediately went to page sixty-seven. 'This author can write good sex – listen to this.'

Jenny began to read.

Alexandra had nearly finished a bottle of Merlot by three in the afternoon when Milly arrived. The wine had given her the urge to bake a cake for her eight year old, who would be returning from a friend's house in the early evening. Milly gave a derisory laugh at this picture of domesticity as she sat herself at the kitchen table.

'Look at you, prim and proper housewife.' Milly took a sip from the glass of wine Alexandra had poured her, topping up her alcoholic intake from her pub lunch.

'Piss off Milly, I do what I want,' exclaimed Alexandra as she returned to pounding dough at the other end of the table. A few seconds later a ball of dough hit Milly on the shoulder. The play fight had begun. Cake mix, flour and dough was flying around the kitchen with their raucous laughter. Soon they were wrestling on the floor. Knowing Milly's weak spot for tickling, Alexandra squeezed her ribs. Milly responded by grabbing her friend's hair and gently tugged her face towards her own. They looked at each other for a second before kissing, full on the mouth, slowly at first, and then with more passion. Both women were responding to their childhood memories, to their childhood friendship; the experimentation of curious thirteen year olds on holiday with Alexandra's parents in southern France.

Milly moved her mouth down onto Alexandra's right breast, pushing her mouth over the outline of the nipple that lay under the white cotton top. Milly felt the nipple harden, reaching upwards for more of her mouth.

Alexandra tugged her top up to let mouth and breast be united…

'Is that good?' asked Henrik, his question startling them both as he approached. Both women had been huddled together, caught up in the scene Jenny had been reading in hushed tones.

'Good enough for me,' declared Pernille as she took the book from Jenny and headed for the sales counter. Henrik joined her, his book on motorcycles under his arm.

Jenny smiled; this was going to be a good trip. Like a *Tail Of Two Women*, the writing was in the build up, in the anticipation – she felt some kind of hope with Pernille.

Chapter Four

Evening cloud drew in over Edinburgh, bringing a humid atmosphere to the city. The tour party had freshened up after their first day, and were congregating in the hotel lobby; a further opportunity for the party to get to know each other better and reflect on the day.

Gill and Robert Hunter, an English couple, were settling into the Nordic company with the ease expected of two retired primary school teachers. Robert especially liked the look of the Scandinavian women, making a special effort by buying a new shirt for the evening – more colourful than his usual choice of garment. He had also acquired a pair of stylish sandals – like the ones Adam and Mats wore – discarding his old training shoes.

Teaming up with the Fricks and the Anderssons, the Hunters were now pleased they were on this non-English trip.

As Bob left his hotel room that evening, he bumped into Marc, whose room was adjacent. Bob spoke first.

'How did the tour go?' His tone was genuine.

'Okay,' came the sullen reply.

Arriving at the lift. Marc stabbed at the call button. He did not wish to chat, not granting any eye contact.

Bob noticed the white lumps on the back of Marc's hands. The lift was taking its time, forcing the guide to talk.

'How was your afternoon?' His question bordered on civility.

'Good. I took Eva and Christina to the *Jolly Beggar*. Then we walked down to Hollyrood Palace.' Bob smiled to himself

– it had been a good afternoon. He'd got them both to do the talking, mostly about themselves, and discovered they were both recently divorced – two women who had set out on this vacation to enjoy new-found freedoms.

Christina was a team supervisor for a computer supplies company. Eva was still to find a job she liked, but was not too worried as her divorce settlement was sizeable.

Christina had a seventeen-year-old daughter, Eva no children. Bob sensed this was a sensitive issue.

After two drinks in the pub, Bob escorted them both along Princess Street for some shopping. He had made up the Hollyrood Palace visit.

The driver had had the opportunity to give some social commentary too. Christina commented on how loudly the Edinburgh people spoke. The city was still a small enough conurbation for people to reach the centre quickly, and socialise in the midst of the tourists. Bob felt their unconscious reaction to the visitors was a territorial one by talking loudly.

By the time they had returned to the hotel just after four o'clock in the afternoon, Bob had decided which one of the 'girls' was up for it. He'd asked her for her mobile phone number while the other was in the bathroom, and she had given it willingly.

The lift arrived for Marc and Bob. When the doors opened again on the ground floor, the Scandinavian chatter in the lobby, a relaxed murmur of human voices, greeted them.

'Marc?'

Marc was accosted by Miriam who looked a little tense.

'We won't be coming along to the dinner show. Gregory is tired from today. We've booked at table in the restaurant.'

'No problem.'

'You'll like the food here,' commented Bob, delivering his winning smile.

'Good. That's good,' replied Miriam, sensing the driver's gaze resting on her chest.

The entrance to the 'Scotland's Journey' dinner show

establishment was deceptive. Located in the Old Town, it appeared to be an old building from the outside. Two burly doormen in full highland dress ushered the party inside and down some twisting steps, which gave way to a room with a high ceiling, a vast cellar-like hall.

The rectangular hall was decorated in a Scottish-castle style; flags and banners, claymore swords, round shields on the walls. Replica tapestries depicted battles from history. Gaelic music played in the background.

Three sides of the hall had tiered seating with tables facing into the centre of the room to a low square stage. The remaining wall had a red velvet curtain across it.

The tour party filed into their designated seats led by one of the young waitresses in traditional costume. The room was filling up quickly with other tourists, including a large group of Japanese.

Bob sat between Eva and Christina. Jenny sat on the next table, Henrik and Pernille on either side.

A loud drum roll called the audience to silence. From behind the curtain strode a tall white-bearded man in full highland dress. He took the stage in a single bound.

'Good evening and a big warm welcome to Scotland's Journey. My name is Fergus and I will be your host for tonight. So enjoy the food and drink we have prepared for you, and let me take you on a journey of discovery through this land's history.'

The Japanese group started clapping as Fergus disappeared behind the curtain.

The first course of the meal was ferried in; vegetable broth with bread rolls and a choice of beer or wine, served from earthenware jugs.

The tour party were getting into the spirit of the evening, even petite Anna Unge, the twenty-eight-year old niece of Jessica Boll. Anna had agreed to accompany her sweet natured aunt as she was still working in her replacement hip. Anna was sweet-natured too, but on seeing the 'bunch of old crocs' at the ferry port, she had felt her spirits dive – this trip would be so boring. But the convivial atmosphere of the dinner show now lifted her somewhat.

Again Fergus began his narration. 'We start our journey in 1057 with Malcolm the Third of the House of Canmore!' And so the show commenced with a quick twirl through Scottish history; William Wallace, Robert the Bruce, Mary Queen of Scots, the Jacobite Rebellion. The players enacting the key scenes in historical dress, rolling around the stage in mock battles, whooping up blood-curdling cries, waving swords, and rounding off with highland dancing to skirling bagpipes.

Christina and Eva's eyes were fixed on the theatre of the show. The choreographed sword fights, the 'fight for freedom' speeches, the bad guys, the good guys, the rousing music.

Christina also had another sensation from the show which she knew was exclusive – Bob's firm hand regularly giving her left thigh a little squeeze – an assured physical signal passed from a man who sensed mutual attraction in this woman. Each touch triggered a pleasant feeling into her middle, then up into her chest. It had started in the *Jolly Beggar*, the increase in eye contact between them, the openness in the body language, the invisible heat only they could see.

But Christina had to be careful. Eva liked to get the attention of any males they encountered – her insecurity was the main reason she had lost her husband to a younger woman. The affair had had a negative effect on her self esteem, her bubbly surface was a thin veneer over a brittle core.

Christina had found her divorce liberating. Her relationship with her husband coming to a natural end without any external factors or influences. Being independent had a diverse effect on both women; Christina had become stronger, Eva a little weaker.

Jenny, Pernille and Henrik were enjoying the show too. Henrik had sweet-talked the waitress into two helpings of the main course. The women's newfound friendship was being well oiled with wine. They had become 'giggly' at their observations of the show's players.

'Mary Queen of Scots looks like a man. I'm sure she has a moustache,' commented Jenny.

Pernille laughed. 'Look, one of the Scottish warriors has dropped a mobile phone from his pocket. So much for historical accuracy.'

Pernille liked Jenny; the warm openness she exuded put her at ease.

She liked the way Jenny brought out her fun side – the carefree aspect of her nature, which was only triggered by a handful of people. When she was a teenager, a girlfriend by the name of Alex had had the same effect. They had had great fun, especially with the boys at school – teasing, flirting, daring each other to discover more about the opposite sex. Pernille felt she was having the same type of interaction with Jenny.

Jenny felt it too. She found her new-found friend easy to be with, conversation coming easy. More to the point, Pernille listened, really listened, to what she had to say.

Jenny could hear someone else's words while watching the show – a narration of sorts, drifting from the tall guy behind, the one who seemed to spend most of his time with the two Swedish women.

'He seems to know what he's talking about,' suggested Pernille. She moved her eyes upwards to indicate the man behind them.

'He must think this is a school trip, and he's the teacher,' quipped Jenny.

'If he does, he must be hoping to give some sex education later. He's had his hand on the brunette's thigh a few times in the last half an hour,' whispered Pernille.

'You must have eyes in the back of your head.'

'I caught them in my vanity mirror when I checked my lipstick. I checked again five minutes ago.' Pernille looked pleased with her spy work.

Jenny made a quick glance behind her.

Sure enough, his hand was on her thigh.

'A perk of the job I would imagine,' added Pernille.

Jenny looked quizzical.

'He's the coach driver. Our coach driver.' Her tone was hushed; she looked ahead.

The bus driver, mused Jenny.

Another person was listening to Bob's comments. Marc was sitting directly in front of him, next to Henrik. Marc tried not to listen, knowing Bob's comments were winding him up. What had started as irritation had now turned to loathing. He detested Bob's superior tone, just like the one his own father used.

Marc felt the next nine days stretch out before him with a gut-sickening dread and in that instant made his mind up – he was not continuing with this. He would quit!

Tomorrow, he would get a train back home to Liverpool, get a budget airline flight to Ibiza, or maybe Greece, and pick up a rep's job, wherever he ended up.

Fuck it, he'd made his mind up. As the audience stood to cheer the players, Marc cheered too, not for Scotland's freedom but his own.

'It's not the Dorchester,' quipped Gregory, spooning fish soup.

'It's okay though, good value,' stated Miriam, looking around the half-full dining room of the hotel. She would have loved to have gone to the dinner show; the tour party's excitement in reception had been obvious.

'Value! When were you ever one for value, Miriam? I can remember you telling me once you only ate in the most expensive places, but then again you wouldn't be paying for it.'

Miriam ignored his comment, but did fleetingly recall a wonderful restaurant in the hills outside Cannes which her second husband, Frank, had taken her to. How different he had been to Gregory, pulling himself up from a working-class background to build a successful pharmaceutical company. He had been dynamic, impulsive, a larger-than-life character, even a little crazy. She turned the diamond encrusted ring on her index finger; the one he had bought her in Las Vegas.

'Which one gave you that?' sniped Gregory, quickly gulping down a large glass of red wine.

'You should know by now,' replied Miriam, holding up her right hand which dripped with rings. All four fingers sported precious stones, encrusted bands; each one from a different ex-husband.

'Naturally, I know the one I gave you, but the others, haven't a clue.'

'The sapphire is Frank's.'

'That makes sense, all gaudy and vulgar,' stated Gregory playfully, the alcohol taking the edge off his dark mood.

'Frank wasn't vulgar, he just liked to make a statement, that's all. A statement of his love for me.' Miriam felt relieved at Gregory's shift in spirits.

'Some statement from the man who could not keep his hands off your friends,' chortled Gregory.

'You're one to talk. Wasn't it Ellen's cousin you were caught in bed with, or was she the one you had in the stables?'

A dark shadow glanced across Gregory's features for a second, but it wasn't the mention of his infidelity; it was the word stables.

He did not reply, but chewed on his steak, giving a small smile of appreciation for the food. Miriam began to eat too, wishing she had not brought up the topic of horses. Even if they were watching a movie with a horse-riding scene, the former surgeon would ask Miriam to switch channels. For it had been in a polo competition a year earlier that Gregory had been thrown from his horse and the base of his spine permanently damaged, confining him to a wheelchair for the rest of his life.

But it was more than the loss of his mobility, it was the forced ending of his career; the one thing in his life which defined him so perfectly. He had been a god, now he was a mortal.

'Well, if the worst comes to the worst, we'll have your jewellery to sell,' scoffed Gregory.

'No way! Never,' panicked Miriam, clutching her hands.

'Might have to. You know how tight things are. Why else are we on this coach tour with these people. It's not what we're used to. It's not St Moritz.'

Miriam leant over and squeezed Gregory's hand, 'What does it matter, at least we tasted luxury living, so many don't.' But she knew he was right.

Chapter Five

By 9.15 a.m., the coach was loaded with the tour group, the luggage in the hold. The morning sunshine was a little bright for some of the tour group's eyes, bleary from the previous evening's alcohol. Bob had secured Gregory behind the tour guide seat. He would have a good view from this position. Miriam fussed over him as usual.

Lisa Hedlund, a shy burly lady was complaining to her friend Carmen Karlsson that the previous evening's meal had given her terrible wind. Rather than quietly exhale in her seat, she kept disappearing into the ladies toilet at the rear.

Bob, in his burgundy blazer and grey flannels, stood waiting at the vehicle's door for the other burgundy blazer to show. A faint breeze kept him cool.

They were leaving Edinburgh now, heading north into the Scottish highlands.

There was no sign of Marc. Bob looked at his watch, 9.25 a.m. They needed to be on the road for half past.

Then he swung into view, dressed in faded jeans and T-shirt, his brown leather holdall slung over one shoulder. He was also carrying his company uniform on a plastic hanger.

Walking with purpose towards Bob, he wore a sort of smile, more of a grimace. Bob sensed the young tour guide's manner was confrontational.

Pulling himself up to his full height, the coach driver readied himself for a spat.

'Sinclair! I want you to know, you have been an inspiration to me.' Marc's voice was loud, the words sounding rehearsed.

'What do you mean?' asked Bob, frowning.

'An absolute fucking inspiration on how not to end up,' his Liverpool accent was in full force. Thrusting his uniform onto Bob's chest, he continued, 'You fancy yourself as a fucking guide, don't you? So here you go, wear the fucking suit for the fucking job...' Marc paused before uttering his final words, 'and another thing, old man, you can tell head office, I've quit!'

He turned and quickly walked down the street, his skinny shoulders trembling.

'I fucking quit, quit, quit, fucking quit!'

Bob felt the eyes of the passengers on his back. It would be obvious to all what had just happened. Got to keep cool, he thought.

Stepping onto the coach, he took the PA microphone in hand, flicking the address system on, and stood facing the sea of questioning faces.

'Due to technical difficulties with our tour guide, we will be without this service temporarily. Normal service will resume shortly. In the meantime, I will do my best to make the trip as enjoyable as possible.'

There was murmur of voices, but no protest.

Turning the key, Bob brought the coach to life. He found this reassuring; the diesel engine thrumming, the gentle vibration from the gear stick, the forward movement he controlled. The journey would give him time to think. Collect his thoughts and the words he would use when informing Head Office of Marc's resignation.

His sudden departure would reflect badly on the young man, but Bob had to make sure it did not reflect badly on him too.

The coach was soon travelling across the Forth Road Bridge, the massive steel and concrete suspension structure running parallel to the Victorian rail bridge; two ages of engineering spanning the Firth of Forth estuary.

Bob glanced in his internal mirror. Christina smiled at him,

Billie Watson

but Eva did not. She looked sullen; maybe feeling the effects of too much drink the previous night. *Old man.* Marc's insulting words stuck in Bob's mind. Not many verbal missiles pierced Bob's sense of self, but these words stung deep. The dread of old age passed through the coach driver. He had to think positively. Looking in the mirror at the coach full of dozing passengers, Bob felt their dependency grow as each mile clicked past.

Another positive was Christina. Eva still looked down, but then it dawned on him; she was jealous of the attention he was paying to her friend.

This was a typical problem he had encountered with female friends travelling together. Last year, there had been Margaret and Jane – two divorcees from Bournemouth. Margaret, a petite lady in her late fifties with a raucous laugh, had proven positive to Bob's advances. But Jane was not laughing. Her jealousy had manifested itself by cornering him in one of the hotel gents' toilets.

Bob would rather have faced another man in the boxing ring than a woman like Jane. But Christina had her own mind, and if he were discrete, Eva need never know. Bob decided he would text Christina when he stopped at the motorway services – something like; *realise Eva upset – be discrete – daylight contact reduced – speak to you in evening.* Women liked a little intrigue, though Bob, it added to the excitement. The stop would also give him the opportunity to call the Scotia Tours office to inform them of Marc's departure. No doubt the company would arrange for a replacement guide to join the tour later.

Glancing at Marc's burgundy blazer that hung on the door handrail, Bob wondered who would be the replacement.

Maybe another young upstart without a clue, dependent on him, more of a hindrance than help, not knowing their arse from their elbow. *He might as well do the guide job as well as the driving*! This thought made such utter sense. He could run the whole show; it was a perfect solution.

ortt8

All these years of listening to Elspeth on the road, his own historical knowledge! His own brand of hosting had always proved popular with the party. Bob looked again at the blazer with the badge – TOUR GUIDE. All he had to do was swap his badge over when not driving.

Ideal. I-fucking-deal!

Bob smiled a large satisfied grin. He was still smiling thirty miles later.

The party could not take their eyes off the breathtaking scenery unfolding before them as they headed into the Central Highlands; the dramatic beauty eluded to in the tour brochure.

Starting with the green lushness of the Perthshire hills, the contour of the terrain began to change as the rugged uplands came into view – the unfenced wilds of natural vegetation, rising to the blue rock mountain peaks of the Cairngorms. Swathes of bottle-green Scot's pines broke up the heath landscape, while cutting down through this country were the many rivers and streams, the arteries of water shedding months of collected rainfall.

'This is wonderful,' exclaimed Gregory, soaking up the landscape. Miriam cooed in agreement. It had been her idea to come on the trip; she was pleased when he was pleased. Not being able to drive had been a factor in deciding to take this holiday, but if she was really honest, it was also having other people around. Miriam was hoping the presence of other holidaymakers would lighten the load of being with her first husband, reduce the strain of being with the caustic character he had become.

'Aren't those mountains awesome,' he informed, swivelling his head.

'Quite something,' agreed Miriam, happy to see him enjoying the journey. He was like his old self, the gentle Gregory, the considerate man she had known for nearly thirty years. Over this period, she had felt he was too soft, too generous, and had on numerous occasions warned him of those who had tried to take advantage of him. He was the only person she had ever felt protective of.

'I'm enjoying this, Miriam, I really am.'

Sinking into her seat, she let out a long sigh, felt some of her nerve ends stand down from full alert. Miriam recalled the sight of him lying in the spinal injuries ward shortly after the accident, a hollowed out husk of his former self. She had flown back from the United States as soon as she had heard about his misfortune. He wouldn't look at her, or even converse. Looking back, his first words were the start of a constant tirade. If she had known that now, would she have stayed?

'You still here, but then again that makes sense, vultures tend to hover first before they fly in to pick over the bones! Well, there's nothing here, nothing at all, so fuck off back to where you came from!'

But she had had nothing to go back to; her fourth husband Ollie had divorced her three months earlier, and the pre-nuptial agreement had made sure she was near penniless. And there lay the problem; Gregory believed she was only at his side out of desperation. Circumstantial evidence appeared to undermine her reasons for wanting to care for Gregory.

But could she blame him? What was it he said on the day she picked him up from the hospital, 'you've always worshipped false gods, Miriam, as long as I've known you, so don't think this Mother Teresa act is going to fool me.'

He wasn't just referring to the plastic surgery; it was the 'gold digger' stigma she had picked up after getting through four husbands, all of whom had not been short of money.

Was Gregory her salvation? Was this the reason she was sticking it out with the cantankerous cripple who belittled her every day. Maybe he was right after all – was it all about what she wanted? Maybe she was trying to prove to herself she could care for someone, but the question remained – was it him?

Pitlochry, the very picturesque village off the A9, catered for tourists in the most typical of ways; the sloping main street was stuffed with shops selling all things *Scottish*. This was the next stop for Bob's tour group.

In the wool shop, Mats took an interest in some tartan trousers, but was soon put off the idea by the ridicule fired from his wife Lotta and the Anderssons.

Inside the gift shop, Christina and Eva were engulfed in a typical range of tourist tack. Martha Vavan, one of the tour group, a red-headed semi-retired nurse from Gotonborg, could not resist the obvious souvenirs and keep-sakes. Back at home in her apartment, the equivalent Spanish, Italian, Mexican, and English versions filled each room.

Bob had driven into the public car park just after 12.30 p.m. He had given some thought to how to make this stop a little more interesting than just trooping round the various gift emporiums.

In his eight years of coach driving for Scotia Tours, Bob had been like a rolling stone, gathering a thick moss of friends, acquaintances, and contacts. He had called one of these associates from his mobile phone, while stopping for fuel. Bob's request had been positively received.

'Ladies and gentlemen, your attention please.' The party was moving out of their seats, preparing to walk around the little town. 'I'm sure some refreshment would suit you after a look around and I would like to recommend a little place I know.'

There was a murmur of approval from the group.

'Please meet me at one of Scotland's finest tearooms, Molly's Rest, in half an hour.' Bob glanced at the tour guide badge on Marc's burgundy blazer; he was tempted to pin it on his own blazer, but resisted. Too early still, he thought.

Bob's boast regarding Molly's Rest was not without good reason.

Situated off the main street, the snug little establishment had traded for twenty-five years under the ownership of Molly Wilson, a silver-haired lady in her mid-fifties. She was a round person; a round body with a round smiling face, large round breasts, large round hands with large round fingers that baked fabulous round cakes, scones, and biscuits.

Later as the group arrived, Molly's young waitresses started taking orders. Bob chatted with the owner, a mug of tea in hand. Arms folded, rocking back and forward on the balls of her feet, she listened intently to Bob's tale of the 'deserter' tour guide.

Twenty minutes later, a tall angular chap in dungarees, worker's boots and a flat cap entered the tearoom. This was Molly's husband, Andrew. He was in his early sixties, his face weathered from outdoor work since the age of fourteen.

The coach party looked on as his wife gave him some instruction. Bob asked for everybody's attention.

'Folks, I have a little treat for you. Andrew Wilson will now entertain you with his instrument!'

Bob turned to Andrew who had produced a mouth organ. Within seconds, he was playing it with consummate skill. A combination of Blues, Cajun and Scottish music rolled into a haunting lament. He then played a Country number, which was more upbeat. His little set had the coach party in applause, some of them standing to show their appreciation.

As quickly as he had arrived, Andrew was gone and Bob thanked Molly again for the impromptu entertainment.

After a short tour round the shops, the party headed back to the coach. As they boarded the vehicle, complimentary comments were passed to Bob.

'Enjoyed the mouth organ man, Bob. Is that a regular thing?'

'A special one off for you!' was the smug reply.

Christina stepped onto the bus; Eva a little way behind. 'Well done, Bob!' She quickly whispered her next sentence to him before taking a seat, 'I'm looking forward to my personal tour later.'

Bob smiled again. He reached over and took the tour guide badge from Marc's blazer and put it into his pocket.

Ideal. I-fucking-deal!

Chapter Six

Inverness – the capital of the Highlands was the first day's destination.

As Bob nosed the coach down past the baronial castle, the passengers noticed the contrast with Edinburgh. Structures of historical significance were few due to the city's violent past. A mixture of nineteenth-century buildings and the boxy designs of the sixties and seventies gave the conurbation a certain flatness to the eye.

The Balmoral, situated by the river, was the biggest, and in its owner's eyes, Mr Crosbie, the finest in Inverness.

He stood at the entrance, atop the red granite steps leading into his Victorian 'castle'. Mr Crosbie suited the architecture, not just by his green tweed suit, but also by his bald head, grey beard, bushy eyebrows and austere expression.

With the coach parked in front of the hotel, disgorging its passengers, Crosbie noticed Elspeth's absence.

He looked for the spindly Scotia Tours guide, but could only see the driver approaching.

John Crosbie did not like Bob Sinclair. A number of incidents over the years had reduced their dialogue to a single word; *goodbye*. The feeling of dislike was mutual.

'Where's Elspeth?' enquired Crosbie tersley.

Bob put down the two cases he was carrying to address the hotel owner, taking his time to answer.

'Not well. I'm coping on my own, doing two jobs!' Bob glanced upwards to convey the situation of added responsibility.

'What about a replacement guide?' Crosbie's fears were being founded.

'They sent a boy to do a man's job. He left me in Edinburgh after two days.' Bob sensed Crosbie's irritation at the situation; being forced to communicate with him – *the driver*. Bob on the other hand was enjoying the conversation.

'The replacement's replacement then? When are they showing up?'

'Day after tomorrow? Maybe tomorrow.'

'Well, when you know exactly, tell Miss Forsythe.' Crosbie turned to enter the hotel, but turned back to add a final instruction. 'Liaise with her for all areas concerned with this stay. She knows the drill.' He marched off to his office, relieved to some degree by delegating communication to his deputy.

Bob picked up the cases, and strode into the hotel, recalling the main reason for Crosbie's dislike. The hotel owner was obviously still upset over an incident two years earlier with his niece. Bob smiled to himself. He could still see Amanda Crosbie's nineteen-year-old face in orgasmic pleasure, the two of them in the wedding suite of the hotel; the result of *her* seducing him.

Just before the evening meal, Jane Forsythe knocked on Bob's hotel room. Although the twenty eight year old had a slight frame, her little fist could rap out a loud knock. She had perfected this action when working as a chambermaid years earlier.

Bob greeted Jane heartily. They had a similar sense of humour.

After a few pleasantries, Jane sat on his bed and got to the point.

'Bob, I understand you are the acting guide at the moment.' Her soft Inverness accent stressed the word *acting*.

'Yes,' said Bob, combing his hair into place.

'Tonight before dinner, when you announce the evening's entertainment, you'll need to tell them we have only one accordion player, and no drummer.'

'What's happened to Bert?'

'Flu.'

'But Alastair's accordion needs Bert to keep him right.' Bob had turned to face Jane. 'It won't make for a good evening!'

'It won't be that bad,' replied Jane.

'I have a better idea. Who's playing at *The Pheasie*?'

'I don't know for sure. Some eastern European music I think.'

'I'll give them a quick call.' Bob strode over to his mobile phone on the dresser.

'Mr Crosbie won't be happy,' said Jane anxiously.

'He need never know. Leave it to me. I'm the acting guide, remember!' Bob smiled, but Jane did not reciprocate.

As she left the room, she had to admit, the group would have a better time, but Bob would pay the price tomorrow.

Worlds Apart were a four-piece combo from the Balkans. The lead singer was a Croatian female; tall, long limbed with sultry dark eyes. Her Serbian boyfriend played lead electric guitar. The balding drummer hailed from Bosnia, while his cousin played bass guitar.

Bob had seen them play before in Stirling. They were very good, entertaining with a variety of music from Neil Young to Robbie Williams. As the evening drew on, they played their own native Croat and Serbian songs, with themes of independence and national suffering – popular with any Scottish audience.

Bob was sure the tour group would appreciate the evening, and it was a full compliment of people who followed him into the packed bar known locally as *The Pheasie*. Miriam was without Gregory, who had elected to remain at the hotel. Tonight, the locals outnumbered the tourists easily.

Bob took his group up into the gallery, allowing a great view of the small stage where the band were setting up.

Most of the party found seats and ordered drinks. Below the pub was heaving with locals talking, drinking, smoking cigarettes, and crowding the bar. The clatter of chatter filled the oak-beamed room.

The atmosphere rose up to the gallery. Bob could see the party inhaling the social ozone; lung-filling dollops of conviviality from the people below. Even the most corrosive character could not help but slip into the warm steam of good will which circulated around the room.

He leaned on the gallery rail, smiling. Christina sidled up to him. Eva was talking to the Anderssons, out of earshot.

'I like it here, Bob! Good choice, I bet you've been here before?'

'When this lot gets going,' Bob motioned his head towards the band who were tuning their instruments, 'the roof comes off.'

He stood straight, and looked into Christina's face. She beamed back, and they both sensed their own little climate of excitement wrapping around them.

'I need my roof coming off, Bob.'

'I know just the man,' he grinned.

Ideal. I-fucking-deal!

A young waitress brought their drinks. The band kicked into life as Bob clinked his glass with Christina's. Eva caught the toast from the corner of her eye.

Van Morrison's *Did Ye Get Healed?* soared from the Croatian singer. The band's sound was cohesive from the start. The atmosphere became static with the electricity of people swaying, tapping their feet, pulsing their bodies to the rhythm.

With his eyes on the band, Bob spoke to Christina. 'Back at the hotel, we go our separate ways at the end of the evening.'

Christina was nodding at Bob's instructions, enjoying his take-charge tone.

He continued, 'You go to your room. Make sure Eva sees you do this. Wait till you get my text, which will signal all's clear.' A pause, 'Come to my room. It's safer that way.'

Christina nodded as she gulped her drink. Her insides were turning with fluttering excitement, an all-consuming churning of anticipation. Pushing her lower body against the gallery rail, she felt a little relief through her denim skirt.

'What's happening?' asked Eva, inserting herself between Bob and Christina.

'Just enjoying the band, Eva, enjoying the band,' replied Bob.

The first number had finished, applause, shouts of approval, whistles filled the air.

'Me too,' chimed Christina, putting her arm around Eva, giving a little squeeze of friendship. A whiff of alcohol passed over Eva's face from her breath.

All of a sudden, Eva felt hot. Then she realised why. The people on either side of her were pumping heat out like two raging radiators. Her heart sank.

'Great evening,' said Henrik patting Bob on the back as they made their way back to the hotel through the orange glow of the street lights. Other members of the party in various degrees of drunkenness supported his sentiment.

'Excellent band!'

'People here know how to have a good time.'

'Good fun. Good fun. Can we do it again?'

'That singer could sing.'

'The band were so together.'

The coach driver felt great. He was absorbing praise, drawing it into every pore. Walking in front were Christina and Eva. He kept his eyes on Christina's bottom, the gentle sway of her buttocks like a guiding beacon, beckoning him on.

Ideal. I-fucking-deal!

Like everyone else, Jenny and Pernille had enjoyed the evening. They had descended from the gallery, pushing through the locals on the ground floor, and started dancing in front of the band.

With a few more whiskies, the two women's dancing infected the crowd. The evening's momentum kept building with each musical number. Pernille and Jenny felt their energetic gyrations bouncing off each other.

As the music moved to slower ballads, Jenny motioned Pernille outside for a breath of fresh air. They walked to the river's edge, the half-moon reflected on the black water.

Leaning on the metal fence at the pavement's boundary, Pernille looked into the river as Jenny faced the other way. Both were soaked with sweat.

'Dancing makes me feel so alive,' said Jenny. She felt the nip in the air around her nipples. They hardened slightly.

'We'll feel it in the morning,' replied Pernille.

'Staying alive is not enough for me. I need to *feel* alive!' Jenny turned to speak directly to Pernille. For a few seconds they took in each other's stare, and when both thought this would turn to being uncomfortable, they kept on gazing.

'When you're young Jenny, being alive is acting with compulsion! Living the moment for the moment's sake, nothing else matters!'

'Compulsion,' whispered Jenny, the whisky making her feel light-headed.

'Compulsion,' repeated Pernille, before drawing close.

The two women kissed on the mouth. Slowly, the tips of their tongues met, tasting each other's lipstick, the embrace lasting a few seconds. Pernille pulled away when her front teeth clinked Jenny's. They coiled up in laughter, grabbing onto the metal railing for support.

Back inside, the band were playing a final raucous number, the muffled thwump of the bass catching their attention.

'One more dance?' asked Jenny, pulling her friend by the hand.

'Please,' echoed Pernille.

Jenny knew Pernille would think about their kiss, ponder it, replay the moment. The test would be daybreak, when sober thinking and possible regrets would come. The strands of morning light would either dissipate any effect of their embrace – like rubbing sleep from one's eyes – or fuel Pernille's excitement for more.

Christina's excitement was palpable as she approached Bob Sinclair's room.

Feeling in need of a cigarette to take the edge off her tingling nerves, she now thanked the effects of her snuff – a small teabag-like pouch which was lodged between the gum and the upper inside of her lip. There it nestled, releasing nicotine into the bloodstream. Christina reminded herself to remove the ladies-sized pouch at the first discrete opportunity.

Their text messages had been back and forward; short, sharp, rapid.

Bob had been back in his room ten minutes before Christina's arrival to make the required preparation for his visitor.

He had left the room door slightly open – no need for Christina to knock. He knew from experience, if she did not show in the first ten minutes, she would not arrive at all. There was no embarrassment for either party by letting the lady decide on whether to take up the invitation. Having Bob stand at her room door, with the female having changed her mind was a demeaning experience for both parties.

As Christina entered the room, her make up freshly applied, she noticed how the lighting was low, two bedside lamps casting a warm subtle glow. Bob approached smiling, holding two glasses of champagne.

'A little night cap, madam,' he said gently, pushing the door shut with his foot.

'Oh. Yes, please,' whispered the Swedish woman, taking a glass.

'Please take a seat,' Bob said in a gentle tone, kissing her on the cheek, taking her by the hand. They sat on the bed together.

'I like your outfit,' he complimented, admiring the contour of her ample breasts under the top she was wearing.

'Thank you.'

Bob noticed how wet her lips looked after sipping champagne, glistening red.

Christina felt the alcohol go to her head – it felt good.
They began to kiss, savouring each other's lips. Bob put his
arms around her, pulling her closer, feeling her body give.
Christina felt herself mould into Bob's frame, felt his maleness
as he gently pushed her onto her back, looking into her face
with an easy smile, pushing his hand through her hair.
Kissing her again, Bob tasted her eagerness, the increased
saliva of arousal, a burning taste in her mouth – *she was hot.*
He felt her tongue, spirited, probing his own mouth – *and that
burning taste again.* He now felt something at the back of his
throat, like a grape or something. He gulped, but the object
was gone down his gullet, a tracing taste of tobacco followed.
Bob broke free from the passionate embrace to see an
apologetic Christina looking at him.

'Bob, I'm sorry, but have you just swallowed my snuff?'

'Snuff!' choked Bob, gulping down champagne.

Christina explained what she had in her mouth. They fell
about the bed laughing – the ice was broken – well nearly.

'Do you want to stay?' Bob asked.

Christina nodded, eyes wide. She was giving herself.

Bob was on the verge of a sensitive threshold; crossing over
required careful staging. Women of Christina's age were very
conscious of their bodies – they needed a modest way to
disrobe, reveal themselves on their own terms.

'I need to visit the toilet.' He lifted himself from her,
holding her gaze, smiling. 'Make yourself comfortable,' he
said as he entered the bathroom. This was her cue.

Alone, Bob slipped out of his clothes. He stood naked in
front of the full-length mirror and complimented himself on
keeping his body in shape. He applied some aftershave to his
face, chest and between his legs. His penis was fully erect – a
gentle stroke to his cock – it felt good in his hand, it always
felt good.

'Ready, soldier,' he whispered staring down at his hardness.
'Duty calls.'

He put on a bathrobe – modesty for the lady's sake rather
than his own.

Emerging from the room, Christina lay in bed, her head and naked shoulders visible above the duvet. He slipped under the covers, holding her gaze. The sensitive threshold was still being crossed. Lights off for this one, he thought, clicking them into darkness.

Bob moved from kissing her mouth to kissing her breasts, which he cupped to push the nipples up towards his mouth. The nipples were large, which he liked and he could tell they were very sensitive. He nibbled gently to see if this excited her further; it did. He felt what little tension Christina had slip from her body, as she realised Bob's skills in the bedroom were those to match his driving.

Bob pushed his thigh into the parting of her legs, felt the material of her knickers covering her mound. He liked this last piece of modesty; a cotton barrier to pry off when the time was right. Final nakedness had to be won.

His fingers travelled to her vagina, sensing wetness through the cotton fibres; the inviting heat of her pelvic platform cupped in his hand. Soon his hand slipped down her knickers. She drew in her breath, indicating her breach was giving – his touching encouraged to supply greater stimulation.

He gently kissed the nape of her neck. Her nipples were hard under his chest. The undulating rhythm of her lower body turned Bob's mind to his 'steering in the bedroom' thoughts. He had often drawn parallels with the handling of women and his bus.

Both needed a sensitive approach, but also the assurance of a firm hand. Pushing the right levers, in the right order, at the right speed, were all part of moving a woman and a bus forward in the desired direction.

Coming off at the first bend was no use. Gentle acceleration of his 'attention', would lead to gaining her 'interest'. Breaking at the right time, shifting gear to accommodate the terrain would build 'desire'. All the time, being sensitive to the different 'chassis' designs.

These women were mostly mature builds who had gone through a shape change in later life and needed a certain handling – a 'classic' vehicle to be driven with care and consideration.

Putting all his driving skills together delivered the 'action' he was seeking; a great ride, sliding through the gears of sexual transmission to the satisfaction of both parties.

Bob found these thoughts adding to his pleasure – the combination of the mental with the physical heightened his enjoyment of sex.

Christina was moving her head down to his middle, eager to reciprocate with some oral sex. Bob lay back while she took him in her mouth, tugging her out of the cotton knickers. He ran his hand over her back, tracing his fingers down to the cleft of her buttocks and into the wetness of her vagina.

Intercourse beckoned them both. He slipped into her, finding her short gasps of reception a turn on. Soon the rhythm of this intimate slotting began to find its own pace; their bodies meeting with synchronised union. Christina's breath coming in shorter and shorter gasps.

'Fuck me, Bob. Fuck me!' she uttered in his ear.

Bob felt her climax coming to meet him; the tightening of her lubricated casing around his hardness.

'Harder. Harder!'

He drove deeper into her, reaching with his erect gland to fill the smooth pulsating muscle, which engorged him. Christina came, crying out something in Swedish. She arched her back in the explosion of female ejaculation; then fell back into the mattress with the subsiding ripples of orgasm, decreasing spasms of pleasure that Bob viewed with satisfaction.

His own release was now desired as he withdrew. But he would not show this straight way. Laying on his back, cradling her head on his chest, Bob felt Christina's post climactic state settle – the need to pull the duvet tight around her as a little shudder transmitted from her body. Lying in the dark stillness was something he always enjoyed after the woman had climaxed; knowing his *soldier* was yet to fire. Time to ponder in what fashion this was to be. In Christina's case, it would be with her breasts. He had decided this when he had first cast his eyes on her.

She felt his tight scrotum. 'Are you ready to come?'

'I am.'

Moving onto his knees, he retrieved a tube of lubricant from under his pillow and smeared some of the substance onto her chest.

'I want you to push them together.' His tone was firm. She liked that.

Christina knew what he wanted now, and complied with the request. As she crouched on her knees, he pushed the swollen cock into her cleavage. Bob gently thrust himself into her breasts, the tip of his penis moving closer to her mouth until she received it there too. Cupping his balls, Christina liked this vulnerable position. She could also feel the build of his orgasm – the onslaught of his pleasure – the quickening spasms heralding the climax. She withdrew her mouth.

He let himself go, firing his sticky load of seed into her breasts with several pumps. Bob gave a muffled cry. Christina felt the coach driver's body above her tighten with the release. Dropping to his knees, he kissed her on the forehead.

Slumping into the sheets, the fog of sleep quickly gathered around them; she snuggled into his side.

Bob's closing thought, as always after these bouts; Sinclair, you have the ideal job for a man of your talents.

I-fucking-deal!

Chapter Seven

The morning light prised open Christina's eyes. Bob's breathing indicated his continued sleep. The digital alarm clock read 6.31 a.m. She felt a sudden urge to be back in her own room, in bed with her thoughts about last night, to reconvene with herself.

With stealth she dressed, left the room and quickly made it back to her own. After a quick shower, she slipped into bed, her mind turning over the previous night's events. Her emotions swung back and forward like a pendulum; from a tingling sensation to the creeping regret she was possibly just another of the coach driver's conquests. Bob was an expert lover – as she had wanted him to be – but was he too much of an expert. Was she one of many? How many? Was he another notch on his steering wheel? Another divorcee, widow or bored middle-aged woman seeking excitement?

She felt a little foolish at her naivety. The thought of being on a conveyor belt of such women, all steadily moving towards this man, sating his sexual appetite and ego, gave her a sick feeling in her stomach.

Last night was a fling; enjoyable sex between two consenting adults. A holiday romp she was as entitled to as much as any other person. But a one-night fling was how it would remain. She was in the driving seat now.

Bob had had a very satisfying slice of cake last night, but Christina was not letting him have any more portions.

Despite putting her thoughts in order, one aspect of last night nagged in her mind; the way Bob had had the tube of lubricant so conveniently placed under one of the pillows. Too presumptuous!

As he showered, Bob ran over the night's events in his mind Christina had been good. He felt his soldier harden at the thought. But he knew she was possibly undergoing shades of regret. There would be a pulling back now, a restraint on the physical urges as her mind took control of the situation. If he had the measure of Christina, as he thought he had, she would be having mixed feelings right about now.

He could now expect a 'cooling off' period – this would suit him fine. Last night was the first part of his seduction plan, but he didn't only have Christina in his sights.

There was also Eva. He wanted to bed her too. The key to having both women was working out which one to take first. Experience had taught him well. Two female friends could be divided into two halves: one would have a 'nuttier' harder centre, the other, the 'caramel' would be softer in the middle.

The nut was more secure in herself – less open to flattery, attuned to identifying people's real motives.

The caramel was prone to being insecure, seeking reassurances to her attractiveness, easier to seduce. The secret to enjoying both these chocolates was picking the right one first. Going for the soft centre straight away would not deliver the desired result. The hard centre would react by becoming harder. But the reverse took affect when the 'nut was cracked first'. The insecure female, the caramel, reacted by giving herself to prove she was just as desirable and attractive as her friend.

This chain reaction all hinged on the closeness of the females' friendship; their instinctive sensing of each other's state of mind and body. And also the simple truism of women not being able to keep a secret – of having to tell, to talk, to share what they were feeling and thinking with each other.

Bob knew all of this – he could have written a manual on the feminine psyche. His school of learning, his classroom so to speak, had been the coach, and the teachers were the many women who had embarked on their summer vacations with Scotia Tours.

*

'Good morning,' said Jenny, seeing Bob leave his room. She had just come into the hallway, two doors down.

'Good morning...' Bob could not remember her name.

'Jenny!' She smiled as they fell into step on the way downstairs.

'Any news of the replacement tour guide?' she asked, as he pushed the lift call button.

'Takes a couple of days for the new person to arrive.' He glanced over at Jenny – glad she could not read his mind. He was surprised at himself for not noticing her before; she was the best-looking woman on the bus. But then again, he had been focusing on Christina.

Jenny sensed Bob's cocksure attitude was at full throttle this morning. She surmised there must have been a 'lucky lady' last night. Which one of the Swedes had it been?

'Good night last night?' said Jenny in a half question, half statement tone.

'Yes. I thought so.'

The lift arrived. They entered. Bob glanced at his reflection in its dark mirror-like walls, believing Jenny had not noted such a subtle check on his appearance, but she'd seen this demonstration of vanity.

'I like to see people enjoying themselves, and if I can help to make that happen,' stated Bob, looking into her eyes, his aftershave filling the lift compartment.

'No denying it, Bob. You're certainly a good host.'

Bob smiled. Jenny looked at the tour guide badge on his blazer as the lift stopped.

'When did you say the new guide was coming?'

His smile faded.

'Sometime. Next couple of days.' He strode out of the lift in a purposeful manner.

Bob did not get far across the lobby. Crosbie was waiting for him with a flaring scowl across his face.

'Sinclair! In my office now!' Crosbie strode behind the

reception desk. Bob followed, the door closed after him with a bang.

It was a cramped room, space only for a desk, a PC, two filing cabinets, a chair, and stacks of filing. Photographs adorned the green walls – mostly of Crosbie with his hunting and fishing pals.

'Explain yourself?' declared Crosbie indignantly.

'Explain what?' replied Bob, equally indignantly. The coach driver liked to see Crosbie heated up.

'Last night, that's what! Taking the tour party to that pub when they should have been here!'

Bob gave a look of *but why?*

'When they're here, they're eating and drinking and I make my bloody money. Why else do you think I give Scotia Tours such a good room rate?'

The hotel owner thumped the desk, scattering papers on to the floor. 'That's the deal you fail to understand. I run a business here, Sinclair!' Crimson rage was spreading up into his face, eyes fierce with anger.

Bob tried to say something.

'Save it.' Crosbie glanced at the tour guide badge on Bob's blazer. 'You would have known that if you were a proper guide. Anyway, you won't be wearing that for much longer.'

Bob sensed from the last statement, the hotelier knew something he didn't.

Crosbie now felt he was getting his point across. He noticed Bob crossing his arms defensively.

'I know about the replacement guide! Or should I say phantom guide?' Crosbie was starting to enjoy the driver's uncomfortable stance. 'I called your office this morning and they knew nothing of you doing two jobs. They were naturally concerned, very concerned!'

A fist of fear punched Bob in the stomach. 'What did they say?'

'It's what you're going to say to them I want to hear. They want you to call and explain yourself.' Crosbie gestured to the telephone. He had enjoyed reigning down the verbal blows. 'Mrs Hoxley wants to speak to you directly.'

'Mrs Hoxley?' repeated Bob.

'Yes, I went straight to the big boss. She reassured me the proper replacement guide will be with the party first thing tomorrow.'

Bob mouthed the word shit and started dialling Scotia Tours.

'Stick with the driving, Sinclair,' laughed Crosbie as he closed the door behind him.

Eva and Christina sat at the table in the bay window of the dining room.

Eva spoke first. 'You're quiet this morning, Christina.'

'Am I?' replied Christina, aware she was. Her mind was still preoccupied with last night's events.

'Are you feeling okay?' asked Eva as she buttered some toast.

'Yes. A little tired that's all.'

They were speaking in their native tongue – it felt good for the words to come easily. Christina's scrambled egg arrived.

Eva continued her gentle inquisition. 'Maybe too many vodkas last night?'

Her friend did not reply. A part of her wanted to discuss last night, but she was concerned about Eva's reaction.

'No sign of Bob for today's briefing?' said Eva looking around the half-filled dining room.

'Maybe we are starting later today,' responded Christina. She sipped her coffee, craving the caffeine.

'He's doing a good job as the stand-in guide, in fact better than that young guy, don't you think?' asked Eva, keeping her eyes fixed on her friend.

Christina nodded. She fixed her attention on buttering some brown toast, feeling her friend's gaze and waiting for the next question.

'He enjoys himself too. You can tell. This is not a job for him, it is a *vocation*, providing for people's *vacations*. A good-looking man like Bob must have the pick of the women on these trips.'

Christina swung her gaze out of the window and felt the game was up. Eva was onto her. She wished last night had never happened.

Eva looked round the dining room. 'I wonder who's next?' Christina was about to say something. Eva continued.

'Easy pickings for a guy like Bob – divorcees, widows or just middle-aged women looking for some fun – women like us. No real male competition when you think about it.'

'I slept with him! Satisfied?' uttered Christina, her voice filled with anger.

Eva sensed she had gone too far, but was pleased she'd uncovered the truth. No more was said. Christina looked out of the big bay window alone in her thoughts.

His call over, Bob replaced the receiver. His explanation had been poor, his apology profuse. He had expected the worst, but Mrs Hoxley had another crisis on her hands – Bob Sinclair was not her biggest problem.

He also found out that the replacement guide was a woman by the name of Patricia White who would be flying to Inverness to join the tour the next morning. Bob took down her mobile number as instructed. He was also ordered to continue with today's planned activities.

Already twenty minutes late, Bob made his way to the dining room to brief the party. He felt deflated, his bubble burst. As he entered, Christina pushed past him, her expression was not pleasant. Eva, a few steps behind her, had a knowing look on her face.

'Bob. Are you here to brief us?' She wanted to say 'de-brief us'.

'Yes!' Bob looked round the room. Eva hovered at his side, like a lost child.

After he had communicated the day's expedition option to the group, the honey-haired Swedish woman asked for a word alone. They stood in the lobby.

'It's Christina. She is a little upset,' informed Eva in a concerned tone. 'Be gentle.' She kissed Bob on the cheek before taking the stairs to her room.

His spirits lifted. The second half of the game had begun, but he would need to speak to Christina.

While Henrik showered before breakfast, Pernille lay on her front in bed, her right hand between her legs, gently touching herself. She thought of Jenny's kiss, the sensuality of their embrace and the fun of it. The excitement of kissing a women in this way was a new departure for Pernille. She felt the vaginal wetness intensify. Her arousal proved the need to investigate further this new dish on life's sexual menu. Pernille tried to imagine the ingredients of such a meal.

There would be the familiarity of another woman's touch; knowing, considered, attentive. The softness of two women together, the reciprocation of touching the same shaped body. Her finger stroke quickened at these thoughts.

Jenny's confidence in this area was now obvious to Pernille. She imagined Jenny coming into the room, slipping off a bathrobe, getting into bed, folding her arms around Pernille. She imagined her hand was Jenny's, gently rubbing forth an orgasm to fruition. Pernille felt breathing on her right ear, large hands across her buttocks. It was Henrik, a towel around his middle, his wet hair dripping onto her back. Her near orgasm subsided quickly, but her arousal did not.

They had sex. She thought of Jenny when Henrik went down on her. She thought of Jenny as a climax seared through her body. It was one of the best she had had in ages. Little did she realise, as Henrik shuddered through his orgasm, he too was thinking of Jenny.

The 'kindness of strangers', the phrase kept coming into Gregory's head, had been obvious since they boarded the coach. The Scandinavians in the group were not only friendly, but also very willing to help. Mats and Adam had taken it on themselves to gently lift Gregory aboard the *Bonnie Prince Charlie*, the large diesel-powered cruise boat, which would take the party down Loch Ness.

If he was honest, he was still getting used to this kindness –

it was a novelty. He had spent most of his adult life with the type of people who found it hard to be kind. Kind to themselves maybe, lavishing their money on self-centred pursuits, one of which had given him an equally spoiled lifestyle; cosmetic surgery.

Wheeling himself to the prow of the boat which now chugged out onto the cobalt-sheen on the loch's choppy surface, Gregory enjoyed the breeze across his face. Musing further, he was beginning to enjoy his honest surroundings, the people, the place, the pace of it all. Maybe he had inhabited his old world for too long, growing accustomed to the one colour without realising it; the colour of money.

'Wonderful views,' stated Miriam, joining Gregory.

'Unspoiled. So unspoiled,' replied Gregory, wishing he was still alone.

The tension between the two hung in the air. Why was he growing accustomed to the kindness of others, but not hers? Gregory could not answer this question. A part of him wanted to believe she loved him, but the cynic would not allow it. He felt his feelings were lashed down, held fast in a black sea storm. 'Letting go' would run the risk of being thrown overboard, left to drown.

The breeze picked up. Miriam took out a light blanket from her rucksack.

'Here, put this over your legs. You'll get cold.' She went to drape the tartan shawl over Gregory's lower half when he swiped it away.

'Leave me alone…just fuckin, leave me alone!'

She did, stemming her tears as she ran to the toilets down below.

The drive along the A82, hugging the northern bank of Loch Ness, gave Bob time to think. The sun poked through a predominantly overcast sky – a cooler day across the Scottish landscape.

Alone with his thoughts, the ride southwards through the scenic Great Glen was an ideal opportunity to calm his mind.

Casting his gaze across the loch, Bob noticed how dark the surface was; the peaty waters, mixing with the black sediment of the loch floor to give an ominous lustre.

Bob considered his situation. Being put back into the driving-only position did not feel good. The tour guide contribution he'd made was worthwhile to the group. Bob did not take to being chastised easily, especially at his age.

On the other hand, he still had his job and the thought of losing his position as coach driver did not bear thinking about.

Taking orders had never really been a problem for him. Army life had prepared him for taking instructions, executing commands, following through other's plans. But over the years, it had begun to grate, especially as the orders were coming from people half his age. The counter balance to these frustrations was that he was in driving control over the tour party, and over the last couple of days, he had had total control. The situation felt good, but Bob wished he owned his own bus.

There had been an opportunity to start up a one-man show ten years earlier. He had had the opportunity with the money his mother had bequeathed him in her will. But his last divorce settlement had seen paid to that sum.

As he turned a corner on the road, a manila-padded package on his dashboard slid across it. The package had been waiting for him at the Balmoral's reception desk. The Cardiff postmark had brought a small smile to his sullen features.

Urquhart Castle came into view, perched on the north-west bank of the loch.

Dating from the fifteenth century, the ruined fortification gave fine views of Loch Ness and was where he would be meeting the tour party later.

Bob nosed the coach into the car park. Turning off the engine, he checked his watch; he had another forty-five minutes before the *Bonnie Prince Charlie* docked at the castle pier. He picked up the manila package. It was warm from being exposed on the dash to the intermittent morning sun. This 'heating' process had been intentional.

Bob peeled back the taped flap of the package and gently compressed the edges of the envelope to create an opening for his nose, which he placed inside. He inhaled the contents. The sweet aroma of Ginny filled his nostrils.

Bob looked inside the bag to see a pair of folded white cotton knickers. He pulled out the note that accompanied the underwear. It read:

Bob, my darling,
Please find enclosed a little something to remind you of me. I was thinking of you when I wore them last. See you soon – very soon.
Love, Ginny XXXXXXX

He took in one more sniff before slipping the package under his seat.

'Are you okay in there?' asked Christina through the closed door in the ladies' toilet. The boat swayed and she fell towards the door just as Miriam opened it. Both women stumbled backwards into the cubicle.

'I'm so sorry,' apologised Christina, pulling herself together.

Miriam was laughing, the type of hysterical spluttering that combines despair and humour. Her red, tear-stained eyes asked for help.

'I heard what he said to you. Terrible, just terrible,' stated Christina as she fished out a tissue from her handbag.

'He doesn't mean it. He's in such pain at the moment,' defended Miriam patching up her makeup in the mirror.

'You mean his physical condition?'

Miriam continued to apply lipstick, grateful this woman was helping her out. The kindness of strangers, she thought. 'It's mostly about losing his position in life, his purpose, everything really. He's not been in that chair a year yet.'

'But it's no excuse to treat you badly…what is it with men? They're so selfish,' exclaimed Christina angrily. 'Will he apologise?'

'Gregory, apologise? I don't think so.'

'Come with me.'

Miriam felt herself being tugged up onto the packed upper deck by the dark-haired Swede. Bearing down on Gregory, who was in conversation with Eva, Christina barged into the wheelchair-bound man's vision.

'It's Gregory, isn't it?'

Gregory nodded quizzically.

'I'm Christina. I would have liked to say pleased to meet you, but after overhearing you speak to your wife like you did, I cannot.' Christina's tone was stern and lecturing. 'I was brought up to respect other people's feelings, consider how they felt, make allowances, understand as best I could. I have gone through life trying to uphold these values, despite the fact so many people do not do the same…until now, right this very second, I'm going to put that rule on hold.'

Wheeling himself around to stare out over the loch, Gregory attempted to ignore Christina until she grabbed his chair and forced her face into his.

'You really are a rude man. This woman cares for you, and from what I can see really loves you.'

'How do you know?' bellowed Gregory, his shoulders rising, his face flushed with anger.

'Because she defended your awful behaviour, she made excuses for you! Despite the fact you are so cruel to her!'

A look of shock replaced Gregory's furious expression.

Bob parked the coach outside the Balmoral Hotel in the late-afternoon sunshine; the grey sky had all but gone. The tour party disembarked, ambling into the hotel with a relaxed air. They thanked Bob for the castle tour, even Christina, who had ignored him in the morning. He had expected the cold shoulder from her later, but she had appeared quite calm when disembarking from the boat serenely. It was as if any negative feelings had been dispatched during the cruise.

He managed to get her alone in the castle gift shop, and

asked if he could have a word outside. Producing his best hang-dog expression, he conveyed his feelings.

'Christina, I don't want you to be angry with me. I sensed you were this morning after breakfast. I just like to have fun, and I thought you felt the same way last night?'

'I did, but I don't want to be used!' she sounded firm.

'There is no way I would stoop to that kind of behaviour. I know I can come across as a little too practical, but it's my way of coping!' Bob gently squeezed her shoulder.

'Coping?'

'Yes, I've had to numb my feelings to a degree since my son's death.' Bob produced the photographs of his family and the wrecked car from his wallet.

'I'm so sorry, Bob,' said Christina sympathetically.

Placing the wallet back in his blazer, Christina gave him a peck on the cheek, before joining Eva back at the coach.

Now, back at the hotel, he removed the tour guide badge from his blazer and placed it on the dashboard as he retrieved his manila package.

As Bob entered the lobby, Jane Forsythe beckoned him to the reception.

'Fax for you, Bob,' said Jane, handing over a white envelope.

Bob tore it open and read the message from Head Office:

Bob,
Patricia White delayed. Proceed as normal tomorrow. She will join you in Skye tomorrow evening.
Regrads,
Mrs Hoxley

'Good news?' asked Jane, seeing Bob smile as he read.

'Absolutely!'

He strode away with a spring in his step to the hotel bar. Eva was waiting for him, perched on a barstool.

Ideal. I-fucking-deal!

Chapter Eight

The shopping trip in Inverness had been brief. Jenny and Pernille had never really had the heart to trudge round the stores. Both women knew it was an excuse to avoid the cruise that morning. Henrik had taken the excursion option.

When Jenny had suggested coffee back at the hotel, Pernille did not hesitate. Nor did she when Jenny suggested they use the coffee making 'facilities' in her room. The chambermaid had paid her visit, they would not be disturbed. Pernille flopped onto the double bed, pushing off her shoes. Jenny boiled the small kettle, got the cups ready and flicked the television on.

'We could have Irish coffees?' said Jenny, pulling two miniature whisky bottles from her suitcase.

'Why not. We're on holiday,' agreed Pernille with a smile.

'How are you getting on with the book, *Tail Of Two Women*?' enquired Jenny as the kettle came to the boil.

'It's very descriptive, very sensual,' replied the Danish woman. She had propped up two pillows on the headboard to make herself comfortable.

'I like the author's descriptions, women's descriptions about how we see and feel.' Jenny handed Pernille the alcohol-laced coffee and joined her friend on the bed; the two of them sitting, cups in hand, the whisky working its warm passage.

Pernille noticed a red tin on Jenny's bedside table. It had a Chinese motif on the lid. The English woman saw the interest.

'My little tin of happiness,' commented Jenny as she leaned over Pernille to retrieve it. 'Helps me sleep!'

Jenny opened the tin. A lump of cannabis resin wrapped in kitchen film, a packet of tobacco, a pack of long hand rolling cigarette papers and a silver lighter lay inside.

'We can have our very own excursion if you want,' suggested Jenny.

'It's been years since I smoked a joint!'

'All the more reason!' Jenny began rolling a long cigarette.

'It was my son who got me into this,' declared Jenny. 'I was suffering from insomnia, so he suggested I try it. It cured my sleeping problems.' She lit the fat joint, inhaling sharply. Handing it to Pernille she added, 'I like the way it makes me feel – light, sunny.'

Pernille drew on the joint, careful not to cough, feeling the sharpness of the unfiltered tobacco on her throat. A wheeze spluttered forth after the second draw. Jenny fetched a glass of water, reassuringly squeezing Pernille's thigh as she drank the soothing fluid.

The joint passed back and forward a few times before Jenny stubbed it out half smoked. They fixed their gaze on the television screen; a daytime chat show flickered back. Soon they were giggling at the presenter and guests. Pernille sensed the euphoric wave of the dope take effect; the increased sense of her surroundings, the relaxed state of being stoned.

Their giggles turned to laughter when an ageing pop star was introduced.

'Jenny, his nose is huge. No, it's more than huge. It's massive.'

'What a conk.'

'What's a conk?'

'English slang for nose.'

'What a strange word. Conk!' Pernille creased up with laughter.

'Conk. Conk. Conk. Conk!' repeated Jenny until she too burst out laughing.

They rolled around on the bed, wracked in laughter. Then Pernille fell off the bed onto the floor with a thump. She was still laughing when Jenny checked her head, looking through strands of hair to see if there was any broken skin. Pernille enjoyed the stroking action of Jenny's hands on her scalp.

'Keep doing that. It feels nice.' Pernille closed her eyes. Jenny leant down and kissed the crown in her hands. Pernille arched her neck back, so her face pushed into Jenny's hands. Jenny responded by dabbing kisses on Pernille's forehead.

They hauled themselves back up onto the bed. The Dane lay on her back as Jenny leaned over and kissed her on the mouth. Pernille felt the fullness of the English woman's wet mouth on her own – the touch of each other's soft lips engaged both women's senses. Jenny unfastened Pernille's top. Buttons springing free to reveal a white bra cupping Pernille's bust – her chest rising.

Jenny moved her mouth down to run a few kisses over the other woman's breasts, which were now free from the underwear holster. Engulfing the hard nipples, Jenny ran her tongue over the rigid breast points with fairness, giving each breast equal suckling.

'Let's get into bed,' suggested Pernille excitedly, eager to move the exploration further. They shed their clothes quickly, giggling like youngsters. Slipping under the covers, pulling the duvet over their nakedness, pushing their bodies into a physical embrace.

Jenny was taking the lead as expected in the situation. Sliding her hand between the other woman's legs, her fingers were greeted with a wet reception. Jenny's sure digits began to gently rub Pernille's clitoris, bringing the small shaft to hardness.

'The clitoris is the only human organ designed solely for pleasure,' informed Jenny, breathing in the other woman's skin. She loved this smell – the scent of intimacy.

Pernille moaned agreement. She lay, eyes closed, receiving the pleasurable stimulation, putting her hand on top of Jenny's to absorb the experienced touch. She then pushed Jenny's hand down to indicate penetration. Jenny eased her index finger inside Pernille, feeling her tremble with expectation. Back and forward with rhythmic motion, Jenny's finger began the priming of Pernille's orgasm, slipping out to trace up over her mound before returning to the soft inflamed tissues of the female pocket.

Jenny could feel the Danish woman on the brink of climax; ready for the switch to another form of sex play. Pernille felt Jenny's head move down to between her legs. The anticipation of what was to come next heightened the excitement further. Pernille was not to be disappointed. Jenny's tongue entered, going deep, triggering the vagina to grasp the friendly invader. Pernille felt a rush of orgasm envelop her – the vibrations of which passed into Jenny who tasted the onslaught of juices with relish.

'Taste yourself,' whispered Jenny as she kissed Pernille on the lips. 'Taste the sweet fruit you are!'

The women cuddled up together, bathing in the intermingled euphoria of intimacy – a pleasurable cocktail of being stoned and the afterglow of sexual interconnection. Their legs entwined, their arms wrapped around each other, their vaginal knolls pressed together. Pernille felt an incredible sense of well being pulse through her – the intensity of this female sex had moved her somehow.

She now wanted to bring Jenny off – to give her partner an equal abundance of pleasure, but where to start? She had never performed sex on a woman before. She so wanted to please this one. Why not use the template of Jenny's moves on her – reciprocate with the same ingredients – and she did.

After Jenny had climaxed, both women lay on their backs, looking at the high ceiling. There had been a delicious illicit feeling to the past few hours – a truancy of sorts. They had stepped clear of another ordinary day, and set course to discover some forbidden place.

After showering, a change of clothes, and reapplying their make up, the two friends descended to the bar for a drink. It was three o'clock in the afternoon; the conservatory at the rear of the hotel was deserted. Taking seats overlooking the garden, they settled into easy conversation.

'Jenny. How did you discover this aspect of your sexuality – I mean women?'

'My husband.'

'Your husband!'

'John had always fantasised about a threesome – himself and two women.'

'Henrik is the same,' chimed Pernille.

'It was a few years ago. An old school friend of mine, Judy, had come to visit. We had not seen each other in years. She had emigrated to South Africa with her first husband, divorced there and remarried. We had kept in touch by Christmas card, but John had never met her. One day, she called me out of the blue – she'd come back on her own for a family funeral. I suggested she visit, stay overnight before she returned home. As soon as she walked through the front door, we were laughing like we were kids again – as if she had never been away.

John liked her straight away, but who wouldn't. Judy was great to be around, full of life and a terrible flirt, causing John to start acting like some bull elephant in season. She was swinging her cleavage about suggestively – we both were. We teased the poor bugger rotten, just like when she and I were at school – right prick teasers we were.'

Pernille was hooked on every word.

'The three of us got quite drunk that evening. Judy hinted at her bi-sexual experiences over the years. I think John nearly came in his pants at the thought of it all. While he was out at the off-licence, she propositioned me in the kitchen, suggesting a threesome. I laughed it off, but it seemed exciting at the same time. Once Judy had gone to bed in the spare bedroom, I told John about her proposition and he nearly shot his load on the spot again.

We were as excited as each other, daring ourselves to go through with it. So we crept into the spare room and slipped into the double bed with Judy. But there was a condition I asked from John – he did not kiss her on the mouth or penetrate her.' Jenny stopped for a moment to sip from her glass.

Pernille was now sitting on the edge of her seat. She was getting turned on again. 'So what was the sex like?'

'Good. John got his fantasy, but it was over for him quite quickly. The combination of the drink and the build up of excitement throughout the evening left him well and truly spent. I got more out of it. Judy and I got down to it with gusto. I seemed to have all this natural 'bi' stuff inside me. It was all so natural; the touching, where to touch and all that. We brought each other off quite a few times. But it was the naughtiness I really liked, doing something which wasn't the norm, that gave me such a buzz. And for her too.'

'Like today. That's what I felt.'

'The key to it all...she was gone the next day. Like a stranger. No complications with John and me. We'd enjoyed the experience, but that was it.'

'Did you do the threesome again?'

'Yes,' replied Jenny, conscious now of Pernille's questioning, delving into her history. 'It happened a couple of times more, that's all.'

'Who with?' Pernille was finding this topic fascinating. Her sex life over the years had been tame in comparison.

'It just sort of happened. Enough of me! What about you?' Jenny wanted to switch the focus onto Pernille. She had given away enough.

'Boring compared to you. Henrik is a considerate lover, but not very adventurous. But I know one thing – he would love to have a threesome!' Pernille's eyes twinkled at the suggestion.

'Hold on, girl! This is not something you rush into. Men are different from us in this area.' Jenny sounded cautious.

'Women are better equipped in dealing with the meaning of sex than men. We can separate love and sex more easily than they can – we can take it or leave it!' Jenny leaned over to be closer to Pernille, increasing the importance of what she was about to say. 'That is why God gave us the sex remote control. If men had it, constant channel hopping, well bed hopping, the world would be a mess!' Both women laughed solidly for a good minute.

'What happened today between us, let's keep it that way.'

Pernille nodded in agreement.

But Jenny knew there would be no more sexual encounters with this woman.

New green chutes of pleasure had sprung forth for Pernille this morning, but the droplets of dew rolling from the unfolding leaf were not to her taste. Jenny had faked her orgasm; she could tell Pernille had not enjoyed going down on her.

Pernille ordered another glass of cola, drinking it quickly.

Chapter Nine

Eva awoke up in Bob's bed alone to the sound of the shower running. Stretching out across the double bed, she felt a little soreness in her pelvic mound; a pleasurable pain as memories of last night's sexual exploits flooded into her mind. Bob had quickly identified her taste for rough play; hard, pounding, ramming-type intercourse – a little foreplay to get started, followed by plenty of penetrative sex as she had hoped for. Bob had provided a variety of positions, one of which was new to her. He called her a *little ball of fuck fun* afterwards.

Eva quickly pulled on her clothes. She was having breakfast with Christina. Her friend had gone to bed early the previous night, leaving the way open for her and Bob.

Bob entered the bedroom from the bathroom, smiling, a towel around his middle, using another to dry his hair. 'Morning,' his tone was upbeat.

'Morning. I better get back. Get packed.' Eva quickly looked in the full-length mirror adjacent to the bathroom door; she needed to do some work to her face.

Bob stood behind her, looking into the mirror, wrapping his arms around her. Eva reached round and tugged free his bath towel. She felt his hardness push into the small of her back.

'No time for this, Bob,' Eva said teasingly. 'I've put my number in your mobile phone, and retrieved yours for mine.'

'Cheers.'

Eva turned and kissed him on the mouth. She slapped his bare buttocks before leaving. They were firm for a man of his age.

*

'You fucked him. Didn't you?' Christina's voice was matter of fact, but with a tinge of rawness.

Eva smiled back from the other side of the breakfast table. She was ravenously hungry and enjoying her fried eggs, sausages, tomatoes and bacon. She buttered a slice of toast as she answered. 'Is it a problem if I did?'

'You did. I can tell. It's nothing to me, Eva. But I don't want to see you getting hurt. Think about it. This man has had the two of us within 48 hours. You had him down as a serial-seductor yesterday and here you are – another notch on his steering wheel!'

'I can look after myself,' Eva said a little defensively.

'Like with Thomas?'

'I was on the rebound,' Eva was finding her breakfast less appetising.

Christina regretted bringing up the subject of Thomas. It had been two years ago; a two-month fling, the first after her divorce, good for her self esteem. But she had landed with a bump when he had dumped her. Eva had got too heavy too quickly.

'I'm your friend. Just be careful,' Christina squeezed Eva's hand.

Eva looked at her friend. She smiled. 'I deserve some fun, don't I?'

'Course you do. Course you do!'

They continued eating in silence, their thoughts turning to the coach driver. They would agree later – he had been good in the sack – though a little mechanical. The dining room was emptying. The party would be hitching themselves aboard the coach for the next leg of their journey.

By noon, the overcast sky had darkened with the inevitability of rain. As the coach pulled into Fort William, a steady downpour was in place.

Situated at the foot of Glen Nevis, at the northern end of Loch Linnhe, Fort William enjoyed one of the best settings in

Scotland. Rising like a colossus, at the northern end of the town was the highest mountain in Britain; Ben Nevis.

Bob advised the tour party the stop was only for two hours, and asked everybody to be back at the coach for 2.00 p.m. The group splintered off into its own sub divisions – now a natural process after five days of familiarity on the road.

Jenny was the exception today. As usual, Pernille and Henrik had invited her to tag along with them; they were keen to find a typical Scottish highland painting to take home. Jenny politely declined, preferring some time on her own.

After a short stroll from the car park, Jenny spied The Tea Cozy. As she entered the small cottage, she noticed Bob was already ensconced at one of the small pine tables, reading a tabloid newspaper. They caught each other's eye. He signalled the empty chair across from him. Jenny nodded. Purchasing a pot of tea from the self-service bar, she joined him.

'It's a dreech day today,' exclaimed Bob.

'Dreech?'

'A Scottish word for a day just like this – raining, not pleasant,' Bob explained.

'We shouldn't complain. The weather's been very good.' Jenny sipped her tea, regretting not buying a scone – they had looked good.

'Are you still enjoying the tour?' enquired Bob, giving a pleasant smile.

'Very much,' Jenny noticed the tour guide badge on Bob's blazer. 'I thought the replacement guide would have joined us by now?'

'They arrive tomorrow. Would you like something to go with that cup of tea, Jenny? I'm going to get a scone.' Bob stood up, towering over her.

'Yes, please.' He had remembered her name this time.

They both enjoyed the scones, the fresh crumbly taste filling their mouths.

Jenny cast her eye over the headlines of the newspaper, which lay folded on the table. 'Much happening in the outside world?'

'Same old, same old. Wars, pestilence, famine. And the Rolling Stones are to tour again!'

'How do they keep going?' asked Jenny. She now had the opportunity to get a good look at him, face to face.

'All in the mind. If you think *young*, you feel *young*, and if you feel *young*, you are *young*.'

Jenny could tell he was proud of his little saying. 'What about energy? Being as energetic as a twenty-something gets harder.'

'Granted, but there are ways of finding the hidden energy we all have. Are you familiar with Far-Eastern health practices?'

'Yoga. That type of thing?' This was obviously one of Bob's pet subjects, thought Jenny.

'Yoga is only one aspect,' said Bob, putting on a knowledgeable tone. He then spent the next ten minutes explaining to Jenny his own personal adaptation of Eastern diet, exercise, meditation and whatever else he did to stay young.

Jenny nodded feigned interest, preferring to speculate on who his sexual conquest would have been last night. Probably one of those Swedes. This guy had quite the life with his own harem on wheels. No wonder he worked so hard on keeping his looks. But it was more than his looks, she could see his easy charm disarming so many, reducing feminine force fields with his oscillating magnetism. Jenny decided to soak up some of this man's rays, why not; it wasn't every day such a charmer crossed her path.

Bob was conscious he was doing all the talking. He took a sip of cold tea before asking Jenny a question. 'How do you do it?'

'Do what?' asked Jenny, caught off guard by the switch in conversation.

'Stay looking so young!'

'Bob, you don't fool me. This is a tried-and-tested line for all your female passengers,' She flashed a big white smile.

'I'm serious. You're fine-looking lady.'

Jenny felt the heat of his compliment rise into her face. She gave away her little secret. 'No Far-Eastern tricks for me, just a blast of cold water on my face, and body, when I'm ready to get out of the shower. It keeps everything taut.'

'I'll try it tonight,' came Bob's reply. He was not joking, he would.

'Tell me, do you have any family?'

Bob breathed in a little. He seemed reticent to answer. 'I lost my only son in a car accident. He left a wife and a child, but I don't really see them much. They're closer to his mother – my first wife.'

Jenny noticed Bob reaching into his inside blazer pocket, as if to retrieve something, but decided against it.

'I'm sorry about your son,' expressed Jenny, feeling a little sorry for Bob.

Bob shrugged his shoulders, wishing to change the subject.

'If you don't mind me asking, have you married again?' asked Jenny.

'Yes, but it sunk without trace, just like my third marriage – three marriages…three divorces! It took that many tries for me to find out I'm not the marrying type. It was more me, than them.'

'Was it the job? Being away from home?' asked Jenny. She was genuinely interested, leaning closer to hear his reply.

'Some of it, but mostly… I'm not easy to live with. I like my freedom and relationships require compromise. It would start well, putting the effort in, but for the most part I would lose interest. My third wife summed me up the best when she described her hopes for me – she thought I would *evolve*. Alice was her name. Met me when I was forty-two – she thought I was at the right age to evolve at last into a marriage. Problem was I didn't – I stayed the same!'

Jenny thought his speech was practised, she could imagine him using it on some of the tour party women who got heavy towards the end of the trip.

'And you?' asked Bob.

'I'm a widow. Lost my husband two years ago. I have a

grown-up son, but he's not married yet, so no grandkids. Straight forward really.' She rattled this out in her typical matter-of-fact tone – she was practised at this type of thing too.

Jenny wondered if Bob would now put her in some sort of group; the lonely widow seeking comfort, taking a holiday to find some romance. She felt the compulsion to ask him, how many widows had he shagged over the years, ten, twenty, twenty-five? Was there a technique he used to get their knickers off? Or maybe, they were more hassle than they were worth, unravelling the memories of the departed husbands as he spliced into them!

Scanning the newspaper headlines, Jenny made a comment to Bob who was preparing to leave.

'There seems to be less give in the world nowadays.'

Bob could not really answer – not one for delving too deep into meanings.

'I really need to be getting back to the coach. I enjoyed our chat.' He stood up, pulling on his raincoat.

'Yes. Same here.' Jenny smiled.

Bob noted the air of respectability this woman possessed. An appearance of restraint that at any moment could transform into a delicious look of wanton sexuality.

'You have a lovely smile!' With that compliment, Bob departed. It did not sound practised, but warm and genuine.

Bob ran back to the coach, striding across puddles to avoid soaking his shoes. Once inside the empty coach, he laid down on the back seat and dozed off to sleep. It would be another hour before any of the group returned. He needed a little nap to ready himself for the next leg of the journey to the Isle of Skye – Eva had been more demanding than anticipated the night before.

The patter of the rain drummed him to sleep.

His mobile phone woke him, the ring-tone startling him. An incoming text message pulled him from his slumber.

WHERE ARE U? WE ARE WAITING TO GET ON THE
BUS. PARTY SHELTERING IN LOVAT ARMS PUB
OPPOSITE CAR PARK.
    EVA

Bob looked at his watch. It was way past two. He had
overslept. Shit! He was running behind now!

He quickly got the coach moving in the direction of the
pub, pulling up sharply outside. He was greeted with a cheer
from the tour party as he arrived. The cosy little public house
was packed; the landlord had kindled the open fire to make
his drinking den more welcoming.

'Where have you been?' asked Eva curiously. She was
putting on her red kagool, her hair matted from the rain.
Christina was doing the same, smiling politely at him.

'I got waylaid on the phone to the office.' Bob knew his
excuse sounded lame. 'Okay everybody, on the bus please. We
can make some time up!'

As the party boarded, he could tell a few had been getting
merry in the pub. More to the point, there would be an
increase in toilet stops to relieve the alcohol-soaked bladders
– more time lost.

Jenny was the last aboard. 'Are you okay, Bob? You look
worn out.'

'I'm fine,' came his curt reply.

Slipping the coach into gear, Bob wheeled the vehicle
around for their journey to the Isle of Skye. It was just after
3.00 p.m. – his safety-time margin had been reduced by about
forty-five minutes. The route to Skye via the bridge at the Kyle
of Lochaish would take four hours. If only the onboard
facilities were working, but he had run out of the chemical
required to run the lavatories.

The other option was to take the A830 to the port of
Mallaig and catch the ferry to Armadale on the southern-most
tip of Skye. An equally scenic route, with less road mileage; it
would save about half an hour on the journey. But there was
one drawback – the ferry stopped running at 5.30 p.m.

Failure to reach this crossing in time would mean they'd have to retrace their journey to Fort William and complete the original planned route of 112 miles to Skye. The result would be a five-hour journey, arriving at the hotel by nine in the evening. Bob could not afford to be late – the replacement tour guide, Patricia White, would be expecting him at the hotel for 7.00 p.m. sharp. A bad report from her would not be good, not with Mrs Hoxley on his case. Better to take the safe option, he decided.

Bob was only ten minutes into the journey on the A82 when Henrik joined him at the front of the bus.

'The Unges are not with us. The old lady and her niece. We think they're still in the pub.'

'What? Say that again!'

'The old lady and her niece, they went to the toilet. They must have been there when we left.'

Bob did not mean to slam the breaks so hard, but he did. The passengers lurched in their seats.

'Shit, shit, shit!' Bob thumped the steering wheel. It was his fault. He should have done a headcount. 'Okay. I'll get turned around.'

The Unges were still at the Lovat Arms. The landlord had made them feel comfortable and was about to phone Scotia Tours.

Regaining his composure, Bob shepherded the couple aboard, but he had lost another half an hour. A couple of people wanted to use the pub toilet, costing him another five minutes. It was 3.33 p.m. as he pulled away from Fort William for the second time. His arrival at the hotel would be after 7.30 p.m., maybe 8.00 p.m. if the bad weather continued. He began to seriously consider the ferry option.

He could be in Mallaig for just after 5.00 p.m. at the latest. The 25-minute ride across the Sound Of Sleat would give an ETA of 7.15 p.m. at Portree on Skye – an acceptable arrival time. The sign for Mallaig indicated the road was bearing up on his right. This was his last chance to choose!

The ferry it was.

As each mile passed, new and dramatic vistas opened up with spectacular effect. The countryside moved from forested green slopes, to barren moors, to sheer mountain sided splendour, appearing like vast painted highland landscapes; as if hidden scene-shifters were constantly trying to outdo the previous canvas displayed for the passengers' viewing pleasure.

By the time they reached Glenfinnan, a few of the party were ready for a toilet stop. The visitor centre had public toilets; time spent at this facility, five minutes by Bob's watch.

He flicked through his ferry timetable. The last one of the day had a latest check in of thirty minutes, but he knew from experience twenty minutes would be fine. He needed to be on the pier for 5.10 p.m. He was on course, his watch read 4.08 p.m. as they pulled out of Glenfinnan. As he passed through Lochailort fifteen minutes later, a sign read: MALLAIG 19 MILES

He still felt confident. The road was quite clear, the steady rain, deterring most tourists from venturing out that day.

A combination of the Lovat Arms alcohol and beautiful scenery was keeping the passengers in rapture. The sheer scale of the mountains rising above them into the mist was satisfying their romantic images of the country. They did not seem to notice the coach clipping along faster than usual.

But Jenny was alert to the increased momentum. She had chosen to sit at the front of the coach to get a windshield view. The oncoming highway was bearing down fast. Jenny also noticed Bob constantly checking his watch; *there was a deadline up ahead.* She felt a little uneasy, thinking how tired their driver had looked when they boarded at Fort William.

There was one sign that gave Bob a start; it was not a road sign, but one made of oak wood with the words ARDNISH HOUSE. It appeared on his right-hand side, three miles from the tiny village of Polnish.

Ardnish House, it must be thirty years he thought! He looked up to his right and there the house stood; the

Victorian-built baronial hunting lodge perched on the glen side, about a quarter of a mile away. There had been trees obscuring its presence from the road, but they were paired back now to show off its stately stature.

He was not the only one to notice Ardnish House. By keeping an eye on Bob's eyeline, Jenny was prompted to look at the house on the hill too. The single-turreted granite building had a gothic appearance. A few lit windows gave it some warmth on this overcast afternoon.

As they pulled round the bay of Loch na Ceall at Arisaig, the sign to Mallaig signalled 9 miles remained. Bob's watch read 4.49 p.m. – on time.

The last village to pass through before reaching Mallaig was Morar. The sandy beaches reaching up from Loch Morar to the village were particularly breathtaking. The silvery appearance of the sand prompted Jenny to shout to Bob.

'Could we stop here? This beach looks wonderful!' She also felt a little sick from the coach movement. It would be a good excuse to get Bob to take a break.

He didn't.

The next sign read: MALLAIG 3 MILES. Bob's watch read 5.03 p.m. – still on time.

It was on this final stretch of the journey Scotia Tours 001 had to slow its pace. Bob had seen the green John Deere tractor at a farm gate just ahead, nudging out, a quarter of a mile away. *Stay where you are,* pleaded Bob in his mind.

The tractor pulled out and set off in the direction of Mallaig. Jenny heard Bob swear and saw the reason for his expletives up ahead. The coach slowed and she felt relieved. But a drop in speed to twenty miles per hour only increased Bob's blood pressure.

'Bastard,' he cursed under his breath. The slow-moving tractor was costing Bob valuable time; somewhere in the region of ten minutes as the road wound its way into the small fishing port of Mallaig.

The bends and contours of the road would not allow him to overtake the agricultural vehicle. The temptation to sound his horn became too much. Bob let off a blast and the tractor slowed down by five miles an hour. More expletives from Bob; the tour group were deadly silent now.

The tractor turned off down a side street. Bob pushed down onto the ferry port. He was slowed again at some traffic lights for a few more minutes. By this time, all the passengers could sense the tension-filled atmosphere – his muttered cursing, his deep sighs.

At 5.19 p.m., he turned into the port, just in time to see the last car being loaded onto the ferry. The slip ramp was closing on a half-full load. The smoke stack pumped diesel fumes into the air as the red-and-black liveried craft prepared to move away. The tethering ropes were hauled aboard as the boat set sail for Skye with a blast from her throaty horn.

Distraught, Bob put his head in his hands against the steering wheel. The passengers, still in complete silence, could see the ferry moving into the grey waters of the Sound of Sleat, choppy foam coming from her stern. Jenny went forward to Bob.

'That was the last ferry for the day, wasn't it?' she asked, sympathetically.

He nodded. She gave his shoulder a little squeeze. He lifted his head and spoke to her.

'We can still get to Skye tonight, but it will be by road. It's a five-hour trip.' He looked tired and drawn, bloodshot eyes under dark lids.

'Can I make a suggestion?' asked Jenny.

Bob nodded.

'Let's stop here for a break, a snack, whatever. Then push on for...' she looked at her watch, '6.30 p.m. I think we're all ready for a stop.'

Bob appreciated her concern. He nodded agreement and handed her the PA, leaving her to address the party.

'Okay, folks! We have a change of plan. As you can see, the last ferry to Skye has gone. We need to take another route, which is going to be a five-hour journey.'

There was a combined groan from the group. Jenny continued.

'So let's spend an hour here in Mallaig to refresh and ready ourselves for the journey.'

The group stirred in their seats, resigning themselves to their fate.

Bob drove them to the only hotel in the port town, The Sleat Hotel.

He did not join the passengers as they squeezed themselves into the small dining room of the hotel. He took his meal in the bar, not that he felt like eating.

Outside, he could see dark clouds mustering a downpour. He felt annoyed with himself, angry and disappointed. By the time he reached Portree tonight, sometime around 10.00 p.m., he could expect another bollocking from the company. He felt like having a drink to drown his sorrows.

A glass of whisky was placed in front of him. It was from Eva. She sat down opposite him.

'Thanks, Eva, but I cannot drink and drive.' He gave her a small smile.

'You looked like you needed something.' She squeezed his hand, her eyes twinkling.

'Sure do.'

'You missed the ferry. So what? We'll get to Skye just the same.'

How could he explain to her, the trouble he was in already.

Eva was not getting the response she wanted. She wanted some reciprocal attention. 'Well we can have a drink when we get to the hotel later.'

Bob nodded while looking out of the window. He turned to look at her, but she was gone. He knocked back the whisky in one go, his throat clenching against the warm bite of the spirit.

Jenny rounded everybody together for boarding. It took longer than she anticipated. By the time the headcount was done, it was 6.45 p.m. She took her seat at the front; this time in the tour guide's seat. She wanted to keep an eye on Bob.

As the coach pulled out of the town, the rain began to fall heavier than it had been all day. Bob's visibility was impaired and he drove accordingly; or so he thought. Dark clouds turned the summer evening to a dusk-like darkness. The scenery of the inward journey now looked bleak and foreboding. The magnificent views of the Hebrides were completely obscured by sheets of rain and rolling mist. The steep-sided mountains now seemed to close in oppressively. The water of the inland lochs, previously shimmering blue, were now slate grey and choppy. The crimson heather moorlands had turned to desolate windswept expanses.

With a distinct lack of cars on the road, the Scotia Tours party felt like a lonesome craft, cutting home through unfriendly waters. Some of the passengers tried to shut out the dreary weather by closing their eyes for sleep. But the winding A830 would not allow such slumber.

Bob adjusted the air conditioning on the bus to drive some heat into the cabin. He felt tired; his nerves strung out from the chase for the ferry. The thought of the long drive ahead was not pleasant.

Jenny could not relax. Maybe she was being over sensitive, but Bob's driving did not seem as assured as normal. She felt the coach sway at a few corners.

Although he was not going as fast on the run back to Fort William, the ride still did not feel safe. Jenny was right to feel concerned.

She had asked the passengers shortly after they left to put on their seat belts as the weather looked nasty. They had all complied. She did not use the PA system, but asked individually as she moved up the coach.

Three miles after Polnish, approaching a tight left-hand corner, Bob misjudged his breaking time by a fraction. He'd begun to slow, but not enough. The bus was moving at 36 mph when he had to take evasive action. Coming off the corner directly was a gravel track sloping downwards. Jenny was the only passenger who saw the corner, felt the speed –

there was no way the bus was going to make the bend. The coach kept going straight, Bob gripping its steering wheel, his foot on the brake, trying to move down another gear. The diesel engine growled stubbornly.

The rest of the group saw some tree branches brush the windows of the coach, like huge clawing fingers, and then felt their stomachs jump as the vehicle nosed down suddenly. Those in the aisle seats craned forward to see a bend approaching through the windshield. The gravel track had its own left-hand corner after 200 meters, and a small river beyond.

This was where the Scotia Tours coach came to rest with a screeching of metal and an almighty bump, which lurched the passengers forward. Thankfully, the gravel track had slowed the coach to something like 15 mph when it ploughed into the River Sneeth. The craggy rocks on the river bottom drove up into the coach's underside and further helped to reduce its velocity. The rocks also sheered the prop shaft and punctured the hold. The engine died suddenly, water flooding over some of the luggage.

The accident had taken less than seven seconds to flip the driver and his passengers into a sudden haze of disorientation, snatching away everyday normality. No one said a word for a further few seconds, sitting, listening to the rain pummelling the wrecked vehicle's roof, as the sound of flowing water came from below. Then Eva let out a cry, followed by some sobbing. A few more of the women followed.

One wheel was still turning though. Gregory's chair had capsized in the crash sending its occupant sprawling down the gangway.

For the second time in the day, Bob cradled his head in his hands. But he felt a different reaction. He too wanted to cry, to let big warm tears flow down his face, but he didn't let them go.

Chapter Ten

'Is anybody hurt?' asked Jenny through the crackling PA system. Her nerves still rattled from the crash, she was the first to regain her senses. By being up front of the coach and witness to the oncoming accident, she had braced herself as best she could for the halting descent into the river.

Bob was trying to force the door open, but to no avail. The front of the coach was firmly embedded in the river bottom, a foot of water seeping into the front step. Miriam and Jenny helped Gregory back into his wheelchair.

There were a few bloody noses, but thankfully no one had sustained any major physical injuries. People were shaken, some in mild shock. Jenny moved up the aisle, identifying those who would need help, and the ones who could give it.

'Kenni, Henrik, Mats, Adam. I'm going to need your help to get everybody out of the bus and onto the bank,' ordered Jenny. Her tone was firm and reassuring.

'Bob. Have you got a way out for us?'

A crash of glass was the answer. Bob had broken the side window directly behind his seat on the right-hand side of the coach. He kept a small hammer for such emergencies.

Jenny and the men joined him at the front. Clearing the window of glass, he swung himself out, dropping into the swirling river, which came up to just above his knees. The distance to the riverbank was not far – five metres – with some large stones to aid passage. Being summer, the river was half its normal height.

Kenni, Henrik, and Mats joined Bob in the water. Adam

stood on the bank ready to haul the passengers to safety. Gregory was the first, then his chair, followed by Miriam.

Between Jenny and Pernille, the two women helped the passengers through the broken window, down into Bob's arms, passing them to the human chain. It took half an hour for the entire party to make it across. Soaked through, they sheltered under some trees, cold eating into their bones, the wind easily cutting through their summer clothing.

While helping people through the window, Jenny saw the lights from Ardnish House up on the hill. She remembered the place from earlier in the day and decided immediately to head there for help.

'Follow me!' Jenny commanded. There were no questions asked; the cold, wet, shaken tour party trudged behind her up the gravel road to the main road. Henrik and Adam supporting Mrs Unge, Mats carrying Gregory on his back.

Bob remained at the rear of the group. Turning round to look at his coach, the rear of which was pitched a metre above the water, the Scotia Tours livery badly scratched. It was a complete write off, just like his coach-driving days.

Choking back tears, he trudged behind the party, trying to work out how the accident had happened, replaying the final moments over in his head; the gut-wrenching feeling of knowing he could never turn back time. Leading at the front, Jenny and the passengers crossed the highway and trooped up the drive to the baronial house, wet clothes chafing their skin.

Several minutes later, the drenched and weary group stood huddled outside the main door of the lodge. Wind and rain pelted their backs; the party huddled together for warmth, pulling themselves into what shelter the doorway would give. Darkness was settling across the bleak terrain.

THUMP, THUMP, pounded Jenny on the door. No answer, no crack in the portal.

'Hello. Anybody in?' cried Jenny, hair matted against her face. She turned the brass door handle; the heavy door gave way into a large hall.

111

A light was on. Collective relief surged through the group as they entered the hallway.

Everybody looked round at the preserved Victorian surroundings of the hallway. The dark blue blousey William Morris wallpaper, the encaustic tiled flooring with a rose patterned effect, all lit by ornate brass lighting fixtures on the walls. But one thing was out of place though; a five-foot plastic statue standing next to the coat rack was not Victorian. The figure was a colourful figurine of a young woman in a black uniform, jack-boots and tied-up blonde hair under a little cap. The face was Aryan-like, the body giving a Nazi salute. Jenny recognised the figure, but could not place from where.

'Hello? Anybody in?' Jenny's call rang out.

A staircase lay at the end of the hall with two further hallways at the foot of the stairs; one leading right, the other to the left. Jenny stood at the crossways.

She could now hear loud music coming from behind a door at the end of the left-hand hall. It was classical piano, Rachmaninov, if Jenny was not mistaken.

A dramatic sequence was playing. The frenetic speed of the piece raced towards a crescendo. Knocking on the door, she waited for a reply. The concerto volume could not be broken by her knock.

Turning the handle, Jenny opened the door slowly. 'Excuse me...' No more words came from her lips.

The occupants did not notice her intrusion straight away – they were caught up in the music playing and the activity they were engaged in.

Facing Jenny, in the middle of the room was a red velvet chaise longue. Visible from the elbow upwards was a naked woman, late twenties, slim, attractive with long chestnut hair. She was in profile to Jenny, her firm breasts rising and falling with the steady rhythm of astride intercourse. Her hand gripped the dark wooden top of the chaise longue, knuckles white with passion.

A few seconds passed before the woman saw Jenny. The

surprise stopped her dead. A man's head popped up from the end of the couch in response to the young woman's reaction. He was older; grey streaks in his longish hair, in his early to mid fifties, a sensitive face behind a greying goatee beard. 'I'm sorry! So sorry!' blurted Jenny as she wheeled round and pulled the door shut behind her. Standing frozen, the image of the couples' exposed sexual position reeled in her mind. Rachmaninov subsided quickly. Stepping forward a few paces, Jenny waited for a reaction from the room's residents. Pernille peered round the corner from the entry hallway. Jenny shooed her away.

'Can I help?' The accent was American, quite soft.

Turning to answer, Jenny took in the tall frame of the man she'd seen on the couch. He was tucking his checked shirt into faded blue jeans.

'I'm so sorry. Please accept my apologies. But we tried the door, and with the rain....'

'Not to worry,' interjected the man. 'You said *we?*' He pushed his hand through his shoulder-length hair.

'Yes. I'm with a coach tour party and our bus has come off the road into the river at the bottom of your road!' explained Jenny, keen to put a sound reason behind her invasion of privacy. She pointed backwards to the hall.

He nodded. 'I'm Mackenzie MacKenzie,' he said, introducing himself with a smile. The young woman's face appeared from behind him, dressed in a baggy white T-shirt and faded combat trousers. They both wore flip-flop sandals.

'Hi. I'm Mrs MacKenzie. But call me Skye.' The young woman's accent was a mixture of Scottish and American, her hand extending to shake Jenny's.

Skye was beautiful. It was the simplest way to describe her; lightly tanned skin, striking face, fine bone structure, an exquisite mouth, and piercing blue eyes.

Jenny held her gaze, soaking up her aesthetic radiation: Mackenzie was a lucky man.

'Let's see what we can do,' offered Mackenzie as he strode down the hall to meet the surprise guests.

Of all the houses to call on for help, you could do no better than the MacKenzies. They threw themselves into the crisis, getting everyone out of their wet clothes and into some dry clothing and fuelling them with hot food and drinks.

Ardnish House had four bathrooms, six bedrooms, a massive kitchen, two dining rooms, a scullery, a large drawing room, a library, and a small sitting room.

Converted stables also housed two studio apartments.

In the midst of the recovery programme, Bob called Patricia White on her mobile phone and explained what had happened. As expected, her reaction was not good. She demanded to speak to someone else; Skye took the call and reassured her the tour party would be well looked after for the evening. Patricia would arrange for alternative transport to pick them up tomorrow – she would leave first thing from Portree to take custody of their welfare.

Finishing the call, Skye looked at the coach driver slumped in a hallway chair. Bob was staring into space, his face drawn, his clothes still wet.

'It won't seem so bad in the morning,' consoled Skye.

Bob looked up at her but did not try to smile. Looking down the hall, he divulged, 'Thirty years since I was last here.'

Skye paused, considering what she had just heard. 'Bet it hasn't changed much. What's your name?'

'Bob. Bob Sinclair.'

The name did not mean anything to Skye. But maybe Mackenzie knew him. So many people had been here in the seventies.

'You need a bath, a change of clothes, something to eat. Come with me.' Skye grabbed her waterproof jacket and led Bob out to one of the apartments above the stables. Clicking on lamps and the immersion heater, she showed Bob the facilities – it was a snug refuge for the night. A chest of drawers contained a pair of pyjamas, a bathrobe hung in the pine wardrobe.

'Come over to the house when you're ready for something to eat,' invited Skye.

'Thank you for all of this...' He did not know her name.

'Skye,' she informed him while opening the door to leave, 'Skye MacKenzie.'

She ran back to the main house, cowering from the rain, to help with the others.

Bob didn't show for food. Skye checked on him an hour later. He lay on the bed fast asleep. Switching off the lamps, she returned to the house.

By 10.15 p.m. that evening, the entire tour party were sitting in the drawing room, clothed in an assortment of garments; jogging trousers, old sweatshirts, denim dungarees, pyjamas, dressing gowns, shirts which had been used for indoor painting, even an old kaftan which Eva wore. It was agreed their personal belongings would be retrieved the following morning.

Their spirits had lifted with a change of clothes, a wash, getting warm and a home-cooked meal.

Polite questions from the group for Mackenzie flowed like his whisky as the evening progressed. They were interested in him and his house. He gave broad answers to their enquiries. A sea of middle-aged Scandinavian faces listened to Mackenzie, as he lit the red-brick fire.

Mats kicked off the questions. 'How did an American come to live here?'

'I'm Canadian. I came here in the early seventies, fell in love with the place.'

'How old is the house?'

'Built in 1867 by the MaCrindle family. They were landed gentry who made their money from Brazilian sugar in Victorian times. They built this hunting lodge for fishing and shooting.'

'Did you have to restore the place?' chipped in Kenni.

'No. This was how I found it, preserved so to speak. The MaCrindle family had, like so many old wealthy families, fallen on hard times since the Second World War. The estates they owned were expensive to run. The last surviving MaCrindle died childless in 1971. The estate was sold off to meet tax demands. That's when I bought it.'

'Is MacKenzie a Scottish name?' asked Marta.

'It is. My forefathers are Scottish. My grandfather emigrated from here to Newfoundland in 1894. So, I guess I've come full circle.'

A gentle laugh passed round the room. Jenny was intrigued with the MacKenzies, their relationship and this house. Wanting to know more, she decided to wait till the others had gone to bed before getting them on their own. Mackenzie topped up the whisky glasses till 11.00 p.m. With profuse thanks, the party made their way to their beds. Skye had been able to sort out sleeping arrangements for everybody through the house.

Jenny still had to take a bath. Her hosts were clearing up in the kitchen.

'Will you still be up for much longer, Mr MacKenzie?' Jenny asked on the way to the bathroom.

'I will. The evening's when I work best,' he replied. 'Lose the mister and you'll be using my forename.'

'Mackenzie MacKenzie,' mouthed Jenny.

'My father was determined we should not lose our Scottishness.'

'I'll be in bed' came Skye's answer to Jenny's question, looking tired from the evening's activities.

Jenny left to take her bath.

'Mac?' said Skye as she cleared some plates, 'I meant to ask you earlier. The bus driver says he's been here before, a long time ago, in the seventies. His name is Sinclair. Bob Sinclair. Does that mean anything to you?'

Facing away from Skye, Mackenzie was relieved she could not see his reaction. He paused before replying.

'Don't know the name. I would have recognised him if he were from the commune time. I didn't recognise him in the drawing room.'

'He wasn't in there. He's in one of the apartments, dead to

116

the world. I put him there out of the way – he looked in a terrible state. Are you okay?' she asked.

Mackenzie sat at a large oak table, staring out of the window in the direction of the stables. It was pitch black outside.

'I'm fine.'

'Is it the situation earlier? That woman coming in on us?'

'No. It's been a busy night, but I'll do some work though.' Mackenzie left the room.

'Good night,' said Skye as he left the kitchen.

Jenny would have soaked in the white enamel bath longer, but she wanted to get back downstairs to find out more. Pulling on a jogging suit, two sizes too big, she wrapped herself in an old, blue, towelling bathrobe.

She found Mackenzie sitting at a large drawing board in the library. His head was resting on the board; a half-full whisky tumbler sat on a stool beside it.

As Jenny came closer, his grey head popped up.

'I didn't mean to startle you,' she said.

'Not at all.' He was glad of the company to stop his mind racing. He might be able to find out if the coach driver was *the* Bob Sinclair.

'Is this what you do?' asked Jenny as she looked at the drawings on his board. He was working on a comic book; he was an artist. The figure in the hall was represented on the page; *Storm Girl*. Jenny's son had been a fan – she now made the connection.

Peter had explained the fictional character to her once. Storm Girl was a resistance fighter. The occupying force were the Nazis; the place they occupied, the world. Storm Girl was Eva Stotz, part of the new post-war generation who became an air stewardess for the only airline – Lufthansa. Through her travels, she realised the Nazi regime was wrong. She fought for justice, but kept her cover as a flight attendant.

'Storm Girl!' exclaimed Jenny.

' That's my little lady.'

'My son was an avid fan.'

'I owe Storm Girl for keeping this place going. I never expected her to transpire into the phenomenon she became!' mused Mackenzie. 'I doodled the character at Berkeley. It was a past time, a break from studying. A friend suggested I create a comic strip and he'd get it published in the University arts magazine. It took off from there.'

He stretched back on his seat, placing his hands behind his head. Jenny thought him an attractive man in the spotlight arc.

'I'm being rude! What will you have to drink?'

'I would love a malt.'

'Laphroig,' informed Mackenzie as he strode over to the antique drinks cabinet. 'Let's get a comfy seat,' he said pointing to two dark leather sofas facing each other in front of the fire.

The malt whisky trickled warmth into her chest. He sat opposite nursing his glass. Jenny was getting her wish to know more.

'I did some more Storm Girl before finishing college. It was the height of the Vietnam war, and the college kids read a lot into the character – fighting imperialism, that kind of thing. I headed for some time out, travelling through Europe, much to my father's disgust. He wanted me back in Toronto to help him out in his steel business.

I had always wanted to see Scotland, the old country. My grandfather had told me all about it when I was a kid. He gave it a mystical air. Like most people who leave their native land – he romanticised it. But I'm digressing. Well not really. It's all the same story – Storm Girl and this place.'

Enjoying the story, Jenny drew her legs up onto the couch.

'I travelled Europe for six months, then made my way here. It was the spring of 1971, I'd just turned twenty-four. I looked like a hippy; I was a hippy. Scotland didn't disappoint me, my grandfather was right all along – it was a magical place. I was reading *Lord Of The Rings* at the time. I thought I had arrived in Rivendell, the Kingdom of the Elves!'

Mackenzie told his story very well, thought Jenny. He continued, after poking a few remaining flames from the fire.

'Little did I realise I was to have my own kingdom! I stayed here for a couple of months, working in the forestry industry. I then got news my father had died from a heart attack – he was only sixty-two. But he had been a workaholic, building up his business through the forties and fifties – he benefited from the Second World War.' He sounded disgusted at the mention of his father's wealth creation from war time.

Jenny could tell there was no love lost between Mackenzie and his late father.

'I inherited a good sum of money, just as this place came up for sale. As far as I was concerned, it was good karma. I had my kingdom, and like a true hippy, I set about sharing it. I opened a commune, but that's another story.'

A good storyteller never shares the whole story at once. Mackenzie was taking a liking to Jenny; she seemed genuinely interested, intelligent and attractive too. He continued his tale.

'Back to Storm Girl. By 1979, times had changed. My money was running out and the house needed work. Then one day, I got a call from my old friend from Berkeley. By now he has his own comic book company, and wanted me to resurrect Storm Girl. He was her biggest fan. I needed the money and he needed to fill his comics – it was perfect really.

I updated the character, and so began my professional career so to speak. She moved into graphic novels in the eighties, and by the early nineties, she was animated for cable channels. As her audience got bigger, so did the pay cheques. The live action movie was released in 1997, and the proceeds meant I need never draw again. Ironic really. From hippy idealist to capitalist in thirty years – how my father would have laughed!' Mackenzie gave a philosophical grin.

'Your family background, is it Scottish?' enquired Jenny, finishing her whisky. She was drinking it quickly and needed to slow up.

Taking her empty glass to the drinks cabinet, he answered.

'Let me refresh our glasses and I will show you something!'
With whisky in hand, he led her into the hallway. On the
wall hung four photographs in burnished-gold frames. The
first one looked very old: it was a sepia image of an old
bearded man and his wife outside their crafting cottage.
Mackenzie gave the background.

'My great-grandfather, William MacKenzie, with his family.
He did well to survive the highland clearances. This was taken
about 1890, before their eldest son emigrated. He knew the
highland life was on the way out, so he saved hard to give his
eldest son, John, the money to start a new life. Stories were
always coming back from Canada from those who had been
shipped out with the clearances – life was hard, but the
opportunities were there.'

Mackenzie moved onto the adjacent portrait: a black-and-
white photograph of a tall man with a moustache standing
next to a woman. She had a stern look to her; he had a
friendly countenance.

'John MacKenzie, my grandfather, emigrated to
Newfoundland in 1894 aged nineteen. He could have gone to
Glasgow, worked in the steel mills, but he liked the
countryside, so he took his chances in Canada.' Mackenzie's
voice was loaded with affection.

'Did you know him?' asked Jenny.

'Thankfully. He lived to the age of ninety-one. I was
nineteen when he died. I used to spend summer holidays with
my grandparents. He would take me fishing in his small boat,
tell me stories of Scotland – his descriptions were prone to be
magical – set my imagination alight. He got me interested in
the old country.'

'Did he ever come back to visit?'

'He could have. My father offered to pay on several
occasions. But he didn't want to – afraid of disrupting the
memories of what he had left behind.'

Mackenzie moved over to the next photograph which was
of a stocky man, forty-something, sitting sternly at a large
desk. Next to him, stood a delicate-looking woman, similar

age, dressed in a long, green dress.

'My mother and father.' Mackenzie's tone had lost its affection. 'Bill and Joan. He had a different strain to him from my grandfather. The steel mills of Glasgow did not tempt his father, but the ones in Ontario did him.'

'What was your relationship like with him?'

'Tolerable. Money was his god. He came home every day and told us how much money the company had made – the amount dictated his mood. The more it was, the more pleasant he would be.'

'And your mother?'

Mackenzie smiled. 'A good, caring person, but very much in my father's shadow.'

'But you were able to buy this place because of your inheritance,' added Jenny. She was finding the family history fascinating.

'I see it more as natural justice. My grandfather had to leave this country because of lack of opportunity. I come back and reclaimed what I could. This house is for my grandfather's memory, not my father's!' Mackenzie spoke with heartfelt conviction, his eyes alight with a combination of anger and pride.

Jenny moved on to look at the last photograph. It was Mackenzie with a woman outside Ardnish House. They both had long hair, he with a full beard. Faded green dungarees for Mackenzie, bright flowery dress for the young woman who was holding a baby – it was summer time.

Jenny peered at the woman's face – she was pretty.

'A boy or girl?' asked Jenny pointing at the child.

Mackenzie hesitated before answering. 'That's my daughter with my wife, Liz. She passed away in 1990 – cancer.'

'I'm sorry.'

He nodded. Mackenzie did not want to talk about his departed wife.

'And your daughter?'

Mackenzie walked back into the library and began turning off the lights.

'She's doing well for herself. She's in the media business.'

Mackenzie's tone had changed. Jenny sensed that discussing his own family was not on the agenda.

'The MacKenzie line? I take it you would like a son to continue the name?'

'It would be good, but unlikely.' The last light flicked off leaving only an outline of Mackenzie, his tall angular frame looking harsh now.

'But with a lovely young wife like Skye...?'

'I think it's time for bed,' interrupted Mackenzie firmly.

'I'm sorry. I don't mean to be nosy, but families interest me. Please accept my apologies.' Jenny felt embarrassed – she had pushed the conversation too far.

'That's twice today you've apologised, Jenny,' he said with a smile.

Jenny blushed. She needed to get some sleep. As she went up the stairs Mackenzie asked a question.

'The coach driver; what's his name?'

'Bob Sinclair. I haven't seen much of him tonight.'

'He's in one of the studio apartments; Skye said he was exhausted. What age is he?'

'Mid-fifties, something like that.'

'Thanks. Get a good night's sleep. You'll be travelling again tomorrow no doubt!' Mackenzie disappeared into the kitchen.

Jenny was sleeping in one of the attic rooms. She slipped into the single bed, curling up into a ball under the duvet. Rain dashed on the sky-light window, but not as heavy as earlier. A few slates lifted and fell from the swell of the wind's probing.

The fog of sleep was descending – just enough time to cast her mind over the eventful day. Then another image creased her mind; Skye on the chaise longue engaged in sensual lovemaking by the look of things – lucky girl!

Sleep took her a few seconds later.

Chapter Eleven

Bob awoke with a start, the sun streaming through the window onto his bed. It took a few seconds to get his bearings, then the previous day's events flooded over him like a pounding wave. Rolling over, he buried his head into the pillow, wishing yesterday's nightmare had been a dream. A sickening feeling of dread pulled at his state of mind, infusing panic. *Fuck, fuck, fuck, fuck, fuck, fuck, fuck – what a fuck-up he'd made!*

A terrible weight pushed down on his chest. He took deep breaths to regain control of his body, fighting a bout of anxiety, which pulsed through him – savage and unrelenting. Two options faced him now; lie there in a state, or get up and take action. Springing out of bed he decided to take action and salvage the luggage. He thought of his photograph album in his briefcase next to the driver's seat – good job it was not in the hold. The thought of it being ruined in the river water made him shudder.

Striding down the drive, the clear blue sky gave him some hope. A couple of minutes later, he was at the crash site. Scotia Tours 001 glistened in the morning sunshine.

Taking his shoes and socks off, he rolled up his trousers and waded into the river. Opening the hold doors he could see most of the luggage was dry. This lifted his spirits a little.

One hour later, the suitcases stood on the bank. Bob lugged them to the foot of the drive, sweat rolling off his body. As he stacked the last one, the local post van turned into the drive.

'Do you need some help?' asked the craggy-faced postman.

'Please,' responded Bob.

Five minutes later, they were going up the drive, the luggage aboard the van, its suspension creaking under the weight.

'Who lives here now?' asked Bob. It struck him for the first time he had no idea who they were?

'Mr MacKenzie.'

'Mackenzie MacKenzie?' asked Bob a little surprised.

'Aye. Been here since the seventies. It's not the hippy place it was then though. He's some sort of artist now. Does very well from what I've been told.'

The van swung in front of the house.

'You must be staying here a while with all that luggage,' quipped the postman as he helped Bob unload.

The postman handed him the mail and sped off. Sure enough, the letters were all addressed to Mr M. MacKenzie.

Entering the kitchen from the rear of the house, Bob could smell fried bacon. Skye turned from the range as the door opened, dressed in faded blue jeans and a turquoise shirt. Flip-flop sandals showed off her painted toenails.

'Morning, Bob. Are you hungry? she asked, frying pan in hand, smiling.

'Please. I didn't eat last night.' Dropping the mail on the big oak table, Bob drew up a chair. Skye turned back to cooking breakfast.

'Thanks for last night. Most appreciated. Is everybody okay?' enquired Bob. Fine ass, he thought, looking at Skye's bottom in her tight jeans. He needed all the distractions he could get.

Sounds of movement from upstairs filtered down into the kitchen; people using the bathrooms, footsteps on the floorboards, the sound of water-pipes rattling.

'I think so. We got everyone fed and watered. We just had enough beds,' replied Skye.

Her slim arms looked toned and strong thought Bob; she

probably worked out.

'I've got their luggage on the drive, ready for when the replacement coach comes,' informed Bob, clutching at any positives.

'Well done!' Skye dished up a plate of fried breakfast. Bob had another good look at her.

'Thanks,' he said as she put the plate in front of him. 'It's Skye, isn't it?

'Yep, that's me,' she said fetching him some cutlery, a smile crossing her striking features.

'Are you related to Mackenzie MacKenzie? He still lives here?'

'Yes. Do you know him? You said you were here a long time ago.'

'Thirty years ago.' Bob started eating his breakfast with relish, hunger from the salvage operation had replaced the anxiety from earlier.

'That would be when this place was a commune!' stated Skye as she began preparing more breakfast for the group.

'I didn't know what a commune was till I came here. I loved it. I'd been out of the army for six months, split up from my first wife, drinking too much. I was aimless – without direction. This breakfast is wonderful.'

'You're welcome,' said Skye, pausing for a moment, looking at Bob wolfing down the plate of food.

'Would you like some tea?' she asked, turning to pour herself one from a chrome teapot on the range.

'Please.' With food in his stomach and a pretty girl pouring him a cup of tea, for an instant the accident seemed far away.

'The accident. How did it happen?' Her question brought him sharply back to reality.

'It was a combination of things; the weather, and if I'm honest, my own poor judgement.' He noted her fine figure again, her firm, slender frame. Fuck, what he'd give to be half his age again.

'You weren't the first, and you certainly won't be the last. It's claimed a few lives too,' Skye said.

'Well it has probably cost me my bus driving life. I can't see Scotia Tours keeping me on after this one – they're strict!' He wanted to get off this subject. 'So who are you in relation to Mackenzie,' Bob asked.

She paused for a second. 'His wife. Second wife.'

Bob nearly choked. Lucky bastard, he thought instantly. But what had happened to Liz? Skye got there before he had the chance to ask.

'Did you know his first wife?'

'Yes, I did. Lovely woman. What happened? Did they break up?'

'You don't know.' Skye paused and sat opposite him. 'She died from cancer.'

Bob felt a jolt of shock. Liz's face came back to him – her lovely face, just like Skye's. It now made sense. Mackenzie had gone out and married a similar looking girl – a replacement for his late wife with the added bonus of her being half his age, probably the same age Liz was when they first met.

Ideal. I-fucking-deal!

'You've met then.' Mackenzie stood in the doorway giving them both a jolt.

Recognition passed between the two men, two people stepping back inside an overlap from the past.

Bob got up to shake Mackenzie's hand. Mackenzie waved him to sit down.

'Don't get up, Robert. Finish your breakfast.' His tone was firm, no nonsense. He poured himself a cup of tea and stood facing Bob.

'You're looking well Mackenzie. Must be something in the water up here!' complimented Bob, sensing the other man's territorial presence in the room.

'Not looking too bad yourself, Robert. I understand you drive a coach for a living now?' His tone was pleasant, but forced.

Bob sipped his tea before answering. 'Yes. Have been for eight years.'

Mackenzie and Skye nodded.

'The house is looking good,' commented Bob.

'Well it's not a commune any more. We all moved on. I make my living from being an artist.'

'Your drawing was always good. You've always had talent in that department.' Bob sounded too eager to compliment now, not liking himself for it.

Skye sensed the history between the two men wasn't good – this was turgid conversation with Bob doing all the work.

'I was just saying to your wife, how the commune helped me back onto the right road so to speak.' Bob was trying to be positive.

'We helped a lot of people. It was the ones who helped themselves a little too much, we had to be wary of!' said Mackenzie, fixing Bob with a solid stare.

'Breakfast, Mac?' asked Skye, attempting to relieve the growing tension.

'What happened last night with your coach?' enquired Mackenzie, ignoring Skye's offer.

But Bob did not get a chance to reply. At that moment, Jenny entered the kitchen, answering for him.

'It was bad luck, pure bad luck! Wouldn't you say, Bob?' squeezing his shoulder sympathetically.

Bob nodded as he stood up. 'I better call Patricia White. There's stuff to sort out.' Bob went outside to make the call, relieved to be absent from Mackenzie's company.

Jenny grabbed a mug of tea and joined Bob outside in the morning sunshine. He stood in the courtyard, deep in thought. Jenny walked up to him.

'Bob? Are you alright?' she asked concerned.

'Fine,' he lied.

'What's with Mackenzie? He doesn't appear to have much time for you. Do you two know each other?'

Bob looked a little taken aback.

'I heard what he said to you from the hall,' confessed Jenny.

Turning to look out at the view, Bob sought solace from the

mountainous blue peaks, the rugged beauty of the West Highlands sprawling into the distance.

'I was here in 1972. Mackenzie had just bought the place and opened it up as a commune. I had not long been out of the army. After seven years of structure, being told what to do and when to do it, civvy life came as a bit of a shock.' Bob was speaking fast, not wishing to dwell on the negative aspects of his earlier life.

'I had served in a Scottish regiment, so I bummed around here for a while, working up on the ferries at Mallaig. Some guys in a pub told me about this place, so I thought I'd give it a try.' He paused, pulling on thirty-year-old remembrances like a fisherman hauling in a net of memories.

'I loved the whole thing; living together, sharing, looking out for each other like one big family. Mackenzie's idea was great. We were all equal and all that hippy stuff – peace and love. I even grew my hair long. Anyway, I suppose I didn't fit in when it came right down to it. To be honest I took the 'love in' thing too far. Do you know what I mean?'

Jenny nodded. She could imagine Bob in his prime back then. Probably treated the commune like it was his harem, like he did with the coach parties today.

'I upset the delicate balance. That was how Mackenzie described it. He asked me to pack my bags and leave – the lot of them had voted on it. Fair do's, I thought. I was off the drink, getting a bit tired of sharing my wages anyway. I left in early seventy-three.'

Bob's mobile phone rang. He looked at the display; it was Mrs Hoxley calling. Taking it from him, Jenny answered it. Bob thankful for her quick thinking.

'This is Jenny Jenkins, one of the passengers. Bob is sorting out the luggage, can I help?' Jenny repeated key phrases to give him the gist of what Mrs Hoxley was saying.

'Bob is to stay put. You will be here by late afternoon.' The call over, Jenny relayed Bob's instructions.

'You need to make arrangements for an overnight stay for Mrs Hoxley and a Mr Entwhistle.'

'He's the head engineer,' informed Bob as he sorted through the luggage.

'They are flying up to Glasgow, hiring a car and they want to see you and the coach.'

'Standard procedure,' Bob said wearily.

'Why don't you see if the MacKenzies can put you all up? Offer to pay them.'

'I think there's a problem. I'm not welcome!'

'But what happened was thirty years ago.'

Bob looked away. There is more to this story, thought Jenny. She made a suggestion.

'Look, there's no harm in asking, is there?'

'I think it's better if I get some rooms at the Arisaig Hotel,' said Bob, taking control of the discussion.

Jenny nodded. She knew she was trying too hard now, and made her way back into the house.

The entire party was now in the kitchen, working their way through Skye's breakfast, apart from Gregory and Miriam who were taking theirs in the drawing room.

Informing them of the arrangements Mrs Hoxley had conveyed, Jenny noted the group's spirits had lifted after a good night's rest. Deciding she wanted to change into fresh clothes, Jenny went upstairs. As she turned onto the landing, she bumped into Henrik.

'Sorry, Jenny,' he smiled knowingly.

'No problem.'

He paused a second, about to say something else. 'I know about you and Pernille. She told me everything and I want you to know I'm okay with it. If there's a next time, I'd like to be part of it.'

With a wink he was gone down the stairs, a jaunt to his stride. Little did he realise, he'd just helped Jenny make her mind up about something.

Jenny asked if she could have a chat with Mackenzie and Skye. They complied with her request, retreating to the drawing room.

'First of all, thanks for everything you have done. From what I gather from Scotia Tours, your expenses will be reimbursed,' announced Jenny.

'No problem!' replied Skye.

'There is one other thing I want to ask.' Jenny paused. 'If Bob and the two Scotia Tours' people cannot get accommodation around here for tonight, can you put them up? They will pay for their board.'

Mackenzie looked unhappy.

'It was okay to do last night, but bed and breakfast we are not!' responded Mackenzie curtly.

Skye interjected.

'Can you give us a minute?'

Jenny withdrew into the hall, closing the door behind her, wishing she'd not asked. She backed down the hall, not wanting to be too close to the door when the MacKenzies came out. Thirty seconds later, the door opened to reveal Skye smiling. Mackenzie was not.

'Jenny,' said Skye, 'that's fine. We'll sort something out with them if they cannot get a place to stay.' Mackenzie pushed past her, disappearing into the library, closing the door firmly.

'Don't mind him. It's his artist's temperament,' intimated Skye, as they walked down the hall.

'One other thing, I'm not going on with the tour, I'm going back to Yorkshire. I'll get the train. Is Fort William the closest station?

'Sure is. I can run you there.'

'Are you sure?'

'Absolutely. I need to get some supplies anyway,' confirmed Skye, a big smile putting Jenny at ease.

The bruise on Gregory's head was quite large by the morning – a blue swelling on the bridge of his nose. Taking a tray from his lap, Miriam looked at him with concern. He'd hardly spoken since the crash, his eyes glazed, his demeanour distant. Miriam would have been reassured with a few caustic remarks – some proof he was returning to his normal self.

'Gregory. Are you okay?'

'Thinking, just thinking,' he replied in a barely audible tone.

'Do you want me to get a doctor?'

'No need. Physically I'm alright. I just need some time to think.'

Miriam retreated to the kitchen, the banter of the party a welcome escape. Gregory was not so much traumatised by the coach accident itself, but the incident had catapulted him back to a year earlier when he had fallen from his horse. Forced to recall the tragedy, the former surgeon was reliving the moment he felt himself leave the saddle, glide through the air and tumble onto the sun-baked grassland. Before passing out with the pain, he glimpsed a bale of straw just feet away and knew in an instant it might have broken his fall, to the extent he might not have been crippled. If only.

A slow realisation was dawning in Gregory Spittlewood's mind – an emerging awareness of the real meaning of something being there to break a fall, to save the damage being done. It wasn't a something though, it was a somebody.

Just after midday, Patricia White arrived at Ardnish House in an old, yellow school bus, pulling onto the drive in a flurry of diesel fumes.

'It was all I could get in Portree,' she explained in her husky smoker's voice to the assembled group. 'The replacement coach and driver will be with us tomorrow,' informed Patricia.

The words 'replacement driver' cut through Bob like a sword. He felt a little shaken. A sick taste invaded his mouth, acidic, unwanted. Fear tightened around his scrotum, and then moved up into the middle of his body. This is it, he thought, it's all over for me.

Jenny noticed Bob's reaction. She felt sorry for him – Patricia might as well have shouted 'timber' instead of 'replacement driver', and watch Bob, the mighty oak, come crashing down.

Bob and Patricia spoke for a few minutes, before she herded everybody aboard. Jenny explained to the new guide she was not continuing.

'That's a shame, Mrs Jenkins,' said Patricia, checking off the tour party's names on her trusty clipboard – she was a clipboard-type person.

Skye and Jenny received profuse thanks from the group as they boarded.

Bob got a kiss from Eva, a hug from Christina, and nearly everybody shook his hand. It had all been a bit of an adventure. Bob stood, trying to smile, but his heart was not in it. His hand felt limp when the tour group shook it – as if the very blood was draining out of his body. Pernille held Jenny tightly and fought back a tear.

'Take care, Jenny! Please visit us if you come to Stockholm.'

'I will, I promise, I'll be in touch soon. Enjoy the rest of your trip, and make sure Henrik gets enough to eat.'

The two friends chuckled as Pernille, the last to board, waved goodbye from the rear window. Jenny had enjoyed her time with the Danish woman, but seemed to find it easy to break such transient friendships – she knew before the other woman when the encounter had run its course.

As the words CAUTION – SCHOOL BUS receded from view, leaving an empty silence Jenny and Bob's solitary pieces of luggage sat on the drive stared back.

The group were gone. It felt like being a child again, thought Jenny. Dropped off after a day out on a school trip – pressed together for all those hours, enfolded by the group, enmeshed in each other's words and deeds, but now alone.

Mackenzie was still in the library, working. After the bus pulled away, Bob asked if the pathway up Ardnish hill still existed. If so he would take a walk, be back later. Skye confirmed it was.

'Take care, Bob,' said Jenny. 'I'm off shortly to get my train.'

They hugged.

'Thanks for all your help, Jenny.' He turned and headed off for his sojourn, carrying his bulky briefcase.

'The view from the hill is wonderful on a day like this,' said Skye as they watched Bob go through a small gate at the side of the stables.

'He needs to clear his head, I think,' said Jenny. 'Poor bloke. Looks like his bus driving days are over.'

'I don't know. He seems a strong man to me.'

'I don't think it's the actual driving he'll miss. It's the lifestyle!' suggested Jenny, watching Bob disappear into the purple heather.

'I will get the Landrover,' said Skye, heading for the garage.

Jenny thought about saying goodbye to Mackenzie, but thought better of it – she could communicate her thanks through his wife.

The run down to Fort William was pleasant. Skye tended to drive fast, but Jenny felt safe in her young hands.

The scenery was breathtaking in the early afternoon sunshine. Scotland's West Highland terrain stood dramatic and magnificent. A red deer bolted across the road, handsome, sleek, swallowed up by birch trees in an instant. Did she really want to go home – the thought flashed through her mind. The encounter with Henrik had been the clincher, not so much his words, but the knowing look he had given her. How long before he told the other men? It was better to cut her losses, face up to returning home.

As they entered the small village of Lochailort, two miles from Ardnish House, Jenny spotted a small store. She wanted to buy Skye something, a present to say thank you, this would be the only chance she would have.

'Can we stop here for a few minutes?'

'Why?' suddenly Skye's tone was less friendly.

'I want to look in that little shop. Just a few minutes.'

Skye seemed hesitant to break the journey, but pulled into

the small petrol forecourt opposite the shop. 'Okay,' she said. 'I need to get some diesel. But you need to be quick if you want to make your train.'

The small store was empty except for the lady owner reading a newspaper on the counter.

Jenny quickly looked round the rustic trinkets, tourist tat, and found a little seal moulded from clay – it was the best there was.

Skye had slipped into the store and paid for the diesel.

'Let's make a move, Jenny. You don't want to be late,' said the young woman, going back outside. The owner smiled.

'A friend of Skye's?' she asked.

'Yes. I was in a coach accident at the bottom of their road. The MacKenzies put us all up – very good of them.'

The woman nodded.

News travels fast round here, thought Jenny as she paid for the present.

'They're a lovely couple,' added Jenny.

'Lovely couple?' asked the woman quizzically.

'Yes. Skye and Mackenzie. I know she's half his age, but if they're happy!'

The woman looked confused.

'I think you've got the wrong end of the stick, dear. Skye isn't Mackenzie's wife, she's his daughter!'

Jenny's legs felt like they were going to collapse as she crossed the road to the Landrover, the engine already running, belching blue fumes as the motor revved. She pulled herself into the passenger seat, staring forward; she could not look at Skye.

The vehicle pulled away quickly.

Silence. Not a word between them. Jenny's mind was stuck with one image – Skye naked on the chaise longue, going up and down; *fucking, fucking her father, father fucking daughter*. Her stomach was now queasy, she might be sick.

'Are you okay?' Skye asked, concerned.

Jenny's face was ashen white. She nodded. It remained

silent for another two minutes as they drove along.
'You know, don't you?' blurted out the young woman.
Jenny nodded. Skye slowed the vehicle and completed an aggressive three-point turn before heading back the way they had come. Jenny hardly noticed.

Five minutes later, they drove into a car park that looked over the splendid views of Loch Ailort. Skye killed the engine. Both women stared over the sheen of blue water; it was a beautiful sight.

Taking a deep breath Skye spoke, her voice loaded with emotion. 'It was never his idea. It was *me*. I seduced Mackenzie! It's always been me!' She broke down crying uncontrollably.

Chapter Twelve

'Jenny, I need you to listen to what I have to say!' pleaded Skye through her tears.

'You deserve an explanation, and I need to talk to someone about this. Mackenzie and I have been carrying this 'thing' on our own for too long, far too long!'

Jenny could feel the young woman's distress – a stranger she had grown to like over the last twenty-four hours. Turning to look at Skye, Jenny gave her a reassuring smile, found a tissue in her handbag and dabbed her face, like a mother would her child.

Skye pulled herself together, preparing to tell her story.

'Take your time,' said Jenny, preparing herself for what was to come.

'What you saw yesterday, when you came into the library...you must understand, it's only happened a few times. You must believe me.'

The chaise longue images flashed through Jenny's mind. She nodded.

Skye continued.

'The affair began after my mother's death. I was seventeen, but I suppose the seeds were sown while I was growing up. They say little girls practice the art of attracting the opposite sex on their fathers.'

Jenny nodded.

'We realise this power early, don't we?'

'Yes,' agreed Jenny, recalling her ability to get pretty much what she wanted from her own father, putting on the cutesy daughter act, the little princess.

'I was no different with Mack, except I called him Macky when I was a kid, not Daddy. I should have called him Daddy, maybe this might not have happened, but we were an alternative family. Anyway, while I was going through puberty, I flirted with him all the time.' Skye made it sound like it was some sort of teenage normality.

Jenny wanted to say, but he should have discouraged you, but thought better of interjecting – she did not want to interrupt Skye, now she had begun to explain her situation.

Skye rolled down the window, letting a soft summer breeze enter the cabin. It felt refreshing to both.

'My mother's death was traumatic for both of us – we were a close family. Mack locked himself in the library for days. I felt I had to get some normality back into the house. I took on all my mother's roles. That was one of the first mistakes, thinking I could replace my mother in all ways.

The other thing with living in Ardnish House is the isolation – you can easily create your own world...nobody from the outside will really challenge it. Mack does not really interact with people – the artist's solitude. I preferred adult's company as a child, there weren't really any other children in my life, apart from school.' Skye took a deep breath. Tipping her past into someone else's lap felt good. The release, as she expected, was cathartic, but draining.

'Are you okay,' enquired Jenny. Reaching over, she took Skye's hand and held it. The human contact felt good for the young woman – she really appreciated Jenny's kindness.

'I'm fine, thanks. Three months after my mother died, Mack and I got drunk and stoned one night. He broke down. We held each other and kissed. On the cheek at first...'

'Skye, I don't need the detail,' reassured Jenny seeing a few tears cascade down the young woman's face, but also wanting to spare herself the sexual specifics of an incestuous relationship.

'I know, Jenny, but I need to tell you how it was. We kissed on the mouth; it felt strange, and yet good. Could it have been the grief – now we had a release of sorts. All I know is I wanted him, I mean *really* wanted him in a physical sense.

I suggested we sleep together – to be close that night. He was really out of it – he didn't know what he was doing, but I did. I knew what I was doing, seducing him.'

Skye closed her eyes, the memory of the evening vivid in her mind. She felt Jenny squeeze her hand and she began to sob uncontrollably. It took a few minutes to regain her composure, Jenny pulling the young woman closer, Skye's head buried on her shoulder.

'The next morning, I awoke to find him in a terrible state. We vowed it wouldn't happen again and not to talk about it... *ever*!

But being in the house together alone, it was a strain. We knew it was wrong, but I sensed he wanted me. It happened again, when I was eighteen. I was set to go to University and having a romance with a local boy, Callum McCreadie. Mack was really protective – he never liked him. Looking back, I think he was jealous. This time Mack instigated it. Afterwards we knew things were getting out of control – we both had to get our own lives. He needed to start a new life with someone else.'

Skye paused, wiped her cheeks with the tissue and continued.

'As part of the film deal for Storm Girl, he got an agreement from the Hollywood studio that they'd give me a job in California. I left when I was nineteen and to be honest, I've never looked back.' Skye smiled at the talk of her career.

'But what happened yesterday evening?' asked Jenny, not wishing to bring the subject up, but knowing she had to.

'A slip up,' said Skye defensively.

'How many slip ups have you and Mack had?'

'None!'

Skye was close to tears again. 'Now and again. Oh what the fuck, every time I come home to Ardnish House. Every summer.'

She held her head in her hands and broke down again. Jenny pulled Skye's head into her chest and hugged her.

'You have to understand something – it's not as bad as it sounds.' Skye sat up, wiping away the tears, her eyes puffy, cheeks streaked and red.

'Mack is not my real father. He's not my biological father.'

Slamming the passenger door behind her, Jenny walked to the water's edge. The peaty water lapped the smooth pebbles. The sun was now in the west, its heat beginning to fade, the light breeze felt good against her forehead.

How she longed for home. This incest thing was someone else's dirty secret – like acrid fumes blowing over from some dirty chimney, inhabiting her clothes and skin. She'd come to Scotland to escape her own past, not to be confronted with another emotional time bomb.

She had never met these people before. Now twenty-four hours later, she felt bound to them, especially this young woman who was literally crying out for help.

Jenny felt she was flailing in some invisible net; one minute swimming freely, the next, swept up by a passing person's despair. Skye appeared at her side, joining the older woman at the water's edge.

'Help me, Jenny. Please!' she pleaded.

Bob stood at the end of the gravel road – the exact spot where his coach-driving days had ended so sourly.

Mrs Hoxley's hired car was parked next to the police Landrover. She and Mr Entwhistle were at the crash scene with Officer Wilkie.

All of the sighing and tutting had become too much for Bob, including the ones from the tow-truck man, Alistair Gibb, a burly, balding man in his forties. The inquiry into what had happened had lasted an hour after they arrived at Ardnish house, just before 3.00 p.m.

Mackenzie had made them all tea, as they conducted their questioning. Bob sensed the artist was enjoying his plight and was relieved when Mackenzie excused himself to work outside.

Procedure called for Bob to give a detailed statement as to what had happened to Scotia Tours 001. Mrs Hoxley had been thorough as usual in her questioning and appeared impartial, not implying any negligence on Bob's part.

Mr Entwhistle though, came over as judge and jury from the start. The tall, gangly Yorkshire man had been the senior engineer at the company for twenty years. He referred to the coaches as 'his ladies', taking great pride in all aspects of their mechanical running and appearance.

Seeing one of his ladies in the River Sneeth had brought on a cold sweat.

Bob was just about to go back down to the riverbank when he saw the MacKenzie Landrover turn the corner. As it swished past, he was surprised to see Jenny in the passenger seat. It stopped a few metres ahead. Jenny stepped out and walked towards him.

'I thought you were on your way back to Yorkshire?' enquired Bob.

'Have you found a place to stay tonight?' she asked quickly, ignoring his question.

'Yes, I have. Myself, Mrs Hoxley and Mr Entwhistle are staying at the Arisaig Hotel.'

'I need a favour. Can you stay at the MacKenzies' tonight. Just you though – I'm staying on?'

'But I've a room. There's no need!' Bob sensed Jenny wanted his support, help, something.

'We'll tell the MacKenzies there were only two rooms available,' suggested Jenny. Her eyes were pleading.

'Okay,' he agreed. Given the choice of having Mackenzie glowering at him for the evening, or Hoxley and Entwhistle's company, he would rather be at Ardnish House. Bob was also intrigued by Jenny's request. Maybe she wanted him in other ways?

'I'll explain later,' she said, before returning to the idling Landrover. It sped off towards the house.

As they approached, Skye asked Jenny, 'Please don't confront Mackenzie with this. He has a terrible temper!'

'I won't, but he needs to know I know, otherwise, this thing will get out of hand.'

Skye nodded.

'Skye. When did you find out Mackenzie was not your biological father?'

'It all came out after my mother died. He'd returned to Canada for a couple of months in 1972 to sort out his father's estate. The commune was in full swing; my mother was left in charge. When Mackenzie returned in the fall, my mother told him she was pregnant. It was obvious I wasn't his; she'd had an affair within the commune, but they still loved each other.'

The tractor mower was completing its sweep of the front lawn as they pulled into the drive. Mackenzie was astride the vehicle, enjoying the task; a contrast to sitting at his drawing board.

Looking up, he was surprised to see Jenny stepping out.

Skye disappeared into the house quickly – she looked upset.

He killed the engine. Jenny stood looking at him.

She knows! he thought. She fucking knows! The woman knows everything! Starting the mower engine, Mackenzie drove the vehicle into the large workshop at the rear of the house. He was still sitting on the machine when Jenny appeared in the doorway.

It was now early evening. A light breeze moved through the trees – all sounds baffled and muffled by the season's vegetation, noise soaked up by spongy green. A curlew's cry carried shrill, the only note capable of piercing the surroundings.

Mackenzie spoke first.

'How is Skye?' he sounded concerned.

'Upset. But I think she feels better for talking.'

In that instant he resented Jenny, this stranger who had come into their lives, literally walking into their most private affairs.

'I have this under control, and to be frank, this is none of your fucking business!' His voice was beginning to verge on the confrontational.

'I know, but Skye wants me to stay, and I think she needs help.'

'Who the hell do you think you are?' Mackenzie shouted as he bounded off the mower, his frame taut with aggression. He placed his face close to Jenny's; she flinched, trying not to tremble or show her fear. She backed away a few steps; he stayed with her.

'Mackenzie, please. You're scaring me!' Jenny appealed to the man who'd drank whisky with her a matter of hours earlier.

He straightened up, turned and put his hands on his head. Walking back into the workshop he turned to speak, the rage gone from his voice. 'Don't judge me, Jenny.'

'I'm not a judging person, Mackenzie. I've been through enough myself at the hands of others.' She could understand his feelings right now; his life stripped bear, an emotional nakedness, a complete stranger looking on. She wanted to redress the balance.

'I would like you to see something which will prove I'm not judgmental.'

He followed her into the house, through to the library. Looking at his computer sitting next to his drawing board, she asked, 'Can you get me onto the web with this?'

He nodded. Within a few minutes the screen was alight with an array of colours and messages.

Taking the black leather office chair, facing the screen, her fingers darted over the keyboard. Looking over her shoulder, Mackenzie saw a website home page materialise; black background, red lettering. The words read: WEBSITE SUSPENDED.

'It's not active at the moment,' remarked Jenny. She clicked on the web-host's logo, typing in her username, password and the website address; www.mature-emporium.co.uk. Hitting the submit button, Jenny leaned back to let her inactive website appear.

The home page transitioned into view; black background, red velvet letters spelled 'THE MATURE EMPORIUM'. On the screen was an image of an attractive couple in their fifties, holding each other, naked from the waist up with the strap line below; *Welcome to a place where mature couples can find discreet fun.*

Jenny clicked onto the Guest Book tab and the page changed to a list of comments from subscribers. One read:

Thank you MATURE EMPORIUM for the fun times we have had. Through the site, we have met similar couples and individuals who want to make new friendships, widen their social circle and have some 'discreet' fun together. So many sites are tacky and explicit, but MATURE EMPORIUM is a credit to our generation for subtlety. Thank you.
Margaret and Stephen, Dorset

'You run a swingers site?' asked Mackenzie. There was derision in his voice.

'I did, until my local newspaper ran a story on me.' A realisation struck Jenny in an instant, she should have held her head high and not run away to Scotland. In the grand scheme of things, her drama was insignificant in comparison to the MacKenzies.

'I get your point about not being judged, and I appreciate your understanding, but I fail to understand how you can help Skye and me,' said Mackenzie, feeling stronger with the knowledge he now possessed.

His words made Jenny feel trivial, bothersome and out of her depth. But there was one thing she had to know before she left.

'Tell me one thing and then I'll be gone.'

'I don't know if I will give you the answer, but ask anyway.' He sensed her leaving – thank fuck!

Jenny braced herself and fired off the question.

'Who is Skye's real father?'

Mackenzie's rage jumped back into the ring, but after a few

tense seconds, he forced a controlled reply.

'I'm not going to divulge such information; it's none of your fucking business. Skye doesn't even know.' He turned to leave.

'It's Bob? It's Bob Sinclair, isn't it? That's why you don't want him here!'

Mackenzie stopped dead in his tracks. Without turning round, he answered calmly, but his fists were clenched.

'Knowing who her *blood* father is will just complicate things, and you have no right to speculate on who that is, and certainly no right to be involved in informing her'. He turned round. 'Do you understand? Now as I said, this is none of your business. Please get your things and leave. I'll call you a taxi.' He marched from the room.

Jenny felt degraded, by the situation and herself.

As she stood up, she glanced over the sketches on Mackenzies's drawing board. Black-and-white images of Storm Girl stared back; her leaping through the air, performing martial art kicks into Nazi-thugs faces, buxom breasts bulging out of her air-stewardess tunic.

A sheet lay below the one she was looking at. A speech bubble caught her eye.

Excuse me, I'm Jenny, I didn't mean to interrupt!

Jenny looked up. It sounded like Mackenzie had gone upstairs, checking on Skye no doubt. She had to look at the drawings below. The compulsion was too strong to ignore.

Jenny lifted the top page and followed the story strip – except it was not about Storm Girl. The characters were Mackenzie, Skye and Jenny in an Ardnish House setting.

It started with Jenny coming into the library and discovering Mackenzie and Skye having sex. The black-and-white images were drawn in the same precise way as Storm Girl – Jenny's character had a remarkable likeness. What unfolded in the strip was not what had actually taken place the night before. Instead Jenny was asking if she could watch the couple having intercourse – the speech bubble coming from Jenny, '*Don't mind me, I like to watch people fucking.*'

A panel later, Jenny was illustrated with her hand down her

knickers, masturbating, and in the next panel she was sucking on Skye's nipple as she sat astride Mackenzie. By the end of the sequence, Jenny was being taken from behind by the artist, as Skye slapped his bottom with a dildo – the speech bubble from Jenny, '*Fuck me harder, Mack, I may be a bit of old, but I still need a good fucking.*'

She felt a terrible urge to get away from Ardnish House, to go now. She didn't even want to say goodbye to Skye.

Skye! Jenny felt the conflict instantly. Panic fluttered in her chest.

This young woman needed to know what type of person her step-father was. Jenny was frozen to the spot – what should she do?

Confusion reigned – fight or flight, but it wasn't her fight!

'Jenny?'

A voice came from the hall.

'Hello. Anybody here?'

It was Bob. Jenny was relieved. She could have kissed him. He stood with his briefcase in his hand, like a travelling salesman.

'I'm glad you're here,' her voice was loaded with relief. 'Come quickly, outside!'

She and Bob stepped into the summer evening. Taking a deep breath, she surveyed the scenery; the mountains in the distance, the wooded slopes, the sheer openness of the sky and outdoor surroundings – freedom.

Jenny looked down towards the drive; it beckoned. This was it – time to leave.

She turned to Bob.

'Bob, let's go. We can stay at the Arisaig Hotel.'

Naturally, he was confused. 'But I thought you wanted us to stay here tonight?' he asked wearily.

'I've changed my mind.'

Jenny started walking down the drive. Bob kept pace.

'Jenny, what's wrong? Has something happened?'

'No, I'm fine. I just want to get away from here,' she replied with a quaver in her voice. Bob was concerned.

'Has Mackenzie upset you?' he asked, walking faster to keep up with her. She did not answer.

'I know what he's like,' Bob continued. 'We had a few run-ins when I was here before. He had quite a temper on him. I remember once, when I first got here in 1972, he...'

'1972?' interjected Jenny, sitting down on a low stone dyke, her frame shaking with agitation. The evening was getting colder. The sun was beginning to set in the west – a pastel-red sky behind the mountains.

'Yes. What about it?' asked Bob. They faced each other.

'Nothing.'

'Is this about Skye and Mackenzie?' probed Bob.

'Were you here all of the summer?'

'Yes, I came in the May.'

'So. You were here when Liz got pregnant?

Bob strained his memory. 'Yes, I was.'

Jenny looked back at Ardnish House; it looked sinister and cold.

'Bob, answer me something honestly?'

'Sure, ask away.'

Jenny paused for a second.

'Did you have an affair with Liz MacKenzie back then?'

Bob was taken aback.

'Please, this is important,' implored Jenny.

'No, I did not!' his tone was indignant. 'I wanted to, but she was devoted to Mackenzie. Absolutely devoted.'

'Was she involved with anybody? Anybody at all?'

'No, she wasn't like that. Some were and believe me, I had my fill, but not Liz.'

'Why did Mackenzie ask you to leave then? What was his problem with you?'

Bob took a seat beside her, still unsure of where all this was going.

'Competition, pure competition – and I mean *fucking* competition. Liz didn't share it out, but Mackenzie did. That's why he started a commune, so he could have all the women he wanted.'

'Until you came along,' said Jenny

'Absolutely. I started getting more than him. He was like a lion with his pride, almost a cult leader. I showed up, and started taking some of his action.' Bob allowed himself a smile, his male ego inflating, before asking Jenny, 'What's this all about?'

'It's about Skye. She's not Mackenzie's wife – she's his daughter!'

'I know,' said Bob quickly.

'How do you know?' exclaimed Jenny.

Bob opened his briefcase and pulled out a leather-bound photograph album. Flicking through the pages, he found a photograph he had come across earlier.

Jenny saw the album was brimming with snaps of women, and guessed this was his 'souvenir' scrapbook of passenger conquests – his trophy cabinet. Taking a photograph from a transparent pocket, he gave it to Jenny.

'That's Liz, she was a beautiful woman.'

The photograph showed a young woman sitting on a grassy knoll, wearing a simple red-tie-dyed dress. She looked exactly like Skye – a carbon copy.

Bob confirmed, 'When I saw the photograph, the exact likeness, I knew she must be his daughter.'

'But didn't you think it strange they made out they were man and wife?'

Bob was about to answer, but Jenny beat him to it.

'Let me guess. *You* thought if *he* thought you knew he had a daughter, you would try and hit on her and Mackenzie could not have that.'

Bob smiled. Jenny knew at this exact moment, she was in the company of one of the most vain men she had ever met – a conceited individual who believed he was God's gift to women.

She looked back at Ardnish House as the dusk closed around them, a few squares of light were on in the house. She shivered a little in the dusk air. Bob gave her his jacket.

'We better make our way to Arisaig. We should be able to hitch a lift,' suggested Bob.

'Shit, my case. It's still at the house. We'll have to go back,' exclaimed Jenny.

Bob nodded and they began to trudge up the driveway.

'You thought Skye was my daughter. What made you think that?' asked Bob.

'Sorry, I should have not been so presumptuous. I got the wrong end of the stick. Forget it.'

'Don't get me wrong, but I would have loved to have got to know Liz in that way, but apart from her not being interested, Mackenzie was always around, never took his eye off her for a moment.'

Jenny could not resist her next comment. 'I didn't think that would have bothered you, a bit of a challenge. Anyway, weren't you tempted when he went back to Canada for his father's funeral?'

'He was here all the time – he never went back. His brother sorted everything out. He hated his father so much he never even went back to pay his respects.'

Jenny stopped dead in her tracks.

Chapter Thirteen

Before knocking on the large oak door, Jenny turned to Bob in the half dusk and stated her game plan.

'We get my case, ask to use the phone, order a taxi and get out of here.'

Bob nodded. He felt a surge of excitement – it was like she was speaking a line from a movie.

Thump, thump, thump.

Seconds later, Skye opened the door.

She hugged Jenny, 'I knew you hadn't gone. I knew you'd stay!'

'We've decided to stay in Arasaig tonight actually.'

Jenny sensed Skye was a little fragile.

'Come in. Come in. I've prepared supper for us,' exclaimed Skye, refusing to listen.

Entering the lobby, both Jenny and Bob could see Skye was in a sort of uniform. As she passed the Storm Girl figurine, they could see it was the character's outfit; the black tunic, the short skirt, the knee-length boots.

'I need my case. It's in the Landrover and we need to use the phone...'

'Yes, your luggage. I have it up in the spare bedroom,' informed Skye, ushering them into the dining room. The long, dark wooden table was set for four; shining silver cutlery, wine glasses, side plates, all perfectly set under a glinting chandelier. Skye's eyes beseeched them to stay.

No words came from Jenny and Bob; they could not find any. They glanced nervously at each other.

'Mackenzie will be down shortly – he's getting changed,' explained Skye. Her voice moved down to a whisper as she moved closer to them. 'He's calmed down since the afternoon. He'll be okay now.' She smiled before returning to a normal tone. 'Now look at you two! You can't dine with us till you've changed for dinner, and as you can see,' she looked down at her uniform, 'we're in costume tonight. I think I can get you both fixed up with something suitable.' Her accent was more American than usual.

Jenny and Bob remained silent. Jenny had been all set for a confrontation on returning to Ardnish House, but was knocked sideways with the pleasant welcome.

Climbing the stairs, the three of them met Mackenzie on the landing.

He was wearing full highland dress including a tartan kilt. The ensemble included black brogue shoes, knee-length woollen socks, a black velvet waistcoat and a green 'Bonnie Prince Charlie' jacket. Mackenzie stood proud.

'Tell me. What do you think?' he asked smiling, arms outstretched sideways.

'Impressive,' replied Jenny, thinking how different his demeanour was from the afternoon's angry outburst.

'A lord if I have ever seen one,' commented Bob.

'It's the MacKenzie tartan!' he proclaimed.

'And the clan motto?' asked Bob.

'*Luceo non uro* – I shine, not burn.' Quite apt for me I think. See you at dinner.'

'This is the dressing room,' explained Skye, leading them into a room furnished with four dark pine wardrobes, two chest of drawers, and a large full-size mirror, taking up one of the walls. Two over-stuffed red velvet chairs sat in the middle of the room.

Opening the wardrobe doors with a flourish, Skye illuminated, 'I'm sure we will have something here for you both. What about Southern Belle for you, Jenny?' she asked pulling out a dress and holding it.

The wardrobes were stuffed with various fancy-dress outfits – a whole host of themes to choose from.

Jenny took the dress and looked at herself in the mirror – the scarlet satin cloth looked good against her skin.

'And Bob? What about this?' Skye held up a white officer's uniform from the United States Navy Airforce. 'It has a cap too,' said Skye placing it on Bob's head.

Jenny and Bob opted for their host's choices; it seemed the polite thing to do.

An hour later, having taken showers and slipped into their costumes, they looked at themselves in the mirror.

'Don't ask me why we are doing this,' said Jenny.

'I wasn't going to. I'm trusting you on this one,' replied Bob, checking the fit of the trousers around his bottom. 'I'm enjoying this already. It's like being in a movie, or in a book. I don't know the ending, but I'm part of it.'

Jenny smiled at Bob through the reflection in the glass. This was when he was the most charming, she thought; when he was not trying.

Just as they were about to walk downstairs, Skye passed on the ground floor on the way to the dining room.

'Stay there!' she shouted and disappeared.

Twenty seconds later, a classical piece of music blasted out. It was Carl Orff's *Carmina Burana* – Opening Chorus 'O Fortuna – a tremendously dramatic segment. Jenny and Bob descended the stairs on Skye's command. Mackenzie looked on with a glass of whisky in hand, bemused.

Taking her hand as they came down the wide staircase, Bob gave Jenny a smile, a smile of reassurance in their surreal situation.

'You both look wonderful,' complimented Skye as they entered the drawing room for drinks.

The fire was ablaze in the fireplace, peaty flames giving the room a welcoming, hearty feel.

'What would you like to drink?' asked Mackenzie. He was now behaving like the man Jenny had first encountered; the perfect host, the gentleman, not the one she had had words with earlier.

'Whisky please,' requested Bob loudly, looking round the room and taking in the fine Victorian decoration. He felt he was in some kind of play, treading the boards.

'May I have a gin and tonic?' asked Jenny, looking forward to some alcohol. She needed something to calm her nerves.

With drinks in hand, the four of them sat down on the two leather chesterfield sofas. Jenny and Bob on one, the MacKenzies on the other. For Jenny, seeing them together was strange, knowing what she did of their relationship, but earlier she had decided to push any negative feelings towards them to the side – for tonight at least.

Skye kept nipping to the kitchen to keep an eye on the food which smelled divine. Jenny heard Bob's stomach rumbling on a few occasions.

'How did it go today with your people from the tour company?' enquired Mackenzie, attempting polite conversation.

'Not too bad, I suppose. The damage to the coach means the end of the line for her.' He sounded philosophical, but Jenny knew he was putting on a brave face.

'And for you?' asked Jenny.

'The same I'm afraid.' Bob forced a smile.

Jenny squeezed his arm. Mackenzie noticed the contact.

Bob continued. 'These things happen for a reason. The main thing is no one was hurt. It could have been worse, much worse.'

'It could always have been worse!' said Mackenzie. 'What a strange saying that is. What if things are actually at their worst, like if you were in a concentration camp. What would people say then?'

'Still the same I would imagine,' added Jenny. 'To say it, you'd have to be alive, and the worst would be being dead!'

Bob nodded, but Mackenzie seemed to ignore her theory, finishing his malt before asking Bob, 'So, where from here?'

'Just like thirty years ago, Mackenzie, I've to make some

new choices. Ironic really, sitting in the same place and having to ask myself, where to now?'

'But you're thirty years older. Can an old dog really learn new tricks?' quipped Mackenzie as he refilled his glass.

'I'm ready for a change. It's time to slow down a bit, get away from the pressures of being a coach driver. I can still drive. It's not as if any road offence charges are being pressed. Scotia Tours want me to take early retirement.' His voice sounded sad when he said the words. He looked down into his drink, not wishing to make eye contact with the others in the room.

Jenny tried to find some positive words.

'It could be a change for the better. Many people find themselves redundant, only to go on and find something which is more fulfilling!'

Bob looked at her, appreciating the reassurance.

'Dinner is served,' announced Skye from the doorway, her accent sounding fully American. She looked lovely, and sexy in her Storm Girl outfit. Jenny noticed Bob taking a good look at the young woman and imagined what he was thinking. At least these thoughts would take his mind off the feeling of being unwanted.

Mackenzie sat at one end of the long table, Skye the other. Jenny and Bob took their seats, facing each other in the middle of the table.

They ate well, very well; carrot and coriander soup followed by a choice of vegetarian or mince lasagne, garlic bread, and salad with a variety of dressings completed the tasty menu. The intake of food and good wine relaxed the conversation of the company.

Bob even felt safe enough to reminisce about his commune days.

'Mackenzie, do you remember the night we had a party in the summer and invited all the local people too?'

Mackenzie laughed. 'Absolutely. It was one of the funniest evenings we ever had!'

'What happened?' asked Jenny intrigued.

Bob took up the tale. 'Well, imagine all these hippy types! There would have been about forty commune people, and about the same number of locals – farm workers with wives and girlfriends, their kids, people from the surrounding villages. They came mostly out of curiosity. They wanted to see how the hippy folk lived.'

Mackenzie interjected. 'At that time, we had people living in static caravans at the back of the house, and a few visitors in tents. I had hired a marquee for the party. We also wanted to keep on good terms with the locals – we worked with them and they were good to know if we needed some work doing; cutting down trees, putting in drainage, that type of thing.'

Skye and Jenny were enjoying the tale, imagining a more carefree time.

Bob continued. 'We had some musicians in our midst, guys on guitars, a fiddle player. The locals were getting into the swing of things, drinking and dancing, and trying out our dope in the bong tents.'

'The barriers went down,' explained Mackenzie.

'Do you remember those two brothers?' asked Bob. 'Two bachelors, real party animals?'

'Wull and Davy,' answered Mackenzie, smiling as he recalled their craggy faces.

'What a pair of characters,' continued Bob. 'They liked to drink, and after some big joints, they put on a show. They stripped down to their underwear and got their chainsaws from their van. They then started them up and did this circus act with these dangerous power tools! One would throw his saw up into the air, the chain blade spinning round about ten feet high. As it dropped to the ground, the other brother would catch it by the handle. Amazing!'

Mackenzie joined in. 'One would lie on his back, legs in the air and the other would put a chain saw on the soles of the feet, and he would rotate it around, real fast. If it had fallen onto him, he would have been seriously injured.'

Both Mackenzie and Bob recalled the incident with fervour, as if they were back at the party.

'Good times,' remarked Bob.

'The best of times,' agreed Mackenzie.

'What happened to Wull and Davy,' enquired Bob, curious to know the outcome of these two character's lives.

'Both died, a couple of years back,' informed Mackenzie. 'One was from lung cancer, the other a broken heart.

'Broken heart?' asked Jenny.

Bob was silent – taken aback at the two men's demise.

'When Wull died from cancer, Davy never really got over it. He missed his brother terribly. He parked his van in the garage, closed the door, put a hosepipe to the exhaust and took his own life.'

Mackenzie seemed to enjoy bringing the convivial atmosphere in the room to a sudden end.

'Enough of this depressing talk,' exclaimed Skye, standing up.

Taking some plates to the kitchen, she asked for Jenny's help. Alone in the kitchen, Skye spoke in a low voice, 'I'm so pleased you're here!'

'No problem,' replied Jenny, placing cutlery in the dishwasher, her face close to the young woman's.

'I would like to extend the invitation. Would you spend a few days, you and Bob? You could stay in the studio apartments – finish your vacation here. You had another few days to go, didn't you?'

'I'm not sure. I need to get back home,' replied Jenny, taken aback at the request.

'I'm here for another week before going back to the states.' Skye paused, 'I don't want to be here on my own...'

'With Mackenzie,' said Jenny, finishing the sentence.

Skye nodded, an expression of pleading crossed her face.

'Let me have a word with Bob, but I can't promise anything.'

Touching Jenny on the shoulder, Skye kissed her lightly on the cheek, 'It would mean a lot to me.'

'What about Mackenzie? Is he okay with this arrangement?' asked Jenny.

'He knows he overstepped himself today, and he doesn't want to upset me again. He'll be fine.'

Laughter came from the dining room. Mackenzie's mood was obviously improving. A waft of cannabis hit the two women as they returned to the room. A large joint was being passed between the two men. Mackenzie offered it around. A mellow air pervaded across the four dinner guests.

Retiring to the comfort of the drawing room – stoned as they were – Jenny and Bob now felt more at ease in these surroundings.

Skye and Mackenzie took a chesterfield couch; Bob and Jenny sat in matching armchairs opposite the MacKenzies.

'Why the fancy dress, Skye?' enquired Jenny.

'It's something we do with guests,' she replied. 'Dressing up like this redefines a person to a degree. With everybody in costume, we're equal. There are no preconceptions of somebody because of what they're wearing.'

Mackenzie added, 'It breaks down the social barriers. You get to know someone quicker and its fun to do.'

'I like it,' agreed Bob. Turning to Jenny he asked, 'Do you feel like a Southern Belle?'

'Well I do, kind sir!' replied Jenny in her best deep-south accent.

They all laughed.

Addressing Jenny in a passable American accent, Bob said, 'It's been a pleasure escorting you to dinner, Ma'am.'

The evening had turned out to be a good one. A mixture of serious and light conversation revealed some insights into each and every one of the party.

Although relaxed, Jenny still felt a little uneasy in Mackenzie's company – not only did she know about his incestuous activity, but his demeanour tended towards the overbearing. He was an urbane individual who cast a long shadow.

But being with Bob brought some light into the shadow, thought Jenny.

Here was a man she felt safe with, and in certain ways, Mackenzie was in Bob's shadow. Although Mackenzie was the same height as Bob, he did not have the bodily stature or presence the coach driver displayed.

Bob had a quick fluid movement to his body; the tautness of his frame could be seen under his garments. Jenny would not be surprised if Bob had boxed in his past. Taking it to a primal level, Bob would win a physical fight with Mackenzie – probably in just a few minutes.

These thoughts gave Jenny a sense of being protected – it was a warm sensation.

On a few occasions, Mackenzie had tried to needle Bob, but the simple truth was Bob's thick skin repelled any clever remarks the artist made, like rain being dispelled from a wax-coated jacket.

Listening to Mackenzie was not always foremost on Bob's mind, sneaking looks at Skye was more interesting, especially in the Storm Girl outfit. When his leching was bordering on the obvious, Jenny gave him a sharp prod in the ribs.

'So tell me you two, how did you meet?' asked Bob of the MacKenzies.

Jenny flinched. Why was he asking *this*? Testing their pretence no doubt.

'LA,' replied Mackenzie. 'Six years ago.'

'Mackenzie was over in Hollywood,' added Skye. 'To tie up his movie deal. I was working in the development department of the studio.'

'I took a meeting with the studio suits, and she walked into the room,' explained Mackenzie looking at the young woman with a smile.

'We looked at each other across the table, and that was it!'

'There you have it!' said Mackenzie completing the answer.

Rehearsed to perfection, thought Jenny.

Skye added one more comment. 'I was in awe of this man

who created Storm Girl, and then I met him – I found him to be so charming,' she cooed.

'So how come your accent is a mixture of Scottish and American?' enquired Bob, enjoying the charade.

'Being in Scotland I suppose, and talking with Mackenzie – it all rubs off,' answered Skye smugly.

These streaks of deceit, thought Jenny, they seem to come so easily to this woman.

'Whose for coffee?' asked Skye, wanting to change the subject, her accent showing no trace of Scots.

'Please,' responded Bob.

'Same here,' chimed Mackenzie.

'I'll help,' said Jenny, following Skye into the kitchen.

Her voice low, tinged with frustration, Jenny asked, 'What's that all about – the "how we met" story?'

'It seems practised, doesn't it?' replied Skye not looking at Jenny directly.

'It started when we went on holiday together; we went a few times after Mum's death. The only explanation I can give is that people assumed we were a couple – it must have been our closeness and the fact we shared a room.'

'Shared a room!' exclaimed Jenny.

Skye indicated to Jenny to keep her voice down. 'Yes, it seemed normal at the time. We both found it hard to be alone after Mum going, so it was easier to just say we were married on these trips.'

Skye came over to Jenny and hugged her, before the older woman could say anything else. In Jenny's ear she heard the words, 'I feel stronger when you're around. Just you being here is making a difference – enough of a difference for this whole thing to be finished with.'

Skye's words sounded sincere.

They finished making coffee. Before entering the drawing room, Skye asked, 'You will stay a few more days?'

'I'm still thinking about it. I'll give you my answer in the morning.'

'Mack and I need to go to Fort William in the morning for

groceries. Will you stay till our return at lunchtime?' asked Skye.

Jenny agreed.

After coffee, Jenny hinted to Bob about saying their good nights. Bob shook Mackenzie's hand at the back door – a symbolic gesture for both men.

The women gave each other a hug, Skye whispering into Jenny's ear, 'Thank you.'

Bob carried his and Jenny's cases up the wooden steps, which led to the apartments above the stables. The steps joined a wooden veranda that gave entry to the doors of the two apartments. The night air was refreshing on their faces as they said goodnight to each other – again it seemed like a scene from a movie. Bob paused for a second, looking at Jenny. He was about to say something.

'Bob,' said Jenny. 'Sleep well. You look like you need a good rest!'

He nodded and dabbed a kiss on her forehead before disappearing into his room.

Jenny's apartment was almost identical to the one Bob had slept in the night before.

Slipping out of her costume, Jenny could hear Bob preparing for bed next door. It was comforting to have him so close.

As she lay in bed, she could hear the wind in the trees outside. Turning over the events of the last few days in her mind, Jenny tried to piece the MacKenzie puzzle into a coherent picture.

Why was she interested in making sense of it anyway? she asked herself before drifting to sleep.

Her passage into slumber was disturbed by a creaking noise outside. She awoke with a start, her nerves tightening. Again a creak, coming from the veranda! Turning to look over the lip of the duvet, she saw a shadow pass her window. Through the thin drawn curtains, it looked like the shadow of a person.

Her mouth dry, Jenny lay, heart pumping for several

minutes, listening for further sounds. No more came. Getting out of bed, she crept to the door. Edging out, she checked to see if any one was on the veranda. It was empty. The cool night air stung her face. She quickly entered Bob's apartment.

Bob heard a voice in his ear; he was half asleep.

'I don't want to sleep on my own, but don't get any ideas!' Bob understood Jenny's no-nonsense tone immediately. Her hot breath in his ear felt good though.

'I hope you're not a fidget,' he replied.

Jenny slipped quickly into the warm double bed. Lying on her back, she felt instantly safe beside this big bear of a man.

How strange they had been thrown together, she thought, this womanising coach driver, this sexual conquistador. But she was beginning to catch glimpses of his inner core – an unselfish part which would try to do the right thing.

'Bob, I have a question for you?' she asked.

'Try me,' came a sleepy reply.

'Sinclair is a Scottish name. What's your clan motto?'

A pause.

'Doesn't really suit me. It's Commit Thy Work to God.'

'Sounds noble,' replied Jenny.

'The crest badge is more me,' added the coach driver. 'It's a cockerel – a great big cock standing proud.'

He was asleep in another minute.

Sleep soon arrived to pick Jenny up for the night too. She accepted the offer of the lift.

Chapter Fourteen

'Portree Cycle Hire,' answered the voice on the other end of the telephone line.

'Hello. I wonder if you can help me?' asked Miriam. 'When I arrived yesterday, we passed your shop and I saw you had a tandem cycle out front. Can I book it for today?'

'No problem, not many people take it out.'

Miriam then asked for a few little modifications to be made. The man at Portree Cycle Hire agreed.

Coming off the phone, Miriam bumped into Christina and Eva who were going for breakfast.

'Hi. You look pleased with yourself?' commented Christina, noting Miriam's tight-fitting lycra shorts over her toned legs.

'I am. I've got a little excursion of my own planned for today,' chirped Miriam.

'Well, the weather looks good. It's going to be hotter than yesterday,' added Eva.

'Good. I'm sorry, but I need to check on Gregory,' replied Miriam, bounding up the stairs.

'Who does she think she is?' asked Eva, pulling up a restaurant chair. 'All fake tan, wiggling her skinny bottom around.'

'No need to be so harsh. Miriam is okay. She has a lot on her plate with Gregory.'

'He's been really quiet ever since you gave him a piece of your mind on that boat,' said Eva.

Christina blushed a little before answering. 'I felt sorry for

her. I was being supportive. Anyway, things must be going
okay with them, she looked happy just now.'

Gregory had made no progress in uncovering the surprise
Miriam had planned for them. She had asked him to be
open minded for their 'excursion' this morning, one which did
not involve being on a coach. This was good news, the ride on
the old school bus the previous day had been a bumpy
affair. The entire party were relieved when they had made it to
Portree.

The taxi had collected them from the hotel five minutes
earlier and was now winding its way through the harbour
town, traversing the narrow streets, passing the low
whitewashed cottages which formed the main conurbation of
Skye. Pulling up in front of Portree Cycle Hire, Gregory gave
Miriam a quizzical look.

'You've got to be kidding?' he exclaimed as he was helped
into his chair.

'Don't be too quick to judge. Hear me out,' replied Miriam
as she sought out the man she had spoken to earlier.

Bill Tann's eyebrows knitted over when Miriam explained
the purpose of the tandem. He'd never had this type of request
before.

'Let me understand this. You want me to get on the tandem
with you, and you'll do all the pedalling? All I've got to do is
keep my balance,' said Gregory, shaking his head.

'You know what they say – nobody forgets how to ride a
bike. I have the strength. I work out all the time and I'm
positive I can pedal for the both of us. It will be such fun,'
pleaded Miriam.

She wanted this to work, more than Gregory could realise.
Little did he know, but this was her way of deciding their
future. Since the coach crash, she had felt a sense of futility
with their relationship. She now sought ways to test his
commitment. If he could make the effort to join her on the
tandem, it was a positive sign, something to build on.

Sitting in his wheelchair, head down, he felt her willing him to agree. Bill Tann and the taxi driver looked at each other, waiting for the silence to be broken.

'I'll do it, but if I don't feel safe, we stop.'

Giving a shriek of delight, Miriam asked Bill to help her get the disabled man on the bike. The cycle-shop owner tied Gregory's shoes into the toe-clip pedals and walked with the tandem as Miriam launched off. A couple of circuits around the car park proved the couple's balance was okay.

'See, I can pedal for the both of us,' said Miriam excitedly.

There was no doubt about it. Although Gregory's legs were going with the revolutions of the pedals, he could still ride a bike. With a wave, Miriam headed off as Bill and the taxi driver looked on: they were tempted to clap.

For the first fifteen minutes of the ride, mostly downhill, Gregory's heart raced with excitement. The wind in his face, the sun on his back – this was a truly wonderful experience. He felt free of his disability for the first time in a year. Miriam too was overjoyed at her idea working so well.

'Where are we going?' shouted Gregory.

'Wait and see. I have it all worked out.'

Gregory felt a twinge of appreciation for the woman in front of him, well more than a twinge, a surge. He could see her legs working hard, pumping the pedals. Her lycra-hugged bottom leaving the saddle slightly in rhythmic movement. Gregory had always liked her ass – it was completely natural. He'd never had to do any cosmetic work on it; it must have been the only part of her body with that honour.

Half an hour later, Miriam turned down a track. Gregory could see a white sandy beach approaching. Slowing the tandem, Miriam stopped at an open gate. Salty air and the sound of surf swept over them.

'Yahoooooo,' screamed Miriam. Gregory laughed.

Undoing his shoes from the pedals, Miriam helped Gregory over to a dune where they sat looking out over the shimmering sea.

A few minutes later, a van with 'Royal Portree Hotel' on its side pulled up at the gate.

'I bet you could do with some lunch,' said Miriam as she strode over to meet the driver who was carrying a cardboard box.

The picnic was delightful. Gregory could not remember when he had felt like this since the accident.

'Thank you so much for all of this, Miriam. It's wonderful.'

'I'm pleased you're enjoying it. I wanted it to be special.'

Gregory looked out over the sea at the diving seagulls, thinking carefully about what he was about to say. 'I want to say how sorry I am. I should have treated you better. I've been such a prick.'

'But you've been through so much since the accident,' replied Miriam, squeezing his hand.

'Not an excuse really. I can't blame such misfortune for my behaviour towards you. But I couldn't understand why you were caring for me in this state. I'm only half of who I used to be.'

'You're not half a man to me, Gregory.'

'But I feel I am. How can you love me, if I don't love myself?'

Taking him in her arms, she pulled him close and felt a barrier fall.

'You'll grow to like yourself again, it's what I believe,' said Miriam, 'And do you know why I believe this?'

'Tell me.'

'Because *you* taught me how to love when we first met. I didn't know it till I was going up the aisle with all those other guys.'

They kissed for ages afterwards and then lay in the sun, looking up at the clear blue sky. Miriam's thoughts circled like the seagulls above, positive thoughts on a warm updraft of feeling. She was feeling good about herself and her connection to Gregory – she felt they had a future.

Just before they headed back, Gregory spoke about something he'd never mentioned before.

'I look at my hands and cannot believe they've been reduced to pushing the wheels of my chair.' He held his long soft hands up to her. 'These have given so much, to my clients, to me, and although they still function, they're useless because my legs don't work. That's fucked up, isn't it?'

Miriam smiled, unsure of what to say, and dabbed a kiss on his forehead. He still took great care of his hands – as much as when he was a surgeon. She was always doing things to save him picking up a scratch or getting them dirty. That was the thing he despised the most – any form of filth coming into contact with them.

She wiped down the handlebars before they left the beach.

The return trip was not so easy. Miriam had enjoyed the downhill run to the beach so much, thinking about the uphill slog back had not crossed her mind. Gregory had wanted to take the front saddle on the way back, his confidence high.

The mid-afternoon sun now beat down on Miriam's back relentlessly. Her lungs and legs ached with each revolution. Powering them both was becoming increasingly difficult.

Wiping the sweat from her eyes, Miriam could see the road still pitching up before her, a relentless swathe of tarmac to sap her receding energy.

The day had gone as planned, so well up to this point. Her water bottle was now empty, her mouth creased with dryness, her face burning with exhaustion.

The sighing had started too, the agitated exhalations from Gregory that Miriam dreaded. She knew what he was feeling, loathing himself for being a passenger on the tandem, unable to help her. It was only a matter of minutes before his self hatred was turned on her, his fiery words scolding her.

Miriam had thought the test was over when they kissed on the beach, but now the swooping carefree thoughts of earlier had migrated. She realised it was never going to be over. The man in front was not really going to change.

Although she felt her spirits dip, Miriam was determined to beat this last hill. Rising out of the saddle, she pushed down with all her weight and kept the tandem moving. But they were now going precariously slow, their balance unsteady. Gregory's shoulders had tightened, his head lowered, obviously preparing the first salvo of abuse, thought Miriam.

Traffic sped past, people staring, adding further pressure. The strain on Miriam was nearing breaking point, every physical fibre tensioning to the point where not much else was left to give.

She heard the sound of a tractor behind her, the throaty diesel nudging closer. It passed, belching fumes. The driver gave a smile. He was pulling a trailer which reeked of cow dung, large dollops fell onto the road with sticky splats.

Miriam looked down, concentrating on giving the pedals one final turn before having to give in. Suddenly, she felt a lightness envelope her legs. Was she passing out? Gregory would never forgive her.

But looking up, she could see they were still moving along without her pedalling, the tandem picking up speed. Then she saw why.

Gregory had put his hand out as the trailer had passed and grabbed onto the rear of it, his right hand holding onto a dung-encrusted rail. He glanced around and smiled, shouting the words. 'We're going to make it, Miriam! We're going to make it!'

And they did.

Chapter Fifteen

'Cup of tea?' asked Bob, his voice easing Jenny from sleep. The digital clock read 9.38 a.m. The previous evening's joints had knocked her out. It had been a long time since anyone had brought her a cup of tea in bed – the last person had been her husband, John. What would he have made of her getting into this situation with these MacKenzie people? she wondered.

She could hear his response in her head, 'Jenny, in my view you are a human pot-holer – you enjoy nothing more than burrowing inside people, crawling into their innermost dark caves and recesses to see what you can find, but one day you'll get stuck – trapped in a hole – and you know what happens to pot-holers who get stuck in the caves – some of them drown!'

If she was honest with herself, her attraction to the darkness in people had been the reason she had stayed as a guest of the MacKenzies last night.

Peeking over the edge of the duvet, Jenny could see Bob was emptying his suitcase, putting clothes in the light pine wardrobe.

'Staying on?' she asked.

'Well, I thought so, after the MacKenzies' offer. It's not as if I've got anything to go back to.' He paused. 'I got the impression you're going to stay on too?'

'I don't know,' replied Jenny. She took a sip of tea. Suddenly an idea flashed into her mind. 'Why don't we leave together, get a hire car for the trip south?'

Bob didn't reply straight away, pondering her proposition. 'Only if I can do the driving. That's if you trust me with such a task.'

'I do, I do! Let's get a car organised for this afternoon,' replied Jenny, getting out of bed, checking to see the buttons on her pyjama top were done up.

Opening the door to let the morning sunshine cascade into the apartment, Jenny exclaimed, 'The weather is glorious. Let's make the most of it!'

'Why not,' said Bob, taking in Jenny's figure, silhouetted by the light from the open doorway.

Her slim legs looked good, he thought.

A second later she was gone, returning to the adjacent apartment.

Forty-five minutes later, Jenny called on Bob to accompany her to breakfast. She looked carefree in stone-coloured knee-length shorts, a light blue baggy T-shirt and navy suede slip on shoes. Her hair was tied pinned back, the first time he had seen it this way, revealing such delicate little ears.

'How did you get on with the hire car?' she asked as they descended the stairs.

'It's all sorted, but it won't be here until tomorrow morning.'

Jenny felt a bump of disappointment. She had wanted to be gone this morning.

As they turned into the courtyard, the MacKenzies pulled up beside them in their Landrover. Skye addressed her guests through the window.

'Sleep well?' Her blue eyes sparkled in the morning sunshine.

'Sure did,' replied Bob, glancing down at Skye's cleavage in her white blouse.

'Like a baby,' chimed Jenny, catching Mackenzie's eye. He smiled.

'So have you decided? Are you staying another day?' asked

Skye.

They glanced at each other for a second before Bob answered.

'If it's okay, we would like to. But we'll be off tomorrow.'

'Excellent,' replied Skye.

'It's going to be hot today,' said Mackenzie, 'The two of you should go for a swim. There's a rock pool not far from here.'

'Near the waterfall,' said Bob, his memory jogged.

'Help yourself to breakfast,' offered Skye.

'We're off to Fort William. Make yourself comfortable. We'll be back in the afternoon,' added Mackenzie, putting the vehicle into gear and speeding off down the drive.

A selection of breakfast cereals, fruit, yoghurts, croissants, jams, and marmalades were arranged in the kitchen. Jenny made some coffee, while Bob worked the toaster. The wooden patio furniture looked inviting in the back garden and they decided to take their breakfast in the open air.

Making himself comfortable on the sun-lounger, Bob remarked to Jenny, 'This is the life!'

'I could not agree more,' replied Jenny, sipping her coffee and looking at the back of Ardnish House.

'I'm up for a swim, if you are,' suggested Bob, his eyes closed, head pitched at an angle to catch some rays.

'What's this rock pool like?'

'From memory, it's great. I went there all the time when I was here before.'

'Okay. I'm up for it. But after lunch. Let's just take it easy this morning.'

'Fine by me,' agreed Bob, slipping into a sun-bathing doze.

Looking at the house gave Jenny an overwhelming urge to explore the building while the MacKenzies were away. It was snooping, she knew, but this was probably her only chance. The pull of the human pot-holer.

'I am going to look for a book in the library.'

Bob mumbled something sleepily in reply.

*

169

At the top of the stairs, running off from the hallway, were six doors. Four led to bedrooms, one was a large bathroom, and the remaining one opened onto a small staircase, which led to the attic.

The master bedroom was large with a sweeping view from the front of the house. This was obviously Mackenzie's bedroom, his kilt outfit still hanging on one of the open wardrobe doors. The centre-piece of the room was the large four poster bed – gothic in style with red velvet drapes tied back. The bed was made, so Jenny could not tell if two people had slept in it the night before.

Two other bedrooms lead off from the upstairs hallway. Simply furnished, one had a double bed, the other two singles. They were light and airy, the least Victorian in the house.

Next up was Skye's room – the words painted on the door like a shrine to her childhood. Inside nothing seemed to have been altered since she was ten or eleven years of age – the single bed, the pile of soft toys on the window sill, the girlie knick-knacks on a desk. On one wall was a painted frieze of a unicorn, standing on a mountain, the sun rising behind. A little girl sat astride the mythical animal. Mackenzie's handiwork, thought Jenny.

Back in the hallway, Jenny studied the photographic gallery on the walls, which charted the last thirty years of the house's occupants.

Several of the framed photographs were of the commune period; Mackenzie standing with Liz, people gathered around at the front of the house on a summer's day, all looking hippyish and happy. Jenny strained her eyes to see a young Bob, but he was not visible; the picture must have been taken after he'd gone.

There was another commune photograph which must have been a few years later. Skye was included, a sweet six or seven year old, holding hands with her mother.

There were a few more pictures of Skye. In puberty, she was quite plain, thought Jenny. But the ones taken in her late teens, revealed the beauty she was turning into – *from ugly duckling to a swan*.

Further down the hallway was a photograph of Mackenzie and Liz at some sort of black tie ceremony. He was holding up an award, the inscription read – *Storm Girl, Graphic Award Novel 1985*. They both looked wonderfully happy, in the prime of their lives, and enjoying it.

Jenny spotted a picture of Mackenzie and Skye, taken just a couple of years earlier outside Mann's Chinese Theatre on Hollywood Boulevard. Behind them on the theatre frontage were the words – *Now Playing, Storm Girl the Movie*.

Mackenzie and daughter were smiling, Skye the image of her mother.

Better get that book, thought Jenny, descending the stairs. In the library, she looked through the floor-to-ceiling bookcase and soon found one of her favourite novels, *Catcher in the Rye*. Leaving the room, she glanced over to Mackenzie's drawing board. Compulsion took hold again – just a quick look to see if any further flights of fantasy had been committed by his graphic pen.

A large sheet lay spread out – one panel completed in the top left-hand corner. It contained a picture of Jenny in the costume room, standing in the Southern Belle dress, her shoulders bared as the dress was slipping down, the stays pulling apart. A speech bubble from her mouth read, '*Can you help me out of this?*'

Jenny could not see to whom she was making this request. No more of the story had been drawn.

'Don't burn,' advised Jenny as she lay down on a sun-lounger next to Bob. Relieved to be awoken from his dream, Bob sat up. It had not been a pleasant one. He was riding a bicycle up a steep hill, and he felt fat and heavy. The hill seemed to go on forever. A coach passed him, full of women of all ages. They were laughing at his strenuous output. Feelings of humiliation and loss poured over him.

'Are you okay?' asked Jenny.

'Nothing a swim won't put right,' he replied.

After Jenny had packed a small picnic, they headed over to the rock pool, courtesy of Bob's memory which did not fail him. A twenty-five minute walk later through open fields, the couple arrived at the natural swimming hole.

The air was heavy with the hot sun; the temperature reaching the high seventies. A dark patch of water lay below a long waterfall. Canopied by trees, it still looked as Bob remembered. Access to the pool's edge was negotiated from the lip of the waterfall. Jenny felt safe as Bob helped her down, his strong arms lifting her at one point, his breath brushing past her face.

Peeling off their clothes excitedly to reveal their swimming garments, they quickly glanced at the other's physiques.

Jenny was not surprised to see Bob's firm body, the slim muscles, and his athletic legs.

Bob was impressed with Jenny's form. He had spied bits and pieces in the last few days; her slimness, neatly tapered neck and shoulders, the shapely legs in the sunshine this morning.

Without hesitating, Bob dived in. Jenny was not so brave, slipping into the cool water slowly. As he broke the surface, hair plastered down over his eyes, he heard Jenny ask, 'How deep is this?'

'About fifteen feet, maybe more.'

Jenny broke into breaststroke, her heart rate increasing as her body temperature dropped. Gradually, the coldness was replaced with the enjoyable sensation of weightless exercise in fresh water.

With confident strokes, Bob swam back and forward across the pool, his shoulder blades working furiously. Twenty minutes later, the two of them climbed onto the smooth expansive rock jetty where their towels and clothes lay.

The rock felt warm from the sun that was now directly overhead. After drying off, they made themselves comfortable on the platform. Bob lay on his front, his head buried in a pile of clothes. Jenny lay beside him on her back, shielding her eyes with her arm. The latent heat of the rock seeped into their bodies, warming their bones. Jenny decided to ask a question of Bob. 'Why did you ask the MacKenzies' about their first meeting? You know their real relationship.'

'To see how they would react – very convincing I thought,' replied Bob.

'But don't you think it's all a bit strange, pretending to be man and wife.'

'I know Mackenzie from old. He's alternative, and so is the daughter from the looks of things. He's always liked playing games with people's minds. Like dressing up last night, pretending to be somebody else. It's not as if they are playing for real, is it? Sleeping together,' said Bob. 'Now that would be sick!'

At that moment, Jenny wanted to tell Bob what she knew about the MacKenzies' incestuous relationship. But she was unsure of his reaction. Once she'd told him, the knowledge could not be taken back.

It would be good to talk it through with somebody, thought Jenny. The question though, did Skye have the right to know who her real father was?

Human pot-holer...beware! You might drown! John's words pulsed through her mind.

Looking at Bob's naked back, Jenny's mind turned to her new found companion. She wanted to know more about the coach driver's personal life, especially the socialising aspect of his job.

'I hope you don't mind me asking...'

'Go on. Ask what you will,' replied Bob. He liked personal questions; it was attention.

'That photograph album you have, the one with the photo of Skye's mother...'

Bob turned over, intrigued by where the questioning was going. 'Yeah,' he replied.

'Who are all those women?'

173

A large grin creased Bob's features; he pushed his matted hair back from his forehead.

'Trippers – women from the tours.' Bob smiled knowingly. 'You've had all of them, haven't you?'

A moment of silence hung between the couple.

'Everyone was special in their own way. Yes, I have been with them.'

'How many have you had exactly, Bob? I'm sure you've kept tally?' enquired Jenny, curious to see how boastful he would be.

'I don't have a number because I don't keep a count,' he answered with a playful look on his face.

'I thought you would be like a rock star, secretly keeping a figure in your head, but making vague references to some number between one and two thousand.'

Turning his head to face Jenny, Bob looked a little taken aback.

'I'm selective, I'll have you know,' responded Bob, getting defensive.

'I'm not judging, but tell me honestly. Do you ever feel anything for these women or is it just sex, recreational sex?'

Bob looked across the rock pool, considering his answer. 'It's a bit of fun for all concerned. It's as simple as that. I like certain women, they like me, we have some fun. It's the holiday environment, no strings attached, no harm done, the open road...'

'Open legs more like,' interjected Jenny with a smile.

'You're taking the piss now!' Bob sat up on his elbows, indignantly.

'I don't mean to. Please don't get me wrong. I appreciate your honesty. Tell me, is it the open road you like or the open field with loads of cows and you're the big bull who has to service them?' said Jenny with a near straight face.

Bob chuckled. 'You're something, do you know that. You're quite liberal, although you don't look it.'

'There's more to me than you think Bob,' said Jenny, flirting slightly.

Billie Watson

'Well that's all in the past,' remarked Bob. He gazed across the pool for a second before continuing, 'I do like Scotland, the sheer openness of it all. I'm going to miss this country!'

'Maybe you can get a driving job locally,' suggested Jenny, squeezing Bob's hand. 'Anyway, I hope you didn't mind me being so direct?'

'No, not at all. I really like that about you – your no nonsense ways. It's good to be so...'

'Open!'

'Yeah *open*. It's been a while since I could be this way with a woman.'

'You know why that is, don't you,' said Jenny, preparing to get into the water again.

'Why? What do you mean?' asked Bob, shielding his eyes from the sun, staring at her bathing suit form.

'*Seduction*! You cannot be entirely honest when you are seducing a person, can you? And you are the James Bond of bus driving, aren't you? In fact, when I think about it, the phrase *Busman's Holiday* was coined for you,' exclaimed Jenny before diving into the rock pool.

Bob was after her in a second, the calm surface of the pool broken by the couple's noisy invasion. After completing a few lengths, the conversation continued, as they treaded the dark peaty water.

'When I said it's been a while since I was this open – I meant it. It's good to be just myself with you.' He sounded serious, genuine.

'Is that because we're becoming friends, as opposed to the other type of relationship?' pondered Jenny out loud. She kept her gaze on Bob, monitoring every twitch. He looked boyish in the pool, his hair askew.

'I suppose so,' replied Bob. 'I've never really had a woman as a friend before.'

'What about a good male friend?'

'Not really. I'm a bit of a loner really.'

'A gregarious loner,' commented Jenny as she swam towards the waterfall. She sensed he was a little disappointed

175

with the way she had described their relationship. At the waterfall, Jenny turned and made a suggestion. 'Let's stand underneath this. I bet it's really refreshing.'

Bob hoisted himself up onto the smooth rock ledge, which lay at the bottom of the thundering waterfall. Crouching, he reached down, extending his strong arms to help Jenny up, the water crashing off his shoulders. Putting her hands in his, she felt him lift her onto the ledge.

'Watch out, it can be slippery,' he advised.

Their backs against the sheer face of the rocky outcrop, they stood under the constant avalanche of white water.

'Relax your body,' suggested Bob.

She did, and nearly slipped. Bob caught her hand and Jenny held onto the clasp of his strong grip.

He leaned over and spoke directly into her ear. 'According to your theory, if we stay here long enough, we'll look ten years younger in no time.' He was referring to Jenny's skin tautness technique of bathing in cold water.

She was touched he remembered.

A few minutes later, they stepped out from the waterfall.

A voice above suddenly made them look up.

'Stay where you are!'

Discovering the source of the interruption, Jenny and Bob saw Skye's face leaning over the top of the waterfall, directly above them.

'I'm going to jump in from up here!' indicated Skye as she threw her towel onto the stone jetty where Jenny and Bob had been sunbathing.

Then she was gone.

'It looks dangerous,' remarked Jenny, annoyed with Skye's sudden intrusion.

Seconds later, Skye dropped from the sky. Her sleek nakedness shot past them; feet first, long legs, bare buttocks, taut back and windswept hair, no sign of a bathing costume.

Looking at the foam and ripples moving across the rock pool surface, Jenny and Bob waited for Skye to reappear; one second became three seconds. After almost a minute, Skye's face, shoulders and breasts broke the surface.

Jenny scrambled back to the sun-bathing rock, conscious of her body now in the company of Skye's lithe nudity.

Covering herself in a towel, Jenny watched Bob's sexual metabolism turning in the direction of Skye. She felt disappointed in him.

Like some adolescent boy, he was out to impress Skye, swimming back and forth across the pool in quick time. Only a matter of time before he would try the dive from the top of the waterfall, thought Jenny.

Sure enough, Bob jumped out of the pool and began the climb up to take the big dive.

'Be careful,' shouted Jenny, genuinely concerned.

Skye swam over to the sun-bathing rock, extracting herself from the water and into her towel. Jenny kept her eyes on Bob who disappeared over the outcrop of rock at the top of the waterfall.

'He's in good shape for his age,' commented Skye as she dried her hair.

'Sure. But he thinks he's younger than he actually is,' said Jenny pleasantly, not looking directly at the younger woman.

Bob walked a few paces back along the rock he would be coming down to make his jump. Skye's clothes lay next to him on the smooth rock surface. Bob could see her white cotton knickers inside her jeans. He stared at the garments, tempted to inspect further. An erection pushed into his trunks.

It was for this very reason that he did not get the full running speed required to launch himself into the rock pool dead centre.

Landing in the water, a little too near the waterfall, Bob caught his right foot on a sharp rock under the surface.

He thought it was a scratch, until he hauled himself up onto the rock where Jenny and Skye waited for him.

Blood oozed from a five-centimetre gash. The women surveyed the damage with concern, and in Jenny's case, some annoyance.

'What were you thinking of,' she scolded, wrapping a towel around his injury.

Bob shrugged his shoulders, chastened.

'We've a first-aid kit back at the house,' informed Skye. 'Mackenzie can look at it, it may need stitches.'

'Are you okay to walk?' asked Jenny, her voice softening.

'Sure, I've had worse.'

The picnic was hungrily consumed to sate the swimming appetite the three of them had developed. Shortly afterwards, Skye excused herself to get back to Ardnish House.

Bob and Jenny did not say too much for the next hour before attempting the return journey to the house. The momentum of the earlier conversation had been lost.

Jenny also felt the excursion had gone flat after Bob's manly display for Skye and now his injury.

He had acted stupidly by trying to act half his age, but part of his attraction was being young at heart. Bob could never be accused of being dull.

Bob felt a little silly. Things were fine before Skye 'dropped in', he thought. Showing off to a woman half his age – he should have known better – especially in front of Jenny. He was growing to like her more and more, her directness and the way she was easy to be around.

Hobbling back to the house through the fields, his voice tinged with regret, Bob said, 'I shouldn't have done that jump.'

'You think you're younger than you are.'

'There is that, but I didn't have to make an impression on you, did I?'

Jenny took Bob's hand, giving him a smile.

'You've certainly made an impression on me.'

Sitting on the patio in the early evening sunshine, his face pinched with pain, Bob watched as Mackenzie drew the last stitch to close the gash in his foot. Mackenzie had enjoyed doing the medical repair, smiling slightly when performing the task.

'How's that feel?' he enquired as he packed up the plastic first-aid box.

'Okay, thanks.' Bob stood up to see how much weight he could put on the injured foot. Not too bad, he thought, gently passing weight onto his right leg.

'Will you be able to drive?'

'Maybe not tomorrow, but the day after probably,' answered Bob, slipping his foot into his training shoe, gingerly.

Jenny came into view from the courtyard, Bob's mobile phone in hand. Wearing a cotton summer dress with a dark red oriental pattern, both men thought she looked great.

'Good news on the hire car. They were able to order an automatic. I'll drive tomorrow.'

'Drink?' offered Mackenzie.

'Glass of white wine please. Chardonnay if you have it.'

Mackenzie disappeared into the house.

'You look great,' complimented Bob, taking in her whole appearance.

'Thank you. You don't look too bad yourself.'

Attired in a blue checked short-sleeved shirt and chino trousers, Bob accepted the compliment readily.

Handing the glass of wine to Jenny, Mackenzie walked on to attend to the brick barbecue which would cook that night's supper.

'He's ready for us to go,' remarked Jenny as she sipped some wine, the chilled sharpness refreshing to taste.

'So am I. I was thinking. Let's make our return trip scenic, head down to Oban maybe?'

'Sure. Take our time. Get some bed and breakfast stops,' added Jenny.

Bob smiled at the mention of 'bed and breakfast'. He liked the way this *friendship* was going.

Jenny glimpsed his smile and smiled to herself.

'Hi, guys.' Skye came through the conservatory doors. She glided over in dark blue knee-length shorts and a baggy green sweatshirt, a glass of red wine in hand.

'How's your foot?' she enquired.

'Fine. Just a scratch.'

'I like your dress,' complimented Skye to Jenny.

'Thank you.'

'Better see how the master chef is getting on,' said the young woman, moving across the patio to join Mackenzie at the barbecue. The food smelled great, wafting over to the guests in the evening air.

Leaning over, Bob dabbed a kiss on Jenny's forehead.

'What's that for?' asked Jenny politely.

'For you being you. For you being you.'

Chapter Sixteen

The barbecue food tasted excellent. Mackenzie even provided his own coleslaw and barbecue sauce.

All four of them were sitting down to eat when Jenny saw an opportunity to sneak a look at the 'comic strip' in the library, curiosity getting the better of her. Excusing herself to go to the bathroom, she went straight to the drawing table.

Sure enough, another four panels had been added. The second showed a near naked Skye helping Jenny out of the Southern Belle dress. The third panel was Skye planting a kiss on the back of Jenny's neck as her hands cupped Jenny's bare breasts. The fourth was of the two women kissing full on the mouth, their naked bodies entwined on the chaise longue.

The fifth scene showed Jenny's head buried in Skye's crotch, a speech bubble declaring, '*I had a hunch you were into women too, Jenny!*'

A noise in the kitchen made Jenny freeze. Someone was getting something from the fridge. A few seconds later, some footsteps leaving to go outside.

Joining the others in the garden a minute later, Jenny avoided eye contact with Mackenzie. Her mind was still digesting the content of the drawings, a conflict of thoughts criss-crossed each other. Jenny understood the need for people to fantasise – MATURE EMPORIUM was all about escape, a consensual fantasy meeting place for people to test their imagination in reality. Jenny had enjoyed being privy to this when logging onto the site, so why was she so surprised at her feelings of revulsion at Mackenzie's flights of fancy about her?

Her appetite had waned. She was looking forward to leaving Ardnish House tomorrow. She was also looking forward to spending time with Bob.

'Not hungry, Jenny?' asked Skye, staring hard at the older woman.

'I will probably eat some later.'

'As you're off tomorrow, I would like to take you up Ardnish Hill this evening to catch the sunset. It's a wonderful sight, a must see while you're here!' invited Skye.

'That'll be lovely,' accepted Jenny, the less time in Mackenzie's company, the better, she thought.

The view from the hill was worth the forty-minute hike up the narrow path to the summit. Looking out westwards across the Sound of Ardnish to the small isles of Eigg and Muck was wonderful. The sun was an hour from setting, but already streaks of ochre red clouds were gathering, shifting into place for a beautiful dusk display.

'What a fantastic sight,' exclaimed Jenny.

'It's beautiful,' agreed Skye. 'I used to come up with my mother all the time when I was little. We never tired of the view.'

Perching themselves on a flat rock, the two women absorbed nature's spectacular vista; the dramatic dominion of sky, sea, and mountains, stretching for miles in a three hundred and sixty degree perspective.

A minute later, Skye broke the silence.

'My mother was a geologist. Living here was ideal for her. All around here are many examples of rock formations, and she would take me exploring,' she continued, 'I learned a lot about how these mountain ranges were formed when massive continental plates folded into the earth's crust...' Skye trailed off.

'Go on. It's interesting,' encouraged Jenny, wanting to know more.

'You've probably heard Scottish people going on about how their country is separate from England, well they have a point. Around 400 million years ago, the part we know as Scotland collided with an area which would become known as England. That explains the very different terrain for the two countries.'

'You've a great memory for this kind of thing,' complimented Jenny, impressed at the knowledge being imparted.

'I hung on every word my mother said, her words stuck like glue in my head.'

'So that's how all of this came about?' asked Jenny, feeling like a tiny speck of sand in the country's long enduring formation across the millennia.

'Pretty much.' Skye had enjoyed showing off her intellect, pleased with remembering so much and communicating it so eloquently.

'Jenny, I hope you don't mind me asking, but are you and Bob involved?'

The question caught the older woman by surprise.

'We're good friends.'

'You just seem a bit more than that,' remarked Skye, prodding for more information. 'He's an attractive guy.'

'Granted, he is. But I need to be attracted to the person as equally as I am to their looks.'

Skye mused on Jenny's explanation before nudging the conversation down the same track. 'So, is there someone special?'

'No. Since I lost my husband, I have not really felt the compulsion to find someone. It's not easy to become involved again at my age.'

'But you're an attractive woman. I thought you would have had the pick of men,' complimented Skye, hoping flattery would lever more information.

'Not the ones I want though. Anyway, I enjoy my independence too much.'

'How do you meet new people then?'

This girl was driving at something specific, thought Jenny. 'Taking a coach tour holiday is a good start.'

'What about the *Internet*! I know a lot of people use it to meet people,' offered Skye, rolling down her sweatshirt sleeves.

MATURE EMPORIUM! Mackenzie had shown Skye the site, thought Jenny. 'I've heard it can be good and bad,' she answered.

'I think it would be good for Mackenzie to meet some women of his own age, don't you think?'

'Maybe. But you can't always tell the age of the person, or what they are really like,' responded Jenny.

'Do you know of any sites he could use?'

'Why don't you come out with it, Skye?' said Jenny, locking eyes with the young woman.

'Come out with what?' Skye tried to look innocent.

'MATURE EMPORIUM, that's what. My website!'

'I'm sorry. I didn't know how to bring it up.'

'No need to be coy with me for Christ's sake. I've seen you shagging your father!' The second she heard herself say it, Jenny regretted the words.

'STEPFATHER. He's my stepfather!' Skye's face creased with hurt. Tears welled up in her eyes; she turned away, hugging herself.

Jenny put her arms around the young woman. Skye's tears soaked through Jenny's cotton dress; warm droplets seeping into her flesh.

No words were uttered on their descent to Ardnish House. The dusk half-light made their progress slow as they negotiated the winding path.

As they crossed a field towards the house, Skye slipped her hand into Jenny's. A smile passed between them.

Bob and Mackenzie were watching television in the drawing room. The sound of the set broke the silence, the booming echo of the presenter's narrative. The four occupants had run out of things to say to each other.

'I need to pack,' said Jenny, excusing herself.

'I need to check out my e-mails. I'll be in the library, if anybody wants me,' added Skye.

In the studio apartment, Jenny busied herself with packing. Her outburst on the top of Ardnish Hill nagged away at her thoughts. This young woman seemed to be placing Jenny in a surrogate mother role, wanting to get close. Jenny felt for Skye, a genuine sympathy for her troubles, but this was way too much to cope with as a stranger who accidentally stumbled onto the dark family secret.

'Are you okay?' Bob stood in the doorway, using the frame as a support to keep the weight off his injured foot.

'I'm fine. A little tired,' answered Jenny.

'I'm whacked. I'll pack in the morning. Off to bed for me.' Bob's face was flushed with the day's sun.

'I'll be off too,' said Jenny wearily approaching Bob and giving him a kiss on his hot cheek. She went to close the door – he got the message.

Jenny heard the flush of Bob's toilet next door. Then no sound, he was probably asleep.

Looking at her bed, Jenny would have loved to slip under the covers, but Skye was on her mind again. She should go and speak to the young woman – advise her to get professional help. She lived in California; the right place to seek some sort of counselling.

Jenny entered the house through the unlit back door. Moving down the hallway to the library, she could see light coming from under the half-open door. Jenny thought it wise to peer through the crack in the door jam to check that her entry would be clear – images of Mackenzie and Skye on the chaise longue returning.

Skye was perched at the drawing board, intently sketching something. She obviously had artistic inclinations.

A piercing realisation entered Jenny's mind! A stab of thought which pushed her into the room and over to Skye's side to see what she was drawing. It only took a second.

On the board lay the comic strip Jenny had seen earlier – it had one more scene added courtesy of Mackenzie's daughter's pen!

The latest panel showed Jenny on all fours as Skye took her

from behind with a strap on dildo – the speech bubble from Jenny read, '*Fuck this old bitch hard, fuck me till I'm sore. Fuck me!*'

Jenny and Skye locked eyes, taking in each other's reaction to the graphic sexual images, which stared back from the drawing board.

'You did this, all of this!' screamed Jenny, looking down at a smiling Skye.

'Absolutely. All my work. Don't you like it? I think I've caught you well – it's a good likeness, don't you think?'

Jenny moved back a pace, her mind reeling with the discovery of the real artist.

'You thought it was Mackenzie, didn't you, Jenny? You thought *this* was the product of *his* sick mind, but instead you find it's been me all along.' Standing up, Skye moved away from the drawing board and closed the door. Turning around, she spoke with an edginess to her voice.

'As you can see, I inherited my *father's* artistic talent, and also his imagination.'

'You said father,' retorted Jenny, conscious she was beginning to see this young woman truly reveal herself. *The human pot-holer felt the ceiling of the cave bear down on her, constricting forward movement.*

'That's right. Father. Not Stepfather, but father. I know he's my fucking father! I've known all along. He was the one who came up with the stepfather thing to try and protect me, but he ended up convincing himself. If you tell yourself something often enough, for long enough, you eventually believe it!' Skye moved across the room to close the curtains.

'But the things you told me in the car about when you were seventeen, your mother dying, taking up her role...'

'It was true to a degree. I did seduce him. I was the seducer – always have been, always will be. I wanted to see how fucking weak he was,' snarled Skye, turning from the window, the red drapes framing her like she was on stage.

'I knew he'd cheated on my mother countless times. I heard the arguments as a kid, and saw how unhappy he made her.

So, yes, in the midst of my grief, I set out to punish him with his own weakness; lust, sex, a desire for his own daughter. He's been fucked up about it ever since, fucked up about fucking his little princess. He's the one you should be trying to help!'

That's why Mackenzie had wanted Jenny to leave. He was concerned about what Skye might be capable of doing. Jenny felt very uncomfortable; this young woman was unbalanced.

'But using sex as a weapon is not the answer!' declared Jenny.

'We all use what we can to get what we want. I use sex in all kinds of ways. I've found it to be more rewarding than anything emotional. It's an instant gratification, an investment with an instant payout. Unlike a relationship – all that energy – for what? To be shat on. To be fucked over.'

'You need the two, sex and emotion,' replied Jenny, wondering where this conversation was going.

'Not for me, I inherited another thing from my father; his insatiable appetite for sex,' explained Skye in a matter-of-fact tone, coming closer to Jenny. 'I want it so much, it does not matter what I fuck. Men, women, it's all the same to me. I thought you would understand, someone as liberated as you.' Skye was now standing inches away from Jenny. 'So what do you say, Jenny? What about you and me getting it on?' purred Skye in a lascivious manner.

Jenny stepped back until she felt the chaise longue on the back of her legs. Her mouth was dry, her throat would not let any sound come out, even if she had had the words. She felt terribly threatened by this young woman whose prior sweet guise had been completely removed to reveal some sort of sexual deviant – grotesque and bitter. *The human pot-holer was trying to back out of the cave on all fours, but the walls stuck fast, trapping her! Panic mounting in her chest.*

Jenny felt Skye's hands cup her breasts firmly through the thin cotton material of her dress.

'Not bad for a woman of your age, quite firm,' remarked

Skye as she moved her mouth to Jenny's. Jenny took Skye's upper arms in her hands and pushed her away.

Encountering resistance to her advances, Skye violently pushed her back onto the chaise longue. Jenny did not expect such force. Fear flashed across her face as she landed on the piece of furniture, all composure gone.

'Skye, this is getting out of hand. Stop it, this is not right!'

Bending over, Skye clasped the back of the chaise longue with one hand, while holding Jenny's shoulder with the other, pinning her into the couch.

The cave was filling up with water now.

'Why did you stay? Morbid fascination? Most people would have run a mile once they knew about me and Mackenzie. Father and daughter fucking like rabbits!'

'I stayed to help you. *You* asked for help!'

'You can help. You can help by letting me *fuck* you! You stayed to be fucked Jenny!' exclaimed Skye, her teeth flashing, spittle spraying from her mouth, her breathing rapid.

'Now you know the whole sordid truth. But that's your thing, isn't it?' Skye was now stroking Jenny's face, her forefinger running up and down the older woman's tense features. 'Sordid sex for the sad swinging middle aged. You with your *mature* web site, getting those wrinkly fucks together – you in the middle of it. Tell me? How did it work? Did you get to try out the new couples first?' asked Skye, her voice loaded with aggression.

'It's not like that,' said Jenny, regaining her composure as best she could. This situation was getting frighteningly out of hand. Unless she fought the fear, she could not overcome this woman. *The cave in the water was now at shoulder level.*

'Tell me what's it like then,' said Skye, going to a chest of drawers by the door.

'It's not the way you described it,' replied Jenny, trembling.

Jenny heard Skye pull open a drawer.

Standing at the foot of the couch, Jenny could see Skye holding a long, black instrument with a harness attached. Skye pressed the tip against her mouth. Jenny recognised the six-inch plastic phallus as a strap-on dildo, like the one in the comic strip – *the one Skye had used to fuck Jenny*. The young woman tossed the sex toy onto the couch.

Skye removed her sweatshirt to reveal her breasts. 'I like fucking older women. I can see how *young* my body is compared to theirs – how much *tighter* my skin is, how much *firmer* my limbs are.' She then dropped her shorts, completing her nakedness. 'I feel so superior, like I'm part of a superior sex race!'

Jenny looked away, disgusted with what she was hearing, not wanting to look at her tormentor anymore. The cold clammy perspiration of fear encased Jenny's body. *The cave water was filling her lungs.*

Skye continued with her acidic abuse, clearly enjoying insulting the older woman.

'You should think yourself lucky I want to have sex with you. You should want to bury your head in my crotch and taste youth again! That's the attraction of the old getting it on with the young – they get to feel young again!' Leaning over Jenny, the young woman continued her verbal assault.

'By the time I've opened you up with this,' Skye grabbed the strap on dildo, pushing the tip against Jenny's lips, 'you'll be screaming for more, you'll see.'

Skye's naked body trembled with a mixture of sexual arousal and anger.

'Now, take your dress off, bitch!'

Jenny closed her eyes, folded her arms and shook her head. 'I will not.' She was quivering, holding herself tightly. Right now she wanted to flee. She felt prevented by Skye's state of near violence.

She was now drowning in the cave, losing consciousness.

'I am going to give you one more chance. Take your lousy fucking dress off now!' screamed the young woman, hot spittle from her mouth hitting Jenny's face.

Bracing herself, her heart racing, Jenny was ready to lunge upwards and make for the door. *Push forward through the cave, not backwards – one last chance!*

189

Skye let out a long deep sigh, her voice dropping in an instance from anger to a softer tone. She backed away from Jenny, perching onto the drawing board.

'I thought the *dominatrix* thing would have worked with you? Obviously not – a lot of the older bitches like it in LA.' Skye sounded resigned to not having her way. She got up, and walked past Jenny who sat looking down, wishing her tormentor was gone from the room.

The cave, emptying of water, air rushing back into her lungs.

Jenny heard the door open, but her ordeal was not over yet. Skye leant over from behind and whispered in her ear.

'I would never force myself on anyone, especially on an old crone like you. I don't need to. But I do need some fucking tonight and I know a man who'll be very willing to feed my desires.'

Then she was gone.

Jenny heard the door slam. She sat alone, letting large tears pour down her face. A mental rape had taken place, a violation. The urge to vomit swept over her.

She lay slumped in the cave, waiting to be rescued.

Although he felt tired, Bob had trouble getting off to sleep. The woman next door kept coming to mind. What was it she had? He never usually dwelt too long on a woman if he couldn't get his way. But Jenny Jenkins was different.

Did she want him? He wanted her to want him. Maybe that was it, wanting equal attraction, equal desire. As a rule, Bob measured out his desire in an almost calculated fashion; unlike the women he went with who had trouble restraining their urges. He liked being in the stronger position. With Jenny, he felt the opposite was going on.

The digital clock tripped the minutes. His foot throbbed from the stitches. His bladder nudged sleep away. He needed to take a pee. He went into the bathroom, leaving the light off.

As he stood, letting go a thick strong torrent of urine, he heard the door of his apartment open and close.

Could it be her? The thought flashed through Bob's mind sending a pulse of excitement.

'Jenny, is that you?'

No reply. Maybe she'd got into the bed, maybe she wanted to surprise him?

He wanted to stop peeing, and get back as soon as possible. But the jet of urine was only at the mid-way point.

Bob felt bared flesh press onto his own naked back – this woman was full of surprises! Two slim hands passed by either side of his waist and took hold of his peeing cock. He took his hand away, leaving the intruder to continue with the task of directing piss into the toilet bowl.

He'd never had this before. Bob was beginning to feel aroused, blood pumping into his organ. The sound of urine on water ceased as the jet of pee climbed the back of the toilet bowl as his stiffening cock raised its aim.

Shit – the last thing he needed was a fountain of piss going everywhere. Bob leaned forward to keep his soldier pointed downwards; he felt the weight of the naked body move with him, resting on his back. The sound of fluid on fluid returned. The flow began to reduce.

As he turned around, feeling the hands disengage, his cock became rigid again at the thought of confronting Jenny.

'You've done that before?' said Bob.

Flicking the mirror light on, Bob looked down to see Skye dropping to her knees, his erect cock in her hands, her open mouth moving towards the tip.

What happened next to Bob was also a new experience. Something that had never happened before – *his head ruled his penis for the first time ever!*

His cock softened in Skye's hands. Like a clay pot on a potter's wheel, one second it was a warm, smooth, tall object, the next it disintegrated into a soft shapeless mass where no efforts could return it to its former glory.

Seconds passed as their emotions tried to find the appropriate reaction. Bob got there first. 'Skye! No offence, but this is not right!'

She stood up quickly, and fled into the bedroom, grabbing her jacket from the bed.

Bob followed her, trying to find some more words. He was not ready for Skye's torrent of abuse.

'If I was that *bitch,* Jenny, you would be ramming it down her throat by now!'

'How dare you use that word about Jenny,' shouted Bob angrily. Anger and protectiveness flared inside him. Had Jenny heard Skye's outburst as she lay in bed next door? He hoped not.

Throwing the door open, Skye retorted. 'Fuck off, old man. You two deserve each other – with any luck you'll both catch clap from her web site!' Then she was gone, footsteps racing down the stairs.

Bob bolted over to the open door, in time to shout out. 'You're disgusting! Do you hear me, Skye. You'll never be half the woman Jenny is!'

Bob's angry words carried out across the still night, across the courtyard, across the stable rooftops; every word winged its way to where Jenny and Mackenzie stood by the back door of Ardnish House.

After Skye's assault on Jenny, the older woman had sat on the chaise longue for a few minutes, jettisoning her fear. But Jenny had realised she had to pull herself together. A voice from the doorway surprised her.

'Are you alright?' It was Mackenzie, genuine concern in his voice. He came over and sat beside her.

'It was Skye, wasn't it?' he enquired, seeing the dildo lying on the carpet.

She nodded, wiping her tear-streaked face. 'I need a drink!'

'I'll get you one.' He was back in thirty seconds with a tumbler of malt whisky.

Jenny took a few gulps. A warm sensation filled her chest. 'I need some air,' she declared.

Moving through the house, they stopped on the back doorstep. The cool still night touched their faces. The cloud-free sky glinted with stars.

Mackenzie wanted to ask questions, but did not know where to start. Running his hands through his hair, he went to say something, but Jenny spoke first.

'I now know why you wanted me to leave.' She cupped her whisky close to her chest, shivering a little. Mackenzie fetched a jacket from the utility room, putting it around her shoulders.

'Thank you,' said Jenny. How ironic, she now felt safe with Mackenzie around.

'Skye is my penance,' uttered Mackenzie. 'I deserve all of this for fucking it up with her mother.' His voice sounded emotional, almost tearful. This was the man Jenny had first met when the tour group had been seeking shelter. A kind man – a man who sat and told her all about his family history with such passion.

'What you did was wrong, Mackenzie, no denying that, but people do wrong things in life. It's how you can best put it right that counts.'

'Putting it right. I have tried, really tried, but she's a …' He could not find the words.

'A siren. Like the women who called the sailors from the cliff shores,' offered Jenny. 'The call was so strong, they could not resist going to them, but the sailors knew they could wreck their ships and lose their lives.' Jenny felt herself begin to steady, like a little boat which has survived a storm, rocking back to equilibrium.

'My daughter the siren,' agreed Mackenzie. 'You know I'm her father then?' He looked drawn and washed out with the weight of his secret.

Jenny nodded.

'How did she upset you?' asked Mackenzie, fearing the worst.

'I don't want to talk about it, but she needs help badly.'

'I need a drink,' said Mackenzie, going inside the house. He returned a minute later with a glass of malt.

'Do you know what tears me apart about all of this?' he announced, looking into the night sky.

'No?'

'The family name – *MacKenzie*. All the work and effort from previous generations – our bloodline has been sullied by this fucking *thing*! My forefathers would have been mortified – it's the shame of it, the waste of it.' He sounded like he was going to weep, wiping the corner of his eyes with the back of his hand.

'Do you know where she's gone?'

'I thought she was with you!' exclaimed Jenny.

A wretched feeling of despair filled Jenny as an image of Bob fucking Skye took hold in her mind. The feeling of nausea returned once more. It was at that precise moment both she and Mackenzie heard Bob's cry from the stables.

In the weeks, months and years that were to follow, Jenny would think back to the precise moment she heard those words and know this was the very second she began to fall in love with the busman.

Jenny ran to the apartments, Mackenzie behind her. As she rounded the corner into the courtyard, she was met with the sound of the Landrover revving up and the glare of its headlights coming towards her. Jenny stopped and stepped back as the vehicle swished past her; Skye hunched over the steering wheel, her face contorted with rage.

They saw each other. The vehicle skidded to a halt, dust rising from the wheels in the gravel. Bracing herself for confrontation, Jenny knew what she was going to do.

The driver's door swung open. Skye leapt out, clad only in a fleece jacket, striding towards Jenny with her head lowered like a stampeding bull. She was screaming abuse at Jenny.

'Get off my property, you fucking bitch, you fucking...'

Jenny's right fist smacked into Skye's face just below her left eye with the solid dull noise of knuckled bone hitting flesh. A jolt of pain shot up Jenny's arm, but pumping adrenalin diluted the feeling.

The young woman was sent reeling onto the drive. She lay in a state of shock. Her father was at her side in seconds.

Jenny, nursing her fist, walked past both of them, looking up at Bob on the veranda. He looked in a state of shock too. By the time Jenny joined Bob, Mackenzie had taken Skye back in the house.

'What the hell was that all about?' Bob asked as he closed the door behind her.

'Hold me, Bob. Just hold me!'

He did. She felt a warm safe sensation wash over her as she folded herself into the enclosure of his body.

'You don't need me to look after you, do you?' he whispered.

'But I do. I do!'

Slipping into bed, they cuddled up together, her head on his chest.

What had happened between Skye and Jenny? Bob asked himself.

'I'll explain it all later, I promise,' said Jenny as she pulled in tighter, soaking up his presence.

The warmth of each other's bodies pressed them into sleep an hour later.

Chapter Seventeen

Next morning, the hire car was delivered on time, a mid-sized, metallic-green hatchback. The sky was overcast, darkening clouds from the east looked like rain to Bob as he lugged their luggage down the veranda.

Jenny got to the delivery driver just as he was about to knock on the front door of Ardnish House. He was a stocky man with a thick Glasgow accent.

It only took a few minutes for the paperwork to be completed. Meanwhile, Bob was loading the car up with the cases.

Another vehicle drew up with a middle-aged woman at the wheel from the car hire company to collect the delivery driver.

Bob got in the front passenger seat as Jenny pulled her seatbelt into position. The front door of Ardnish House opened. Jenny's heart quickened with trepidation.

Mackenzie appeared in a green threadbare dressing-gown. He looked tired, as if he had not slept.

'We're off now,' said Jenny.

'Safe trip.'

'Thanks,' said Jenny, her right hand on the ignition key. She just wanted to be gone from this place.

Mackenzie leaned down to address them through the window.

'I'll make this simple,' he said seriously. 'I'm very sorry for everything that's happened, but please understand, I'm going to get help for Skye. I will do all I can. I wish the both of you all the best.'

Jenny thought he looked terribly unhappy as he turned away and closed the front door behind him.

The car came to life as Jenny turned the key and it sped down the drive.

'Slow up a bit,' advised Bob. 'You don't want to end up in the river like me!'

She took her foot off the accelerator slightly. She felt like a getaway driver, eager to be gone from the scene of the crime.

Turning in the direction of Fort William, Jenny felt relieved as Ardnish House disappeared from sight in her rear view mirror.

By 10 o'clock they were pulling into Fort William. Very little conversation had been made. Their individual thoughts about the previous evening had preoccupied the two of them.

Jenny wanted to stop thinking about the MacKenzies, especially Skye. The image of her naked, brandishing the dildo was an oppressive one that brought a twisting sensation to her stomach.

Bob, on the other hand, was accumulating questions.

He had assumed Jenny had heard Skye's insult about her from the adjacent room. But Jenny had come from the direction of the house, not the studio apartment. Something must have gone off between the two women earlier.

Then there was Skye's last insult at both of them, something about catching the clap from Jenny's web site. What web site was this?

Before they left, Mackenzie spoke about getting Skye some sort of help? Could this be something to do with the MacKenzies' 'married couple' charade? Jenny probably knew something about this, but had decided not to share it with him – that explained the conversation they had on the drive two nights back.

Glancing at Jenny, it struck Bob, she knew more about him, more than anyone had done in a long time. But he knew very little about her.

Bob decided to broach the subject of the previous night.

'About last night, it's come to me...'

Jenny cut him off. 'I don't want to talk about any of that today. Let's just try and have a normal day. It will all come out in due course. I can assure you of that, but when I'm ready.' Her voice was terse and tired.

Bob stared ahead.

'What about some breakfast,' he said after a few minutes. 'I'm starved.'

A full Scottish breakfast of fried sausages, eggs, tomatoes, breakfast, sliced haggis, baked beans and potato scones served with toast sated the couple's appetite. They had returned to the Tea Cozy, the little tearoom they had had a chat in several days earlier.

'So Bob, where to?' asked Jenny sipping her mug of tea.

'Oban.'

'Oban?'

'I know a lovely hotel, great views. What do you say?' Bob smiled with a little egg yoke around the corners of his mouth.

'Sounds good,' answered Jenny reaching across the table to squeeze his hand. Bob reciprocated.

The trip to Ballachullish was a scenic run past Loch Linnhe. The clouds were starting to part, streaks of sunshine piercing through to glance off the water. Turning onto the A828, a sign to Oban said 34 miles.

Again the views were spectacular, Loch Linnhe opening up into the Firth of Lorne, the expanse of water stretching out to their right. On their left, the craggy hills and slopes bristled with summer health as the clouds scattered to let a blue-sky morning herald their journey. It was good to be moving. Jenny was enjoying being behind the wheel.

Both were absorbing each other's presence – a little craft of anticipation rocking with gentle excitement.

By midday, they were dropping down into the centre of Oban, the large ferry port busy with vehicles loading for the Isles of Colonsay, Mull, Coll and South Uist. Driving along the Victorian promenade, Jenny thought the town would not have looked out of place on the southern coast of England.

The Isle View Hotel was perched at the northern end of the town, overlooking the sea. Bob had stayed there on numerous occasions as a Scotia Tours driver.

Entering reception, Bob was warmly greeted by Jean Howie, head receptionist, a middle-aged woman with a round, smiling face.

'Bobby!' She was the only person who called him by this name. 'I did'na know you were staying with us. There's no Scotia booking!' Jean checked her computer screen.

'I'm on my own this time, well with my…' He did not know how to describe Jenny.

'Partner. Hi, I'm Jenny.' She did not like using the word, but using the term 'girlfriend' seemed ridiculous at her age.

Jean smiled broadly. 'So, how long are you staying for?'

The couple had not discussed the duration of their stay; they looked at each other before Jenny gave an answer. 'Two nights.'

'What kind of room? Twin, double?'

'Double,' replied Jenny, excited and scared at the same time for proposing such an intimate arrangement so early into this foray with Bob. The last couple of days had been so surreal in the grand scheme of things, a double room seemed trivial. Anyway, she could always get a single, if things became uncomfortable.

'Any chance of a sea view?' requested Bob.

'For you Bobby, not a problem.'

As they walked towards the elevator, Jean called out to Bob.

'I have a parcel here for you, it came about a month ago.'

Bob returned to the reception desk to receive an A4 padded envelope.

Recognising the postmark and packaging, he slid the item into his briefcase. Jenny noticed this movement from the elevator.

The room had great views overlooking the sea and the Isle

of Mull. Jenny turned around and gave Bob a big kiss on the mouth. They locked in the embrace. She felt Bob's cock hardening against her.

'Let's wait till tonight,' suggested Jenny.

Bob nodded.

Ideal. I-fucking-deal!

'I need to go to a chemist for some bits and pieces,' said Jenny.

'No problem. We can also get a drink in town.'

Bob pulled out a little rucksack to take with them.

'Can you put my mobile phone in your bag? There's not enough room in my little handbag.'

Bob obliged. It felt good to be participating in such two-some activities – he could not remember the last time he spent time with a woman in this way.

Oban was bustling with day trippers. Bob looked at a couple of the coaches as they crawled along the esplanade. Was this aspect of his life all over? he thought.

Jenny tried to distract him by visiting a few gift shops. But his eyes were drawn through the windows as the coaches drove past. At the chemist door, Bob declined to enter, preferring to wait for Jenny on the other side of the road on the esplanade front. She disappeared inside.

Soaking up the view, Bob's sightseeing was disturbed by a ringtone coming from the rucksack. It was Jenny's phone. Bob took the call.

'Hello?'

'Good afternoon. Is that Mr Jenkins?' asked the caller.

'No. I can take a message for *Mrs* Jenkins?'

'This is Mark from Alpha Web Services, the web-hosting company the Jenkins have an account with. I'm calling to discuss the renewal of their domain name and I would appreciate if she could call me back on this number.'

'Sure I'll tell her,' assured Bob. 'But which web site is it? She has a couple.'

'Mature Emporium,' came the reply.

'Mature Emporium!' repeated Bob. 'I'll get her to call you.' He had the *web address*; all he had to do was check it out on the net.

Putting the phone back in the rucksack, Bob saw a café across the road with a sign in the window – INTERNET ACCESS AVAILABLE.

'I'm next door in a café,' said Bob as Jenny deliberated over which mascara to purchase.

'I'll be with you shortly. Get me a coffee,' she replied, smiling.

The café was basic and mostly catered for the young people in Oban. After paying for two coffees and the use of the Internet, Bob took his seat in front of the screen and keyboard.

Typing the web address into a search engine, Bob linked straight through to the Mature Emporium. A page came into view – the site was inactive, suspended.

He would have to ask her about it. Probably a rational explanation, something to do with aromatherapy, or something similar for older people.

Checking his hotmail address, Bob trawled through a handful of messages, looking for anything from Scotia Tours as regards his redundancy offer.

Sure enough it was there. The pay-off came to £10,500. He'd hoped for £15,000.

'Good news?' enquired Jenny, standing behind him.

'Not really.' Bob flicked off the PC. 'Just my redundancy notice, the amount of money I'll get.'

'I know it's easy for me to say, but this redundancy could be the beginning of something new and exciting.'

Her words did not lift him or his head, a sinking feeling spreading throughout.

'I know. But at the moment it just feels so final.' Bob could smell Jenny's perfume waft towards him. 'You smell nice.' He looked into her eyes.

'Thank you! I tried a few squirts at the perfume counter. Tell me. Which one do you like? She extended her arms to put her wrists under his nose.

'I like this one.' At least he had Jenny, for the moment.

'I have a message for you. Your mobile rang.'

Sipping her coffee, Jenny looked quizzical. Bob continued.

'Some man from your web company, the hosting company I think. I've the number saved in the phone, something to do with Mature Emporium?'

Jenny did not give a reaction straight away.

'Oh that! My late husband built it for the vintage car club he was in.' She paused, looked away. 'I should have given the responsibility to one of his club pals.' The explanation was as unconvincing to her, as it was to Bob.

She was lying. They both knew it.

There was the first lie, thought Bob. Further disappointment added weight to the heaviness he felt inside already.

Jenny felt bad. How ironic. After everything she had been through in the last couple of days with the MacKenzies' secrets and lies.

'Bob, forgive me. I lied.'

He gave a startled look.

'My late husband and I set it up together. It's called Mature Emporium. Basically it was a...' she paused. 'A swingers site for mature couples. But please understand; it wasn't a sleazy, explicit thing with pornographic photos and the like. It was designed to appeal to discreet people who wanted to meet like-minded couples, people who wanted to inject some fun into their lives.' She stirred her coffee, searching for the next sentence. 'It's history now anyway, I closed the site down.' Jenny felt herself blush, looking away.

'Thank you for your honesty! It's refreshing,' said Bob. He had to admit, she was full of surprises.

'It's why I was on the coach tour,' continued Jenny. 'The local paper did a piece on me, an exposé; *Swinging Pensioners – local woman arranges sex for the over sixties*'. She held her hands together to stop them shaking. 'In my hometown, it was awful to have this type of thing come out. So I ran away and here I am.' Jenny felt her top lip quiver; her eyes prickle with tears. She pulled it all back inside.

Getting up, Bob sat beside Jenny, putting his arm round her, pulling her closer. 'Well, as far as I'm concerned, your local paper did me a favour. Otherwise I'd never have met you!'

She let a tear go. He wiped it away.

'I have a confession too,' divulged Bob, realising he had lied to Jenny on a prior occasion.

Now Jenny's heart sank. He had a wife, that's all she needed!

'Go on,' she prompted.

Bob reached into his wallet, and pulled out the photograph of his son, daughter-in-law and grandson, handing it to Jenny.

'I told you my son was dead, killed in a car crash. Well he wasn't.'

Bob paused and then continued.

'I tell people he's dead, because as far as he's concerned, I am. He hates me so much for what I did to his mother. I was never a husband to her or a father to him. As a little boy, he heard us fight all the time, not a happy home I'm afraid.'

He paused, feeling a lump of emotion. 'When he grew up, he asked me never to contact him. So, I pretended he was dead to me to ease the guilt and the shame. And if you keep saying something often enough, you begin to believe it yourself!'

A shudder ran through Jenny. This was the second time she'd heard this type of explanation in twenty-four hours.

She hugged him.

'What's his name?' she asked.

'Daniel. I called him Danny boy when he was little.'

The couple sat for a few minutes, no words passing between them. Thoughts turning, past events prodded alive, lumps of personal history swelling, waiting long enough for the itching heat to subside, for the memories to fall back into line.

'Time for a drink, I think,' suggested Bob. 'All this honesty makes you thirsty.'

The Whin On The Hill was a cozy little pub on one of Oban's back streets. Catering for the locals, the smokey den could have done with a refurbish; as could some of its patrons. But Archie the landlord, a small man in his sixties, filled the place with his big personality and raucous laughter.

'Hello, stranger,' cried Archie as Bob entered the pub with Jenny. After they exchanged pleasantries, the couple took their drinks to a table under one of the frosted-glass windows.

Nursing her vodka and tonic, Jenny decided to keep rowing the honesty boat, which she had launched in the café.

'What's in that envelope you picked up at reception when we arrived?'

'I didn't think you saw that,' answered Bob, taking a gulp from his pint of Guinness. Bob grabbed one of the oars in the honesty boat. 'It was a pair of women's knickers!' he awaited her reaction.

'From one of your admirers?'

'Yes.' He took another sip from his pint.

'Did she wear them before sending them?' asked Jenny.

'Maybe.' Bob wondered where this questioning was going.

'What do you do with these knickers?'

'I use them as rags to clean the bus.'

'So you get this underwear on a regular basis?'

Tricked into admitting this, Bob smiled and tried to change the conversation. 'Now and again. Anyway, what about you and this web site?'

'Get me another drink,' replied Jenny gulping down her vodka, 'and I might tell you some more.' Her eyes flashed with mischief.

As Bob got up to go to the bar, Jenny caught his arm. 'There is no way you're using my knickers for your windshield.' They both laughed.

Keeping him on a reel like a fish, Jenny slowly pulled Bob in towards her past life. Each round of drinks uncovered a little more information, another juicy morsel of sexual adventurism. The heady mixture of alcohol, confessional story-telling and the subject of sex excited them both. A cocktail of openness and release surged through the couple; an intoxicating discharge to tell it all.

Bob tried to pin Jenny down on her own personal experiences from the web site. He got one. Jenny had been widowed for eight months and had naturally lost interest in Mature Emporium. But she needed some company, and female company was what she was after. Starting with e-mail correspondence, she got involved with a woman called Veronica who was also recently widowed. Chat room conversations were fun, and when they saw each other via a web cam, they decided to meet.

Choosing a hotel they both knew, their first meeting went well. Veronica was the same age, attractive, a little larger than Jenny and fun to be with. They met again; this time at a pub and decided their next meeting would be Veronica's home – Jenny could stay over if she wished. They both knew what this meant. The evening arrived; Jenny found Veronica's smart bungalow. Two hours later, an Indian take-out and two bottles of red wine, the women were rolling around with each other on the black leather sofa in the lounge, photographs of Veronica's dead husband looking on.

Up to the bedroom they went, giggling like schoolgirl chums, half dressed. They were in bed about ten minutes, when Jenny heard a noise coming from a wardrobe in the room. A few minutes later, she heard it again and saw the piece of furniture topple over onto its side. The doors opened and a skinny man in boxer shorts with a camcorder spilled out onto the floor. He looked like the man from the photographs, the 'deceased' husband. He was very much alive and had been hiding in the wardrobe to film his wife and Jenny.

Veronica and her husband apologised profusely. They found it difficult to get women to join them for threesomes, so they opted for this scam instead, getting off on watching footage of Veronica with other women. Jenny stormed out of the house, taking off into the night, swearing she would never get personally involved in Mature Emporium again! She would run it, but not use it to meet people.

Telling this recollection had her laughing. Bob too.

Getting up to visit the ladies', Jenny nearly toppled over.

She was drunk. Archie organised a taxi for them both. The late afternoon light hurt their eyes as they left the pub.

They were still laughing when they got back to their hotel room, imbued with an afternoon of drinking; the couple were enjoying the abandoned feeling of running with their impulses. Staggering over to Bob's briefcase that stood on a chair, Jenny retrieved the padded envelope. Swaying a little, she ripped it open and fished out the black satin French knickers.

'Oh, I say. These are certainly for the larger lady,' mocked Jenny at their size. Straddling Bob, swaying a little, she brushed the knickers across his face.

'Sinclair, you're a liar. You do more with these than use them to clean your bus. You give them a good sniff, don't you? And the rest!' exclaimed Jenny playfully.

It was at this moment that the alcohol sluicing around Jenny finished its euphoric journey – it took her to the emotional cliff edge and dropped her. She felt down in an instant, almost desperate, everything welling up inside, set to explode. Jenny now tried to push the knickers into Bob's mouth. Although his senses were slowed, he felt the sea change of emotion in the woman above him.

'Here, eat the fucking things. You vain prick!'

Bob wrenched the knickers from her, throwing them onto the floor.

Jenny pushed her face close to his. She came out with another anxious explosion.

'Who did you fuck on this trip? Was it that Christina, or was it Eva? You probably had them both, didn't you? Both at the same time I bet!'

Bob tried to get up, to take control. But she sat right on his chest.

Hot tears fell from her eyes. Everything now felt out of kilter; this affair with the Cassanova of bus drivers, the shame of leaving home, the trauma of Skye, too much honesty about her past, all these things collided into one another. Thoughts searing her mind, making her feel sick. Sick – *she was going to be sick!*

Gripping the toilet bowl, she threw up the remains of the fried breakfast from the morning. Mushrooms slid down the porcelain, the vapour of puke filled her nostrils, bringing on more retching. Slumping onto the bathroom floor, the cold tiled floor felt good against her forehead. My dignity is now gone, she thought, and I haven't even slept with him.

Crawling back into the bedroom, and up into bed, she noticed Bob had passed out. Burrowing her head into the pillow, she sought the refuge of sleep.

Head pounding, Jenny flickered awake at 7.56 p.m. She heard the sound of splashing water from the shower. Lifting her head, she realised she still felt a little drunk. Flopping her head back into the pillow, she remembered why she preferred smoking dope. There was not this aftermath. The summer breeze coming through the open window was refreshing on her face. Bob had probably had to open the window to free the room from the odour of vomit.

There was a knock on the door. That was all she needed, a hotel staffer seeing her like this. She hid under the covers.

Answering the door in his bathrobe, Bob took delivery of a tray with two long glasses containing a pinkish-coloured fluid.

Jenny watched as Bob emptied two sachets of Alka Setzler into the strawberry flavoured milkshakes.

'This will do the trick,' he said, handing her one of the glasses. He sat on the bed and gulped his down in one go. 'Great for clearing the head.'

It took a few attempts, but she got the ice cream congested drink down.

'I'll run you a bath,' said Bob, disappearing into the bathroom.

'We need to be out of here by nine. I've a table booked,' he informed her.

Slipping into the soap-sudded hot water, Jenny felt the heat easing into her bones. The sound of the television in the bedroom brought calmness to their surroundings, an every-day normality. Looking around the bathroom, she realised

Bob must have cleaned up her mess from earlier, what a sweetie.

Although she had left behind Ardnish House and the strange events of the last few days, the strangeness was still in motion with the situation with Bob. This dizzy little affair, spinning along like a child's top, but would it stop with a jolt – the jolt of reality, as certain as the holiday coming to an end?

The milkshake started to take effect and by the time Jenny was drying herself, she felt a lot better. There was a gentle throbbing in her head, but her stomach was settling. Make-up would sort out the rest.

By 8.55 p.m., they were ready. Jenny looked good in a blue summer dress. Bob had donned chinos, a denim shirt and loafers. His foot was still a little sore. Their taxi waited.

They drew up outside a fish and chip shop on the sea front – Luigi's.

Disembarking from the car, Jenny looked for a bistro-type eating establishment. She was a little taken aback when Bob escorted her into Luigi's with the words 'the best fish and chips you will eat in your lifetime!'

Joining a long queue of tourists and some locals waiting to be served, Jenny started to feel disappointed.

'Bob! How are you?' welcomed a stocky Italian man in a Scottish accent.

'I'm good, Michael. How are you?'

'Busy, Busy! But not complaining,' replied the fryer, nodding towards the queue. 'Go on through. Your table is ready.'

Taking Jenny by the hand, Bob led her into the back of the establishment where ten tables with red checked tablecloths formed the eating area. The 1920s art-deco fittings were acutely preserved; it was like stepping back in time. All the tables were filled, except for one at the back of the room, in the corner, affording privacy.

Taking their seats, the couple were joined by a slim woman, Alexandra, Michael's wife. Her red hair spelled Scottish extraction.

'Good to see you, Bob,' said Alexandra.

'Good to see you, Alex. This is Jenny.'

'Pleased to meet you, Alex.'

Jenny picked up the menu.

'No need to look at the menu,' remarked Bob. 'Cod and chips will do nicely.'

'Same for me,' chimed Jenny, enjoying the coach driver's control.

Ten minutes later, their order arrived. They ate with vigour. Bob's recommendation was absolutely spot-on. They were the best fish and chips ever, Jenny could not disagree. The couple felt a renewed sense of well-being return to their constitutions.

Holding hands across the table, the couple didn't say much, their bodies busy absorbing the meal, their thoughts absorbing each other.

Following the meal, they walked along the esplanade as the sun started to set on the outline of the Isle of Mull. The couple put their arms around each other.

Stopping a passer-by, Bob got the young man to take their photograph.

'That's Kerrera over there,' informed Bob, pointing to a strip of coastline across the water. 'I promise to take you there tomorrow.'

A passionate kiss infused Jenny and Bob with the desire to make a hasty return to their hotel room. Bob didn't care if his stitches burst as they raced along the esplanade.

Chapter Eighteen

The climax flooded through Jenny, fusing all her senses together in an expanding rim of pleasure, a shock wave of completeness throughout body and mind.

Bob was two seconds behind; her contracting and expanding sexual muscles pulled his erection to ejaculation with pumping spasms that further heightened her orgasm. Thousands of nerve endings in both their bodies bristled with sensory excitement; alive, aware, connected.

Held together in the engorged outpouring of this sexual union, Jenny and Bob looked into each other's faces with fixed intensity.

Bob loved the little crow's feet, radiating from the outside corners of her eyes. They had their own perfection.

Jenny found Bob's mouth intriguing to study, it was expressive and beheld much sensitivity.

Her eyes are so full, thought Bob, like some aquarium, little tails of colour flashing.

His forehead is so smooth, thought Jenny, an impenetrable rock-face.

He pulled himself gently free from her vault, rolling onto his back, the sheets felt cool under his body. She snuggled up to his side, feeling the enclosure of his strong arms around her.

Their breathing returning to a steady beat, basking in the afterglow of their passionate lovemaking.

Lovemaking! It was indeed lovemaking. Not just sex, but full on lovemaking, the way it should be.

Right from the start, they were burning up. As soon as the

door closed behind them, they locked onto each other with fevered kissing, undressing each other with impatient fumbling, pulling the bedclothes over their nakedness, pushing their bodies towards each other, excitement building with every touch.

Setting out to explore with mouth, tongue, and fingers, Jenny and Bob were instinctively pleasing each other.

Taking his hard cock in her mouth, she felt the stem quiver with near ejaculation as her tongue ran around the crown of the penis.

Intent on bringing each other to the successive levels of arousal, buried in each other's bodies, their minds raced on the fuel of pleasure, till they were ready to complete the joining.

Jenny thought she was going to climax when Bob entered her, sliding himself with sensitive care into her receptivity, seeing her quiver with the drive of his vein-splitting hardness.

Pausing for a few seconds, they then began the gentle meeting and retreating strokes of intercourse. He felt the pulsing wrapping of her – she felt the swollen filling of him.

With assured strokes, he found the mutual pace of this glorious act. She guided his trajectory with a firm grip of his buttocks. This was not going to take long, they both knew that. Days of anticipation welled forth with increased penetration and motion.

Rising together to climax, clasping each other tighter with expectation, Jenny and Bob plunged together into the fire of the final act.

The morning light striking through the hotel room window was ideal for Jenny to apply her make-up. Her face glowed, beamed with the radiance of the night's lovemaking. Between her legs twitched with physical annoyance of the aftermath, but the inner glow of satisfaction more than compensated.

She reached for the hairdryer. Flicking the switch produced nothing.

'Can you see if reception have a spare hairdryer? This one isn't working.'

Buttoning a shirt, Bob entered the room from the en-suite bathroom, 'No problem. I will call them.'

Jean was on duty in reception and confirmed there was a spare one downstairs. Bob left the room to complete his errand.

Looking for the hairdryer, Jean Howie checked all the usual places while Bob waited.

'Sorry, but it's not here,' apologised Jean.

'Hi, Bob,' said a New Zealand accent. A middle-aged man, dressed in a dark blue suit walked towards him, Harry Patterson, owner of the Isle View Hotel.

Bob turned to greet him. 'Hello, Harry. How are you?'

'I'm fine, just fine,' responded the hotelier, shaking Bob's hand. 'What are you doing here? I know we've no Scotia Tours bookings at the moment.'

'I'm nothing to do with them anymore. I'm here of my own free will.'

Harry looked puzzled. 'But, I thought you would have been buried in your bus! Like some Viking in his blazing long-ship!'

'It's a long story,' said Bob wearily.

'Walk with me, Bob. Give me the short version.'

Keeping pace with the energetic hotel owner was no mean feat.

Visiting the hotel's housekeeper in the basement was his first inspection, before going onto the kitchen, where the breakfast shift was beginning to wind down.

Despite the interruptions, Bob did manage to convey the recent downturn in his coach tour career.

By the time they reached the lounge bar, where the barman was undertaking a stock check, Harry had some questions for Bob.

'So, have you thought of setting up on your own, getting your own bus?' he asked.

'I hadn't actually?'

'Well you should. What's stopping you?'

'I suppose it's lack of business experience.'

'But you have years of driving experience, and plenty of contacts,' said Harry, heading to the office with Bob in tow.

'Money. I'd need to get enough cash to get a coach of my own.'

Harry mused for a few seconds, before making a suggestion.

'You could get a loan based on having a contract with a company who'll supply you with the passengers.'

'Where am I going to get a contract like that?' replied Bob, following Harry into his office, an untidy room with two chairs and a desk heaped with papers and a phone.

Harry indicated to Bob to take a seat.

'The reason Scotia Tours are no longer booked in here, or in any of my four hotels, is because I told them to fuck off after they tried to screw me down again on the room rates. It was getting ridiculous. What they were *expecting* for how little they were prepared to pay.' Harry swung back in his black leather chair. 'The thing is, coach parties fill up hotels quite nicely and I could still do with the business.' He leaned forward in his chair, staring hard at Bob. 'So, I'm going to organise my own coach tour holidays. I'll do it myself, it shouldn't be too difficult.' Harry paused. 'But I need a man with his own coach, a man who knows how to handle this type of thing?' Harry left his suggestion in the air, awaiting Bob's reaction.

Stuck for words, Bob finally stammered a reply, 'So what you're saying is you're looking for a driver?'

'More than a driver. A driver with his own coach. I'm not talking about giving you a job, it's a business opportunity. I've been successful because I've seen opportunities and taken action, moved when I saw my chance. Give some thought to my proposition and we'll talk again.'

The conversation was over. Bob moved to the door. 'Thanks, Harry. I'll come back to you.'

Bob bounded up the stairs to the room with the energy of a man half his age.

'So, what's it all about?' asked Jenny as they slid into their chairs in the breakfast room. Bob had conveyed some of the conversation he'd had with the hotel owner as they came downstairs.

'Harry Patterson is not taking any more Scotia Tours parties. I know Scotia are tough, but it looks to me they were asking for too much. The straw that broke the camel's back.'

The young waitress took their order as she dropped off a jug of coffee. The couple poured themselves a cup each. Bob continued. 'The thing is, Harry still needs the business from the coach tours. He's got three other hotels as well as this one. So, he's thinking about organising his own tours. That's why he's interested in talking to me.'

'So, would you drive a coach for this guy?' asked Jenny. 'That's great news – back in the saddle already.' She felt genuinely excited for him, but she was also sceptical.

'That's where there might be a problem. He's not looking for a driver; he wants a man with his own coach.' He let out a long sigh.

'Could you get yourself a coach,' she remarked. 'A second-hand one?'

'With what? I don't have the money, even a second-hand bus is expensive.'

'Re-mortgage your house, get a loan, there must be something you can do to raise the capital.'

No reply. He sat watching her, his shoulders slumped.

Negative thoughts permeated the coach driver's mind.

He knew nothing of running his own business? Where would he get the money to finance the purchase? Wasn't he too old now for this type of thing? What if it folded – and he owed a lot of money to people?

'Is there something up?' enquired Jenny.

Bob screwed up his face.

'You were full of beans a minute ago.'

'Well that's just it. It's a business proposition and I've no idea about this sort of stuff. I can do the work, but it's getting started. I don't know where to begin.'

Jenny had not seen him like this before, so helpless. She offered some support.

'I won't pretend I know a lot about setting up a business, but I grew up in a house where my father was self-employed, and I was always interested in my husband's career. I wasn't one of those wives who could not be bothered with the business talk. I made sure I had some grasp of what was going on.'

Listening intently, Bob was impressed with what Jenny had to say.

'So what's the first stage?' he asked hopefully.

'Write a business plan. You do the research, work on the numbers and put it all into a document which explains to people what your business is all about. It also helps you make the decision to go through with it or not.'

'I've no idea how to do such a thing.'

'I'll help you. There are books on the subject. Is there a library in Oban?'

'I think so,' replied Bob, beginning to smile, his enthusiasm returning.

Jenny continued. 'Let's get on this straight away. We need to know the cost of a second-hand coach. You must have some contacts you can call to check it out?'

'I have a couple of people I can ring to get some ball-park figures.'

'Great.'

They both smiled.

The library was near empty. The building had been built in the seventies and a lack of local government funding was beginning to show, peeling paint here and there, a few rotten window frames, some original furniture from the opening day.

Mrs Dunlop looked like she needed some repair work too, but her unbridled enthusiasm shone through her face. She helped Bob and Jenny find the books they needed, and got them onto the Internet.

Bob surfed the net to gain pricing information on coaches while Jenny drafted the business plan based on the library books Mrs Dunlop had provided.

Bob made some calls on his mobile phone to double check the information he had secured.

By midday, they had enough notes to convene and work up a first draft in the reading room. By 2.00 p.m., Jenny was typing up the plan on the PC.

The morning had been fun. The couple had still found time to convey their affection for each other; dabbing kisses on the cheek, a little squeeze of the hands, and catching each other's eye as they worked. It was like a school romance, Mrs Dunlop like a friendly teacher, turning a blind eye to the goings on. By 3 o'clock, they had finished.

The old photocopier managed to crank out five copies of the plan. Bob had bought a box of chocolates for Mrs Dunlop to say thank you for her help. She was quite touched as they said goodbye and headed back to the hotel.

In their room, Jenny made a suggestion.

'When my husband was working on a presentation, he would get it all done, and then leave it for a couple of hours, even a day. Then he would go through it with fresh eyes and make the corrections and improvements needed. We should do that.' Jenny tapped the stack of five copies on the dressing table.

'Well, if we have some time to kill...' suggested Bob as he took Jenny in his arms, planting a full kiss on her mouth. 'I want to show my appreciation of your hard work!'

'I can feel your appreciation pressing against me.' His hard cock was pressing into her body. Arousal's small embers flickered inside the couple.

'You're like a sexual compass,' stated Jenny, fondling his erection through his trousers, 'always pointing north!'

Sex in the afternoon was a particular favourite for Jenny. A sort of truancy from the constraints of everyday life. As her orgasm cut through her body, she thought of those people at work; stuck behind desks, working in factories, delivering things, talking on the phone, doing their jobs. This thought seemed to give added excitement to their lovemaking.

Dozing for an hour, Jenny came around before Bob. She fetched a copy of the plan and slid back into bed, propping herself up with the pillows to digest the contents. But her mind soon wandered as she began to think about the rapid train of events in her life since she had boarded the coach in Edinburgh a few days earlier.

How surreal it all seemed, the way life crawled along; days, months, years of everyday mundane living. The daily cycle of work, family, commuting, chores, paying the bills. The repetition of it all – layers of habit building up like sediment. Everything remained the same until a massive tidal wave of change came rolling in at once, shaking the floor of existence, stirring up all the sediment.

The question she asked herself was, where in the cycle of change was she right now – in the middle, near the end, or were there more waves to come?

Looking at Bob sleeping, Jenny thought how apt the saying was; you wait for a bus, and you wait, and you wait, and then three come along at once. She returned her attention to the document in hand. Bob stirred and gave her a smile.

'Is this the figure here for buying the coach?' asked Jenny.

'Yeah.'

'Can you raise this amount? It's a lot of money?'

'I don't know. I can probably get half, but that's all my savings and my redundancy.'

'What about using your house to get a loan for the rest,' offered Jenny.

'What house?'

'The house you live in when you're not on the road.' Jenny sensed she was touching a sensitive subject.

'I don't have a house,' he replied sharply turning his back.

'Where do you live?' She leaned over, putting her chin on his shoulder.

'I have a static caravan in Derbyshire. That's what's left after a lifetime of failed marriages,' he replied bitterly.

Jenny felt sorry for him. No wonder losing his job was such a real body blow.

There was a long silence as his enthusiasm ebbed again at the thought of not being able to raise the capital needed.

'Harry Patterson,' said Jenny. 'Harry Patterson might be the person who could lend you the cash.'

Bob's expression was pensive. Jenny could see the whole thing was worrying for him.

'Let's show him this business plan. He's the businessman. If he thinks it's sound, ask him for the money you need to get the coach, make him a partner!' Jenny was pleased with her idea.

'Worth a try, I suppose.' Bob felt a little more positive. All he wanted to do was drive a coach again, and if that meant being self-employed and having a partner, so be it!

'You've nothing to lose, and everything to gain,' said Jenny.

Bob called Harry while Jenny soaked in the bath. The conversation was brief.

'Game on!' shouted Bob. 'We're meeting him later.'

Ideal. I-fucking-deal!

Descending in the lift, Jenny checked her appearance in its smoked-glass interior. The blue dress was the most flattering of her summer wardrobe. She wanted to make a good impression on Patterson, as well as make Bob feel proud. He also checked his appearance, dressed in light chinos, a dark blue shirt open at the collar and a lambswool sweater draped over his shoulders.

As they walked into the bar, Jenny guessed instantly who Harry Patterson was. He had an entrepreneurial air to him, the confidence, the bearing, the self-made-man persona that exuded from him. His suit looked expensive. He was talking to a man who had his back to Jenny and Bob.

Harry locked onto Jenny as soon as she walked in. She knew the type, like her late-husband's boss, the owner of the company, same breed, clever and smart in business, but not the most mature when it came to the opposite sex.

'Hi. You're Bob's partner,' said Harry introducing himself to Jenny with a handshake and a smile. Expecting a strong grip, she found his hand quite limp.

'Jenny, this is Harry Patterson,' said Bob, knowing he had a real asset in Jenny. He felt lucky tonight.

'Pleased to meet you. I would like to say what a nice hotel you have.' Jenny knew from experience that flattering a man's ego was a good way to start.

'You should see the The Grange, one of my other hotels just outside Stirling. It's my flagship.' He grinned with pride.

'Excuse me. Where are my manners. Let me introduce you to Michael White, he's considering coming to work for me,' informed Harry.

'Pleased to meet you both,' said Michael, extending his hand outwards to the couple. He was early-to mid-forties with an average build, but not an average face. Jenny found it interesting, the type of distinctive features that seemed to belong on television, like those of a newsreader. She especially liked his piercing blue eyes.

'Can I get you a drink?' asked Harry.

The bar was filling up with guests for pre-dinner aperitifs. The clatter of chatter resounded around the room.

'So, might you be working with Harry?' asked Jenny.

'Yes, but it won't be the first time, will it?'

Both men laughed heartily at some shared history.

'We first met when starting out in this trade as trainees. We were both as crazy as each other.'

'I'm a chef by trade. Harry wants me to head up his catering staff for all his hotels,' Michael explained.

'He's fantastic. He should been on telly,' added Harry.

Michael winced a little at the hotelier's comment and downed his glass of orange juice.

Jenny felt the men's eyes on her and was flattered. She remembered her earlier thoughts, you wait for a bus and then three show up at once.

Excusing himself, Michael wished them a pleasant meal. As he made to leave, he shot a look at Jenny with his striking eyes.

'Pleased to meet you, Michael,' said Jenny.

'Call me, Chalky. Everybody does. Bye.'

Bob was eager to get down to business. 'We have a plan for you to look through, Harry.' Bob pushed the document onto the table. 'I've never done anything like this before, so excuse its...'

'Virginal content,' added Jenny with a cheeky smile.

Harry gave a slight chuckle at Jenny's wording. He picked the document up and flicked through the pages quickly. 'I'm impressed. I only spoke to you this morning, and here you are with a proposal.' Harry sipped on his malt whisky, looking at some of the profit and loss numbers. He could tell this was not all Bob's work. 'Joint effort?' he asked, looking at Jenny.

'Yes.' replied Jenny in her best business-like tone.

Harry flicked back to the first page of the document, his sharp mind digesting the information quickly. He started asking questions, which Jenny fielded. Questions about the amount of money Bob would charge for his services. Jenny knew she was not in Harry's league for such discussions, and Bob would certainly not stand a chance.

But her late husband had passed on a few tricks. The one that came to mind was – *stall for time to think*, and if you still can't come up with something you're sure of – *delay to negotiate another day*.

'Do you have a calculator?' asked Jenny.

'There is one behind the bar, I'll get it.' Harry left for a moment.

'I wish I could say more,' said Bob in a whisper.

'You're doing fine. This is exciting, isn't it?'

Bob nodded, squeezing her knee under the table.

'Here you go,' said Harry, handing the calculator to Jenny. 'I have some more drinks coming over.'

Jenny randomly punched in some numbers, looking like she knew what she was doing, while thinking about the answer to give. She felt a trickle of sweat drop down from her armpits. She needed time to work some more on the figures.

Harry spoke. 'Come back to me in the morning if you want. Do you two play golf?'

'I don't,' answered Bob, feeling inadequate.

'It's been a year since I last played,' remarked Jenny.

'Bob,' asked Harry. 'Would you mind if I take Jenny out for a round of golf first thing? There are some questions I have on this plan and Jenny seems to be the person to talk too. We can go through these on the course.' He flashed a smile.

'Sure.' There was some reticence in Bob's reply.

'I will bring my wife's clubs,' commented Harry. 'Have you folks eaten?'

'No,' they chimed.

'Good. Let me treat you.'

Harry ushered them into the hotel restaurant, taking a good table by the window. The evening sunset was spectacular over the Isle of Mull.

Over the meal, Harry got to know the couple better, more than they did of him. Bob found his form again as the business talk was out of the way, regaling Harry and Jenny with stories from his army days.

Around 10.00 p.m. the couple excused themselves, thanking Harry for the meal. Jenny agreed to meet with Harry the next morning in reception.

Flopping into bed, the couple both felt exhausted. Snuggling up together, Jenny rested her head on Bob's chest, listening to the steady thump of his heartbeat. His breathing was moving into the rhythm associated with sleep. Just before slipping into the undertow of slumber, he uttered a few words.

'Thanks, Jenny. Thanks for everything today.'

She smiled to herself.

Jenny found being awake next to a sleeping person was always quite calming, even as a child, sharing a bedroom with her younger sister. Listening to Margaret's laden exhaling and inhaling soothed Jenny to sleep. She had experienced the same when her husband was alive.

This peaceful interlude before closing her eyes was ideal to reflect on the day's events. Some people used it to think about what the next day would bring, but she always used it to go over what had passed.

Again she dwelt on the recent events since she had set out on the tour coach; seducing Pernille, the coach crash, the MacKenzies, becoming involved with Bob, more had happened in a week than in the last five years of her life.

But the big question was, where was this affair going? Was it just a holiday romance? A brief adventure? Could it be the start of something? Was he even capable of loving one woman? Could she make another life with this man? If so, it would probably be here in Scotland – did she want that?

Chapter Nineteen

With three holes completed, Jenny was finding her form. On the par three fourth hole she watched the ball fly down the fairway as the *whack* of her driving swing resounded across the hilly course. It travelled a good distance on the dew soaked grass, stopping just ten metres from the edge of the green.

'Shot,' complimented Harry as he lined up to take his drive.

The freshness of the morning air tinged Jenny's face as she looked across the fir tree lined fairways towards the Isle of Mull, sitting on the other side of the shimmering Firth of Lorne. The sun was burning off a few clouds to clear the sky for another beautiful day. Waiting for Harry to take his shot, she noticed how creased his blue checked trousers and red cashmere sweater were.

Harry's ball sped off down the fairway, landing close to Jenny's.

'Fantastic view!' exclaimed Jenny.

'The best of all worlds! You get to play golf in one of the most scenic places in the world.'

They started walking down the fairway.

'But your native country of New Zealand is a stunning place from the pictures I've seen,' remarked Jenny. She noted the swagger to Harry's walk, like a young man's swagger, full of attitude, out to prove something.

'It's very similar, and it's why a lot of Scots who emigrated to the country feel comfortable, people like my parents.'

'When did they go out?' enquired Jenny.

'In the fifties. They loved the place as soon as they got off the boat. They were disappointed in me when I flunked out of college and kept running the country down. I was twenty and looking for excitement. Wellington didn't have it as far as I was concerned. They thought by sending me to live with my uncle in Glasgow for six months, they would make me appreciate their adopted country. They thought Glasgow was like the place they left in the fifties; dark, post-industrial, slums, no hope. But by the early eighties, the city was on the up again, full of opportunities, an exciting place to be. I loved it and that's where I got into the hotel business.'

They had stopped to take their second shots. Jenny was enjoying the game. Harry noted the number 9 iron selected for her next shot, a good choice. He also noted the nice shape of her bottom, the smoothness of the buttocks against the cotton of her trousers.

The ball was chipped onto the green with precise ease, coming to rest very close to the flag.

'I think you're lying to me about your handicap, Jenny,' exclaimed Harry.

'It's luck, just luck. I've not played in a year.'

'Well you're a natural then.'

Harry took his shot. However, he over-clubbed it and the ball flew right through the green.

Jenny putted out, the ball dropping into the hole with ease.

'Your hole,' conceded Harry.

Picking up their balls, the pair continued their conversation.

'So how did you get started in this business?' asked Jenny.

'I got a job as a trainee manager with a big hotel group, real hands on stuff. You do all the jobs there are to do, from working in the kitchen, to changing beds, to serving in the bar. Long hours, but I loved it, really loved it; the variety, moving from hotel to hotel and I could see an opportunity to progress. By the time I was twenty-six, I was managing one of my own hotels in the group. It wasn't one of the best, but I turned it around, valuable experience. By the time I was thirty, I had completed a management buyout of one of the loss-making hotels the group wanted to get rid of, and I was on my way!' Harry's face was awash with pride at this story, which Jenny could tell he'd told on many occasions. He was typical of most entrepreneurs; driven by ambition, the odds being stacked against them, taking risks, proving to themselves and others they could pull it off.

'So your parents did you a favour!' commented Jenny.

Harry nodded. 'They're proud, I'm pleased to say. Everybody deserves a chance. I'm looking at a fifth hotel now.'

As they made ready to tee off on the fifth, Jenny had another question for Harry.

'You want to give Bob a chance, don't you, Harry?'

'Absolutely! He would be ideal. I've seen him with the guests in the evenings. He's a good host. He adds to their enjoyment of the trip. There aren't many like him. The timing is perfect, I have enough hotels to develop my own coach tour business, and Bob is available.' Harry stopped talking while Jenny concentrated on her drive, which delivered a good *thwack* to the ball, sending it speeding straight down the fairway.

'But I have one concern. Is Bob up to the commercial side? He doesn't strike me as a person who can run his own business?'

Caught off guard by the question, Jenny also felt very defensive.

'He needs some guidance, I admit, a little help in the beginning, but he would repay that over and over by doing the job really well.'

'But that's just it! It's not just a *job*. I hear what you're saying about some 'mentoring', and six or seven years ago I could have fulfilled that role. But with a fifth site coming on line, I simply do not have the time!'

Harry took his drive. It was not so hot. They started walking down the fairway.

'The other concern I have,' said Harry, 'is the money. Does

he have enough capital to put into the venture? I want to contract out the coach tour facility, I don't want to worry about him folding.'

Harry was taking in her expression, monitoring the reaction. She had to appear strong, and in control. She had to pitch Bob hard, better still, the opportunity.

'The amount of money he needs to get started is tight. But as you can see from the business plan, it can work. You know that, because it's your idea.'

Harry nodded.

'I understand what you're saying about your time, but putting some of your own money into the venture could give you comfort.' She heard the words come out of her mouth and was impressed.

Harry gave a little chuckle. 'I appreciate your directness, Jenny. But if you think it's such a good investment, why don't you put *your* own money in!'

The hotel owner's suggestion took her by surprise. Investing in Bob and his coach business. Well she was already involved with him in this affair, but that could finish tomorrow.

She stopped in her tracks, stuck for a reply. Harry turned to see her expression, a little stunned. He had predicted the outcome of this conversation.

But by the same token, he had decided how to play the next part of these discussions by the time he'd finished having dinner with Jenny and Bob the previous evening.

Harry made another suggestion.

'Tell you what, I'll do a deal with you. I'm always looking for good people for my organisation, people who are not only capable, but can demonstrate some flair, and I need someone to run the new coach tour division. If you give Bob the financial commitment needed to get him on the road, I will in turn give *you* commitment. How about coming to work for me to run the new division?'

Harry paused, taking in Jenny's wide-eyed expression. Eventually she found some words.

'I don't know what to say!'

'Think about it, I don't need an answer straight away.

By the time they had played the fifth hole, Jenny had asked some questions about the role, what would be involved, how much responsibility she would have. All the answers excited her, it sounded great.

The big question was salary.

'How much does this job pay?' They were coming off the seventh hole.

'Twenty-three thousand plus benefits!'

'I'm on twenty-four thousand at the moment.'

'Okay! Play you for it. If you win the next hole, you can have your twenty-four thousand – that's if you decide you want to take the job.'

She won the hole.

Jenny was on a roll.

'Harry, *if* I'm coming to work for you, and I'm saying if, I need to do one more thing.'

'Name it?' Harry was enjoying the rapport, which was growing between them.

'I need to act in Bob's best interest to get the best price for his tour service.'

'And also protect your investment,' he replied with a smile.

'Yes that too. But seriously, he needs the monthly revenue amount we quoted over dinner last night.'

Harry paused. 'You have just confirmed again why I'm hiring you. Okay, you have the figure Bob needs if you win the next hole.'

Jenny won that hole too.

Waving Harry off, after dropping her back at the hotel, Jenny skipped into reception as Bob was coming up from the swimming pool.

Jenny gave him a huge hug, wrapping her arms around his dressing-gowned body. He smelled of chlorine.

'Have I got some news for you, honey!' she exclaimed excitedly.

Bob listened to Jenny relay her golf-course conversation with Harry as they headed for their room. She was speaking fast, burning with the initial excitement of being offered a new job.

While swimming, Bob had felt a little worried at the thought of Patterson trying it on with his girl. But now this seemed remote, as Jenny trotted out all the things they had discussed, and her shoes were marked green from the course, proof they'd played nine holes of golf.

'We're going to have to forgo today's excursion,' informed Bob as they ascended in the lift.

'Why?'

'I need to spend some time on the phone with Scotia Tours. Mrs Hoxley and Human Resources need to talk me through my redundancy details.'

'No problem, I've some shopping to do,' she replied giving Bob's buttocks a squeeze.

Back in the room, Jenny managed to infect Bob with some excitement on his future possibilities and soon he found his spirits lifting as they talked about the positives of making a new life in the Highlands. They were pumping each other up, discussing the myriad of possibilities for the venture; an adventure they would have to decide upon in a month's time, the deadline set by Harry.

Oban was busy as usual, milling with tourists. Jenny was enjoying ambling through the streets, popping into stores if something caught her eye in the window.

Turning a corner, her heart quickened a beat as she saw an empty Scotia Tours coach parked near the ferry terminal. Could it be the party? She didn't fancy making pleasant chit chat with any of them, she'd moved on. They had probably taken a ride on one of the sight-seeing boats anyway.

As she started walking in the direction of her car, she could see Pernille and Henrik coming towards her in the distance. She'd only seconds to hide. Turning right into a shop doorway, she entered the establishment and found herself in a barber's shop.

Some men and young boys waiting for their haircuts gave her a look, as did the two middle-aged barbers.

Jenny felt silly and knew some sort of explanation was expected. A friendly, familiar smile reflected in one of the mirrors gave her an excuse.

'I'm waiting for him,' Jenny indicated towards Chalky, sitting in one of the barber's chairs.

He nodded and gave her a wink as she took a seat next to the waiting customers. The barber continued with Chalky's trim.

Five minutes later, he was finished and heading out the door, his holdall over his shoulder.

'Buy you a coffee? My train is not due for another forty minutes,' he offered.

'Sure.'

'I take it you were trying to avoid someone when you ducked into the barber's?' he asked as they walked out onto the street.

'Was it that obvious? I saw a couple of people from a coach tour I could not be bothered making polite conversation with.'

'In that case, let's go to the station café for a coffee, less chance anyone will know you there.'

Within ten minutes, they were sitting in the deserted café, two coffees placed before them by a young waitress. The décor had seen better days.

'Harry's offer of a job. Is it tempting?' enquired Jenny, seeing the opportunity to get some background on her potential new boss.

'Absolutely. The chance to work in this beautiful place instead of the city. I just need to consider the role. It would be a change, being in charge of other head chefs. It would be my first time in management.'

'But you know, Harry. You've worked with him before?'

'That's just it, worked *with* him, but not *for* him. But

you've got a point, I do know him and he's one of the good guys.'

'We've something in common. I'm considering coming to work for him too,' informed Jenny.

Chalky smiled. Jenny glanced away, finding his stare a little too intense, but flattering.

'Harry is like a medieval king, but in the good sense,' he added. 'He leads by example, at the front of the line, charging into the thick of things. He's firm, but fair and like a king, you just need to make sure you're behind his sword, not on the tip of it.'

'You paint quite a picture,' said Jenny, impressed at his eloquence.

'I'm a chef. I'm creative.'

Jenny went on to explain her and Bob's business plans and Chalky gave full encouragement.

'In a lifetime, you'll be lucky if you get a couple of chances to do something that will make you happy, and by the way you're talking, you and Bob should go for this one.'

'Do you think so?' asked Jenny.

'I do. Take it from a man whose had his chance and blown it,' replied Chalky philosophically.

'Do you mind if I ask what happened?' asked Jenny. Chalky was likeable and easy to talk to.

'No. Not at all. I was working in one of London's top hotels in the early nineties, and I regularly advised a TV company on a food show they produced. They liked what I had to say and asked me to host a new show.'

'How exciting. What happened?'

'I didn't treat it seriously enough. I didn't make the effort to follow it through. Now television is wall-to-wall chefs.'

'Maybe this is your next big chance, working in Scotland,' offered Jenny. 'Do you have any ties?'

'No. Just myself to think about.'

She found his manner generous towards her, but being a chef, she could imagine him being less pleasant in a busy kitchen environment.

'Same for me,' replied Jenny, 'leaving Yorkshire would not be that difficult. It's just being sure about making such a life changing decision, especially at our age.'

'I agree. Anyway, I'm superstitious. I look for certain signs to help me make my mind up.'

'So have you had any so far?'

He gave a big grin as he stood up and hauled his holdall over his shoulder.

'Nothing until today.'

'What was it, tell me?' asked Jenny as she accompanied him onto the platform.

'I need to think about it, turn it over, make sure it was a positive sign.'

He scanned the departures and arrivals board to see if his train was on time, it was.

'I'll see you off,' offered Jenny, still intrigued at what he had just said.

'No need, but as no one ever sees me off, I accept your offer,' he replied.

There now ensued a few seconds of silence before they both tried to speak at once. Chalky asked her to go first.

'Strange how the crossroads in life appear so quickly, don't you think?'

'It's because there's no road-markings or sign posts, Jenny. But the main reason is because we're not looking. John Lennon put it well, life is what happens to you when you're busy making other plans.'

'So true,' Jenny nodded.

She wished Chalky's train would be delayed, and they could continue their conversation over another cup of coffee. For the first time in a long time, here was someone she could really exchange with conversationally. She wanted to find out more about him, he seemed to have depth.

The diesel locomotive came into view and within seconds was pulling into the station. Turning to Jenny, Chalky dabbed a kiss on her cheek.

'Good to meet you. Take care, I hope everything works out.'

'You never know, we might be working together,' she replied as he closed the carriage door behind him. She watched him find a seat. The train did not pull out straightaway and she noticed he was scribbling something on a note pad.

Then as the train belched fumes and creaked forward, he pressed the piece of paper against the window for her to read. The message read: *Jenny, you are my sign.*

Chapter Twenty

Bob wanted their last night in Scotland to be special and had arranged to move to the best suite in the hotel as a surprise for Jenny on her return. This was all new terrain for him – usually such effort was reserved for the seduction process, but now, he felt the urge to continue pleasing her – unconditionally. A combined sensation of exhilaration and fear seared through him; heady stuff indeed, he mused.

Touched by the gesture, Jenny gave Bob a big kiss. Soon she was slipping into the large corner bath, the hot water pushing heat into her bones. Scented bath oils filled the air as Bob handed Jenny a glass of champagne.

'Cheers,' he said clinking their glasses.

He then proceeded to sponge her back, squeezing warm water across her shoulder blades.

Moving onto his knees, leaning into the bath, he planted a kiss on her lips; the taste of champagne intermingling with the fresh smell of sea salt, which was impregnated in both their hair.

'There's room in here for two,' suggested Jenny, flashing a cheeky smile.

'I hoped you were going to say that.' Bob slipped out of his dressing-gown and eased into the bath, facing Jenny, careful to position his long legs on either side of her.

Rain now pelted the bathroom window with little strumming noises against the panes of glass. The steamy bathroom was a cozy little haven. Taking the sponge, Jenny swabbed Bob's chest, then his stomach before moving down to his genitals.

'Up periscope!' she announced as his erection broke the surface.

Her mouth dropped to kiss the crown of his veined hardness, her tongue rolling around the tip before taking it inside. She felt his legs quiver on either side of her hips. With her mouth around his stem, she took him close to climax with her sensual fellatio, she pulled her mouth away to put a kiss on his lips.

'I have an idea,' said Jenny, stepping out of the bath, and disappearing into the bedroom, clad in a towel, rummaging around in her suitcase till she found the little tin with the Chinese motif.

Eyes closed, Bob felt Jenny slipping back into the tub a few minutes later, a large joint protruding from her mouth; the smell of cannabis hit him.

Five minutes later, the joint had passed between them several times, and the effects were taking over. The deepening of the physical and mental sensory perceptions added to the couple's enjoyment of being in the bath. Jenny loved the feeling of the warm water clasping her, enveloping, holding her in the large porcelain bowl. Bob dipped his head below, the pleasure of being submerged, cocooned in fluid.

He reached for the shower attachment, turning on a hot jet of water. Kneeling over Jenny, he began to wash her chest, sponge in one hand: the showerhead in the other. His touch was very sensual, thought Jenny, resting her head on the lip of the bath, pushing her breasts clear of the water's surface. Bob angled the jet of hot water to create a tingling effect on her nipples, bringing them to hardness.

For some reason Chalky came into her mind. He didn't strike her as particularly sexy, but more emotionally tuned to a woman's needs. That was the conundrum with men, Jenny thought. Individually they had different strengths; some leaned more to the mental, communicative, others were sensitive and affectionate.

With Bob, it was his sure-footed understanding of himself and the confidence of his physicality. If only he had some finer points, like Chalky's expressiveness.

She felt a surge of warm water radiate down onto her neck, across the shoulder blades, down her back to glance spray off her buttocks. His free hand soaped her body in a caressing fashion. Looking over her shoulder, Jenny saw how intense Bob's concentration was on hosing her body.

'You probably have the same facial expression when you're washing your bus!' quipped Jenny, imagining him soaking down his vehicle with the same application.

'But I can't do this to my coach,' came his reply as he gently slipped his thumb between the cleft of her legs.

'I say Mr Coach Driver, should you be doing that,' replied Jenny, pushing down onto his sure digit, feeling the rise of arousal spread through her stoned self; a warm, fuzzy mass of pleasure, particles of sex colliding in harmony.

The sound of water splashing onto the bathroom floor alerted the couple to reconsider their frolicking.

'Time to pull the plug,' said Bob, amidst laughter, turning off the shower.

'But you're not pulling the plug on me!' exclaimed Jenny, wrenching the chain to release the contents of the bath.

Still wet, they fell on the fresh white linen sheets under the red velvet awning of the four-poster bed. Aroused, excited, feverish with passion for each other; the physical nature of this session seemed more heightened than before.

Going down on Jenny, Bob tasted her wetness instantly, his tongue driving into her vault with sure strokes. She felt his index finger pry around her anus, nudging the closed bud.

'Put it in,' she commanded.

Vaginal juices lubricated this anal entry, the finger moving easily up to the first knuckle. Jenny's pelvis thrusted upwards, as she cried out in pleasure.

Soon she would be ready for him to take, he thought. His cock twitched in anticipation, the soldier prepared to go over the top.

'I want to take you,' Jenny exclaimed, sitting up on her elbows. 'Get on your back.' She liked being in control.

Bob did as he was told.

Taking his erection in her right hand, she guided it into her vagina, moving to complete the astride position, her body weight perched on his middle. He liked the feeling of being pinned down.

Inflamed, Bob felt his cock enter the hot sleeve of Jenny's sex, wrapped in warmth, encased in a place where nature's snug fit is perfect.

Lowering herself onto the shaft further, Jenny received his stem with an intake of breath, the engorged sensation of filling herself with this man, his swollen rigidity, brought her near climax.

Eyes locked on each other, both turning on this point of complete joining, encapsulated in the moment.

A few seconds of stillness, and then Jenny began to take him. He felt submissive below her, she felt in control above him.

Looking into the contorted female face, eyes closed, Bob felt Jenny was riding him all the way to the finishing line with furious thrusts. He gripped her buttocks; breasts brushed his face, sweet fruits to suckle as they hang from the tree.

Jenny's gasps were closing, getting shorter with each plunge of her body on his manhood, till with one final searing stroke her climax was unleashed.

Grinding her pelvis with each pleasurable moan, Jenny collapsed onto Bob, her orgasm slowly quivered to a standstill.

Their hearts pounded in unison through the contact of their chests.

Minutes passed. They lay locked together, the wind whipping against the window, the evening light fading.

Sliding off Bob, Jenny moved her head down to his middle, crouching on all fours, taking the still hard member into her mouth; tasting herself.

She also took Bob's right hand and placed it under her chin, so he could feel the movement of her throat as she sucked on his cock.

Gently squeezing his warm sack, still bathed in her juices, Jenny set about milking this man with her mouth. It would not take long to siphon his seed.

Sure enough, she felt the travel of sperm, like putting an ear to a train-track to anticipate the coming of a locomotive; the tightening of his balls, the final stretching of his glands to push forth the ejaculation.

Locking her mouth on him, she braced herself to swallow, knowing this act would reverberate into Bob's hand.

Bob pumped his tide of well-being into Jenny with several jolts; she took him down, fully accommodating. He felt her gullet contract and expand, then contract and expand again, imagining his emission travelling into this woman.

'Taste yourself,' she said, embracing Bob passionately. He returned the intensity.

Drained from the physical exploration, the couple's fusing of the senses pulsed on emotionally. The post-coital connection of mind and body laid bare their innermost feelings, and it was Bob who felt the need to articulate.

Clasping each other in the darkness, he found himself launching a string of words, previously unknown in his vocabulary.

'I think I'm falling in love with you, Jenny.'

A few seconds before her response came out of the night.

'Me too – scary, uh?'

Wrapped in this emotional exchange, the couple fell into the undertow of sleep.

Just before Bob slipped under, his mind turned over amidst the feelings swamping him – the pleasurable submerged desperation of falling in love. She was right, it was scary, but wonderful.

Jenny awoke a few hours later. Bob was dead to the world. She instantly recalled his last words to her, I think I'm falling in love with you and felt a serene wave push through her. He had an expressive side to him after all.

Adjusting her pillow, she felt an object underneath and

retrieved it. Not wanting to wake Bob, she took the item into the bathroom.

It was a small jewellery box and it contained a silver Celtic cross and chain. He must have intended giving the piece to her, but their lovemaking had taken over to the exclusion of all else.

He had probably bought it in the hotel gift shop while she was out in the afternoon and for a few seconds she felt bad as the sight of Chalky entered her mind's eye. But, here she was with Bob, sharing a bed with the man and her feelings were now lapping around him, like his around her.

Slipping into bed, she put the little box back in its hiding place and with her head on the pillow believed she had been sent a sign.

The following day, the cross on its silver chain nestled on Jenny's chest, where she played with it on the journey south to Glasgow.

Bob kept glancing at it from the driver's seat. But then again he liked looking at Jenny's chest. It was a rare combination, he thought.

The Highland scenery began to give way to a more arable landscape by the time they reached Callander. The towers of rock, the rugged blue mountains, were behind them now. Jenny was going to miss those rangy peaks, the long, narrow lochs; the sheer drama of the place. She decided; the north-west coast was her favourite part of Scotland.

Going home to reality sobered the both of them from the alcohol of holiday dreaming. But there was one part of the dream, yet to explore.

Bellshill was their destination now, a working town to the east of Glasgow. Approaching the place, the surroundings were typical of any country's economic heartland. Johnstones Coaches was on a sprawling industrial estate; a landscape of sheds, warehouses, factories, trucks and vans.

Parking up in the car park, next to a dozen used coaches, Bob suggested Jenny stay in the car while he checked out the bus he'd made an enquiry about from the Internet. Jenny agreed, closing her eyes.

Billy Johnstone was a hard man; grey wiry hair, steely eyes behind large, dark-rimmed glasses and a stern narrow mouth, his frame was bulky, his fingers nicotine stained.

'Can I help you?' his loud Glasgow accent boomed in the cabin office.

'I'm Bob Sinclair, we spoke on the phone yesterday.' They shook hands.

'Ah, yes. The Volvo.'

'That's right.'

'Let's take a look then,' said Billy taking a set of ignition keys from a board dripping with many others.

Outside, the Volvo coach, in black and gold livery gleamed in the afternoon sunshine. Bob swung into the driver's seat, taking the keys from Billy, who sat in the front passenger seat.

'One owner! An old boy who retired for health reasons. He loved this coach.'

'It shows,' said Bob, taking in the spotless condition of the driving controls and seating area. 'Can I take her down the motorway?'

'Aye, you can.'

Coming to life, the diesel engine gave a throaty roar, sending a tingle down Bob's spine. An ever so slight vibration travelled through his frame as he meshed the gears to move the coach forward. Stopping at the hire car, he sounded the horn, giving Jenny a jolt from her doze.

Bob's grin beckoned her aboard. She took the seat behind Billy.

Slipping onto the motorway, Bob's senses were seeking out any glitches in the ride.

The coach felt good. He felt good. Back in the saddle. Back where he belonged. *Ideal. I-fucking-deal!*

The motorway clipped below him, cars pushing past, the pulse of traffic as familiar as ever. Bob seamlessly merged back into the bloodstream of internal combustible transport.

A permanent smile took residence on the coach driver's face.

Jenny was pleased to see how happy he was. Inspecting the upholstery, she could see the condition of the bus was very good. The coach had been well-cared for.

They returned to Billy Johnstone's compound after twenty minutes. While Bob inspected the coach with one of Billy's mechanics, Jenny had a confab with the owner to establish the feasibility of somehow reserving the purchase of the bus for a short period.

Explaining the business offer they had had from Harry Patterson, she and Bob needed a few weeks to consider and decide on their new venture.

As hard as he was, Billy Johnstone could not refuse a pretty woman's request to hold the Volvo for a couple of weeks on the basis of a three-hundred pound deposit. They shook hands on the deal and Jenny took down the details of the coach and the purchase price. She would check out later how competitive it was to buy this vehicle.

Joining Bob in the car park, the couple looked at the black and gold vehicle.

'She's the one,' stated Bob, an expression of desire on his face.

'Well, she may well be! I've just put a deposit down to hold it for a couple of weeks till we decide what we are doing.'

He scooped her off the ground in his arms, twirled her around and planted a big kiss on her lips. 'You're amazing!

An hour into their southbound journey on the M74, dropping down through the steep sloped valley of Beattock, Bob posed a question to Jenny, something that had been on his mind since they left the MacKenzies. She did not expect it.

'What happened between you and Skye on the night before we left the MacKenzies?'

Taken by surprise, Jenny stumbled over her response.

'I don't know quite where to begin...it was all very upsetting. I still don't know what to make of it all now...'

'If you don't want to talk about it, I understand,' responded Bob.

There was a long pause, just the open road clipping along outside.

'No, I *do* want to talk, and I *do* want you to know what happened,' replied Jenny, thinking the car was an ideal place to recount the Skye incident. By facing forward, looking through the windshield, not facing Bob, she could discharge the events more easily.

'Skye *assaulted* me, in a way I could not imagine possible.'

Bob shot her a glance.

Jenny continued; images of the young woman holding the dildo flooded her mind, followed by a tightening feeling of revulsion in the stomach.

'She's not what she appears to be. This is a woman who is a master of disguise, a person capable of hiding her real self, a wolf in sheep's clothing!'

Sensing some distress in her voice, Bob took his left hand from the steering wheel and squeezed Jenny's right hand reassuringly.

Pouring out the sordid details, Jenny recounted the comic-strip drawings and how she thought they were Mackenzie's work. How Skye made her move in the library, how she undressed herself and threatened Jenny with the dildo. But it was the relaying of the acidic insults Skye had unleashed, which brought forth the tears from Jenny.

Pulling into a service station, Bob comforted Jenny by holding her.

Flushed, dabbing her teardrops with a tissue, Jenny had a question for Bob.

'What did she do when she came to your room that night?'

Answer carefully, thought Bob, not wanting to upset her further.

'She tried to get into bed with me. I threw her out.'

Her composure returning, she nodded, 'I heard you shouting at her, telling her to go. I knew then I was falling in love with you!' She pressed her head into his shoulder.

Bob restarted the car and joined the motorway again.

'She really had a thing for you then?' he enquired.

'Gender doesn't matter to Skye, nothing stops her. If she wants to fuck someone, she will. Not even being related makes a difference.'

'What do you mean not being related?'

'Work it out, Bob!' Jenny wanted to stop talking about the subject. 'You're a man of the world.'

'Mackenzie?'

Jenny nodded.

'Her own father!' he said incredulously.

'Her own father,' repeated Jenny wearily, reclining the seat so she could be more comfortable. Closing her eyes, Jenny indicated the conversation was over.

His imagination flickering with images of Mackenzie and Skye. Bob turned over the facts he'd been made aware of. So much so, he forgot to wake Jenny up as they crossed the border from Scotland into England as she'd requested.

Scotland fell behind them, the early evening sky darkening with heavy rain clouds, like a theatre curtain coming down on the final act.

It was strange waking up in a house, thought Bob. He seldom slept in one. Hotels and his static caravan were his usual abodes.

A house was quiet compared to a hotel, the coming and going of people, staff and guests, banging doors, the hum of hotel life. Here in Jenny's home at the end of a cul-de-sac overlooking some Yorkshire farm fields, there was pure, quiet and utter peace.

Turning over, he could see the room in daylight, a light airy colour scheme prevailed. It had been dark when they had arrived from Scotland the previous night, and they had only enough energy to drop their luggage in the hall, have a cup of tea, and flop into bed.

Alone in the double bed, the digital alarm clock read 8.33 a.m. The smell of fried bacon hung in the air. Slipping on his boxer shorts and a shirt, Bob padded out onto the landing. At the top of the stairs he could see three doors to his left, and two doors to the right. This was a good-sized house, almost too big for someone living on their own.

Joining Jenny in the kitchen, he kissed his dressing-gowned lover as she stood watching the bacon grill.

'How did you sleep?' she asked.

'Like the just – the sleep of the just.'

'Are you hungry?'

'Starved,' said Bob, sitting down at the pine kitchen table.

Ten minutes later, they were enjoying bacon, eggs, tomatoes and mushrooms with buttered toast and mugs of tea.

'It's a strange feeling when you get back from holiday,' stated Jenny, 'you have a feeling of disorientation, of not knowing where to put yourself.'

'I wouldn't know, being on the road all the time. I'm used to it now.'

'It's not so much the return to normal surroundings, it's the return to everyday routine; daily life, work, chores and the rest,' Jenny reminded herself to put another load of clothes in the washing machine. Should she offer to do Bob's? This would mean him hanging around for another couple of hours. Not that she did not want him around, but at this precise moment, she wanted to be on her own; see how it would feel, test the holiday fling ardour. Would it fade when they were apart?

'I need to get back home,' said Bob, 'Can you drop me off at the nearest rail station.'

'No need, I'll take you back to your place. Chesterfield isn't far.'

Jenny sensed his reluctance. Her heart skipped a beat. Had he still something to hide, a wife and children after all?

'Are you sure?' Bob pressed.

'Absolutely.' Jenny started clearing the kitchen table, nagging thoughts abounding.

'Okay, I would appreciate a lift. I'll have a wash first.'

Feeling relieved that Bob had nothing to hide, Jenny was eager to see his static home. Maybe that was why he was so reluctant about taking a lift, thought Jenny, he didn't seem too proud about his home.

Jenny was right. Bob did feel this way about being driven back to his caravan.

Turning into Dunmoore Park just after 11.00 a.m., Bob gave directions through the lines of large mobile homes to his unit; a white and green caravan on the edge of the site, overlooking the Derbyshire countryside. The words MALPASO were painted in ten-centimetre high letters to the right of the door.

'Good view,' commented Jenny switching off the engine of her little car.

'It may be, but you feel the wind coming off those fields in the winter.'

A musty smell hit them both as they entered the static. Opening windows, Jenny could see the bareness of the interior. Bob disappeared into the small kitchen to brew some tea and empty the shopping bag of provisions they had bought earlier.

Entering into the lounge area, Jenny slipped into one of the built-in cushioned seats, which sat on either side of a formica table.

Looking around, she could see this was a place for Bob to hole up in between trips. A few photographs adorned the walls. One looked like his parents. The other was of a young couple with a five-year old boy, the same photograph of Bob's son and family he kept in his wallet.

A portable television, a half-full bookcase, a drinks-cabinet were all the furniture the room could afford.

'Do you want a biscuit with your tea?' asked Bob, his head peeking out from the cramped kitchenette.

'Please.' Jenny felt she had to be positive about MALPASO for Bob's sake.

'It's cosy.'

'It's practical. And if I go back to Scotland for this thing with Harry Patterson, I'll take it with me.' He sounded matter of fact, looking for the positives.

Reference to a possible future in Scotland unlocked several

thoughts for Jenny.

When should they see each other again? Would the relationship they embarked on have a chance? If so, would it all work out in Scotland if they took up Harry's offer?

Placing a tray with two mugs of tea and some biscuits on the table, Bob slipped into the seat facing Jenny.

Sipping their drinks silently, the couple wondered who would speak first. It all felt a little uncomfortable – all too real since the holiday was over.

The fuel of their romance seemed to have run dry, thought Jenny. Or was it just the transition of returning to their ordinary existence?

Determined not to give in easily, Jenny made Bob an offer. 'Why don't you come up and stay with me for the weekend. We both have things to do this week. You no doubt will need to sort things out with Scotia Tours.'

'Yeah, I do,' he paused. 'I would like to come and see you.'

They were both pleased that an arrangement was now in place for them both to meet in a few days time.

On her return journey, heading north on the M1, Jenny slipped *The Very Best Of Supertramp* into the car's CD player. Cranking up the volume, she lost herself in the music. *Goodbye Stranger* reminded her of Bob. Well how Bob used to be, until he met her.

But it was *From Now On* which gave her hope. From the opening piano chords, into the laconic vocals, the song's sad beginning, building steadily and surely with lyrics turning upbeat to the theme of finding romance and a shared world.

The words, *I guess it will always have to be, living in a fantasy, it's you for you, and me for me, from now on*, swept the climax of the song to a positive finish.

The song brought forth images of Bob, herself, and a coach-load of trippers wending their way through the Scottish uplands on a beautiful sunny day, singing the song together.

From now on, she thought, it was going her way...from now on.

Chapter Twenty-one

'So what's he like?' asked Margaret, eager to know everything about her sister's holiday romance.

The department store cafeteria was half full, typical for mid-week in Leeds city centre.

'I don't know where to begin,' replied Jenny stirring her filter coffee, her mind swimming with images of Bob; some she could not share due to their explicit nature.

Margaret was not as liberal as her sister. Two years senior to Jenny, she looked older than her age. She was one of these people who, when they turned forty, took the conscious decision to become sensible and middle aged.

Margaret had never really made the effort to keep up with changing fashions anyway, but she also let herself go a little too. But then again her husband Steve had taken the same route, so 'why bother' had been Margaret's excuse.

Jenny had given up trying to coax her sibling to do more with her looks. Seeing her puff and pant as they climbed the car-park stairs, brought Jenny close to saying something, but she knew it would upset the sister whom she dearly loved.

At school, Jenny had looked up to Margaret with pride. The robust girl had been a popular student and captain of the girl's hockey team.

Steve had to take some of the blame, mused Jenny. He was more interested in satellite television programmes than his wife's appearance.

Margaret's big warm smile shone out from her round face. A smile directly connected to a big warm heart.

After the local paper expose, Margaret was the first person Jenny went to, knowing she would not judge. Margaret didn't approve, but caring about her sister was more important.

'I have a photograph,' replied Jenny fishing out a print of Bob, placing it on the table. It was the one of the couple in Oban, standing on the esplanade in the evening.

'A good-looking man,' stated Margaret. 'You two look so relaxed together, as if you've been together for a while.'

Jenny nodded, looking at the photograph. She had thought the same when picking up the prints the day before.

'He's in Chesterfield you said. That's not far. You can keep in touch,' said Margaret looking at her chocolate éclair.

'Well that's just it! He might be moving to Scotland.'

'Oh well, you can visit. You loved it up there.' The éclair began its journey to Margaret's mouth.

'It might be easier than that.' Jenny braced herself for her sister's reaction to telling her about the possible move north.

'What do you mean?'

'I've been offered a job in Scotland, working for a hotelier who wants Bob to do coach tours.'

Margaret's eyebrows darted upwards. Her mouth stopped moving around the sweet cake. She gulped down a mouthful before replying.

'You're leaving Yorkshire to go to Scotland? Starting a new life, a new job, a new relationship with a man you barely know?'

Jenny nodded. This was not going well.

'I think it's wonderful! A wonderful idea and you should go for it.' Margaret's tone was genuine, with a smile and a tear in her eye, she reached out for Jenny's hand and squeezed it. 'I'll miss you, I really will, but I can visit. How exciting!'

Relief spun through Jenny.

'You and Steve can come and visit. It's beautiful; you really have to see it. I can show you both around!'

'Who said anything about Steve. I'll have no fun if he comes along. I'm coming on my own. Look at the fun you had!'

They both laughed.

Jenny would miss these shopping trips with her sister. They got up to leave a few minutes later. As they left, Margaret took her by the arm.

'Look, Jenny, this sounds like another chance for you. You're still young enough to give something like this a try. Losing John was hard I know, but your life can go on. Even if this Bob guy doesn't work out, the change of life in Scotland would be good. And if the worst comes to the worst, you can always come back here.'

Jenny put her arms around her sister. They hugged.

'Go for it girl!' said Margaret tenderly.

Tears in both their eyes, Jenny wiped a little chocolate smudge from her sister's cheek.

Nerves. First date nerves prickled through Jenny. How ridiculous, she thought. Ever since late afternoon on the Friday of Bob's arrival, she had felt a little anxious about their meeting. She wanted it to be good. A perfect weekend full of passion, the passion they had experienced in Scotland. Her anxiety was brought on by the thought of no passion – the spark having disappeared – just nothing.

As each day passed, she had missed him a little more. The telephone conversations and the texts were all positive; missing you, looking forward to the weekend, can't wait to see you, can't stop thinking of you.

Final proof would be tonight.

It was a lovely late summer evening, and Jenny had taken plenty of time to get ready for her man; a long soak in the bath, shaving her legs, scented bath oils permeating the air, spending ages on her hair, and as long again on her make-up, and on deciding what to wear.

The final decision was a viscose silver grey v-neck tunic, with white boot-cut trousers. Slipping into smart mules, Jenny looked at herself in the full-length mirror in the corner of the bedroom.

She still had it. She still looked good. Jenny had dreaded her forties, remembering how her mother's features began to change; the thickening middle, the slippage to her facial features, nature sapping her firmness.

But she had her father's genes – he had one of those faces, which never seemed to age. Now, in her forties, expecting her looks to diminish, she was staring at a woman who could pass for late thirties.

Last to be applied, but most important, was the little cross that was now her favourite piece of jewellery, rarely taken off. She gave it a kiss.

After a few squirts of perfume, she went down to the kitchen to check on the meal she had cooked for Bob.

Jenny was a competent cook, but not the most daring. Scanning her recipe books the day before, she settled on a meal that could be prepared prior to her guest's arrival. She did not want to be wasting time in the kitchen, or getting all steamed up pulling it all together. She wanted to look sleek and desirable at all times.

The meal consisted of hot tomato mozzarella salad to start, followed by honey orange glazed chicken, served with new potatoes, and fresh vegetables. The table was set in the dining room, best place mats and crystal wine glasses.

With Supertramp playing on the CD player, she stood at the patio doors, staring down the garden, holding a whisky, the malty aroma reminding her of Scotland.

Checking her watch, it was just after seven. Where was he?

Too fidgety to sit down, she checked on the meal again. It was fine, the enticing tang of the chicken floated into the air as she closed the oven door.

Slipping her hand between her legs to adjust the new black silk knickers, she felt her wetness. He better show up, she thought, even if it was just for sex!

Jenny was imagining Bob's fingers inside her when the doorbell rang. Quickly, she checked how she looked in the hall mirror.

Swinging the front door open, Bob stood smartly dressed in

249

a light suit and a pale blue shirt with cuff links. He smelt of aftershave.

Holding a bottle of red wine and a bunch of lilies, his face beaming said it all. He was glad to see her.

'Come in, come in,' she said, barely able to conceal her excitement.

Without saying a word, he put his finger to her mouth to indicate no more words were required.

Closing the front door, placing the flowers and wine on the floor, he took her by the hand up to the bedroom.

Passion was well and truly alive! Intense lovemaking, powered by an aching desire satisfied the couple's lust for each other. But it was more than lust. It was Jenny and Bob turning on a fused axis of the physical and the emotional.

They climaxed quickly and in union. Eager to sate their appetite, they took each other partially dressed.

It was good, fucking amazingly good – enough sparks to make an arsonist happy.

Ideal. I-fucking-deal! didn't seem to do their lovemaking justice anymore thought Bob, he needed a new mental phrase – *I-fuuuuuuucccccckkkkkiiiing-deal!*

The food was good too. 'This is excellent,' said Bob, clearing his plate, sitting opposite Jenny in his boxer shorts and shirt. His hair a little tussled, cheeks flushed.

'I'm glad you enjoyed it.' She too had been ravenous after their session in the bedroom. Her short light dressing-gown showed off her gleaming legs.

As she got up to clear the table, Bob pulled her onto his lap sideways. Her dressing gown rode up, his right hand supported her back, his left hand gently placed on her upper left thigh.

'I want you, Jenny.' His voice was loaded with emotion, looking into her eyes. 'I want you for good!'

They kissed.

Jenny had been hoping for Bob to express himself in this way, thinking it would have been later in the weekend.

'I feel the same. I want to make a go of this too.'

A moment sealed.

'And Scotland?' she asked.

'That too if you want to?'

'I do. I do!' She pushed her hand through his hair. 'I want the two of us to make a go of it. I want to help you.'

'Help me?' he moved his hand further up her thigh, to the cleft between her legs.

'Help you get that bus, get you started, get you back on the road.'

There was a moment's silence.

'It's a lot of money,' said Bob, pursing his lips.

'It'll be a loan, if that makes you feel better about it?'

He considered the offer for a few seconds, as he pushed his index finger into her wetness.

'And what about the rate of interest?' His finger was advancing and retreating rhythmically inside her.

'Let's say you've just started paying it right now.'

'Well, if that's how I'm going to pay interest, I never want to pay off the loan!'

They had a great weekend. No, a brilliant weekend! It was one to be remembered, everything falling into place; a drive into the Dales, a long walk, followed by a cozy pub lunch, meeting up with a couple of Jenny's close friends. Bob charming them all, including Margaret.

Sunday morning, lazing in bed, some more passionate lovemaking, down to Jenny's local pub for a roast lunch. Convincing Bob to stay Sunday night, which was not too hard. Getting a video from the local rental store, but only getting half way through it before rolling around together on the couch.

Holding each other, drained, satisfied, finished in the after-burn of lovemaking. Slipping into a semi-awake haze that spent lovers find themselves basking in.

Consuming each other like this was exhausting, thought Jenny, but how alive she felt. *Long may it continue* thought Bob.

251

'I'm serious about Scotland,' whispered Jenny from her listless state.

'Same here.'

'We'll be happy, won't we?'

'Sure we will, as long as we have each other,' he replied.

'I'm too old to be chasing dreams.'

Jenny nuzzled into Bob's chest.

'One last go on the merry-go round, my darling. But it's our merry-go round,' affirmed the coach driver, enjoying the new found sensation of being in love. He'd never imagined it possible for the loner he was.

Jenny felt she was absorbing his easy confidence as she pressed against him, like heat rising from sun soaked rocks, passing into the flesh and bones of a sunbather.

Six Months Later

Chapter Twenty-two

The watery February sunshine slid through the clouds onto the motorway.

The M62 was not too busy, Saturday football traffic mostly. Jenny's car was packed with the essential possessions for her new life in Scotland; clothes, crates of books and CDs, her midi hi-fi centre, and some sentimental knick-knacks.

There was a tearful farewell from Margaret, with whom she had been staying for a week.

The last six months had flown past with so much to do in preparation for her new life in Scotland. Taking a local taxi job in Chesterfield, Bob had been able to see her every second weekend, driving up to Yorkshire on a Friday evening, returning on a Sunday.

Enrolling in a twelve week tourism course at her local college, Jenny had been busy familiarising herself with the new industry she would be working in.

There had been a four-day trip to Oban to meet with Harry Patterson in October to agree the details of Jenny's new job, and for Bob to sign the business contract to provide the coach tour service for the Patterson hotels. It was also on this visit she was informed by Harry that Chalky had decided to join his management team. Jenny was looking forward to meeting him again, someone else new to the area.

Harry took them on a tour around his new hotel in Fort William, The Nevis Grange, still being refurbished.

The hotelier pointed out the half-constructed offices, where Jenny would have a desk, including a wonderful view across Loch Linnhe. A spot for Bob's static caravan was also arranged behind the hotel, at the end of a track, overlooking some fields. Jenny could live in the hotel, if she desired, offered Harry. The couple would decide on the domestic arrangements when they arrived in the new year.

As it turned out Bob had to come north three weeks earlier than Jenny with his static on a large truck. A truck-owner friend of Bob's could only transport the caravan in January. Some casual work in the near-completed Nevis Grange gave Bob some money as he waited for Jenny and the coach to arrive.

The coach was still at Johnstones Coaches in central Scotland. Bob had used the redundancy money as a down payment to secure the vehicle. Billy Johnstone agreed to store it over the winter on the understanding the final payment would be made in February.

The bankers draft in Jenny's handbag for forty thousand pounds was for just this purpose, finding the money in part from the sale of her house.

Over the six months, despite being caught up in the euphoria of romance, she had her moments of doubt about committing to the 'Scottish Expedition', her descriptive term for the move north of the border.

The relationship with Bob still burned brightly, probably helped by only seeing each other every second weekend. The real test was yet to come when they would be living and working together.

It might be an idea at first to live in the Nevis Grange in a room in the staff quarters as Harry had suggested, mused Jenny while driving. The thought of staying in Bob's cramped static caravan in winter – not the most comfortable residence – was not entirely appealing. Through time no doubt, they would get a house together, ideally a cottage, maybe one of those crofting places.

Communication in the last three weeks had been sporadic. Bob was busy with Harry, getting the hotel ready to open for

March 1st. Text messages and mobile phone conversations were short, but sweet.

She had missed him. But there were times she knew *she* missed him more, than *he* missed her. Jenny put this down to the man's independence; he'd been on his own for a long time. Bob had spoken of the need for solitude now and again. But most men were like this; her late husband had gone night fishing for just this very reason.

Supertramp's From Now On came on through the car audio system, prompting her to sing along. The image of the full coach returned again – the musical fantasy.

Turning onto the M1, the signs read: Carlisle 92 miles. She would be in Scotland in two hours, at Billy Johnstones in over three hours and at the little bed and breakfast in Tarbert in five to six hours.

Attempting the entire trip in limited daylight hours was too much. Anyway she wanted to be fresh when arriving to surprise Bob – he was expecting her to show the following day. A smile crossed Jenny's face at the thought of the look on his face when the knock on the static door turned out to be his lover; she could hardly wait.

Motorway driving never really intimidated Jenny like some people. She enjoyed the steady pulse of the lanes, moving in between the traffic, pondering the other vehicles occupants' reasons to journey.

The commercial travellers were easy to spot; typical fleet saloon cars, the single male or female passenger, pressed shirts and a sense of purpose to their expressions.

In the main it was leisure and pleasure traffic; many families, some carrying grandparents, sitting cramped in the rear with the grandchildren. Some fraught expressions for the family trippers, impatient children, fathers irritated with yet another toilet stop, mothers trying to keep the peace.

It had struck Jenny on previous journeys that the travellers who seemed the most relaxed and happy were the young and old.

Boyfriends and girlfriends away for the weekend, visiting

parents, seeing friends, enjoying each other's company – a girl's hand on her boy's neck, gently massaging away the strain of the driving.

Retired grey-haired couples taking a break, some with caravans, some with dogs, putting along serenely. With their work lives over, every day was Saturday, and these excursions were promised to each other in pre-retirement days.

In the past, Jenny had not really taken much notice of coaches while driving. But now, she checked them out. Was the livery attractive, sleek and eye-catching?

Did the passengers look happy or bored? At service stations, how attentive were the guides with the party?

Making mental notes to make sure her and Bob's service would be of the highest quality. Detail, detail, detail; this was the key in providing the type of service they could be proud of.

Crossing the border into Scotland, the sign read: Glasgow 89 miles. Jenny gave a little whoop of joy.

The Cumbria scenery of arable uplands now gave way to the more rugged landscape of the winter-weathered Scottish Lowlands. Climbing up through the Moffat hills, Jenny felt good to be in her adopted homeland again, soaking up its expanse.

She was making good time, but she had to – Billy Johnstone had made arrangements to meet her at his business premises for 1.30 p.m.

By 1.15 p.m., she was turning into his site on the Bellshill trading estate. Billy was there waiting, sitting at his old desk, reading the *Daily Record*. He was smoking on a brand of cigarette Jenny had only ever seen in Scotland.

'On your own?' asked Billy, smoke swirling around his tussle of wiry grey hair.

'Bob is up north already.'

'I thought he would be here to drive the bus away?'

'He will. I'm bringing him down on Tuesday. There will be no holding him back. Believe me!'

It only took twenty minutes to complete the paper work,

before Jenny handed over the the final payment on the coach. Pressing the ignition keys into her hand, Billy wished her and Bob all the best for their new venture – a genuine sentiment, through a tough, gruff Glasgow accent.

Back on the road, Supertramp continued to score the journey north. Singing along, she felt on top of the world, riding high on all the promise the future could bring, with the man she was in love with and the coach he would drive.

Slipping through Glasgow took no time at all and soon she was wending her way up the A82 to Loch Lomond – the beginning of the Highlands. Fir-tree cloaked slopes ushered Jenny onwards in her climb north. Stopping for a coffee and a sandwich, she checked the roadmap. Another half an hour and she would be at Tarbet. Tiredness was seeping in and Jenny was pleased she had done the right thing to break the journey. The remaining sixty-nine miles would take two hours tomorrow morning, allowing her to arrive fresh.

It was just after 4.00 p.m. when Jenny pulled into the bed and breakfast in Tarbet. Dusk was settling across the little village.

Mrs Wilson, a cheery widow in her mid sixties with white hair and a ready smile, made Jenny feel very welcome. She also cooked a good chicken pie and told great stories of her late husband's adventures on the high seas as a naval officer.

Turning in at 11.00 p.m., a few malt whiskies sloshing around inside, Jenny fell asleep quickly, but not before she set the little travel alarm for 6.00 a.m.

Mr Sinclair – are you in for a surprise tomorrow?

It was still dark when the English woman left Mrs Wilson's just after 7.00 a.m., the bed and breakfast owner braving the frosty morning to wave off her only guest.

The dawn broke half an hour later in a spectacular red glow over the craggy peaks as Jenny motored through a sleepy Crianlarich. The road sign in the village read: Fort William 53 miles.

Only a few cars were present at this time of the morning on the road, traversing across a wilderness of moorland, open and expansive with a frosty overcoat. The descent into Glencoe was an eerie experience after travelling across the unprotected heath. Steep, jagged rock faces hemmed Jenny's little hatch car, as she wound her way down the valley, careful on the breaks, concerned about black ice.

The road sign read Fort William 16 miles as she pulled through Ballachulish, her heart quickening at the thought of sneaking a surprise on Bob shortly.

Imagining him asleep, she would quietly enter the static caravan, undress and slip into bed. The thought brought some tingling to her body.

By the side of the road, a sign read, *Nevis Range Hotel – Opening Soon*. A further pulse of energy shot through Jenny, feeling the new future move towards her, nearing to the point of embrace.

A grin creased her face. She had probably been smiling since leaving Mrs Wilson's, thought Jenny. There was another sign for the Nevis Range Hotel – it stood 100 metres on the right.

Swinging through the sandstone pillared gate, she swept up the drive towards the grey granite country house. The stately appearance of the building reflected near completion of the construction work; much improved since Jenny had seen the hotel the previous October.

Remembering the way around the back of the establishment, she located the track, which led to a clearing in the fir wood where Bob's static caravan was parked.

Crawling along the track, her heart pumping with excitement, the caravan came into view. A green Landrover sat next to the static. He must have borrowed it from Harry.

Parking up, Jenny checked her make-up in the mirror. She was ready!

A seagull screeched a call in the air, the only noise to be heard on this still morning.

Making sure not to slam the car door, she walked towards the caravan, the rear of which faced down the track entrance. The front end was pitched, looking out across some fields that sloped downwards towards a small stream. The view beyond the stream was of a steep slope rising up into the uplands of Glen Nevis.

Because the clearing ground sloped away too, the caravan required securing to a thick steel post staked in the ground with a heavy metal chain on the tow-bar. The rear of the unit was resting on the earth while the front half sat high above the slope. Two wooden blocks wedged the wheels in place, preventing Bob's home from tumbling down into the stream.

Approaching the door, Jenny hoped it would be unlocked.

With her hand on the door handle, ready to turn, Bob's shout from inside froze Jenny to the spot.

'Put it in…that's it…yes, oh yes…a little more…oh that's fucking good!'

Seconds passed.

'Harder …fuck me harder!' came a woman's cry.

Jenny thought she was going to collapse as a flush of nausea engulfed her frozen state; she flopped against the side of the van, the cold surface against her cheek.

She heard a woman's voice again.

'Fuck his ass…fuck it!' She sounded American.

Edging along the side of the caravan, Jenny prayed for one thing; *Bob was watching a porno video.* She knew he owned them, having seen a brown jiffy bag at the caravan back in Derbyshire and confronting him about women still sending their underwear. He'd opened the package to reveal a video with the title, *Hot 'N' Horny Housewives 7.* They even watched it together, but Jenny got bored.

Please let this be a pornographic video, with Bob sitting, trousers around his ankles, please!

The front side window would have let Jenny see into the living room, if the caravan had not been positioned on a slope. As Jenny neared the window, she found herself looking up at the pane of glass, not through it.

Moving back from the caravan onto higher ground, she hoped to get a view into the static. A fir tree pushed against her back, but she now had an accessible view through the open-curtained static.

Jenny now felt she was watching a scene from a movie – disembodied from what was taking place on the screen.

A naked woman was on all fours on top of the formica table. The woman was facing forward, out towards the view of the stream and the glen. Bob was taking her from behind, standing, clasping her hips, thrusting into her with furious strokes.

Jenny looked away, reviled at what she saw, choking back the sickness which wanted to explode from inside.

Looking back again, seeing Bob's big grin, the short-haired brunette being fucked in an animalistic way, Jenny noticed something else. A hand gripping Bob's left buttock; there was someone behind him, not pressed against him, but helping with the rhythmic sexual act Bob was performing. This person was obscured from Jenny's restricted vision, not in sight of the window.

The *bastard* had two women in there.

Her legs felt like giving way. Jenny scrambled back towards the car, tears beginning to flow, stinging her eyes, breathing rapidly, her heart banging on her rib cage.

It must have been the sight of the sledge hammer, laying on the ground near the tow bar of the caravan, which turned Jenny's twisting emotions from flight to fight, converting a panic strewn retreat to something quite the opposite – REVENGE.

Picking up the heavy instrument, Jenny's first thought was to smash her way through the caravan, wrecking havoc, scaring the women and pounding Bob.

But Jenny received a flash of an idea with her mounting rage. Aided by pumping adrenaline, she slipped under the caravan to the sound of muffled sexual cries from above.

Clearness of thought had returned, inciting a quick understanding of what she wanted to achieve in her quest for revenge.

Swinging the hammer at the wooden blocks, wedged under the wheels, she was counting on the strain of the caravan's load being taken by the steel post attached to the tow bar.

Her thinking was correct – a couple of knocks with the sledge hammer and the blocks were knocked free, skidding down the slope.

There was a cry from inside the static.

'Ram it up her...ram it, ram it!'

The woman's voice sounded familiar, but Jenny could not place it. Returning to the rear of the caravan, she wiped the sweat from her brow and lifted the heavy hammer high to swing it down onto the steel post, hoping it would drive further into the ground, popping the release of the coiled metal chain.

The post gave a clang of metal on metal and stayed put.

Knock the chain upwards – bring it off the post, the thought flashed.

Three swings later, and one link of chain held precariously at the top of the post. Gripping the shaft of the sledge hammer, sweat trickling into her eyes, Jenny found a few fitting words for the situation.

'I name this ship Bastard Bob and wish ill on all who fucking sail in her!' exclaimed Jenny as the final swing of the hammer dislodged the chain.

Malpaso, detached from its mooring, began the rumbling descent down the slope towards the stream.

Picking up momentum with each metre travelled, the rear dragging on the ground at first, then the front pitching forward, the lumbering caravan managed to pick speed as it barrelled down the hill towards the strip of water at the bottom of the slope. Brought to a stop as the undercarriage dropped into the stream with a shuddering screech, the metal frame groaned as it bore the strain of such a sudden halt.

This was a defining moment for Jenny as she would recount in the months and years to follow. As the caravan careered off down a Scottish hillside, this was a moment of release – of standing up to adversity at the time it faced you, not running away, but taking it head on!

It was also the moment, it fully struck home what she had just done in a fit of anger as the caravan door swung open, and a figure stumbled out of the crashed home and crumpled onto the grass – Jenny felt a lurch in her stomach.

Bounding down the slope, Jenny was at the naked woman's side in seconds. Skye Mackenzie was dazed and confused with a cut above her right eye. Her sleek naked form was beginning to shiver on the frosty floor.

'Fuck!' said Jenny, with the shock of finding Skye in this situation, injured, concussed, prostate in the field. Skye was trying to focus, eyelids fluttering.

'Skye, are you okay?' came an American woman's cry from inside.

Entering the caravan, Jenny saw the naked woman Bob had been screwing, down the far end, hunched over him. He too was still naked, huddled up in a ball on the floor, writhing in pain.

'Thank God, some help!' the American female exclaimed, turning her head to see Jenny.

The front window was knocked out; clean frosty air blew in, mingling with the smell of sex and sweat – the place stank.

Help. They needed help.

Bob's moans indicated excruciating pain; his face was white, his eyes clenched shut, holding his abdomen.

'He's injured, and it looks bad. It must be internal,' said the American, glancing at Jenny who joined her at Bob's side.

She was mid forties, with a tanned, slim, sinewy, over-aerobicised body, still glistening with sweat.

'We need to get him to a hospital,' said Jenny, regretting her actions – a little.

'Could it be his heart?' asked the American fearfully.

'He would be holding his chest,' replied Jenny. She sensed somebody behind her; it was Skye, staggering, supporting herself against a tall cupboard. Her head was clearing, her eyes scanning around the floor of the caravan, looking for something.

'It's the dildo!' Skye spluttered.

'Dildo?' queried Jenny.

Skye pulled on a denim shirt over her shivering body.

'Are you sure?' asked the American.

'What the fuck are you talking about?' exclaimed Jenny.

'It's not here, and I had it up his ass before we crashed!' retorted Skye still scanning the caravan for the instrument. 'Where else could it be? That's why he's in such pain,' proposed Skye, 'he's got a fucking dildo stuck inside him!'

The women, now realising the cause of Bob's injury, looked at the writhing man on the floor – a man who could barely speak because of the searing pain inhabiting his rectal passage.

'Cassia, check to see if you can see the end of it,' suggested Skye, conscious of the trickle of blood at her temple from the cut above her eye.

Cassia carefully moved Bob onto his side, still in the foetal position. He let out a shriek of pain. Jenny found it strange to watch this stranger look up Bob's crack, gently prising his buttocks apart to look directly into his anus.

'I can't see it. His ass is closed, it must be right inside!' reported Cassia, a pained expression on her face.

'We'd better get him to a hospital,' said Jenny, marshalling them into action.

Cassia pulled on her jeans and a top as Skye found her green combat trousers.

Pulling Bob to his feet, with a cry of pain, Cassia and Skye took one arm each around their shoulders and with shuffling steps moved him to the door.

Finding his dressing-gown, Jenny draped it round his shoulders, tying the middle with the cord as best she could round his hunched body. They got him outside and started making their way up the field to the clearing.

Tears were rolling down Bob's ashen white face. Each step, sending a piercing shot of torturous pain through his groin and abdomen. It took a few minutes to get him to Jenny's car. Realising it was full of luggage and cardboard boxes, she turned to Skye for help.

'Is that your Landrover?'

Skye nodded, making her way to the vehicle as Jenny got the tailgate down.

Dragging forward, and with the help from the three women, Bob crawled inside the back of the vehicle. Cassia joined him, making sure he was as comfortable as he could be on the cold metal floor.

Skye jumped into the driver's seat, Jenny into the passenger's. The diesel engine cut into life, and they moved back down the track. Peering through the metal grill that separated the cabin from the rear of the vehicle, Jenny could see Cassia cradling Bob's head as they clipped down the bumpy road.

'Who is she?' asked Jenny, firing the question at Skye.

'She's my counsellor. My sex counsellor.'

A beat of silence as Jenny digested the information.

'Tell me, having sex with your counsellor – is that part of the fucking therapy?' asked Jenny, her voice traced with anger, incredulous at this discovery.

'Don't you remember, Jenny; you suggested I see someone, a professional. I took your advice!' retorted Skye. 'Can you do something about this blood?'

The trickle of blood had traced its way into Skye's left eye, and was beginning to sting. Her hands gripped the steering wheel.

Looking through the glove box, Jenny found a packet of tissues, which she ripped open. Dabbing and soaking up the blood from Skye's temple, Jenny was struck again at the surreal element of the morning's events.

What was it with this young woman – every time their paths crossed – shit happened!

The Landrover lurched round a corner, throwing Jenny into the passenger door.

'We want to get there in one piece!' exclaimed Jenny.

Skye looked straight ahead, concentrating on the driving as she wound her way through narrow streets to Fort William hospital.

There was a screech of brakes as the Landrover tore into

the hospital car park. Backing up into the ambulance bay, Jenny was out of the vehicle and into the building in seconds, running for help.

Dropping the tailgate, Skye turned to see two female nurses with a flatbed trolley come through the A&E entrance doors.

The blue-uniformed nurses, with the aid of Cassia, slipped Bob onto the trolley.

'What's his injury,' asked the blonde nurse, her heavy-set features displayed a no nonsense demeanour.

Jenny and Skye looked at each other. Cassia gave them the answer; she obviously had some experience of this type of thing from her Californian patients.

'He's had an accident with a cylindrical tube type object, about six inches long. It's lodged inside his rectal passage.'

The two nurses did not bat an eyelid as they sped their new charge off into the hospital.

'I need a coffee,' said Cassia. 'Is there a coffee shop?'

'There's a vending machine,' replied Skye.

After parking the Landrover up in the car park, Skye led Jenny and Cassia to the waiting room.

Coffees in hand, the three women took a seat each. The sound of hospital life filtered through the open door, people being helped and treated, hurried doctors and nurses passing along corridors.

A few minutes' silence passed.

Jenny looked at the floor, contemplating the shattered dream of the Scottish Expedition. The new world was in sight, only for the good ship to run aground on flotsam of jagged ice. The ship was sinking, with no survivors. The blue and white tiled floor stared back, the smell of disinfectant pervaded the air, but could not take away the awful taste of betrayal in her mouth.

Addressing Skye, Jenny launched some questions, eager to find answers.

'How long has this been going on?'

Taking a sip of coffee, Skye replied in a matter of fact tone. 'Last night. This morning was the first time. We met him in a bar by chance. Not much more to tell. The three of us got drunk and he invited us back to his trailer.'

Jenny flinched.

'Was there any mention of me?' asked Jenny.

'He didn't mention you,' offered Cassia, her tone apologetic. 'I'm really sorry, I feel terrible for all that's happened. I know what sexual betrayal feels like!'

'Well that's your stock and trade, isn't it!' quipped Jenny acidly.

'No need to apologise, Cassia. Jenny's had her revenge. Who do you think caused the caravan to crash!'

Inflamed at the audacity of Skye's remark, Jenny stood up, but was unsure of how to react. One part of her wanted to punch the woman for the second time, another wanted to crumple into a sobbing heap. Where do you put such sorrow, thought Jenny. At this moment she wanted so much a pair of arms around her – her spirit seeking refuge in another's crevice of humanity.

A young red-haired doctor entered with a wry grin on his face. Cassia and Skye stood up, waiting to hear the verdict with Jenny.

'Who do I give this to?' asked the doctor, offering a transparent polythene bag with a pink dildo inside.

'I'll take it,' said Skye, extending her right hand and taking the sex tool.

'How is he?' asked Cassia genuinely.

'Experiencing quite a bit of discomfort from the internal bruising, but there's no permanent damage. A few days rest at home and he will be as good as new. Some painkillers will help.' The doctor turned and left the room.

'He hasn't got a home now!' quipped Skye.

It was the way she delivered the sentence, revealing so much to Jenny about the situation.

'This is all about you getting your own back at me for last summer, isn't it, Skye? You're the one who knows all about revenge!'

Skye's face tightened.

'We need to stay calm,' implored Cassia, stepping between Jenny and Skye.

'We're taking Bob back with us. He can rest up at Ardnish House,' stated Skye defiantly.

'Your welcome to the *bastard*. I'm sure the lot of you can fuck each other senseless!' shouted Jenny, making for the door. As she turned to leave the room, she fired off one more insulting bolt, drawing on the most abusive terms she could find.

'I'm sure you'll have such fun, Skye, I can just imagine it – all of you, Bob and your father fucking day and night...it's not just having one old man inside you...that's not enough...you need two old cocks inside you!'

Storming down the corridor, Jenny heard an almost animal cry from the waiting room. A trace of satisfaction seared through Jenny – two can play at the foul-mouthed insult game, she thought.

Locating a public phone in reception, Jenny dialled for a taxi to take her to The Nevis Range.

As she waited outside, three figures caught her eye on the other side of the car park. Bob was being ushered in a blue dressing-gown to the Landrover by Cassia and Skye. His gait was pathetic as he shuffled along, slightly bent. While Skye helped him into the passenger seat, Cassia ran over to Jenny.

Slightly out of breath, she spoke quickly.

'I know you don't believe me, but I'm truly sorry.' Cassia put her hand on Jenny's shoulder. Jenny winced and the American woman retracted her hand.

'There's something else you need to know,' continued the woman. 'It's about Mackenzie...he died last October. It was very sudden.'

The Landrover horn sounded.

Cassia ran back to the waiting vehicle and hopped in – it sped off in a trail of blue diesel fumes.

Chapter Twenty-three

The Nevis Grange was coming to life as Jenny strode into reception. Although it was Sunday, the pressure was on the staff and builders to be finished for the official opening at the end of the month. Painters and decorators were busy putting the finishing touches to the establishment.

Harry Patterson, like a marshalling admiral, was picking out the crew who would help sail this new ship into the waters of Scottish tourism.

With the smell of fresh paint in the air, Jenny walked through to the offices at the rear of the hotel.

Some sort of remote-control motor was driving her limbs, pushing her forward, while her brain functioned at a minimum sensory level; processing her surroundings to allow basic human operation and co-ordination.

Survival instincts had taken over, overriding her reaction to the traumatic events of the early morning. Continue as normal for the moment, she'd told herself.

Entering the open-plan office area, Jenny saw Harry supervising the locations of four desks, which would fill the room. Two young men in overalls were being given the run around.

'Jenny!' exclaimed Harry, pleased to see her, a big smile flashing across his tanned face. 'What are you doing here? I expected you tomorrow?'

'I thought I would avoid the traffic,' she replied, amazed she had found words to reply.

'Excellent,' said Harry, giving her a welcoming hug. Little

did he realise, she could have fallen into his frame and wept like a baby.

But he did feel her hold a second too long and sensed something was up. He took in her eyes, expressing concern at their redness.

'Are you okay? You look tired?'

'Yes. It's been a long drive. I'll be fine.'

'Here is your desk as we agreed,' replied Harry, indicating towards the window.

Walking over to it, the two of them stared out at the view across Loch Linnhe, the surface shimmering under the watery sun of the February morning.

'So, are you ready for this?' asked Harry.

Silence hung in the air. She felt she was going to drop to the floor.

'Where are my manners. Let me get you a chair. Would you like a tea or coffee?

'Coffee, please,' she replied, forcing a smile.

Harry dialled the kitchen and ordered. As soon as he replaced the receiver, his mobile phone rang and he was caught up in a call for a few minutes. Jenny was relieved to be spared his enthusiasm for the moment.

'Here you go – one coffee for the weary traveller,' said Chalky placing a cup on the desk.

'Hi. How are you?' asked Jenny, pleased to see him.

'I'm fine. Busy getting the kitchen up and running.' He sat on the edge of the desk. 'So I take it you've just arrived?'

'Yes.' She wanted to add and I'm just about to leave too.

Harry had finished his call and joined the two of them.

'After you've had your caffeine injection, I'll show you around. There are big improvements since you were last here.'

She wanted to tell him not to bother as she would not be staying, but the ebullient hotelier's mood was too much for her.

A few minutes later, he was guiding her through the hotel.

For someone who came across as brash and flash, Harry had taste when it came to fitting out a hotel.

The gentle colour scheme could not be called bland. A blend of old and new, giving visitors a sense of the past with the comfort of the modern. The furniture was subtle, with a hint of antique. The soft furnishings were stately, but without grandeur. Throughout the building, a Celtic crest with the wording *Caledonian Hotel Group* advertised its ownership.

Sweeping through the building, Harry's pride at his new flagship hotel was obvious.

As they reached the top floor, where the staff quarters were located, Harry asked a question.

'Jenny, have you thought about your living arrangements? I know you were considering moving in with Bob.'

She felt a lump in her throat, a slight tremble in her lip at the mention of his name.

Harry continued. 'Before you answer, I want you take a look at this room...it's yours if you want it.'

He pushed open the door of room 78 to reveal spacious living quarters. An airy chamber with a double-aspect window in the corner, looking out of the rear of the hotel onto a wooded glen; the same view Bob had from his static.

'I don't know what to say,' blurted Jenny, feeling a wave of confusion push in over her senses.

'No doubt you will want to discuss it with Bob, but the room is only designed for one. He'll need to stay in his caravan.'

'I'd like to put him up, but I don't have the space,' continued Harry, 'but he seems happy enough in his mobile home.'

'He won't be now,' Jenny found herself saying. 'Not since his front window fell out and the thing slipped into the stream.' She stayed in the bathroom so Harry couldn't read her expression.

'What happened? I was up there yesterday, it was okay!' replied Harry approaching the bathroom.

Jenny pushed the door closed, indicating privacy. 'I'll be out in a minute.' She had to think quickly, give him some story –

she did not want him to know the truth.

An idea sprang to mind as she flushed the toilet and rejoined Harry.

'It happened last night. One of his friends dropped him off from the pub. They were driving a Landrover and they bumped into the caravan. The next thing, it shot off down the hill.

'I'll get a couple of my men to sort it out,' expressed Harry, stabbing at his mobile phone. 'We'll have Bob back in his home before he knows it!'

So far, Harry had made her feel welcome and she appreciated his efforts. She could tell he wanted her to be part of his grand plans.

But could she be happy here after what had just happened? Her thoughts and feelings were in a state of flux. One second she wanted to flee; the next, to stay and not disappoint those who had faith in her.

She could hear Harry's instructions – her possessions were to be taken to room 78 from the car. Everything was going too fast.

Jenny waved at the hotelier, indicating she wanted to speak to him, but he continued speaking. Suddenly, he broke off to ask a question.

'Jimmy wants to know when the bus is coming? He's busy converting one of the stables into a coach garage and it won't be ready till Wednesday.'

The bus! The fucking bus! her bus! her bus and Bob's bus!

An invisible punch hit her in the stomach.

Harry looked concerned as she took a seat on the bed.

Everybody was expecting it to arrive, realised Jenny, a vehicle that had cost many thousands of pounds and to all intents and purposes was what her future dreams were built on!

'Are you okay?' he asked.

'Thursday. Tell him it will be here on Thursday,' whispered Jenny.

*

To keep busy, Jenny helped Harry for the rest of the Sunday, but when he took himself home at 6.00 p.m., as did all the staff, she found herself in her room alone. She thought about unpacking her belongings, but she could not face the task. Her new surroundings hemmed her in and she decided to keep moving, otherwise her fragile emotional state would disintegrate – an inevitability she knew would come, but not just yet.

The biting winter wind was colder than expected as she trudged through the dark streets of Fort William. She debated going into a pub, just to have other people around, even if they were strangers. But she was never comfortable venturing into one on her own.

Standing in a queue for fish and chips took up a couple of minutes. Overhearing people's conversation kept her mind occupied, but when she came to place her order, she didn't feel hungry and left the shop empty handed.

The town was deserted and her aimless wandering after an hour brought Jenny to the realisation she should make her way back to The Nevis Grange. She felt a terrible wave of loneliness sweep through her like a scythe felling vulnerable stalks.

It was at this point she passed the little town hall, light seeping from the windows. Inside she could see about twenty people sitting in rows, facing a woman. She could hear a wave of clapping through the panes of glass.

There was something open in their expressions, something inviting.

Entering the hall, a sea of faces looked around and friendly smiles beckoned her forward.

'Good evening. Take a seat,' invited a stout lady in a high-pitched Scottish accent.

Slipping into the back row, Jenny felt relieved to have joined this human enclave of sorts. Whatever its purpose – it was better than being on her own.

'Okay, Michael. Would you like to take the chair?'

Chalky stood up and took a chair facing the group. Taking

a deep breath, he spoke. 'Hello. I'm Michael White. I've not had too bad a week. I've been busy with my new job, and that's what I needed, to be kept busy. I get tempted when I've too much time on my hands.'

There was a murmur of agreement from the group.

'It's been seven months now since I relapsed, but I do feel stronger than I have in a long time. I've the chance of a fresh start here.' He gave a smile and some of the group clapped. He continued.

'As you know, some days are better than others, but I've come up with little ways to remind me of the other person I used to be – the man I don't want to be again, the...' Chalky broke off as he had now locked eyes with Jenny who was hanging on his every word. He finished his sentence, 'the drunk who was hell bent on ruining my life.'

A warm wave of applause filled the room, bathing Michael and Jenny equally.

'Jeez, it's cold. I never thought it would be as raw as this,' commented Chalky as they walked up the Nevis Grange drive.

'Visiting in summer is one thing. You can't imagine it gets so cold in the winter,' replied Jenny keeping her head bowed against the wind.

'Are you hungry?'

'I am as it happens.'

'I'll fix us up with something in no time.'

And he did, moving around the hotel kitchen with deft movement, inserting delicious smells into the air, juggling boiling pans across the range with ease. Jenny enjoyed watching him work, a distraction for her frayed nerves – the grinding anxiety she had felt all day seemed to be in some respite.

'I didn't realise the meeting was an AA one,' informed Jenny, 'I just fancied some company.'

'You've not been the first person to come to one of those meetings whose not an alcoholic. I think we send out these signals to people seeking somewhere to feel safe, a place where you can be accepted. That's what I get from the meetings.'

'How long were you an alcoholic?'

'I still am, but we use the term 'recovering' alcoholic. It's a part of me, being addicted to drink, but I know I'm allergic to it – and like any allergy – you learn how to treat it.' He was serving up their pasta dish, a creamy chicken meal for two.

'This looks yummy,' complimented Jenny.

They took a table in the empty restaurant.

'When you arrived this morning, you did not look very well, you looked upset,' Chalky said quietly.

Putting her fork down, Jenny put her head in her hands and tried to find the right words. An intense tearing inside consumed her, a shredding of her feelings, she convulsed into tears.

Chalky was at her side, his hands around her shoulders, feeling the uncorking of her repressed pain, an outpouring of hurt, a knot of anguish which could not have been tied any further.

Sobbing, Jenny clung to Chalky, and it was a few minutes before she could explain Bob's betrayal.

Fetching a bottle of brandy from the stores, Chalky poured Jenny a large glass and handed it to her. She gulped it back, feeling the numbing reassurance of its warm passage.

'I'm so glad you're here. I was dreading going to my room,' said Jenny, regaining some of her composure.

'I know how you're feeling, the dreadful emptiness – the fear of being on your own. It was one of the reasons I drank.'

Over the next hour, Jenny poured out the intense hurt she was feeling, while he topped up her glass, knowing she needed some sort of sedation.

'I need to go to bed now,' said Jenny eventually, wishing for the escape of sleep.

Chalky helped her to her room, making sure she took off her shoes before she rolled under the duvet. Switching off the lights, he made to go to the door when she spoke.

'I have something for you.'

Leaning down to hear her drowsy words, she gave him a kiss on the cheek.

'Thank you.'

Back in the kitchen he cleaned up before retiring for the night. Grabbing the brandy bottle, he emptied the remains down the sink and headed for his room.

As he opened up one of his kitchenette cupboards, he caught sight of one of the photographs pinned to the inside of the door. He stared at the image for a few seconds before climbing into bed.

He felt intense sympathy for Jenny, almost a sort of yearning. Her face kept coming back to him, but not the tear streaked features of the evening, but from last summer when he had first met her.

He had thought of her now and again; a sign – his sign to come here.

Chalky felt all the more sure he had done the right thing to journey north.

Bob tried to get comfortable in the little single bed in Skye's room at Ardnish House. His groin area throbbed incessantly. The dildo had inflamed the tissue lining of his rectal tract to such a degree, the pain felt like some medieval torture – like a hot poker up his arse.

Painkillers had some effect, but to Bob, it still felt like the cylindrical object was lodged inside him. He imagined the dent it had made; a sickly feeling passed into his stomach. His mind flitted between the agony, and thoughts of Jenny.

Picturing her, standing at the hospital, as he sped away in the Landrover.

Probably the last time he would ever see her.

She would be back in Yorkshire by now, taking their Scottish Expedition adventure with her. Without Jenny, the future looked bleak and lonely.

What a fucking fool he'd been! A fucking idiot!

He deserved the pain – all of it.

But, then again, this outcome could have been avoided, if

she had not showed up a day early. He mused on this thought and knew he was only kidding himself.

One last foray into the sex jungle, one last raid on the luscious fruit trees of carnal pleasure, one more indulgence before settling down with Jenny had been the idea – *his justification*!

Working hard with Harry Patterson's head maintenance man, Jimmy Anderson, on the finishing touches to the hotel, had kept Bob busy.

The previous Wednesday, Bob had decided to go into Fort William. He had been standing at the bar in the Cross Keys pub when Skye MacKenzie had walked in with a female friend.

Taking a fleeting glance in their direction, Bob thought Skye looked a little thinner since he last saw her. He continued to watch football on the large television set, wary of any contact with the young woman who'd assaulted Jenny last year.

He heard Skye order two whiskies and from the corner of his eye, could see she was staring at his back. Then she was back at her table.

On his way to the toilet, he had to walk past them.

'Well, it's Bob Sinclair,' said Skye, flashing a big smile.

'Skye, how are you?' replied Bob, hesitating in his stride.

'I'm good. This is my friend, Cassia.'

Bob was introduced to Cassia, an American staying with Skye.

'I thought the Californian sunshine would be more preferable than being here,' remarked Bob.

'Believe it or not, endless sunshine becomes boring.'

'What brings you to Fort William on a wet February evening?' she asked.

'Work. I'm busy up at The Nevis Grange, the new hotel, and I'll be responsible for busing the guests around,' answered Bob proudly.

'Back on the road! Good for you.' Skye picked up her glasses of whisky, 'Why don't you join us? We can catch up.'

'Let me nip to the toilet first.'

As he stood at the urinal, Bob knew Jenny would not be pleased if she found he was conversing with Skye. Best to make some excuse and leave, he decided.

His already made-up excuse was on the tip of his tongue as he approached Skye's table, when the sight of the two women put paid to them being spoken. Drawing up a chair, he decided there was no harm in a couple of drinks.

'Not the ideal time to visit Scotland, you're not really seeing it at its best,' Bob said to Cassia.

'More of an opportunity visit really. Skye has some business to sort out here, so I offered to tag along,' answered the American.

Pleasant chit-chat ensued between the three of them.

Bob could tell they were more than friends. It was not just the usual female tactile exchanges; the two women were connected in the type of 'we know something you don't know' behaviour of the schoolyard; giggling, lots of eye contact, references to previous incidents without explaining their context.

But every time Bob made an attempt to leave, Skye convinced him to stay with a squeeze of his shoulder or thigh. Her flirtatious manner towards him steadily increased over the next two hours. Not once did she mention Jenny, Bob was relieved, wishing to keep the conversation light. Skye started drawing from him some of his coach driving stories, and this he enjoyed.

He then noticed Skye and Cassia were holding hands under the table and this sight started to excite him. Excusing themselves to go to the ladies' toilet, Bob got another round of drinks in.

On their return to the table, the two women, giggling, thanked Bob for their malt whiskies.

Leaning over, Skye inspected Bob's face.

'You have a smudge on your cheek, some dirt I think. Hold still. Let me get my handkerchief.' Reaching into her battered leather handbag, Skye retrieved a piece of white cotton cloth, and dabbed Bob's right cheek. 'That's it, all clear.'

'Bob, you have another mark on your chin,' remarked Cassia, pulling out a light blue handkerchief; she rubbed under his mouth. A familiar odour passed into his nose, but he could not place it.

A look of mischief played across Skye's features. Five minutes later, and much more giggling from the women, Skye made a suggestion.

'Bob. We want you to do something for us, if you don't mind?'

'Tell me, I'll see what I can do.' He was enjoying the attention, but every now and again, Jenny's face came to mind. He drew a mental curtain over her scowling face.

'Will you wipe you nose with my handkerchief.'

A quizzical expression on his face prompted Cassia to explain.

'The way a man wipes his nose, can tell what sort of lover he is.'

Grinning, Bob extended his hand. This was just a little harmless fun.

After wiping his nose, he awaited their reaction. Skye took hold of the handkerchief and let the white cotton unfold to reveal the material was a pair of women's knickers.

The women were creased up in laughter.

'Keep them,' said Skye, pressing the underwear back into his hand.

'Here, have mine too,' said Cassia pushing her blue panties over the table.

'He put the garments in his jacket pocket, mentally noting he would have to hide them from Jenny. A little harmless fun.

The women nodded at each other. This old guy was putty in their hands.

Bob could see a few of the locals looking over at their table with the sound of such hilarity; he basked in the attention, especially being in the company of these attractive women.

'The benefit of no knickers at this exact moment is being able to feel her pussy so easily, and she has such a lovely pussy!'

Bob glanced down to see Skye's hand pushing rhythmically down on Cassia's jeans around the vaginal mound. Cassia winked back at Bob.

'How hard are you right now?' asked Skye.

He wanted to tell her he was rock hard, but a shot of guilt kicked through him.

'I know what you are trying to do here,' replied Bob.

'Do you really?' Skye had taken off her boot under the table and swung her stockinged sole up gently into Bob's crotch.

'You don't need to answer. I can feel how hard you are. I could feel it a bit more if you didn't have any underwear on.'

Bob felt more than her foot pressed against his erection. He felt a vice of conflict close in around him – his feelings for Jenny and the carnal desires these women were arousing in him.

'I need to go to the toilet,' he spluttered, standing up.

Bob felt temptation move towards him, like a warm snuffling snout of some animal, eager to uncover some illicit hidden fruit. Again he knew he should excuse himself and leave, but he found himself removing his boxer shorts in one of the cubicles in the gents' toilet.

On his return to the bar, there was no Skye or Cassia. Their jackets had gone. They had left, probably doubled up with laughter at his gullibility.

Slumping into his seat, downing his pint, the coach driver felt he had been made a fool of and deserved it.

A few knowing smiles from the locals did not lift his spirits either.

Staring into the fireplace, Bob was just about to leave, when a tap on his shoulder prompted him to turn around.

Skye's face pushed up against his own, 'Sorry, but I had to get you back somehow. You spurned me last summer... remember?'

Stuck for words, Bob gave a bemused expression. Skye let forth a chuckle before continuing. 'Why don't you meet up with me and Cass on Saturday night in the Indian restaurant at eight? And I promise. We'll behave ourselves.'

'Okay, no harm in meeting up,' he found himself saying.

With a quick kiss to his cheek, she disappeared into the night.

Bob also made a promise, one to himself about Jenny. He convinced himself that meeting up with the two women was in no way disloyal to her. A little harmless fun. Anyway, he did not envisage getting to sleep with Skye and Cassia.

But when Saturday came, Bob's promise was soon under pressure. Secluded in a booth in an Indian restaurant, facing Skye and Cassia, the seating afforded ideal privacy for their little games.

'Wearing underwear tonight?' they asked. But they did not wait for his reply as he felt two stockinged feet push into his crotch under the table.

'Boxers I think?' stated Skye breaking off a piece of papadom.

Bob nodded, but felt the grip of his promise slip some more.

By the time their samosas were being served, Skye and Cassia had unbuttoned their tops, which they had purposely worn to reveal as much cleavage as they could muster, which was plenty, bending over the table at any given opportunity to give Bob a good view. Clefts of flesh; rounded, rising, falling and inviting.

Ideal. I-fucking-deal!

Over the main course, the threesome turned their attentions to talking about their sexual histories.

'Have you ever had two women at the same time before?' asked Cassia.

'Absolutely – on a couple of occasions. One was with three women,' replied Bob boastfully.

'But, really, having a couple of pensioners must count as one woman of Cassia's age,' quipped Skye.

'They were forty-seven, forty-eight and fifty-one, and believe me, they knew what they wanted. Kept me up half the night.'

'I'm impressed,' said Cassia. 'But we're not your average women, are we Skye?'

'Certainly not, sister! We're very demanding,' added Skye, winking at Bob.

Using the spare set of cutlery on the table, Bob placed the utensils in different positions to explain how he had pleased women in the past.

The women had to admit, Bob had imagination.

The meal passed quickly, Bob wolfing his dish down, his head reeling from where the night might end up.

'So where to now?' asked Cassia as they pulled on their jackets.

'Pubs will be closed,' informed Skye, 'so what about back to your place then?'

'If you want, but it's a static caravan!' replied Bob.

'What's a static caravan?' enquired Cassia.

'What you would call a trailer,' informed Skye, ushering them out the door.

'A trailer! You live in a trailer? Wow that's fantastic. Hey that sounds great. We can pretend we're trailer trash getting screwed by the old trailer park warden.'

'Filthy trailer-trash bitches, that's what we're gonna be tonight,' joined in Skye, holding Bob's eye line.

Fifteen minutes later, they piled into Bob's home, Cassia noting the Malpaso name on the side. 'So complete,' had been her reaction.

Bob noticed a text message on his mobile phone, but he did not read it. He turned the phone off, swearing to himself this adventure would be his last. After tonight, he would be there for Jenny – *exclusively*.

Looking at Skye and Cassia, half dressed, parading around his trailer, dancing suggestively to his Neil Diamond CD, he blocked out any thoughts of his lover.

In the years to come, he knew happiness lay with Jenny, but there was no harm in having some reminiscences to draw on when things slowed up – call it a souvenir for all the times past, one for the road, one last time.

Demanding! They had not been joking. Skye and Cassia were

two of the most intensely demanding women he had ever had sex with. But what fucking it had been…a fuck festival, a fuck fest of incredible proportions. At one point, he thought the caravan would break free from its station.

But that was just it; fucking, fucking, and more fucking. After two hours, hard at it, a thought glanced across his mind, one he'd never had before.

While taking Skye from behind on the bed with her head buried in Cassia's crutch, Bob felt removed from what he was doing – out of his body – not immersed in the sexual act. The initial excitement of getting Skye and Cassia into bed had passed, replaced with a sort of vacuum. So unlike when he had sex with Jenny; the feelings just kept building, rising, gaining intensity.

With these two women, it was all technique, stamina, dexterity, proficiency, being some sort of sex machine, like the men in porn movies.

With Jenny, he had experienced a deeper level of intimacy, a place he had never been to with any other woman.

A pang of guilt seared through him.

'Are you going soft on me,' demanded Skye, sensing his erection was losing some of its rigidity.

Closing his eyes, he thought of making love to Jenny, recalling the many times he'd been with her. Skye felt the rod inside her return to full strength.

'Full steam returned ladies,' shouted Bob, but in his mind, swearing ultimate allegiance to the woman in his life; this was the last fling, the last time, one for the road.

It was 3.30 a.m. before they all slumped into a heap of sleep. By 6.45 a.m. they were rousing him into action again.

'I want you to take me as the dawn breaks. I want to be looking out the front of the trailer, watching the day come as we come,' said Cassia.

He could not deny her as she went down on him to bring his hardness back to life.

Five minutes later, she was on all fours on the table in the living room, facing out of the window, shaking her skinny bottom at him. Dawn was breaking, fingers of light prising the darkness away.

Taking up position behind Cassia, Bob slipped into her.

The view was good he had to admit, looking down on her tanned back, and then out of the window, over the hills to a spectacular sunrise.

Last time, definitely the last time, one for the road!

Bob sensed Skye behind him.

'You're looking a little sluggish there, old man,' quipped Skye, reaching for the pink dildo, which was on the couch. Bob had watched her use it on Cassia the night before.

'He could do with pepping up a little,' came the reply from the American woman, thrusting her behind into the coach driver's crotch.

Bob felt Skye's hand on his left buttock, steadying herself, and then, the end of the dildo being inserted into his anus, the lubricant cold. There was a sharp pain as the plastic tube pushed past the sphincter muscle.

'Put it in...that's it...yes, oh yes...a little more...oh that's fuckin good,' he found himself saying. This was new to him; fucking and being fucked at the same time.

Last time, definitely the last time, one for the road!

'Harder...fuck me harder,' shouted Cassia, feeling Bob lunge deeper.

'Fuck his ass...fuck it,' Cassia shouted to Skye who now found her own rhythm with the sex toy.

'That's better, old man. You're a fucking machine since I used this tool to adjust your motor,' commented Skye, concentrating on pushing the dildo further up Bob's crack, more and more of the pink tube disappearing up his bottom.

A few minutes later, they felt the caravan jolt. The countryside was coming towards them, the static was moving down the hill.

Were they going at it so hard? he'd asked himself, as the mobile home started to gather momentum.

Cassia slipped forward, releasing his cock as she tumbled into the couch. Bob felt Skye trying to steady herself by holding onto him. His legs were pinned against the edge of the table, hands holding onto the formica sides, bracing himself for the impact of the stream, which was bearing up fast.

As the caravan dropped into the water, the wheels locking dead, he felt Skye smacking into him from behind, her whole weight dropping onto his body, forcing him face down onto the table. At that exact moment, as the static shuddered to a halt, searing pain entered the middle part of his body, shooting through him like a hot bolt of lead.

Afterwards was a blur, but he remembered Jenny's voice and the expression on her face. Full realisation of his senses did not return till the young doctor extracted the dildo from his rectum.

Laughter from down the hall, jolted Bob's thoughts. Cassia and Skye in the master bedroom, getting up to their usual tricks. Those two were like sexual scavengers, constantly hungry, picking every bone of pleasure clean; that's how Bob felt – picked clean, well and truly picked clean.

One more thought came to mind as he drifted into a restless night's sleep. One more thought which gave him some comfort.

At least he was still alive. Poor old Mackenzie was no longer with them.

He did not know about the man's departure, till the Landrover swung into the gates of the house and the *For Sale* sign with the *Sold* banner prompted an enquiry.

'Is Mackenzie selling up?'

There was a pause, before Skye answered curtly.

'No, I am!'

Bob probed no further. Cassia filled him in later about Mackenzie's passing.

It had happened one October morning, while he was working on a Storm Girl strip – a massive brain haemorrhage had brought life to an end for the artist.

He was found two days later, by the cleaner, slumped over his drawing board in his dressing-gown. Congealed blood had oozed from his nose and mouth, covering half the page of his last uncompleted drawing, a pen still in his hand.

Mackenzie had managed to scrawl a few final words in his dying seconds.

I shine, not burn

Chapter Twenty-four

It had been two good days. Jenny felt her confidence growing with the progress made in her new role at the Caledonian Hotel Group.

On Monday, she had spent the morning with Harry in his office, getting down to the detail of organising the first few months' coach tours.

The key to its organisation was the transfer of visitors from one hotel to another, and the excursions in between.

With only one coach, her schedule had to be precise, almost military in execution. If demand increased, they would need to hire another coach and driver.

Jenny enjoyed new challenges, regardless of the long hours. The excitement of being involved with a project from the beginning was like fuel, giving her the energy required to see things through.

Throwing herself into this new world was just what she needed to take her mind off Bob in the emotional sense.

Harry's enthusiasm was infectious too. Using the Monday afternoon to get her desk straight, she felt positive about her first day's work.

Harry had invited Jenny out for dinner in the evening with his wife to an Indian restaurant in Fort William.

Liz was not what Jenny had expected. She had imagined Harry to have a trophy wife; younger by ten years, ex model, all surface and very little filling.

But Mrs Patterson was a forceful lady in her own right, the same age as Harry with short auburn hair, sharp blue eyes, and a quick tongue which conveyed her irreverent sense of humour in her soft Dublin accent.

Jenny and Liz got on straight away. Waiting for their meal to be served, Liz dispatched advice about her husband.

'A word of advice. Don't take any shit from this man. If you stand up to him in the beginning, you'll be fine.'

'No worry there,' commented Harry, leaning back in his chair, enjoying the attention. 'Jenny can stand up for herself. I know. I've seen it on the golf course.'

'Great. A new golf partner for me,' remarked Liz.

Feeling welcomed by Harry and Liz, Jenny felt herself relax a little, the first time since arriving in Scotland. But the best was yet to come.

'I want to give you your business cards – they came in this afternoon,' said Harry.

Taking the small white cardboard box from her boss, Jenny opened it to look at the cards. She was taken aback and thrilled at the same time.

Jenny Jenkins
Tour Director
Caledonian Hotel Group

Jenny had been under the impression her title was to be Tour Manager, not the elevated role of Tour Director. Smiling at the Pattersons like a cat who's got the cream, she leaned over the table and kissed them both.

'I've only been here a day and I've been promoted!' Jenny exclaimed.

'Well, I believe you need the internal company clout, and this title gives you just that,' explained Harry, topping up their champagne glasses for a toast.

As the hotelier toasted Jenny's future, she felt the hull of the Scottish Expedition lift off the sandbank where it had floundered a little.

Next day, Jenny met the five mangers of Harry's hotels at their monthly meeting. Introduced as the Tour Director, the only other woman in the senior team, Helen, seemed a little cool towards her. The men were friendly, offering ideas and being generally supportive.

These were the people, the colleagues she would be working with in pulling the tour side of the business together. At the end of the meeting, Harry took Jenny aside.

'You made a good impression. I suggest you visit each of their hotels over the coming days to get further acquainted,' said he, as they made their way back to the office.

'Sure, I'll get it arranged.'

'How's Bob? I haven't seen him yet. Has he gone to get the coach?'

A jolt shot through Jenny, but the truth was simple – her driver and coach were not together yet!

'I'll be speaking to him later. He plans to get the bus tomorrow.'

'Good. I'm looking forward to seeing it.' Harry disappeared into his office, leaving Jenny at her desk, staring at the telephone.

Directory enquiries gave her the number for Ardnish House. Punching in the number, she bit her lip. It rang several times.

'Hello,' it was Cassia.

'Can I speak to Bob Sinclair?'

'Sure, I'll get him,' she replied politely.

'Hello, Bob Sinclair!'

There was a beat of silence.

'It's Jenny.'

Another beat of silence.

'Hello, Jenny.'

'I'll make this quick. We need to talk – sort things out.'

'I agree. But I'm not fully mobile yet.'

Taking a deep breath, Jenny replied. 'I'll come up to Ardnish House tonight, say seven o'clock?'

'I'll see you then.'

'See you then,' uttered Jenny, putting the receiver down quickly. It was strange to speak to him, the familiarity of the voice in her ear. But there was a distance now between them. Not for the first time, she felt a little numb.

Turning into the Ardnish House drive, Jenny noticed the *Sold* banner across a *For Sale* sign.

A few lights were on in the house, which looked ominous to Jenny in the dark. The house in winter had a foreboding feel, with the surrounding bare trees, etching a stark background to the lodge.

Knocking on the door, her stomach tightened further. A tense, anxious feeling had inhabited her since speaking to Bob in the afternoon. She could not eat either; the nausea of trepidation wouldn't allow it.

Bracing herself, she waited for the door to open, the wind whipping at her back.

Bob opened the door in a baggy checked shirt, and loose jogging bottoms. They were not his clothes, thought Jenny. They must be Mackenzie's.

Did he know no shame, wearing a dead man's clothes.

'Come in,' he said, ushering her inside.

The hallway was dark, less inviting at this time of year. Cardboard boxes and crates littered the passage. There was no sign of the Storm Girl figurine.

'Can I take your coat,' asked Bob as they entered the library.

'No, I won't be staying long.' Her reply was terse.

A cold atmosphere pervaded the house. It was half stripped in preparation for Skye moving out. There were spaces on walls where pictures used to hang, empty bookshelves, rolled up rugs. There were no audible clues to Skye and the American woman being in the house.

'Would you like a cup of tea or coffee?' asked Bob, trying his best to make the meeting as comfortable as possible.

'A tea,' replied Jenny, taking a seat on the infamous chaise longue, then deciding against it, opting for an overstuffed dining chair. 'Are you on your own?'

'Yes. *They* thought it wise not to be here. They've gone out for a drink to give us some privacy.'

'How considerate,' quipped Jenny sarcastically, as Bob departed to the kitchen in a shuffling motion.

A few minutes later, he returned with two cups of tea, taking a seat from the drawing table, gingerly sitting on it.

'Still sore?' smirked Jenny.

'Not as bad as yesterday,' replied Bob, putting on a brave face. 'How's your new job going with Harry?' He wanted to get off the subject of his accident.

'It's good. He's pleased with me.' Jenny took a sip of tea.

'Thought he might be,' commented Bob, trying to make eye contact with her, but she would not reciprocate. So she had stayed on to run the tour business, and not run back to Yorkshire! He was now waiting for her to begin the verbal assault he so richly deserved.

'Less of the pleasantries. Let's get things sorted out as best we can.'

'Sure. So what do you want to do about the coach. It's your call?'

Jenny paused before answering.

'We need to proceed as normal, regardless of what has happened. Harry doesn't know about our situation, and he doesn't need to know.'

Bob nodded, thankful for her doing the talking, taking control, but that's what she did so well. The question was, did he have a job driving the coach?

Jenny now felt an incredible compulsion to switch track on their restrained conversation, sensing Bob's guard had dropped slightly – intense emotion was also readying to erupt inside as she looked at the man opposite.

'Just tell me. Why did you do it?' shrilled Jenny, her eyes flashing wide in anger – a hot jet of hurt breaking suddenly, scalding.

Bob nearly fell off the stool, the verbal sideswipe catching him unawares.

'I'm sorry Jenny…I really am. Please believe me,' he stammered.

'Not sorry enough, you bastard!' her voice moved from

outright rage to a tremble – a seesaw of pitch and tone. 'I want to make you feel so sorry that it hurts like how I'm feeling right now!'

Bowing her head, she stemmed her tears as best she could. 'Why, why, why? Why did you need to fuck that bitch Skye? You know what she did to me.'

It was in these moments, the coach driver knew he was failing in more ways than one – not just his infidelity, but by not being able to articulate his feelings of remorse adequately.

'It was a moment of weakness. It's a shit reason, I know, and there is no justification for what I did.'

'Weakness!' Jenny looked up, her eyes flaring. 'We all have moments of weakness. But you give into yours, over and over again. You'll be telling me its force of habit next.'

The phrase struck a chord with Bob, and some words of reply dropped into his head, which should never have been verbalised.

'I've given all of this a lot of thought, and I know I've wronged you terribly, and I'm searching for the reasons to why I screwed up. How can I explain it – I think I've been peddling for so long now, I don't know how to freewheel, just freewheel!' As Bob heard the words coming from his mouth, he hated himself.

Jenny's expression was incredulous below a tear-seared face, which was already flushed with anger and emotion.

Bob tried to get up in an attempt to comfort her.

'Stay away. Stay away!' She found a tissue in her handbag, and dabbed back some dignity as best she could. Jenny now launched her little speech prepared on the drive over.

'You're a *man*, and with such temptation you behaved like any other man. But I wanted more from you. I wanted you to be *special*, someone who held me in such regard that temptation would not weaken your resolve to be with me!'

Her words were crisp, fluid and clear, as if she were delivering lines from a play. She felt good for getting her feelings over so eloquently.

Bob tried to say something. Jenny swiped her hand to

quieten him, continuing, growing stronger with each crushing sentence.

'Let's not prolong this any longer. It's clear to me now, and I should have seen this all along. I was prepared to give you everything, and you were prepared to give me what you could, as much as you gave all the other women... *casual sex!*'

'That's not true, and you know it, Jenny!' exclaimed Bob, feeling wronged by her summary.

'Not true! I know what's true, you fucking two women senseless while I drive hundreds of miles to give the man I love a surprise, believing he would be thrilled to see me!' She was standing up, rage climbing back into her voice. 'Have you any idea how degraded I feel right now, any idea at all?'

Bob could not find the words to respond, his head bowed again, staring at the floorboards.

'You don't know, do you? You've never known how a woman feels after being involved with you. That's it. It's clear now. You're never around long enough to find out...back on the bus, looking in the mirror for your next shag. *Shag 'em and shunt 'em*...that's you all over, Bob Sinclair!'

Jenny undid her jacket; she was sweating profusely. 'The shame of it is, even though you've worked out how women think, you'll never know how we feel.'

He was tired of taking the verbal pounding – he fired back in defence – more out of pride than knowing he had a case.

'You knew the type of man I was when you met me. I just needed some time to make the transition to fidelity.' Bob wondered where this statement came from, probably from watching daytime television during his recovery.

'Transition to fidelity? What the fuck are you talking about? Fuck you. I'm not listening to this!'

Jenny stormed to the toilet, determined to regain her composure.

Five minutes passed. Bob poured two whiskies.

As Jenny entered the room, Bob thrust one of the malts into her hand.

'Drink it!' His voice was forceful. He'd had enough of the arguing, the aggravation.

Jenny had simmered down and she wanted to move the exchange on too.

Knocking back the amber fluid in one go, she spoke.

'We still have to address our commitments,' said Jenny, sipping from her glass.

'Commitments?'

'The coach tour business. We have *both* our futures tied up in it!'

Nodding, Bob felt relieved. He had expected Jenny to scupper his chances of getting on the road again.

'I still want to go on with the arrangement,' stated Jenny, sitting down on the chaise longue.

'I'm a professional coach driver; you can count on me to give my full support. You've seen me work.'

'I've see you crash a bus!' Jenny felt the upper hand return to the relationship, the business relationship; and that was the way she wanted it to be, having the upper hand all the time from now on.

'Point taken, but it would be my bus – I mean our bus. I'm prepared to give this everything!' Bob went to sit down, but as his bottom hit the seat, a jolt of pain changed his mind.

'You said that about me, giving me everything,' quipped Jenny.

Feeling like a post being knocked further and further down into the ground, Bob shrugged his shoulders.

'Whatever,' he uttered.

Jenny saw him now, as she had first seen him, when meeting last summer, weak and strong all rolled together, a tangle of his *best*, and his *worst*, inextricably linked.

With the shine of their romance now gone, the veneer rubbed off, Jenny was looking at the bus driver again, and right now that's what she needed – *a bus driver.*

'Let's get to work,' exclaimed Jenny, standing up. 'I've informed Harry the coach will be arriving tomorrow. You need to collect it.'

'Okay.'

'I'll pick you up first thing tomorrow, be ready to go at seven sharp.' Jenny made her way to the front door. Bob followed, trying to catch up.

Standing in the open doorway, she turned to Bob, doing up her jacket. He noticed something missing in her appearance.

'Where's your cross?' Her neck was bare.

Rummaging in her handbag, she pulled out something, hidden in her fist. Taking Bob's hand she thrust a clutch of silver into his open palm. The keys for the coach stared back at him, with the cross and chain entangled.

Looking up at her, he saw the shape of a person in the driver's seat of her car.

'Who's that?' he asked.

'Chalky. He didn't want me driving out here in the state I'm in at the moment.' She turned, strode to the car, and was gone into the night, a flurry of grit kicked up from the spinning wheels on the drive.

Knocking hard on the front door of Ardnish House at 6.45 a.m., Jenny did not want to spend any more time than need be at Skye's residence. The brass knocker rang clear across the frosty morning, underneath the red-streaked sunrise sky.

Skye answered the door in an old, green towelling dressing-gown, wiping sleep from her eyes.

'I'm here for Bob,' said Jenny, curtly. 'I'll be in the car waiting.'

'He's just out of the bath. Come in.'

Reluctantly, Jenny followed Skye through the hall to the sound of her open-toed slippers slapping on the bare floors.

'Do you want a coffee? I'm making one,' offered Skye, preparing the kettle to be boiled, her voice emotionless.

'No, thank you.'

'Please yourself.'

Jenny sat down. The younger woman attempted some conversation.

'Are you and Bob going into business together?'

'Yes, coach tours.' Jenny found it difficult being civil to this woman, but awkward silences could be worse. 'Your father loved this place.'

Skye didn't reply, her back to Jenny, pouring the hot water from the kettle into the mugs.

'Are you sure you don't want a coffee?' asked Skye again, stirring the mugs.

'No, thanks.'

Skye swished past with one cup. Jenny heard her go upstairs.

A minute later she returned.

'Bob will be another five minutes. Cassia is helping him get dressed.'

The young woman turned to face Jenny, their eyes locking.

'You're right. My father loved this place; in some ways it was his whole life.' Skye sipped on her coffee, her hair falling in front of her face. Looking up, she flicked back her fringe. 'Let me show you something, it will only take a minute.'

Following Skye out through the front door onto the drive, a cold breeze swept over the two women. Skye did not seem to feel it, even in her dressing-gown.

'You see those mountains? I remember my mother explaining their origin. How they were formed, how the entire landscape here came into being.'

Jenny recalled last summer, when the two of them walked up Ardnish Hill, and Skye gave her a geology lesson.

'The final piece of shaping took place when a thick ice blanket eroded and smoothed the rocks. Hard rock is made up mostly of iron and it gives the most resistance, not really changing that much; they are the mountains you see. The softer rocks break up, and are pushed down to make valleys. They resist the least to the glaciers.'

Pausing to take a sip of her coffee, Skye continued.

'In my mind, people fall into two groups, like the rocks; the hard and the soft. The hard rock people don't change, won't change, can't change. The soft people on the other hand are always changing, re-forming due to the external forces pushing them around. That's the difference between Bob and my father. For all my father's ability, his talent, he was a soft rock being ground down over the years until there was nothing left. Now Bob is a mountain. He's never going to change shape or be moved. He's all hard rock.'

'Just like you, Skye,' remarked Jenny coldly.

Skye turned, the dressing-gown flapping open slightly to reveal some nakedness. She stood, looking hard into Jenny's eyes, resolute with her reply.

'No, I'm not any of these. I'm the glacier!'

Climbing into the car, Jenny fired the engine into life. Bob carefully inserted himself into the passenger seat.

'Sorry I'm late,' he said. He still had the same clothes on from the previous evening.

Jenny said nothing till they were turning out of Ardnish House drive.

'There's a bag in the back seat.'

Bob glanced at the black leather holdall and his fleece jacket in the rear.

'Your wallet, shoes and a change of clothes are inside,' informed Jenny in a matter of fact tone.

'Thanks.'

Conversation turned to business, with Jenny bringing Bob up to speed on the plans for the tours, the procedures he would have to adopt, the schedules to be adhered to.

Swinging into Fort William, Bob wondered why Jenny did not continue south on the A82, but parked up at the railway station.

'You didn't think I was driving you down to Glasgow did you? I'm far too busy!' said Jenny.

Pulling back a bewildered expression from his face, Bob retrieved his bag and jacket and got out of the car.

Jenny gave him instructions through her open window.

'You'll be able to get the 7.45 a.m. to Glasgow. The ticket is in the wallet. You'll then have to get a bus out Bellshill to collect the coach. I expect it will be late tonight before you get back,' Jenny had one more thing to say, 'I want to make something very clear about our business relationship. The first time you fuck up will be the last time!'

This was no idle threat – the seething anger in her voice conveyed there would be no second chances.

Throwing his bag over his shoulder, Bob turned and walked towards the railway station. He stopped in his tracks after a few paces and turned around. He approached the car just as Jenny was pulling away. She stopped, dropping her window to hear what the coach driver had to say.

'Jenny, I know I've fucked everything up. But I'm going to prove to you, I'm the best bus driver for this job, who'll do the best job possible. And hopefully, I can prove...I'm the man you thought I was, when we met on the last bus I drove!'

Not waiting for a response, he disappeared into the station.

Chapter Twenty-five

The snow had been falling steadily since lunchtime. Jenny's meeting with Callum Alexander at the Avimore hotel had taken longer than expected. But as she was travelling back with Chalky, who'd also had a meeting with the hotel's head chef, she felt confident about making the journey in the worsening weather conditions.

'Ready to go?' asked Chalky in Callum's office doorway.

'Sure,' replied Jenny, packing up her briefcase.

'Are you sure you two should be heading back in this?' asked Callum, his young brow creased with concern.

'The roads will be gritted, won't they?' asked Chalky.

'It'll need more than gritting for this. It needs snow ploughing.'

'We'll be fine. I need to get back, I've a meeting with Harry first thing tomorrow,' added Chalky.

Jenny thought he looked a little under pressure when he mentioned Harry's name.

'Make sure your mobile phones are fully charged,' suggested Callum as he saw them out to reception.

Chalky offered to drive Jenny's car and soon they were pushing back to Fort William.

'I've never seen snow like this,' stated Jenny peering through the windshield at the flurry of large flakes falling before them.

'If we take our time, we'll be okay. I'm going to take the back road back, it will be quicker.'

'But shouldn't we stick to the main route,' asked Jenny with

300

concern in her voice.

'You heard Callum. The snow ploughs will keep the roads open.'

'How did your meeting go?' asked Jenny.

'Okay. But I had to get a little heavy on their inventory,' replied Chalky, a trace of annoyance in his tone.

'How are you finding things in general?'

'I'm still adjusting to this management lark,' he replied, hunched over the steering wheel. 'After all these years being a chef – it's a little weird.'

'It'll take time. It's a transitional thing, I'm going through the same thing,' replied Jenny encouragingly.

Chalky didn't reply.

The light was fading and their speed was slowing as the landscape around them disappeared beneath a thick blanket of white. Jenny was relieved not be alone on the return journey. Her friendship with Chalky had grown in the last few weeks, calling on her and texting her to keep her spitits up. She appreciated such concern and was open to his suggestions for meeting up for drinks in their spare time – when they had some. Both had been busy with their new jobs, and Jenny was thankful for the frenetic activity to keep her mind off Bob.

Chalky was easy to talk to, a little like talking to a girlfriend. When she thought about it, his comments demonstrated a sensitive side to his nature – he was a thoughtful man.

Jenny knew this layer of his character was reserved for her. To the world in general he displayed a veneer of masculinity – a persona that offered protection from what lay beneath.

'How are you getting on working for your friend?' asked Jenny.

'Alright. Considering it's been years since we worked together.'

'He's so much energy.'

'Yes,' replied Chalky. 'I thought he might have slowed up a little, enjoyed the good life a bit more.'

Jenny detected her friend was holding something back. 'It

301

takes time to get used to a new job, never mind working with an old pal.'

'I suppose so. It doesn't matter what I have a go at – in the beginning I always think the worst. I believe I'm going to fail.'

The car skidded a little, the wheels spinning, grasping the snow-covered road for grip. Chalky brought the vehicle back under control, a light film of sweat bathing his forehead.

'Sorry. You need to concentrate. I'll shut up,' said Jenny.

'No problem, I just need to slow up a little. Anyway, I like our talks.'

Jenny nodded, but kept quiet. Pitch darkness had now completely enveloped them, and there was no sign of the snowstorm abating. The hills were proving difficult to ascend, forcing Chalky to move into bottom gear. Wind whipped off the moors to bank the snow where it could. It was just such an obstacle they encountered as they turned a corner and the car ground to a halt, stuck in a drift of white.

'You take the wheel. I'll get out and push,' suggested Chalky. A couple of minutes of wheel spinning and Chalky jumped back into the car, shaking from the cold.

'We're stuck, aren't we?' asked Jenny.

'I'm sorry. But, yes, we are.'

'We both decided to risk it,' offered Jenny. 'I know one thing – we're supposed to stay in the car till help arrives. A plough will be along soon.'

Nodding, Chalky turned up the heater to get some warmth back into his frame.

'We can have one of our chats,' suggested Jenny.

'Sure.'

'So tell me. Why do you think you're going to fail at things? You're a proven chef, respected in your field.'

'I know. But I think it stems from childhood. My father never gave me any praise, just put me down all the time. I grew up thinking I never really had any worth.'

She leant over and gave his hand a squeeze.

'He was a drunk too,' continued Chalky.

'You're not a drunk.'

'Remember when I told you about the chance I had to be a TV chef?'

'Yes.'

'I blew that because of my drinking.' He closed his eyes.

Planting a kiss on his cheek, Jenny felt for her friend.

'We need to conserve fuel. Let's put the engine on to keep us warm when it gets really cold,' said Chalky.

The snow did not relent and an hour later they could not open the doors. Running out of petrol was not the problem. The starter motor froze up and the engine could not be started when they needed the heating. Not being able to get a signal on their mobile phones, a cold night ahead seemed inevitable.

But they talked, and kept each other going. Although Jenny did not want to talk about Bob, the conversation drifted onto the subject of relationships.

'Who was the first woman you really loved?' asked Jenny, determined to keep the focus on Chalky.

'Claire Roberts.'

'What was she like?'

'A lovely woman. She was a banqueting manager at one of the hotels I worked at. I fell for her straight away, but she was a little reluctant. So I wooed her with my cooking. You know the saying, the way to a man's heart is through his stomach. I reckon it's the same for women.'

Jenny laughed through chattering teeth.

'It's true. Took me a few months, and many dishes, but it was my tapas that did it.' He smiled, recalling the past.

'So why did that meal do it?' asked Jenny.

'Because we were using our fingers. It's a very sensual way of eating – especially when you feed each other.'

'So what happened to her?'

'Same old problem. My drinking. She really tried to help. But with alcohol, you're living in a haze, not able to see things as you should. So the day came when she left me, and although I was pissed, I can still remember it as if it was yesterday. She stormed into the bedroom, holding a bottle of brandy and threw at it me. Her parting words were, "here you are, the other woman in your life, you can fall into her arms every night".'

A blast of wind buffeted the car. Jenny did not know what to say. She so wanted to reach out to him. She recalled just two weeks earlier, fetching a mug from one of his kitchenette cupboards and being taken aback with what she found pinned to the inside of the door; a photograph of his face, battered, cut, a tooth missing, an inebriated expression. More of these images were placed around his home, a constant reminder of his past.

'I'm so cold,' she uttered.

'We're going to have to cuddle up, use our body heat.'

'But I thought it was your cooking you used to seduce women?'

He laughed.

There was an attraction between them, but it was subtle, unobtrusive – the reassurance of someone close by, harbouring such feelings was comforting.

Let's get into the back seat,' suggested Jenny.

Chalky climbed into the rear of the car and Jenny followed, gently lying on top of him. Whatever was happening outside, they could not be aware as the snow was frozen to the windows – they were cocooned. Sure enough, their combined body heat brought some relief from the cold. Lying on top of him, Jenny could feel his warmth radiate. He was excited by having her so close, and she was soaking up this aroused energy.

She cuddled her head into his chest. She felt him gently stroke her hair.

'Jenny.'

'Yes.'

'Do you remember the day you saw me off at the station?'

'I do.'

'Do you remember the note I put to the carriage window?'

'Course I do, I thought it was lovely.'

She felt him fumble with his jacket, pull out his wallet and retrieve the same note and hold it before her eyes.

She looked up at him. 'You kept it?'

He replied by kissing her full on the mouth. It was halfway through his embrace that Jenny realised he kissed like a woman, with tenderness.

They had drifted into a light sleep, despite the cold. Jenny was drawn awake by a bright light coming through the snow-covered windshield. Raising herself, she could see the growing glare of headlights approaching through a little gap in the windscreen.

'Chalky. Wake up. The snow plough's coming.'

'I hope it can see us.'

'We need to get the warning indicators on,' suggested Jenny.

Chalky dived into the front seat to activate them. He tried to lower the driver's door window, but it was frozen stuck.

'I don't think they will see the indicators. They're under the snow,' he said, clambering back into the rear.

'I think we need to brace ourselves.'

The snow plough's beam grew steadily with the sound of its engine.

'They must be able to see us by now,' said Jenny.

'Not if the driver's suffering from snow blindness.'

Still the plough kept coming. They could feel the car reverberating from the shares of snow being dispensed ahead. They tightened their grip on each other.

With an almighty bang and screech, Jenny and Chalky felt the front of the car take the full brunt of the large vehicle as it bore into them. Now the car was being pushed back. They looked at one another with a combination of fear and disbelief.

A few seconds later, the moving car ground to a halt. Then a mitt was wiping at the window and a middle-aged man staring in.

'Are you awright in there?' he asked sheepishly.

They nodded with relief.

John Baxter was profusely apologetic for the entire journey back to Fort William. Jenny and Chalky were glad to be in his warm cab and asked him not be so hard on himself – it could have happened to anyone.

It was three in the morning when they were dropped off at the Nevis Grange and Chalky suggested a cooked breakfast before going to bed. They ate heartily. The time came for them to go to their respective rooms.

An awkward silence hung between them as they climbed the stairs, Jenny sensing Chalky's desire for her. But the attraction she felt for him was still swimming upstream against the recent events of Bob's betrayal.

'I understand how you must still be feeling about your last relationship. I'm here when you're ready.'

He kissed her on the forehead and was gone down the corridor.

Climbing into bed, she felt tiredness swamp her senses and willingly gave herself to sleep. But not before smiling at the thought of Chalky's kiss.

* * *

'I can't get the hang of this,' stated Chalky, throwing his hands up in frustration at the computer on his desk.

'I'll be over in a second,' offered Jenny, picking up her ringing phone.

He was struggling to get a monthly report ready for Harry – the deadline was only two hours away. Glancing out the office window, he could see springtime sunshine brighten the loch's surface and thought of asking Jenny to join him for a day fly fishing.

'You won't get your work done looking out of the window,' joked Bob as he walked past.

'I know,' replied Chalky, irritated at the comment.

'That's what I like about my job, being on the move all the time. I couldn't be stuck in front of one of these.'

'Shouldn't you be on your way to Glencoe with the German party?' snapped Jenny, her question curt and no nonsense.

'On my way now,' he replied before disappearing from the room. But not before glancing back to see Jenny leaning over Chalky, helping him with his computer query. She seemed very attentive towards him, thought Bob and he felt a little emotional arrow pierce him inside.

As he swung out of the Nevis Grange, not even the reassuring pulse of his coach, could suppress the niggling suspicion that Michael White was involved with his ex.

He'd had these little pangs of anxiety before when he saw them together in the Indian restaurant. At first he thought the nausea was from something he ate. But then he made the connection when he thought of Chalky with Jenny. For this was the first time in his life he had felt jealousy – and a part of him was disappointed at such a reaction – his world of total self reliance seemed to have lost something.

But then again, he knew for sure, he still loved Jenny, even if she did not feel the same way about him.

'It's a good report. Everything is in it that I need to know,' complimented Harry.

'Thanks,' said Chalky, as they left the meeting room.

'No problem. You'll get the hang of it soon enough,' replied Jenny.

'I hope so.'

'Let's get a coffee.'

He nodded and for a split second resented her confidence. She seemed to be getting more assured in her job by the day. Whereas he felt he was not coping with his new career choice, slowly going under. To buoy his spirits and his confidence, he had taken to covering for the hotel's head chef on his day off.

The bar was filling up with guests taking pre-dinner drinks. They found a little table in the corner.

Jenny sensed her friend's heaviness, a weight she wanted to help lift.

'Look, I'm getting my new car tomorrow. Harry has managed to pull a few strings with one of his pals and get me a deal on this smashing little convertible. Why don't we go out for a drive? You never know, we might even be able to get the top down?' suggested Jenny.

'Great idea. I'm up for it,' said Chalky, happy to spend more time with Jenny.

She was a beauty; metallic blue, sleek, sporty. The car made Jenny feel sexy – the first time she had felt that way in a long time.

Sliding into the leather upholstery, the engine growled into life, sending a tremor of excitement through Jenny. Looking upwards, the clouds looked like they were breaking. Closing his door, Chalky felt the acceleration as Jenny swung out of the garage forecourt and took to the road.

'Whoa, she's nippy,' said Jenny, smiling broadly.

'Steady, you need to get a hang of it first.'

Restraining her enthusiasm, Jenny spent the next half an hour gaining a feel for the car. They wound up into the mountains and by the time they had reached a picnic area in the Glen Nevis forest, she felt firmly in control of the vehicle.

The sun had broken through the clouds and it did not take long for Chalky to set up his primus stove. Soon he was preparing a seafood dish as Jenny unpacked the rest of the picnic.

They ate heartily, enjoying being outside in the leaf-budding woods. After a leisurely walk, they packed up and headed off in the car, the convertible top down. With the wind in their hair, they both felt a surge of freedom as they took to the road.

'This is living!' shouted Jenny.

'Too right,' replied Chalky. Glancing at her, he found her sexiness heightened by being in control of the sporty car. She looked great, but she always seemed to look good. He wondered what she saw in him sometimes.

As they closed in on Fort William, Jenny recognised her coach ahead, going in the same direction. Chalky noticed a grin crease Jenny's face as she put the accelerator down hard.

In her mind a couplet of words sprang forth.

Ideal. I-fucking-deal!

Bob saw the sports car tearing up beside him in his rear-view mirror and thought nothing more of it, until the streak of blue pulled in front of him. Jenny briefly waved and Chalky gave him a thumbs up as they sped off.

The coach driver slowed slightly – he was going to be sick.

'I found some of those photographs I was telling you about when I had just come out of catering college. Do you want to see them?' asked Chalky as they entered the hotel.

'Sure. It will be interesting to see what you looked like.'

She was still heady from the afternoon's excursion, and to top it all, burning up Bob on the road had felt wonderful.

In Chalky's room, she flopped onto his bed while he rummaged in a drawer.

As he was bending over, Jenny knew she was going to sleep with him. The inevitability of it all had been in the air all afternoon.

He'd only got to the third snapshot when they kissed. A passionate embrace which saw them fold into each other. She had imagined him to be a sensitive lover, ever since they kissed in the snowstorm, and she was not to be disappointed. Taking his time, he undressed her slowly, enjoying the unwrapping. As each piece of clothing was removed, he embraced the part of her body which was revealed.

She noticed how he seemed to inhale her, breathing in deeply when pressing his face close to her body.

'I love how you smell,' he whispered.

Slipping under the duvet, he held her close, as if absorbing more than her physical presence. Steadily arousing each other, Jenny found his mouth particularly assured when exploring her body. While intent on pleasing him, he conveyed his pleasure to continue giving to her. Jenny accepted.

As he entered her, she felt him tremble and realised this man was deeply emotional about this part of the sexual act. It was not so much his physical weight she felt as he began to take her, more the heaviness he seemed to carry inside. Through their sexual connection, she felt she was sharing in it – this was all new to her, but somehow familiar.

His hands held her buttocks, raising her lower half to increase the reach of his member. It was plunging with a steady searching rhythm, delving, reaching to pleasure her further, but also wanting to be as lost in her as much as possible.

Pushing against him, Jenny felt the build up of her climax. The quickening pulse of imminent release drew their eyes to lock together. As her orgasm came, Chalky kissed her passionately.

He followed a few seconds later with a shuddering discharge, spasms of ecstasy reverberating into Jenny.

The sexual smelting over, the couple enjoyed the heat of intimacy. Jenny felt him place his head on her chest, and hold tight, almost as if he wanted to burrow into her, to prolong the intensity of their physical attachment.

No words were exchanged, the two of them listening to the evening birdsong which carried through the slightly open window.

Reconciling her thoughts, Jenny felt joined again to the world of affection and pleasure with a man. But something was different about Chalky. It then struck her what felt so familiar about sex with him; he made love like a woman.

Chapter Twenty-six

The remoteness of his journey and the bus being empty allowed Bob's mind to churn to over – something he had been trying to avoid in the past few weeks.

Normally he was too busy to let any negative thoughts permeate his days.

Shuttling the guests between the hotels was straight forward enough and being able to add his tour guide experience to the journeys was icing on the cake. He had to admit he was back in the saddle, but losing Jenny still nagged at his sense of completeness.

The early-evening light was beginning to fade as he drove through the tiny hamlet of Whitebridge. Supertramp was blasting through the bus. He should switch it off, he thought. Maybe he was punishing himself.

The constant recurring image that flooded his mind was of Jenny and Chalky, swishing past him in her new car over a month ago. He'd tried to discover if the two of them were involved, but they were very discrete about their affair. But there was evidence enough, a few little signs of closeness.

Jenny kept her relationship with him on a strictly business level – she was very much the governor; cracking the whip, issuing curt instructions, chasing him for updates, requesting written reports, authorising his expenses, querying any issues that would arise.

Bob didn't blame her. He deserved the treatment. But then again, the harder she pushed, the more determined he became to deliver the most professional service possible – no slip ups from Bob Sinclair, he didn't want to give Jenny the satisfaction.

Bob sensed she was also trying to catch him out as regards his weakness, the old tricks. Was he playing about with the female tour members? His policy of shag 'em and shunt 'em.

But he felt he had changed. He was reminded of one of his favourite Westerns, The Wild Bunch. William Holden and Ernest Borgnine played two gunslingers who realise it's time to hang up their weapons as the new west was bearing down on them. Bob imagined himself as a sort of cock-slinger who had decided it was time to be faithful to one woman – escape over the border to build a new life with Jenny, not to Mexico, but Scotland.

Sweeping round a bend, his mind still on Jenny, Bob had to jam on the breaks hard to avoid a figure in the middle of the highway.

Dressed in camouflage combat fatigues, and wearing a gas mask, Bob found himself bearing down on a person with their arm held outwards, signalling the coach to stop, commanding the vehicle to halt.

With a screech of tyres, Bob pulled the bus to a stop only a few metres from the soldier in the road. What struck Bob as impressive was the way this guy did not flinch an inch as the coach bore down on him, standing impervious to the large oncoming vehicle. He has balls of steel, thought Bob.

Wiping a film of sweat from his brow, he pushed the lever to open the coach door; the sharp evening air wafted in, refreshing him.

The soldier embarked still wearing the gas mask.

'Please do not be alarmed. I'm part of an army exercise and I need to engage the use of your vehicle. I'm commandeering this coach.'

Smiling, Bob was instantly taken back to his own army days. He too had commandeered a couple of bicycles with his sergeant to slip past the enemy while on training.

'Where are you going, soldier?' asked Bob, his heartbeat returning to normal. This could be fun, he thought.

'Fort Augustus,' replied the figure, who seemed smaller as he faced the driver.

'No problem,' offered Bob. 'Gas training?'

'No,' said the soldier, reaching up to remove the mask. 'Protecting our identity in the process of identifying friend or foe.'

The mask came off to reveal a pretty-faced woman, in her mid-twenties with blonde hair tied up. She finished her sentence.

'In your case, *friend* fits the description.' Officer Hilary Bowes-Turner gave a perfect smile. She darted her head out of the door, shouting at some gorse bushes.

'Private, all's clear.'

A tall, masculine woman with short, dark hair and sullen features broke free from her concealment with a lumbering gait.

Getting on the bus, she glanced at Bob and gave a cursory smile, before standing next to her commanding officer.

'Your name?' asked Hilary politely, conveying authority. Her face belonged to one of those English upper-middle class families – she probably came from generations of officers, mused Bob.

'Bob Sinclair.'

'Do you have any armed services record?'

'The Argylles, Ma'm.' Bob felt the hierarchical soldier surface from his past.

'Excellent regiment! Well, we are evading capture, and as you know, a soldier must use their initiative to overcome many obstacles to achieve their goals.'

'What obstacles?' enquired Bob, checking the mirror to see if any cars were behind him.

'A road block just ahead, and a helicopter scouring the open country. We need to hide aboard your vehicle.'

'Sure. But won't my coach be checked over?'

'It will, so we need to be well hidden.'

The coach driver was enjoying the situation, the suddenness of being thrown into this adventure, being part of it appealed to his sense of daring.

'No problem,' replied Bob.

'Time is also a factor,' added Hilary. 'We need to be at the rendezvous for 20.00 hrs to qualify successfully.'

'We should manage that,' remarked Bob, lifting the luggage doors open at the side of the coach. His watch read 7.20 p.m.

The hold compartment was empty apart from the provisions Bob carried to make the journey more pleasant for the passengers; crates of bottled water, carbonated drinks and some boxes of crisps.

Bob crawled inside the hold and began arranging the load to create a false wall at the rear of the vehicle's underside; the two soldiers could be hidden in a narrow gap, undetected from a cursory inspection.

The two soldiers got into position and Bob built the false wall around them.

'Best of luck,' offered Bob as he put a box of salt and vinegar crisps in front of Hilary's face.

'You'll get us through, soldier,' replied the female officer, her white smile flashing.

Seconds later, Bob had closed the doors, and was back in the driving position. He moved off taking it steady, conscious of the concealed cargo.

The light was fading. The darkness would aid their mission to beat the road block.

Three miles from Fort Augustus, a swathe of searchlights from above cut across the road ahead. Dropping the driver's window, he could hear the sound of helicopter blades chopping through the night.

The unseen helicopter, trailing its searchbeam would have radioed ahead to alert the road block of the coach's impending arrival.

Sure enough, a mile outside the town, an army road block appeared. Several green army Landrovers straddled the road. Squaddies were stationed next to them. Pulling up, Bob waited to be approached.

Two men signalled to him to open the door. Bob obliged.

'Can I help you?' asked Bob politely.

Pulling himself aboard, Major John Strummer cut an overbearing physical presence as he locked eyes with Bob. He was mid-forties with a slit for a mouth: this was a tough bugger, thought Bob.

'Sir, we are engaged in a field-training exercise to locate and capture two terrorist individuals. Although this is a simulation, we treat the situation as serious. Have you seen any individuals on your journey who would fit this description?'

The forced politeness could barley hide this man's frustration, thought Bob. Anger lay just below the surface, some sort of verbal outburst seemed inevitable.

'No I haven't,' replied Bob, pulling a convincing innocent expression.

'We'll need to inspect your vehicle. They may have boarded without your knowledge. Do we have your consent?'

'Go ahead.'

Stepping off the coach, the major barked the order for the inspection to take place – his harsh Scottish accent propelling the men into action.

One private scoured the seats, while Bob hitched up the luggage doors. Although this was a game, Bob's adrenaline was pumping furiously.

His watch read 7.40 p.m.

Two soldiers flashed their torches in the empty hold, the beams glancing off the crates and boxes.

The major was pacing around the coach irritably, keeping his gaze on Bob all the while.

'Who're you after?' asked Bob to one of the soldiers as he swept his torchlight into the darkness of the coach's underbelly. He looked tired.

'One of our officers and a private,' he revealed in a hushed Liverpool accent. 'The major has a perfect record though. He hasn't been beaten yet. He always gets his man'.

'Hoskins!' shouted the major. 'Anything there?'

The soldier's white beam of light rested on the crate of salt and vinegar crisps. 'No, sir!'

The major approached Bob.

'Are you sure you have not seen anything suspicious?' asked the officer, pushing his face close to the driver's.

'Not a thing.' Bob shrugged his shoulders, glancing at his watch casually.

Strummer squinted his eyes. He did not seem convinced. A few seconds passed. The officer checked his own watch.

'You're cleared!' he barked.

Bob felt a spray of spittle fly onto his face.

Within minutes the soldiers had parted the Landrovers and the black and gold coach drove through the road block. As Bob passed the major, the officer gave him a stony look.

I would not like to meet him on a dark night, thought Bob.

But he already had.

With ten minutes to go before the deadline, Bob pulled into the main car park in Fort Augustus, and switched off the engine.

Two minutes later, he was closing up the hold doors, the two female soldiers, smiling like Cheshire cats, stretching their bodies back from their crouched hiding positions.

'Thank you for your co-operation,' said Hilary.

'No problem. I enjoyed it. Is your mission completed?'

'Absolutely,' remarked Hilary, surveying the quiet town centre bathed in the orange glow of street lighting. 'We set a record tonight.'

'Evading the officer at the road block?'

'I'm impressed, Bob, at your intelligence,' complimented the female officer. 'Take care. We need to check in.'

'What's your name,' asked Bob.

'I'm Hilary. And this is Alice.'

Overcome with the regimental record she had just achieved, Hilary dabbed a kiss on Bob's cheek, before disappearing into the night with her subordinate.

A couple of days later, Bob was parked up outside the Nessie

Experience – a visitor's attraction built around the legend of the Loch Ness Monster.

On a rain-drenched day like today, with mist clinging to the banks of the loch, Bob knew the indoor facility would keep his party amused and satisfy their appetites for lunch.

While the party had been sauntering through the gift shop, and exploring the centre, Bob had tucked into a hearty meal of cod and chips, bread and butter, and a large mug of tea.

He fancied a quick doze on the coach; just twenty minutes would be fine.

Striding quickly over to the bus, head bowed from the onslaught of rain, Bob did not notice the column of armoured vehicles trundle past on the road going south.

As he climbed aboard the bus, he still did not see the motorised combat unit slow and come to a standstill, blocking the wide entrance to the tourist spot.

Only as Bob was walking up to the rear of the coach, did he see the camouflaged-clad figure strut over to the bus – the major from the army exercise.

There was a firm wrap on the door.

Bob moved back down the aisle and opened up.

Immediately, the major leapt into the coach, forcing his face close to Bob's.

'I thought it was you!' he shouted.

'Excuse me?' said Bob firmly.

'You're an irresponsible civilian,' barked the officer, his chest heaving with rage.

'Get off my coach,' requested Bob. He wanted to shout back, but this would have only exacerbated the situation.

'*Your* fucking coach, is it?'

'Yes, it's *my* fucking coach!'

'When I stopped you the other evening on *your* coach, I made it very clear the nature of our training exercise. I used the description terrorists to explain the type of people we were seeking to apprehend.'

From the corner of his eye Bob could see another soldier

come around the coach. He felt relieved that a sane person was here to quell this enraged soldier.

'In a real life situation, you would have aided enemies of this country.'

Another beret-clad head appeared over the right shoulder of the major.

'Is this the man, sir?' he asked.

'If you can call him that?'

Bob was taken aback by the behaviour from the soldiers. He was hoping that sanity would return to the situation soon. Then the lieutenant winked at him – unbeknown to his superior.

'He cost me my reputation!' added the major, pushing his face closer to Bob's.

Suddenly the penny dropped. With the two female soldiers completing their mission, this major's field training capture record had been broken – and by two women no less.

'They commandeered my vehicle,' offered Bob, looking for ways to diffuse the situation, which although was plainly ridiculous, he could envisage getting out of hand.

'Commandeered!'

'Sir, I think you've made your point,' commented the junior soldier, realising the situation was escalating.

'I've only just begun to make my point, lieutenant.'

'Where are your passengers?'

'Having lunch,' answered Bob, looking bemused. He looked at the younger man, whose eyebrows shot up in sympathy. 'They will be boarding shortly.'

'No, they won't. I'm *commandeering* this coach as part of an army exercise. Lieutenant, I want twenty men ready to board in five minutes. I'm sure they will appreciate a comfortable ride to the camp.'

'You can't do this!' shouted Bob indignantly.

Jenny's face flashed into his mind, scowling, angry. She would see this situation as his first and final fuck up.

The major sensed Bob's fear and gave his first smile of the day.

'Sir, I think you're being a little hasty,' said the junior officer.

'Its part of the exercise, now get it organised.'

Bob had to think fast to turnaround this situation. Otherwise, he and the party would be stranded, forcing him to call Jenny for help. An idea flashed into the coach driver's mind.

'Sir, as an ex soldier,' shouted Bob to the departing officer, 'I suggest we sort this out man to man, and don't involve any civilians.'

'You were a soldier?'

'In the Argylles,' stated Bob proudly.

'What do you suggest, soldier?' replied the major, intrigued.

'I was a bit of a boxer in my day. Do you box, sir?'

A large grin creased Major Strummer's face.

'I do.'

The lieutenant's expression was one of horror.

'Is it a match then?' asked Bob, 'and we can put all of this misunderstanding behind us?'

'Okay. Come to the village hall at Banavie tonight. See you at seven sharp.' Major Strummer sprang off the coach.

'How good is he?' asked Bob, speaking to the lieutenant as he watched the officer stride back to his vehicle.

'Do you have false teeth, old man?'

Bob shook his head.

'You'll need some when he's finished with you.'

The rain had slackened by the time Bob pulled up outside Banavie village hall. The hall sat at the top of the hill with a row of white-walled one-storey houses sloping down the main street. A lone red telephone box stood at the other end of the hamlet.

The small car park was filled with army vehicles. A handful of squaddies in uniform milled around the front door, lighted cigarettes in hand.

Sighing deeply, Bob moved to the back of the coach to change. As the day had worn on, a sensation of dread had taken hold of his insides, the gut-twisting feeling of apprehension. It must have been thirty odd years since he last got into a boxing ring. He'd thrown a few punches since then, but had not gone any two-minute rounds with a grudge-bearing major ten years his junior.

One positive. On his returning to the caravan, he had found his boxing shorts – and they still fitted. The dark blue silk cloth still looked good as he looked at himself in the mirror. He glanced at his teeth – they belonged in his face, not on the floor.

Stepping off the coach to shouts from the soldiers at his dressing-gown attire, Bob briskly strode past them.

'It's Grandpa Rocky!' guffawed one of the soldiers.

'You might be walking into this place, old man, but you'll need carrying out,' quipped another.

The dark wooden doors of the hall gave way and he moved into the throng of camouflage pressed into the room. The odour of maleness filled the place. His apprehension eased a little at the familiarity of the gladiatorial environment from his past life.

Back then he felt like the fox, as the Scots dogs cheered on their own to fell the Englishman, the Sassenach. But this evening, a couple of remarks whispered to him as he walked to the boxing ring caught him unaware.

'Fuck him up good.'

'Give him one from me.'

'When we're cheering for him, we're cheering for you.'

This officer was despised, thought Bob, not surprisingly. He felt a surge of promise from this support as he clambered into the ring. He was greeted by the lieutenant.

'Looking good, soldier,' he commented, encouragingly, holding out a pair of black boxing gloves.

'Cheers,' replied Bob.

'You are going to need two people in your corner. Let me see who we can get. What's your name?'

'Sinclair. Bob Sinclair.'

'Attention. Bob here needs two people in his corner. Are there any volunteers?'

Two hands shot up, and came forward through the throng. Hilary and Alice ventured forth from the crowd. Wry smiles abounded across a few faces in the village hall. The two soldiers joined Bob and the lieutenant in the ring.

'Fancy meeting you here, Bob,' quipped Hilary, a sympathetic grin creasing her face.

'I understand we have something in common,' said Bob, taking off his dressing-gown.

The private had taken the boxing gloves from the sergeant, and was setting about strapping Bob's hands into them.

'Major Strummer, I presume,' answered Hilary, coming closer to Bob's ear. 'I'm sorry for all of this. It's ridiculous. I never meant for you to get into any trouble.'

Shaking his head, Bob responded. 'I'm a grown man, and I know how to look after myself.'

'You're a fit man for you age, if you don't mind me saying,' said Hilary, glancing at Bob's body as he slipped off the robe.

'Ladies!' the lieutenant addressed the crowd, 'A big hand for the major.'

From a door at the rear of the hall, Strummer stepped out, pumped up in black boxing shorts and red gloves. He held his hands aloft to a roar from his men. With confident strides, he bounded into the ring, jumping on the spot, taking in the cheers from his subordinates.

Bob gave his opponent's stature the once over – the man was exceptionally well toned, strong and solid. But his strength appeared to be in his upper body – his legs looked quite spindly poking out from under the baggy boxing shorts.

The gloves feeling tight on his hands, Bob threw a couple of punches into the air to warm up. Hilary gave him a drink of water and then slipped a mouth guard into his mouth. The clunk of plastic on his gums brought back the past.

Before leaving the ring, Hilary wished Bob well. Alice also had some advice for the older man.

'I think your reach is longer. I've seen him box before. He puts everything into the first few rounds – he's no stamina for the long haul.'

The lieutenant brought the two men into the centre of the ring to give the boxers' handshake.

'This won't be a training exercise,' sneered Strummer.

'And I'm not one of your men,' retorted Bob, feeling his blood rise.

Round one commenced. Strummer barrelled into Bob immediately, but Bob staved him off with some long defensive punches. Dodging back, using a back foot shuffle to keep just out of fire of the piston-punching major.

Getting his breathing into rhythm, Bob was grateful now for the fitness regime he'd embarked on since splitting up with Jenny. Although he'd been working hard during the day, he still found he had some residual energy to be worked off in the evening – a pool of excess vigour which used to be drained from his sexual forays.

Lasting two minutes, the first round seemed to be taking forever. Adopting a defensive position, Bob was constantly body weaving, blocking Strummer's jabs as best he could, but unable to stop a few thumping into his rib cage. Streaks of pain seared across his sides, leaving a dull ache in the kidneys.

But he managed to get one good blow to his opponent's head as the bell rang, a firm punch on the right side of Strummer's face.

Hilary and Alice were in his corner in seconds, towelling off the sweat, swilling water into his mouth, giving encouragement.

'You're doing good,' shouted Hilary over the din of the audience.

'Keep him at bay till the third round,' instructed the Alice.

Holding onto the ropes, Bob could hardly believe the surreal situation he was in.

'The men are on your side,' informed Hilary,' believe me; they can't stand this bastard. They can't shout your name, but it's you they're cheering.'

The bell chimed. Bob span round to see Strummer tearing towards him like a whirlwind, fists loaded with anger.

Blows reigned in onto his head, forcing the older man to

put up his gloves for protection, leaving his torso open to some pummelling. Pain seared into his abdomen.

Pinned against the ropes, Bob could see the fury in the major's face and was reminded of several fights in his younger days where the loss of temper used up valuable energy and the ability to focus – a factor which Bob hoped would be to his advantage.

The trick was to absorb the blows, soak up the other man's output, but as Strummer's pumping assault continued, Bob wondered if he could hold out.

Getting off the ropes, he managed to mount a better defence, using his reach to quell some of his opponent's barrage.

The soldier had the edge, and knew it, relaxing slightly as the round ticked towards closure. Bob's instincts were still there. Sensing a drop in the younger man's guard, the coach driver delivered a missile of an undercut punch into Strummer's chin. The bell rang, the crowd roared and Strummer felt the lack of support from his men.

'This is the round!' remarked Hilary, checking the mouth guard.

Bob knew it was his last round. He had to take the major out, his fifty-six-year-old frame could not go another round – Bob's body was on fire with aching exhaustion and quickly draining of energy.

'You can do it,' said Hilary, holding up the plastic water bottle to his mouth, a white-toothed smile flashing hope.

Nodding, Bob looked out across the crowd of faces, their expressions willing him to knock out their despised officer. This sea of smiles, winks, and expectation helped Bob summon up a wave of fortitude for the big push.

'Go, tiger,' shouted Hilary, her kiss on his cheek lighting the torch paper of attack surging through Bob at the sound of the bell.

The stationary bus caught Jenny's attention as she turned the corner into Banavie, causing her to slow the car down.

What was her coach doing outside the village hall with all these army trucks?

Pulling into the roadside, she was determined to find out. There were no excursions planned for this evening; she knew that for sure.

Approaching the hall, the sound of cheering soon became audible. As she entered the building, the smell of testosterone and cigarette smoke assaulted her.

Packed with hollering soldiers, their backs to her, Jenny could now see they were spectators of a boxing match in the centre of the room. She instantly recalled Bob's stories of his own boxing experiences in the army.

The bell chimed, attracting her attention to the sparring athletes in the ring – where her coach driver was receiving a kiss from a young female, before going into battle with a younger man.

A shock wave passed through her. What the bloody hell was going on? Had Bob gone crazy?

A minute and half into the third round, Bob could feel he was getting the better of the major. His longer reach was now paying off in spades – punches digging into Strummer's face and body, the younger man caught off guard from the opening seconds of the round as Bob came out with the vigour of a man half his age.

The crowd was going wild, transmitting their support with openness now.

'Go on, you old bugger. Take him down!'

'Finish him off, Grandpa!'

Bob was soaking up the cries, channelling the wave of support into the successive piston-punches that were taking the other man apart.

Feeling his arms weaken, Bob glanced to his corner, seeking Hilary's smile to help deliver one last shot to dispatch his opponent for good. It was at this precise second, he saw Jenny's stern face in the doorway.

It was this vital second that cost Bob dear – a moment of lapsed concentration was all that was needed for the major to realise here was his chance to fell the bus driver once and for all.

Strummer's punch went square into Bob's open face with such ferocity that the older man felt the blow resound with a crack down his neck, through his spine and jar his legs, which gave way.

Bob still had Jenny's face in his mind as the canvas floor came towards him, feeling his body crumble into defeat. Then everything went black.

Five minutes later, to the sound of the hall emptying, Bob came round to the sight of Hilary and Alice reviving him.

'How many fingers am I holding up?' asked Hilary.

'Three,' he croaked.

'How do you feel?' she enquired.

'Old!'

Helping him to his feet, the two women helped him out of the ring.

'You did well to go three rounds. We thought you had him.'

'So did I,' replied Bob, pulling on his dressing-gown, looking for Jenny. There was no sign of her.

'You shouldn't drive your coach. We'll get you back home?' stated Hilary.

Nodding agreement, Bob shuffled out into the night, wishing Jenny had stayed for an explanation – why he'd fought to save fucking up.

Tasting blood in his mouth, he also wished Jenny could have taken him in her arms, easing the pain of defeat. He wiped away a small tear before the soldiers could see it.

Chapter Twenty-seven

'Who the hell does he think he is? His face is going to be a right mess. What will the tour party think, that we hire thugs?' asked Jenny in an exasperated tone.

Chalky looked up from reading the newspaper on his bed.

'I'm sure he'll have an explanation,' he replied.

'He better have.' She helped herself to an orange juice from the fridge, but would have preferred something like a whisky. Since becoming involved with him, she had abstained from taking a drink in his company, believing it to be a supportive way of helping her boyfriend resist his old habit.

The truth was, she needed something to steady her nerves. The shock of seeing Bob being punched out had not been pleasant, but the feelings she had felt immediately afterwards of genuine concern had surprised her. A part of her had wanted to stay and see if he was okay – another to be gone from the situation. By the time she had reached the Nevis Grange, she had channelled her conflicting feelings into those of irritation for the coach driver.

'I'll have a word with him first thing tomorrow and find out what he was up to,' informed Jenny.

'He's just one of those guys. He's always getting into scrapes and things. You know what he's like,' said Chalky.

'But he's a middle-aged man. He should know better by now.'

'You said it yourself, he can't be changed,' offered Chalky. 'Harry is the same. In fact most people cannot change their ways.'

'But you did?'

'Yes, but it's a still a battle every day.'

He sounded weary, thought Jenny. 'So how's your day been?' She joined him on the bed.

'So so.' He paused. 'Actually, it's been awful.'

'Why? What's happened?'

'I had a run-in with Harry. He had a go at me about one of the new chefs. He said I should have spotted the guy's shortcomings weeks ago.'

'But that's unfair. You're new to this sort of thing,' said Jenny, putting her arms around him.

'He might have a point?'

'Nonsense. It's just a blip, you'll see.'

There was silence. 'It's easy for you to say, you seem to be doing okay, well better than okay. All I ever hear about from Harry is how wonderful you are.'

Resentment seeped out from Chalky. For the second time in the evening Jenny was taken aback.

'I'm sorry. I shouldn't have said that. Please forgive me,' he asked, looking her straight in the eye.

They made love a little while later. She prompted it by taking a bath in his room and slipping into a slinky night dress. As before, she found their lovemaking to be sensual, sensitive and moving in an emotional sense. But what had struck her was his lack of passion. He never seemed to reach a fevered peak, but swam with a steady rhythm though the sexual waters they navigated. He didn't always climax either, explaining there was no need for this to happen on each and every occasion. But what he did do afterwards was curl up beside her like a cat, gently pawing her arm till he went to sleep.

She awoke a few hours later with a parched thirst. Slipping into the kitchenette, she quietly opened one of the cupboards to retrieve a glass. Too dark to see properly, she opened the fridge door to shed some light.

As she was closing the cupboard, she noticed something was missing from the inside of the door – the photograph of

Chalky's battered, inebriated face. The lack of the image stung her.

Slipping back into bed, she felt disconcerted at her discovery. Jenny hoped she was now his reminder to abstain from the drink.

The only other reason to explain his removing the photograph did not bear thinking about.

Bob's mobile phone rang. He could see it was Jenny calling. He had managed to avoid her for two days now in the hope his swollen face would improve for when they did meet.

'Where are you?'

'At the cable cars,' he replied as he herded the Italian party towards the entrance of the Ben Nevis Cable Car Rides.

'When you've seen them onto it, I need you to report back here,' said Jenny.

'I can't do that. Mrs Ianotti needs some help. She's a little infirm. I'm going up with her.' She could manage on her own, but Bob was determined to avoid his boss.

'Then I'll see you tonight in the bar at the hotel at seven. Be there.'

The call was over.

He did take the ride. Knowing his luck, Jenny would discover if he hadn't. As it turned out, he was glad he took the ride. The panoramic view from the summit of the journey was spectacular on this clear blue sky day.

Bob stared out at the undulating horizon curves of the Inner Hebrides. The Italians cooed at the views and Bob enjoyed the tranquillity of being so high up on the mighty mountain. But it was his descent which was to provide a perspective he found even more interesting.

With a minute to go before the car docked at the base station, Bob could see down through the budding trees to where a few footpaths wound their way through the wooded slopes. A man was walking alone and a few seconds later Bob recognised it was Chalky.

If only he was on his way to meet another woman, thought

Bob, wishing for this to be the case. But what if he was? Jenny would drop him like a stone, and he would have a chance again.

Ideal. I-fucking-deal!

He could follow him just to be sure. Some of the party were still to come down from the top of the mountain. He had a little time.

Bob traced the path Chalky was on and was soon on foot in the woods. It did not take long for the coach driver to catch up with his prey, keeping a safe undetected distance behind.

Chalky walked on at a brisk pace, almost as if he was in a hurry, but showed no signs of stopping. Glancing at his watch, Bob knew he would soon have to turn back. He started to feel a little silly about this spying lark. Then Chalky dropped off the beaten track and stopped next to a large tree.

Taking up a crouching position behind a gorse bush, Bob felt his heart beat with anticipation. Who was the mystery woman?

Checking to see no one was looking, Chalky took a plastic carrier bag from his jacket pocket and slipped it into a hole in the tree. He was all set to retrace his steps, when he retrieved the bag, took a bottle of brandy out and swigged back a few mouthfuls. Then he replaced the bottle back into its the hiding place before heading the way he had come.

Bob lay for a few minutes, realising Chalky did have a dark secret, but not the one he had imagined. Then again, if he was a man who'd fallen off the wagon, he'd fallen into the arms of another – a woman called drink.

As he headed back to the coach, he felt a trace of sympathy for his rival. Bob knew what it was like to have an addiction and seeing Chalky skulk around made the coach driver even more determined to keep his vow of celibacy – until he could win back Jenny.

'You're late,' stated Jenny standing in the bar.

'Sorry, but the Italians took longer than I anticipated doing the distillery tour,' replied Bob, knowing he had in fact spent ages getting himself ready to meet her. Despite his face still looking bruised, he didn't look too bad.

He bought her a drink and they took a seat by the window.

'How's your face?' she asked.

'It looks worse than it is. Before you say anything, I want to say I'm sorry about the fight I got into. I should have known better.'

'How did you get involved?'

'Me and my big mouth. You know what I'm like. I was in a bar and I was going on about my army boxing days to these soldiers, and before I know it, I've challenged one of them,' replied Bob, trotting out a rehearsed version.

'It cannot happen again. We have an image to uphold,' chided Jenny.

'I know, and it won't happen again. How's Chalky?'

'He's fine, busy like we all are.'

Bob would have loved to divulge the knowledge of Chalky's furtive movements, but good sense prevailed.

'You look a little tired,' said Bob.

'I have a lot to do in preparation for the high season. I have a couple of things I want to go over with you now on the business.' As ever Jenny kept their meetings strictly business, and they spent the next hour going over plans for the forthcoming months.

Bob naturally participated, but took the opportunity to soak up her looks, her voice, her movements, which he still found to be a heady draw.

'Bob, are you listening to me?'

He nodded, studying the little lines which radiated out from the corner of her eyes – he adored them, always had.

Jenny would rather not be talking about business. She would have liked to have shared her concerns about Chalky, the suspicions she had about his drinking, get a man's viewpoint. She found it strange talking to Bob, considering his betrayal. But his easy-going manner was comfortable to be around. After being with Chalky these past months, she noticed how much lighter Bob appeared to be. He could be accused of simplifying the world too much, thought Jenny, but his luminosity was like a breath of fresh air tonight.

'Are you having a high-powered business meeting?' came a voice behind them. Harry stepped over and patted Bob on the back. 'That's what I like to see – dedication.'

'You know us,' replied Bob, 'we're a team.'

Jenny gave a genuine smile and noticed the time on her watch.

'Excuse me, gentlemen. I need to be somewhere else.'

She left, leaving Bob watching her every move.

'You still love her, don't you?' asked Harry, sitting opposite Bob.

'Does it show?'

'Sure does, cowboy.'

'How can I get her back?' asked Bob, fiddling with a beer mat.

'I'm not really the man to ask, but from the little knowledge I do have about women, you have somehow got to recreate what you did have. Take her back to the good times you both enjoyed.'

'That's going to be difficult, if not impossible,' replied Bob, slumping his shoulders.

'We need some music in here to create some atmosphere,' stated Harry, getting up to a have a word with the barman.

A minute later, background music started playing. Harry rejoined Bob.

'That's better, don't you think?' asked the hotel proprietor.

'Much better. It puts people in a more sociable mood.'

As Bob said these words, an idea suddenly came to mind. It was such a good plan and filled him with such excitement, he slapped Harry on the back.

Jenny waited for over an hour, but Chalky did not show. The Indian restaurant staff kept asking if she wanted to see the menu, but she declined. His mobile phone was switched off, and a call to his room only found his answer-phone message.

She decided to take a walk and knew an AA meeting would

be taking place about now. As she headed up the street to the little village hall, she prayed he would be there. Pausing a few seconds before entering, she hoped to find him.

The room was busy, but Chalky wasn't there.

It was two in the morning when she got a call from Adam, one of the waiters who worked at the hotel. He had found Chalky drunk to the point of paralysis on a Fort William street, not far from a pub.

Jumping in her car, she sped over to where he lay. With Adam's help, Jenny got him back to his room and into bed. He was covered in sick, had urinated over himself and had a cut above his right eye from a fall.

She was just about to undress him, when she had an idea. Fetching her camera, she took his photographs, sprawled, snoring on the bed.

A few minutes later, Jenny pulled the duvet over him, knowing he was heading for a horrendous hangover in a matter of hours. But more than this, she knew the shame of what he had done would swamp him.

Back in her own room, she could not sleep. The same question kept recurring, the same bloody question, over and over – Why were men so weak, and why did women care so much?

Chapter Twenty-eight

Turning into the Nevis Grange car park, Bob switched off the coach engine, the mid-morning sunshine illuminating the insect film on his windscreen. The sun felt warm on the back of his neck while cleaning the glass. The coach was reliable and had been a good buy.

It was good to be back behind the wheel, to be back on the road, especially as it was coming up to the anniversary of his accident. Although he had less time off, the work for Harry Patterson's outfit was more interesting.

He felt his tour guide contribution had improved over the months, giving a lively interpretation to the region's history as he walked the parties through castles, churches, around monuments and across battlefields.

He loved this aspect of the job, always looking to improve the tour dialogue by reading as many books on the excursion topics and visitor attractions as he could.

Contact with Jenny was still a strictly business affair, especially since she had become involved with Chalky, but he had noticed recently less of a 'bounce in the romantic step' for the couple. He'd seen Jenny going to the AA meetings with Chalky, and he could imagine how determined she was in keeping her boyfriend walking the path of sobriety. The question was, Bob mused, was she happy? Well today would be the day, for this was D Day in Bob's grand plan.

Striding into the Nevis Grange office with purpose, he stopped at Jenny's desk where she was busy on the computer, a concentrated expression on her face. The other girls in the room were busy too. The air hummed with human industry and the buzz of telephones.

'All work makes Jenny a dull girl,' quipped Bob.

Jenny shot Bob a glance, before returning to gaze at the flickering screen.

'I take it party three are on their way up the Railway to the Isles jaunt?' asked Jenny in a matter of fact tone, ignoring his comment.

'They are, and with this weather, the views will be great.' Bob paused a second before making a suggestion.

'Why don't you come with me to pick them up from Mallaig? On a day like this, it would do you good to get away from your desk for a couple of hours – you've hardly been on the coach.'

'I'm too busy. You don't know the half of what's involved in running this business.' Her tone was a little stressed, self important, dismissive.

Addressing the coach driver in such a manner had become a habit for Jenny, but in many cases Bob did not deserve it.

Bob felt his neck redden with annoyance, but he stuck to the plan.

'Put it down to market research. You'll be able to spend time with the party on the way back from Mallaig and get feedback about their holiday.' Bob glanced at Harry's closed office door – where was he? This was his cue.

Jenny looked up, considering Bob's suggestion, but was interrupted by Harry coming out of his office and addressing them both.

'Hi guys. What's happening?' Harry clapped Bob on the back, flashing his smile over the two of them. He was a happy man – the coach tour venture was going very well.

'I was just asking Jenny to join me in picking up one of the parties from Mallaig. It's a good market research opportunity!' informed Bob.

'Excellent idea! Jenny, what do you think?'

They both had a point, she thought, and the weather outside looked wonderful.

'Okay. I'll be ready in a mo.'

As Jenny walked out of the room, Harry winked at Bob, as the coach driver showed two crossed fingers on his right hand.

It was a truly glorious day. There wasn't a cloud in the sky. Ahead lay a canopy of blue, a sunshine escort for Bob and Jenny as they wound their way up to Mallaig.

Hills, glens, mountains, lochs seemed to part for the coach as it rolled through the landscape, beckoning them further into the rich green and blue landscape.

Jenny sat in the front seat, soaking up the views as Bob drove with his usual consummate ease, delivering a smooth ride, taking out all the wrinkles from the road with experienced driving.

Her mind drifted onto Chalky. The argument the previous evening had been a blistering one. She'd caught him sipping from a hidden bottle of wine. He'd been abusive, mocking her dedication to work and implying it was more important than he was. As her relationship with him had developed, she discovered a man wracked with self doubt and low self esteem. Jenny felt he was trying to pull her down, a tactic he denied, but she could tell he knew it was true.

Storming off to her room, he'd come to her door half an hour later apologising profusely. They had made love, but his drinking had put paid to any reasonable performance from him.

Looking over at Bob, Jenny found herself appreciating the coach driver's suggestion of taking a ride out today.

He looked like a man in his element, thought Jenny, and so he should; this was his vocation in life. She felt a little bad about not giving him any credit for making their new venture work so well. But Jenny still felt sore about the betrayal, a lingering hurt; a fresh scar prohibiting any praise for Bob's hard work.

She knew all about his efforts by keeping tabs on him right from the start. Initially, it had been an exercise in making sure he was not up to the old 'seduction tricks' on the female tour members. Jenny did not want the tour service soiled by this type of sordid behaviour.

Using her contacts with the individual hotel managers, Jenny was able to keep tabs on Bob's nocturnal activities.

These reports seemed to paint a picture of Bob's monk-like living. When it came to bedtime, he was going to bed at 11.30 p.m. on the dot when residing in any of the hotels. The reports included positive comments about his contribution to the overall experience for the tour party; helpful, pleasant, and eager to make all aspects of the trip a memorable one. In the evening, he displayed his usual hosting skills, creating a lively atmosphere. As the Oban hotel manager remarked, 'he's a real asset to the company.'

Harry was supportive of him too, unlike that of Chalky whose behaviour meant he would likely be out of a job in the near future. Harry had also let slip that Bob still carried a torch for her.

Wheeling into Mallaig, Jenny was looking forward to pressing the flesh with her customers, getting first-hand accounts of their travelling observations. She would also enquire about Bob.

Parking up in the railway car park, Bob informed Jenny of the five-minute wait for the train to arrive.

'Would you like tea?' asked Bob, pulling out a silver thermos flask from under his seat.

'Yes please.'

A light breeze slipped through the open door of the coach. Jenny closed her eyes, enjoying the air on her face. It was also good to be away from her desk.

The couple stepped out into the car park which overlooked the Sound of Sleat towards the Isle of Skye. There was a wonderful view of the sparkling water and soaring mountain ranges – a gigantic engine of weather and terrain turning together without faltering.

'Here you go,' said Bob, handing a cup of steaming tea to Jenny.

Sipping from the cup, she was reminded of how good Bob's tea was.

'Would you be anywhere else?' asked Bob, looking out across to the rounded summits of Skye.

'No. Nowhere else compares.'

A minute's silence passed as Jenny and Bob stood trance-like in their surroundings.

Both reflecting on the last time they had been here together last summer; the eventful day when Bob had missed the ferry to Skye. The day of the coach crash, they had found shelter at Ardnish House, when Jenny and Bob would begin their personal journey together.

'No regrets?' asked Bob.

'No regrets. We were meant to come to Scotland.'

Bob sensed Jenny's guard was down, relaxed. Good, he thought; the plan was on course. 'It's funny how things work out.'

'Can I ask you something?' enquired Jenny, wishing to confide in Bob about Chalky.

The diesel locomotive's horn sounded, piercing the air, heralding the arrival of tour group three.

'It'll keep,' added Jenny.

The tour party spilled out into the car park, a group of fifteen Scandinavians.

They were smartly dressed individuals, moving towards the bus, smiling at the sight of Bob.

Jenny could see the coach driver's popularity was as strong as ever, his easy charisma radiating, equally appealing to both men and women. He was an asset – she had to admit it.

Lunch was taken in a little tearoom in the town centre. Ideal for Jenny to introduce herself, mingle with the individuals of the party.

Receiving good feedback filled her with a rewarding feeling. Members of the tour party liked the attention to detail, the personal touch of the hotels, the facility to choose from excursion options, not feeling part of a herd, but as a group whose individuality could be catered for.

One consistent remark kept coming up – what a lovely man Bob Sinclair was, what a great tour guide. Jenny was beginning to wonder if Bob was paying these people to praise him.

As Jenny embarked for the run to Fort William, all the party aboard, she leant over to Bob as he slipped into the driving seat.

'Good job, Bob, well done. I'm really pleased!' The compliment was heartfelt.

Bob grinned back, turning the engine into life.

Ideal!

Jenny noticed Bob held the grin for some miles on the return journey to Fort William, as if he knew something she didn't.

The tour group were a lively bunch, chattering away in their native tongue.

Jenny had hoped to doze on the way back, but the audible buzz did not allow it.

The journey was coming to an end, the coach skirting the northern bank of Loch Eil, the shimmering water's surface casting a strong glare.

Bob drew the coach to a stop in the little hamlet of Corpach, a row of white houses overlooking the loch.

Taking the PA microphone in his hand, Bob stood up to address the party. Jenny was expecting some comments on the surroundings – pleased to see how he handled the tour guide aspect of the trip. The speakers crackled to life, Bobs dulcet tones rang through the length of the coach.

'Ladies and gentlemen. We have been together for seven days, and I want to say, what a great bunch of people you are!'

There was a cheer from the passengers.

'Over the last few days, I've asked you to join me in a sing-a-long, which I am pleased to say you have wholeheartedly embraced.'

Another cheer, louder this time. Jenny sensed the

excitement in the bus, the electricity of expectation. He really had them charged!

'Now, I had an ulterior motive for this pastime, and I want to share this with you. One of the songs we sing along to is a very personal one, a song which meant a lot to me and a special lady who came into my life.' Bob glanced at Jenny.

The hairs on Jenny's neck prickled.

Bob paused, the whole coach party, including Jenny, was hanging on his every word.

'I want to dedicate this song to her now, because I want her to know how much I think of her. Jenny, this is for you. It's my way of saying...'

He could not finish the sentence, but turned around, sat down in his seat, fiddled with the CD player and Supertramp's *From Now On* blasted through the coach.

The chunky piano chords brought the song to life as Bob eased the coach back onto the road.

Stunned, Jenny swivelled round to stare out of the windscreen as the song played, and the entire coach party sang along, word perfect, pouring themselves into the song. By the time the rousing chorus kicked in – *I guess I'm always gonna be living in a fantasy, that's the way its got to be, you think I'm crazy, I can see living in a fantasy, from now on, you for you, and me for me, from now on* – tears were flooding down Jenny's face, blinding her vision.

Emotions were blinding her too, a sweep of feelings catching her off guard.

Bob kept his eyes forward, singing along, sneaking a look at Jenny now and again.

The song was nearly finished. The Tour Director stood up and had to shout at Bob to be heard over the clapping of the passengers, her voice angry, charged, explosive, and hurt.

'Stop the coach, stop it now – this is not right what you're doing!'

Taken aback, Bob slipped into a lay-by on the bank of the loch.

'Open the door!' barked Jenny. Bob obliged.

With the tour group sitting in silence, Jenny leapt from the vehicle and walked onto the pebble shore, tears scolding her face.

The Scandinavians, sensing all was not well with their driver and the woman marching down to the water's edge, waited for direction. The PA system came to life.

'Ladies and gentlemen, please bear with me. I need to chat to her.'

All eyes were on Bob as he walked over to join Jenny.

The coach driver took an intake of breath, readying himself to speak to the woman who he had hoped to melt with the busload of singing holidaymakers.

'Jenny, I'm really sorry. Please listen to what I have to say.'

She stood, hugging herself, not wishing to look at him, staring out across the water. Ben Nevis dominated the horizon on the other side of the loch with its sheer size, rising into the sky.

'You know how I feel about that song!' stammered Jenny, 'it's so special, and you've just cheapened it by using it to…' her words dried up, not knowing how to finish the sentence.

'That was never my intention. I was trying to find a way to reach you….to tell you how I feel. I have trouble finding the right words, you know that's my failing!' appealed Bob, trying now to find the words, looking heavenwards, asking for divine intervention.

Turning, Jenny faced Bob. Her face was red from crying, her eyes puffy, mascara smudged on her cheeks. Locking her eyes onto his, Jenny asked him to explain.

'Tell me how you feel, this is your chance – reach me.'

Taking a breath, Bob spoke, realising this would be his only chance.

'Your words from some months back keep going round in my head, about me knowing how women think, but not how they feel. I understand now, because I now know what it's like to feel for a person. The incident with Skye…' Bob halted for a second, seeing Jenny flinch at the mention of the young woman's name, 'it happened for a reason, and that was for me to learn how much I felt for you by feeling absolutely nothing for that woman – something had to be broken, before it could be fixed.' The coach driver paused for breath, awaiting a reaction from the cross-armed woman before him.

'Go on, I'm listening,' said Jenny emotionlessly, her brow furrowed.

Bob would rather have swum the breadth of the loch, knowing he could find the air to fill his lungs than the words to fill the space between him and Jenny right now. On he went.

'I need you to know I've changed. I'm not chasing around after the women like I used to. I know you think that incident with me and boxing the army guy was a ploy to impress those female soldiers – well it wasn't. Believe it or not, I did that to avoid a situation which would have compromised the tour service.'

Jenny looked quizzical.

Bob felt he was losing it, and then a strand of words came to mind, like a rock appearing in the river to step onto while crossing, he knew what to say now. 'I can explain all of that later. What I'm trying to say is, I love you, Jenny Jenkins, like I've never loved anyone before – because I've never loved before!'

He noticed her face soften for a second.

There was one more thing to say, the only analogy his mind had ever offered.

'I have spent a lot of time asking myself, if I'm a good person, or a bad person? If my character were a water well, that question would be the bucket, dropping down time and time again to see what kind of water fills the bucket from my soul.

Is it sludgy, black, undrinkable water, no good to anyone? Or is it a clear, fresh drink to slate your thirst on? The more I sent the bucket down, the more I knew what kind of water was at the bottom! You now need to send that bucket down – you need to see what kind of water the Bob Sinclair well gives!'

He had found the words, like the clear water.

Bob turned, leaving Jenny with his fate. The tour party watched him stride back, drop into the driver's seat and wait for the woman on the shore.

Silence still on the coach as Jenny approached and popped her head through the doorway.

'I need to do some thinking. I'm going to walk back to the office, it's not far.'

He nodded, and turned the ignition.

Forty-five minutes later, Jenny strode into the reception of the Nevis Grange, her mind still reeling from what Bob had to say, his outpouring of feelings towards her.

The walk had been good, allowing her to turn everything over – to drop the bucket down the well, retrieving it again and again to taste the water as Bob had put it, the most eloquent thing he'd ever said. It proved how much the man had been thinking about the two of them.

The coach driver still loved her – she knew that for sure.

She also now felt immersed in a dilemma, one she could not have imagined a couple of months back. Two men wanted to spend their lives with her; two men with their own distinctive strengths, weaknesses, foibles.

A memory interrupted her train of thought on the walk back. One from childhood, a shopping trip she had taken with her mother. It was still so vivid, like it had happened yesterday.

'Which pair do you like?' her mother had asked her as an eight-year-old.

'I can't decide,' replied the little girl, fidgeting on her mother's hand as she stared through the shoe shop window.

'You're no help,' said the mother, taking Jenny into the store.

A little while later, they were back on the street, the new sandals slapping the surface of the pavement with a steady beat.

'I don't like these ones,' said a little voice by the time they reached the grocers.

'Are they hurting you? Is it your toes?'

'No. I just don't like them now. I want the other ones!'

Dropping down to eye level with her daughter, the frustrated mother spoke.

'Look here, young lady. These are the ones you chose. You wanted these sandals and you're going to wear them whether you like them or not.'

The terse tone brought on a flood of tears, which did not subside until the groceries were packed into the car. The silence of the homeward journey was broken a little later by a question from Jenny.

'Mummy. When will I know what I really want? Is it when I grow up?'

A smile creased the mother's face as she glanced at her little one. She considered her reply carefully, knowing a good answer was required.

'Darling. When you grow up you will know what to choose most of the time. But now and again, it will still be difficult.'

'What do I do then?'

'You listen to your heart. Your heart will tell you what to do.'

Little Jenny placed her hand on her chest and gave a quizzical look before asking yet another question.

'But Mummy, what if it's my heart that's asking me what to do? What do I do then?'

Chapter Twenty-nine

Sitting in the public bar of the Cross Keys, staring at the photographs, Chalky felt the gnawing vacuum in his stomach increase in size. These were the images Jenny had captured on the night she had hauled him back in his inebriated state. He looked terrible, caked in sick, dishevelled, prostate on his bed, dead to the world. And that's how low he felt, wishing to be dead.

Sipping his orange juice, he contemplated his future.

He knew Jenny deserved better, and he knew the best thing for all concerned was to end it – finish with her, spare her. But being with her, he felt more connected to the world than he had in a long time, less of the lingering bruise he imagined himself to be. Over the years, he had categorised people into injuries. Jenny was a sharp cut, experiencing a whisk of pain initially, but healing quickly, unlike the sensitive blue lesion he saw in the mirror each day.

He glanced over at the bottles of whisky behind the bar. The urge to have one drink to help his thinking was fleeting; he knew it was never just one drink. A line from one of the AA pamphlets came back to him – *an alcoholic is a person for whom one drink is too many, and a hundred are not enough.* It was the most apt of these sayings he had encountered.

One of his own phrases came to mind – *it was not the loving that was the problem, it was the living* – reference to the daily grind of life; the distractions, the pressure, the setbacks, all the things that can get in the way of two people being with each other.

But he knew he had formed a sort of reliability on Jenny, as he had done with Claire despite promising himself in the beginning not to. Here lay some frustration, at this type of dependency on another. In the past, drinking numbed him from feeling so weak.

And so the cycle turned, chasing his own fears as they chased him.

A sign, he could do with a sign to aid his decision about his future. Checking his watch, he made a move to leave; he had a meeting back at the hotel with a supplier. As he stepped out onto the street, a group of tourists walked by, forcing him to remain static till they passed. Their language sounded Germanic, and then he recalled Jenny saying about some Scandinavians being one of the tour parties.

He followed them down the street and noticed how they all trooped into the small record store at the bottom of the high street. An act of compulsion took hold and he followed them in. The little horde were wall to wall, congregating around one part of the A to Z racks in particular.

Clutching some CDs, they swept over to the counter and made their purchase. A minute later they were gone. Chalky moved over to the rack and scanned the artists the tour party had been looking at. All began with the letter S. He had to know what all the fuss was about. He decided to ask the young girl behind the counter.

'Those tourists who were in here, what did they buy?'

'Cleaned us out. Weird, I had never heard of the band Supertramp.'

Jenny's favourite band.

This was a clue, thought Chalky. A part of the sign. He now felt the irresistible need to unravel whatever *it* was.

He caught up with the tour party as they were walking up the Nevis Grange driveway.

'Excuse me, I hope you don't mind me asking,' he addressed a woman with a pleasant smile. 'What made you all want to buy Supertramp CDs? I saw you in the store. I'm intrigued.'

There was a little chuckle from the group before the woman answered.

'True love.'

Chalky then listened as they told him about the incident on the coach earlier in the day, with the driver proclaiming his affection to his boss, the lady tour director.

Half an hour later, as he turned on his computer and began to type up his letter of resignation, Chalky felt relieved. A little sad too, but mostly relieved.

Bob was the man for Jenny, he was ideal really. He hoped Jenny thought so too.

Striding into the hotel lobby, the receptionist beckoned her over.

'Are you seeing Bob shortly?' the young blonde asked, her sweet smile captivating the guests as they booked in.

'I might be. Why?'

'I have this for him. It came in the post today.' Vicky handed Jenny a padded manila envelope.

'I'll take it,' agreed Jenny, a sense of disappointment at the sight of the package.

On the way up to her room, she looked at the handwriting on the address label, a woman's touch, the swirling neatness of the lettering.

She felt her heart sink. The envelope had somehow pricked fear in an emotion that had been gaining momentum for Bob as she walked back to the hotel – the feeling of still being in love with him.

Climbing the stairs, she felt the parcel. There was a slight lump in one of corners, probably a pair of women's knickers.

Laying the item on her bed, she poured herself a whisky and sat on the windowsill, working out what to do next.

If only she could take the qualities of both men, and fuse them together.

She decided to open the parcel – whatever the contents of the package were, it would be a sign.

Ripping the seal, she pulled out a letter; a woman's handwriting stared back.

Bob sat in the caravan, the early evening sunshine beginning to fade, a malt whisky easing his nerves, the prickle of the day's events tingling through him.

He could do no more now, pinning his all on the speech to Jenny at the loch side.

Opening up like that was a completely new experience, baring his feelings – it felt like a sort of emotional nakedness. He felt like some piece of pine furniture which had been stripped of the many coats of paint that had been applied over the years, but at least the wood could breathe; that was how he felt, being in the open now.

One thing was for sure; he could not go on working with Jenny. If he could not be with her, it would be too painful. He would find another driving job, probably in the south. The coach driver poured another whisky.

His mobile phone rang. Jenny's name flashed in the display, he took the call.

'Hello.'

'Can you come down to the hotel? We need to talk.' She sounded business like. 'I don't like coming up to the caravan.'

She had not been to his static unit once since the Skye and Cassia incident.

'Sure, I'll be down in five minutes,' replied Bob.

'Meet me at the coach, and bring the keys for it.'

The call ended.

Bob's heart sank, plummeting with Jenny's words. This was it – it was all over. The bus was hers, and she wanted to take full possession; Jenny wanted him to go!

In the half-light of dusk, Bob trudged down the track, and around to the front of the hotel where the coach was parked, the black and gold vehicle glinting in the dying strands of sunshine. Jenny stood at the door of the bus, waiting.

'Hi,' said Bob, pulling the keys out of his jeans pocket.

Expressionless, Jenny took the ignition keys, and unlocked the front door.

'Let's talk inside,' she suggested, climbing aboard.

Bob followed, wearily pulling himself up, not knowing where to sit. Jenny had taken a seat at one of the tables so they could face each other. The coach driver slipped onto the velour upholstery opposite. He braced himself for what was to come.

'There's a wonderful sunset tonight. I never tire of them up here,' commented Jenny, looking out of the coach window as the sun's golden orb neared the peaked horizon on the other side of Loch Linnhe.

'It's beautiful, just beautiful. I missed all of this when back in England,' replied Bob, looking at the woman before him, her face in profile, the fine bone structure displayed so well. Jenny's hair was tied up, revealing the delicate lines of her neck.

'Although I've only been here a few months, I cannot imagine leaving this country,' added Jenny, looking directly at Bob, her face a little pinched.

She must be struggling to find the words to ask him to leave, thought Bob, buying time by talking about Scotland. He now wished she'd get it over with.

'I feel the same way as you. Leaving here would be hard for me, but if I had to, I would get by.' Bob managed a brave smile.

Their eyes fixed on each other, two people sitting on a silent coach, darkness encroaching. Jenny pushed a piece of paper across the tabletop.

'I owe you an apology for opening up this letter, which came for you today. But I'm glad I read it. I had to know if you were the man you said you were.'

He reached out for the letter, but Jenny's hand dropped onto his, holding the piece of paper flat.

'Bob,' her voice was strained. 'I want you to do something for me.'

'Whatever,' he replied, holding her gaze, ready for the words to come

'I want you to take a holiday.' Her tone was matter of fact now.

Bob felt his heart sink further. She was pushing him away, believing he was in need of rest and recuperation after this afternoon's outburst. He nodded, head bowed.

'Bob,' she continued, 'I want you to take a special type of holiday.'

Bob shot a quizzical look at the woman opposite, curious at the last sentence – did she mean some kind of counselling? Was what he said this afternoon so bad?

Jenny gave a broad smile.

'I want you to take a *busman's holiday*…and I want *you* to take *me* with you!'

With these words, she pushed the ignition keys into his hand, and made one more request.

'Now, go and put that song on!'

If you had been walking down from Ben Nevis on that summer evening, not far from the Nevis Range hotel as the sun disappeared from view, you would have heard some music echoing through the glen, and if you were familiar with the seventies band Supertramp, you would have recognised the song as *From Now On* – the lyrics carrying through the evening air – *I guess I'm always gonna be, living in a fantasy, that's the way its got to be, you think I'm crazy, I can see living in a fantasy, from now on, you for you, and me for me, from now on.*

Chapter Thirty

June 1st

Dear Bob,

I write on behalf of Daniel, my husband. He found your letter of last week quite a shock, coming out of the blue after all these years. In time, he will contact you. I thought it best to reply for the moment.

Your grandson, Michael, is now eleven years old, and the photographs enclosed will give you an idea of how tall he has become. According to Daniel, his height comes from the Sinclair side of the family. He wants to be a racing-car driver when he's older – no doubt this will change.

Daniel still refers to you as his father, regardless of the fact he still hurts about what has happened. Time has helped heal his memories of the past, and being a father himself has brought further understanding.

We are both interested to know more about Jenny – your hopes to be with her and to make a life together. I know this means something to Daniel – he was always concerned you would end up a lonely old man with nothing to show for your life.

I have returned the photograph you sent of the two of you – she looks like a really nice person. I hope it works out for you both. Maybe we can all meet up in the future.

Please be patient in waiting for your son to make contact, but be assured he will.

With love,
Michelle

Visit **wwatson.net** to post a review for
Busman's Holiday if you feel inclined. Billie appreciates
feedback to aid future writing.